Praise for *Breaktime*:

'Ditto writes about all his exciting encounters, including his first sexual experience, an excruciatingly funny as well as touching scene' *Publishers Weekly*

'An immensely rich piece of work . . . entertaining, stimulating and thought-provoking' *School Library Journal*

'Above all it's very funny' *School Librarian*

'Unusual, clever, fascinating and totally riveting' *NATE News*

Praise for *Dance on My Grave*:

'Clever and imaginative, wide and spacious, vividly creating the atmosphere of summer in a seaside town and the intensity of adult love' *The Evening Standard*

'Refreshingly uncoy' *Daily Telegraph*

T0316095

breaktime
Aidan Chambers
dance on my grave

DEFINITIONS

BREAKTIME & DANCE ON MY GRAVE
A DEFINITIONS BOOK 978 1 909 53135 2

This collection with Afterword first published in Great Britain by Definitions,
an imprint of Random House Children's Books

Collection copyright © Aidan Chambers, 2007

9 10 8

BREAKTIME
First published in Great Britain by The Bodley Head Children's Books, 1978
Red Fox edition published 1995
Copyright © Aidan Chambers, 1978

DANCE ON MY GRAVE
First published in Great Britain by The Bodley Head Children's Books, 1982
Red Fox edition published 1995
Copyright © Aidan Chambers, 1982

Definitions are published by Random House Children's Books,
61–63 Uxbridge Road, London W5 5SA,
a division of The Random House Group Ltd,

Addresses for companies within the Random House Group Limited can be
found at: www.randomhouse.co.uk/offices.htm

THE RANDOM HOUSE GROUP Limited Reg. No. 954009

www.totallyrandombooks.co.uk

A CIP catalogue record for this book is available from the British Library.

Penguin Random House is committed to a sustainable future for
our business, our readers and our planet. This book is made from
Forest Stewardship Council® certified paper.

Printed and bound in Great Britain by Clays Ltd, Elcograf S.p.A.

breaktime

For
Nancy

CHALLENGE

Coffeetalk

'I tell you no lie,' said Morgan, slopping his coin-machine coffee on to the scuffed woodblock floor of the sixth-form common-room. 'Maureen Pinfold is a dream.'

Ditto stared at him in what he hoped was an enigmatic fashion. Since term began he had been perfecting this cool exterior manner, an attitude of unshakable intellectual poise.

Morgan licked dribbling coffee from the side of his plastic mug.

'She's ripe for dissection,' he said, affecting his medical style. 'I plan to operate as soon as the patient is prepared. And a theatre found, of course.' He laughed. 'It might have to be a field trip.'

'God, the mixed metaphors,' said Ditto.

'I do not believe in purity.' Morgan laughed again. He always preferred his own witticisms to anyone else's. His laughter shook another expectoration of coffee on to the abused floor. Surveying the morning-break crowd that filled the room, he said, 'You know the trouble with half this lot?'

'Tell me,' said Ditto indulgently.

'And with you too, I might add.'

'Say on.'

'They talk a lot . . .'

'So do you.'

'. . . but they've done nothing. They talk very knowledgeably about Life and Sex and Politics and Religion and all that guff. But they've got it out of books.'

He lobbed his empty mug like a shuttlecock half across the room, into the metal wastebin by the coffee machine. A group

I

standing by the bin turned and applauded. (Why did he have to be so insufferably gifted, hand and mind, Ditto wondered.)

'What's worst,' Morgan went on as if unimpressed by his skill or the applause, 'they get it out of stories. Out of lit-er-arr-tewer.'

Ditto remained studiously unmoved.

'And what's so bad about literature?'

'Literature is crap,' Morgan said. 'Fiction is, anyway. Novels and stories. It's like that coffee they make us buy. A pretence. Ersatz.'

'They ought to let us make our own,' said Ditto, draining his mug.

'You might say the same about the literature they force on us,' said Morgan and chuckled.

'Midgely says literature offers us images to think with. That its unreality has nothing to do with untruth.'

'Cods,' Morgan said. 'Images out of a book make you think like a book. And old Midge can be a pompous ass. He should have retired years ago.'

'That doesn't diminish the truth of what he's saying.'

'No, but it does make it a lot less attractive.'

'Get back to literature.'

'I'd rather get back to Maureen Pinfold.'

Ditto conceded a smile.

'You're spoiling for a fight,' he said. 'Okay. I challenge you to prove literature is crap.'

'You're on,' said Morgan, rubbing his hands with relish.

The klaxon sounded the end of break.

'Damn it,' said Ditto. 'Can't stay. Got a double period with Midge and Jane Austen.'

'Pity. I'm free. But I'll tell you what. I'll jot down my Charges Against Literature—I mean fiction—and serve them on you at lunch.'

'A subpoena I'll enjoy discharging,' Ditto said. 'But why bother? Just tell me.'

'Innocent!' Morgan said. 'My Charges will give me just the

2

excuse I need to trap Maureen Pinfold behind her typewriter in the commercial room. While she does me the favour of typing my Charges, I'll prepare the patient for dissection.'

'If this was a story,' Ditto said, 'you'd call that typecasting.'

Morgan laughed.

'Thanks for the compliment,' said Ditto, and left.

Gauntlet

CHARGES AGAINST LITERATURE

(I Mean Fiction)

Morgan   v   Ditto

I charge that:

1.   Literature as a way of telling stories is out-moded. Done. Finished. Dead. Stories as entertainment are easier got from film and TV these days. (And what was Fiction ever about except telling entertaining stories?)

2.   Literature is, by definition, a lie. Literature is a fiction. Fiction is opposite to fact. Fact is truth. I am only concerned with truth.

3.   Novels, plays, poetry make life appear neat and tidy. Life is not neat and tidy. It is untidy, chaotic, always changing. Critics even complain if a story is not well plotted or

'logical'. (Life, logical!) They dismiss
characters for being inconsistent. (How
consistent are you, Ditto? Or me?) And they
admire 'the literary convention', by which
they mean obeying rules, as in ludo or chess.
SO:

4. Literature is a GAME, played for FUN, in
which the reader <u>pretends</u> that he is playing at
life. But it is <u>not</u> life. It is a pretence.
When you read a story you are pretending a lie.

THEREFORE:

5. Literature is a sham, no longer useful,
effluent, CRAP.
    As I said.
    Q.E.D. *Morgan*

Lunch Date

The morning over, Ditto joined Morgan in the dining hall.

An aftertaste of Jane Austen lingered in his mind as he sat
down opposite his friend. Often he went only half-heartedly to
Mr Midgely's literature class. (Morgan was right: Midge could
be unbearably pompous.) But somehow the man always riveted
his attention. Uncomfortably sometimes; he was never easy,
never made concessions and could, when marking an essay, be
ruthlessly cruel. Yet he brought to life every writer, every book
he dealt with. He seemed to devour them, making them part of
himself, and then he regurgitated them like spirits, alive, out of

his mouth, by what he said and the way he read aloud. As though he were a magician, a medium even. No doubt about it, a great talker was Midge. Had the gift of the gab, Ditto's father said—all too often these days.

While Ditto pored over the Charges and inattentively ate his lunch, Morgan prattled on. Ditto only half listened. And Morgan's voice, in any case, was almost drowned in the cacophony of three hundred people all talking too loudly as they chomped their way in concert through lumpy mashed potato, soya bean protein disguised as hamburger, and watery cabbage swimming in instant gravy.

Ditto felt sustained against Morgan's diatribe by the lingering pleasure of his morning's work. Wasn't that very pleasure itself proof that Morgan's Charges were false? Could literature really be dead, finished, if it gave him, alive, such enjoyment?

But how, he wondered, could he unsettle Morgan's entrenched prejudice? Not by argument, that was sure. Morgan was bound to win, right or wrong. How then? By demonstrating his error? Perhaps. Be scientific, pragmatic. Morgan would certainly be moved by that. *Show* Morgan he was wrong.

But how?

'You're saying nothing,' Morgan complained when the pudding was served—mushy stewed apple resurrected from dehydration and soused in the customary glutinous custard. 'Here I am, hungry for argument to distract me from the offensiveness of lunch, and you've said nothing since arriving.'

'This menu of your Charges must be digested,' Ditto replied, jabbing his spoon at Maureen's immaculately typed page. 'And your comments on each savoury item have left me no room to say anything.'

'Then ruminate privately,' said Morgan, standing up and clattering his empty dishes into a pile. 'I've a first team practice now, a full afternoon of chemistry, and I've just fixed an evening mixing it with Maureen. So the Charges found their target. See you tomorrow. So long.'

Ditto Goes Home

After school, Morgan's *Charges Against Literature* tucked into his breast pocket, Ditto sets off for home. Mode of transport: a dilapidated bicycle once used by his father to carry him to work. The sprockets squeak at every third turn of the pedals.

Ditto's legs push him on rapidly, for the weather is grey, damp, cold. But his mind is tardy. Home is not an attraction, school a livelier, friendlier place these days. The principal cause of this unhappy state of affairs—so Ditto complains—is his father.

For two years an illness has stalled the man from working. Other afflictions have resulted. A depressed and moody atmosphere in the house. Irritability. A pinching of the family's income. (Ditto's mother has had to take a part-time job behind a grocery counter to supplement their income. She will not be at home when Ditto arrives. Ditto has had his pocket-money cut, he relying on windfalls from relatives and weekend work as a window-cleaner's mate in the streets round his own to provide his private needs.)

Most unsettling of all has been the souring relations between his father and himself. They have reached that pitch where neither can speak civilly to the other for more than a minute or two; more usually, sharp words and barely controlled insults serve as their daily discourse. It pains Ditto; he is certain it pains his father. But the hurt is apparently incorrigible.

Pedalling steadily towards his next parental encounter, Ditto's thoughts travel in another direction. He remembers a time before his father's illness, before, even, he himself had left primary school.

A photograph in Mother's box of family pictures, me thin as a lamp-post on the sprout, ten years old, holding a fishing rod and grinning triumphant at the camera, a dace the size of a stunted sardine hanging from the end of my rod, the dace wriggling still when the picture was snapped by a nearby fisherman who obliged so that Dad could be in the picture too and he is there behind me and to one side, my left side I think, right as you look at the picture . . . Dressed in his work suit, grey and a bit baggy, but a starched white shirt collar and neat black tie, always neat your dad they used to say always just right, his hair still black then, grey now since his illness, and his face full still, moon round still, and used to shine blood-orange red after he'd had a few at the local in the evening or before dinner on Sundays, doesn't bother now, can't I suppose . . . After the picture was snapped he rubbed his hands together as though trying to crack the finger bones, and smiled to himself in the way he does, did, when pleased or proud, he was pleased and proud that day because I'd caught that dace my first and he had been there to see it and have the moment recorded, the capture captured, memorialized by the obliging fisherman.

That same day, yes that's right, just after slaughtering the dace with a sharp blow on its head we saw a snake swimming down the river its head above the surface like a submarine periscope. It turned just below us and writhed ashore entirely confident, not a jot of notice paid us who were standing there aghast agog me, my father, the nearby obliging fisherman, my camera still in his hands. An excited shouting boy came downriver with the snake, skipping along the bank crabwise, pointing at the riverborne reptile and bellowing Look, look, a snake, see, a snake. The minute the snake got ashore this boy and me we fell upon it hurtling stones and beating it to death in the end savagely—were we scared or were we hunting—and while we were assaulting it Dad said You shouldn't kill it. It's only a grass snake you know not poisonous . . . Afterwards he was silent did not celebrate the occasion with wringing of hands and did not join this stranger boy and myself who persuaded the obliging fisherman to take another snap of the pair of us each with a finger and thumb in tentative apprehension holding the snake by its tail end dangling dead between us as we had been big game hunters in safari Africa and our grins are wide and fevered.

If not the snake why the dace? . . . Next day I was disappointed, the snake was like a deflated balloon after a party, but a wrinkled memory of itself not exciting or fearsome any more nor wondrous neither, just empty, and pungent . . . Dad reverently wrapped it in old newspaper and carefully placed it in the rubbish bin.

And said nothing.

Home

Now, thought Ditto, he'll still say nothing. Can he still?

The front door snecked behind him, its phony pane of stained glass window trembling in the concussion. He hoped the glass would shatter one day and was experimenting with various forces of slam to find breaking point. At least when the window splintered the superfluous lead would serve at last some honest purpose and save the pieces from scattering.

Coughing from the livingroom, rich, liquid, gurgling.

A deadly liquefaction, Ditto thought. He's gargling in his own sputum.

He would have liked to climb the stairs at once to the seclusion of his room; but a sense of duty he was trying so far without success to corrupt forced him towards the livingroom. Inside, the air was greenhouse stuffy, smelt of rancid snot, stockinged feet and overheated television set. He tried not to breathe, but the only result was that finally he had to breathe more deeply still and savour the tangy odour. He sat down on the edge of the sofa, prayer-placed hands gripped between pressing knees.

'Home then,' the inevitable conversation began.

Ditto nodded, eyed his father for signs of prevailing mood, slumped there in his bulky armchair with its rubbed-to-the-skin arm ends, his feet resting on a footstool. At the other side of the fireplace the TV flicked its images but the sound was turned off. His father disliked TV sound; said it gave him palpitations, and that anyway he could imagine what was being said because nobody ever said much worth hearing.

8

'What you done today?'

Ditto resisted the impulse to reply not much. He knew too well the fractious talk that would follow.

'Jane Austen,' he said, his throat stiff from restraint.

'What did she have to say for herself?'

Ditto squinted for hint of jest behind his father's deadpan. None was intended, sadly.

'She's an author,' he said.

'O, aye?'

'A dead one.'

'Is she now? So you've been reading all day.'

'For exams.'

'What's she write about, this dead woman?'

'It would take too long to explain.'

A long glance; a smile, sour. 'You mean, you think I'm too thick to understand.'

Ditto knew better than to bite on that bait.

'How've you been?' he asked.

'Fairish. Cough's bad.'

'Had some tea?'

'Couldn't be bothered.'

'Like a cup now?'

A nod; small boy ashamed. 'If you're making one.'

While the kettle boiled, he standing over it, Ditto remembered another day.

He gave me a book that time, how old was I? About twelve, well I must have been twelve because it was my birthday and I had just started at sec school and was getting good reports. He was hand-wringing pleased, his lad was learning French and stuff that would help him get on in life. A proper snot I must have been. Am I still? . . . And he gave me this book, who was it by? I don't even remember. Anyhow I thought it was some god-awful person, not to be seen reading it, and I said, I remember what I said if not who the book was written by, I said, not thinking, you don't when you're a kid like that, I said haughty,

Thanks, Dad, but I can't read this. Why not? he said his face fallen. Well at school they tell us what's best to read and Mr Midgely, he said this writer wasn't very good, so I don't think I can read it you see, I said, right little snot . . . And he just looked and went out of the room, my room, my bedroom it was, I remember now, where they'd brought my presents early to please me and see me open them . . . Mother looked daggers, one of those looks she used to promise me in shops when I was very little and not behaving, If you don't behave yourself I'll give you *such a look*, she'd say, well she gave me such a look then, that day, my birthday, and went after Dad. I don't remember feeling I'd said anything rotten.

Was that the start of it?

Ditto took the cup of tea to his father.

'Ta,' his father said. 'And I forgot. There's a letter for you. On the mantelpiece. Come after you'd gone this morning.'

Ditto took it. The handwriting he knew at once; knew too that he could not read this letter here, in front of his father.

'If you're all right then I'll go upstairs and do some homework.'

'Right-o,' his father said, an agreement heavy with accusation.

Ditto's Room

Upstairs. Front room of three-bedroom, semi-detached, late 1930s speculation-built house, half limey brick, half crumbling pebble-dash with bay-window on ground floor front room, the room below Ditto's.

Inside Ditto's room. Single bed with blue candlewick coverlet. Wardrobe, laminated dark oak on chipboard. Bookcase crammed with books, mainly paperbacks, case made by Ditto himself in woodwork lessons during first two years at secondary school, painted white and looking now to him a hamfisted construction for which, nevertheless, he felt a nostalgic affection. Old, real oak kitchen table, four feet by two, sanded to the bare wood (having once been stained dark in days when virgin wood was vulgar) and sealed with varnish; now used as desk; found by Ditto languishing on a rubbish tip.

On desk: blotting pad, pocked with surreal ink stains, doodles composed mainly of abstract combinations of squares, triangles and hachured shading: product of many hours of brooding contemplation. Portable Olympia typewriter, present from parents last Christmas. Pot, unglazed, red-fired clay bought for five pence at summer fête at school, profits in aid of Oxfam, serving now as pen and pencil holder. Seventy-second scale model of Mark V Spitfire on perspex stand. Rubber pencil eraser; chipped wooden ruler; small calendar cut from last year's pocket diary and Sellotaped to a piece of stiffening cardboard.

The room walls: painted mat sand-brown, the ceiling mat white, the door and other woodwork gloss white. On the walls: pictures, clippings from magazines, posters, record sleeves, bookjackets. Ephemera in profusion. Mostly browned from age and sunlight (which achieved some sort of penetration between the hours of two-thirty and six, *post meridiem*).

The flat-faced window, two-sectioned. One section opening outwards gives view and vent on to arterial road leading to town (or, from, depending upon one's need), centre of town two miles distant, edge of town one mile. His father cannot tolerate noise of traffic, preferring duller, but larger and quieter back bedroom, hence this front room Ditto's. Window veiled by crisply starched net curtains, insisted upon by his mother (you never know what people outside might see inside). For night-time privacy, heavy chocolate-brown curtains drape the windows, floor to ceiling.

The seats. One kitchen chair, uncomfortable, at desk. One old, small, poorly stuffed armchair covered in synthetic fabric stretch-cover, bile-green, bought in Co-op sale and looking it, with bright red loose cushion for highlight. If you slouched across the thing, sitting was bearable.

Letter

He laid the letter on his desk blotter, stood staring at it a moment, savouring its possibilities. Its arrival was entirely unexpected; not even hoped for.

Then, anticipation weakening him so much his hands trembled, he took off his school jacket and tie, heeled his shoes from his feet, unhitched his trousers and stepped out of them, took up the letter again carefully, threw the candlewick coverlet aside, and lay down on his bed.

While calming his breath, he gazed closely at his name and address in the unmistakable handwriting: fluent, firm, yet still echoing a child's awkwardnesses.

The letter, when he slit open the envelope with his right forefinger and eased the page out, was written on one side of a single sheet of school exercise paper. As he unfolded the page, a photograph fell like an autumn leaf on to his chest, picture side down. Deliberately he left it lying there while he read the letter.

Sibena

Wednesday

Hi!

This place is a DUMP — a hole, a DEAD END. Why my crazy parents had to move here I shall never understand. There is one main street about as exciting as Noddyland, no cinema, no caff. As for BOYS — I saw one yesterday. I said

Hello, he said Arrr.

The scenery is quite nice.
But who wants lovely country
without a lovely boy to share it
with?

Which brings me to – YOU!
. How art? And everyone at
the factory? Has Midge recovered
yet from the pleasure of my
leaving? And Morgan?

WRITE, please, soon

The enclosed is to remind
you what I look like.
Hugs –
Helen xxx

Picture

Her of course, the picture is of her, of course, in colour and my
god it's her in swimsuit strip but not stripped enough, must
have been taken last summer before she left while she was still

here and I was lusting after her then and didn't attain what I
dreamt of feeling too cloddish when face to face with her but
she must have known   mustn't she   Morgan wouldn't
have dithered the sod not he and she would· have aided and
abetted him I'll bet   would she me   those legs what
legs what tits and a face to go with them a bit knowing though
and maybe that's what held me back though it doesn't now you
brute   but this letter now maybe all the time she was waiting was wanting was after it me me her after it was she me her
me her legs breasts skin face legs legs o legs her her her
there there there   there   there   there

and it's gone all over my frigging shirt and my hanky's in my
pocket in me trousers on the frigging floor   should have
thought   prepared   but didn't think   didn't
expect her to send such a provocative picture the slut

But she is okay, could almost shoot off again just looking at
her, certainly could in the instant flesh instead of the instant
Kodak, and that's what I'd like, what I need, her in the flesh
and willing.

Does Morgan succeed in all he claims?

I bet he doesn't, most of it plain rodomontade. Randy he may
be but a rodomont he is too by nature. Though even if he has
had only one or even two of the adventures he claims, his rodo-
montades are but decoration to the truth, cos then he's had it,
with his willy or nilly, and I haven't.

What a thing to have to admit at seventeen years plus.

Afterbath

Ditto rose from his rumpled bed, straightened the cover,
examined the scene for clues of his concupiscence, pulled on his
trousers, replaced his damply soiled handkerchief in his hip
pocket to dry in his fleshheat before discarding it in the laundry
basket, and sat at his desk, the better to frizzle his eyes on the

tormenting photograph while musing on his unexpected letter and the inexperienced nature of his being.

Suddenly, in the afterbath of his self-abuse, his room seemed tediously dull, embarrassingly naive. There he was for all to see who had gump to perceive. The inside Ditto. Himself, as he would hide himself.

The furniture was all his parents' except for the rickety bookcase, rudely cobbled product of boyhood, and his desk-table, throwaway acquisition from a rubbish dump. The pictures on the walls, like his bookcase, were stuck there three, even five years ago: expressions of crazes and passions now vestigial only: birds from his nature-spotting days (circa 11 yrs), planes from his flying period (circa 12+), authors and singers going back into primary school years, and finishing up lately with Orwell, Lawrence, Joyce and Richard Brautigan (the authors), Fineguts, Razor, Towlake and Prinwell (the singers).

Even his books were half boyhood favourites, half recent purchases mostly inspired by Midge and bought more—could it really be the truth?—because he believed they were what he should read and possess rather than simply to please himself.

And that damned Spitfire arrested there mid swoop on its transparent stand, motion miniaturized and simulated and made safe for childish hands: another pubic hangover.

All toys, the whole lot, or received possessions of other people. Where among it all was he? Where was the present Ditto, the real, bloodflushed Ditto? WHO was the present Ditto? Was this he? This neatly precise collection of outgrown junk and second-hand propositions? Loads of it crammed into this little box of a room, yet featureless somehow. Absent in its presence.

Was that what Morgan was getting at?

Remembering Morgan, he took from his jacket the *Charges Against Literature* and laid the page out, open on his blotter. By its side he placed Helen's letter and her photograph.

They lay silent there. Together.

Words on paper cheek by jowl with colours in a pattern (a reflexion of light and shadow captured months ago).

Mute. Yet eloquent.

Witnesses come to accuse him.

Opponents in some unlooked-for battle.

Challengers.

Perturbed in the face of his documentary friends, Ditto went to the window, pushed aside the obscuring veil, and glared out at the street.

People and vehicles programmed for home ignored him.

Ditto's Mother Returns

Hello, love.

Hi.

You all right?

Sure. You?

Tired.

Course.

Been home long?

About an hour.

Your dad seems a bit low.

O?

Did you give him his tea?

A cup. All he wanted.

Have a chat with him?

A few words.

You haven't been rowing, have you?

No, not yet anyway.

You should talk to him more.

I had something to do.

He likes a chat with you.

Yes? You wouldn't think so sometimes.

It's his illness.

School all right?
The usual.

I wish you'd spend a bit more time with him.
Ma, you know how it is.
But you could try.
I do.
You know how ill he is.
I know.
It's the illness makes him . . .
It's more than that.

Did you change your shirt this morning?
Can't remember. Think so.
Looks filthy.

Well, I'd better go down and get supper.
Anything I can do?
Lay the table, love, in a minute, eh?
Sure.
I'm worn out.
You do too much, Ma.
Somebody has to, love. But I'll manage.

Set-to at Supper

Father and I had had fights before. And frequently at meals because that was when we spent longest together. At other times, to save the conversation from turning fierce, I could leave the room, or he would feign occupation in a newspaper or the television, or, in desperation, in reading a book. But round the table at meals we were both trapped, literally facing one another, with Mother between, referee, judge, wearied peacemaker.

This evening the conversation began with the topic of my day, a sure-fire success for Father's satiric irony and my tetchiest self-defence.

I had, said Father with a sour chuckle, been lounging around all day talking about a dead writer. I think he intended only to be playful: to tease, not to wound. I sensed the danger, of course; my antennae were by now well trained, and Father's chuckle not exactly deceptive. Mother sensed it too, and her quick glance as she handed me my plate pleaded for neutrality.

I wished no combat; my reply was likewise intended simply as a jest returned in kind. Was apparently received so. Father smiled; Mother laughed (too gustily however; hers was not a response to my wit but an attempt to ensure the conversation was taken at its lighthearted face value).

And now we reach that significant truth which detailed description would only obscure. Despite our mutual intentions, we—Father and I—were soon spilling emotional blood. Even as I snapped pert replies to his gutsy blows, I regretted—more, resented—doing so. But could not restrain myself. I did not mean what I said. I did not hate the man I said it to. I knew what I said to be clever but hurtful, witty but churlish. I knew this even as I spoke the wounding words. Nor did saying them give me any release. Unlike an explosion of temper, or an unlooked-for row, or some final show-down in which the event brings satisfaction, there was no easing of tension. Just the opposite. The longer we continued, the greater the tension became.

Father was bulged and red of face, squared to me and by the end near speechless with rage.

I felt like a twisted elastic unable to stretch any more.

Mother sat slumped, head bowed, defeated.

We reach this point every time we argue without interruption and it is this I resent more than anything, that the tension is a separating wall between us, Father imprisoned on one side and me on the other, and our only means of communication to shout insults at each other across the unyielding density. At least by that one exhausting means we each know that the other is still there.

Of all my father's assaults that evening, only one requires

record. I was, he told me, not just lazy, not just ungrateful, not just loutish and arrogant. No. I was far worse: a twit. I knew nothing except from books, had learned nothing of life from living it. I was a ponce, a parasite. Clever, I might be, but, he concluded, using a favourite phrase of disparagement, if I were faced with a real life problem, I wouldn't know whether to have a shit or a haircut.

Perhaps this evening matters went further than usual; or perhaps I reached the edge of hysteria. Whatever the explanation, I suddenly saw what seemed to me the comic stupidity of this fruitless exchange. Here were a father and son, for no explicit reason, lashing out with sharpened words at each other across a table of neglected food, spectated by a tearful wife-mother. Is that funny, comical? Not so presented. That is why I so present it. But through my eyes at the time it appeared quite bizarre.

And I laughed. Laughed as I used to do when a boy and watching some slapstick farce on television. Laughed uproariously. Side-achingly. Uncontrollably.

Father, finding not unnaturally nothing whatever to laugh at, nothing in the remotest funny, glared across the burdened table at me a moment and then collapsed, unconscious, burying his face in his untouched sausage and mash.

Morning After

'You mean,' said Morgan, 'he flaked out, right there in his mash?'

'Indubitably,' said Ditto, passing off his slopping coffee as nothing worse than yet another accident of the inadequate plastic mugs.

'Where is he now?'

'Memorial Hospital. Mother in evidence and playing at nurse —of course.'

'Christ!'

'He had not arrived when I left.'

'You are tasteless, not to say unoriginal this morning.'

'Put it down to the coffee.'

'Or the shock.'

'Let's walk the perimeter.'

The day was a wrung-out dishcloth.

We stalked the fence that bounded the school playing-field for some yards before either of us spoke again.

Then, 'Is he very ill?' asked Morgan.

'Doctor says he'll be all right in a few days,' I said. 'But that we must realize this collapse is another of the inevitable steps in the deterioration of his health and an added complication.'

'You use language like a civil servant.'

'I use the medic's words exactly.'

'Whatever could have possessed the man?'

'A desire to avoid the words *disease* and *death*, I suppose. They aren't fashionable. Besides, nowadays doctors are civil servants.'

We had reached the sports shed where are stocked grass cutters (various) and equipment (assorted) used by the plodding groundsman. Against the south-facing wall of the shed (which happened also to be the wall hidden from view of the school buildings) was set a wooden bench upon which the groundsman himself usually lazed. Today he was not there.

Morgan and I sat.

'Do you want to talk about it any more?' asked Morgan.

Ditto glanced at his friend stretched at his side, back to shed, hands buried deep in trouser pockets, legs stuck straight out in front, feet crossed, and had a sudden intuition that explained something of Morgan's success with others. Girls especially. He was unafraid to ask questions, to touch on raw nerves, but to ask and touch gently. It was a quality Ditto had not recognized in Morgan before and admired the more for wishing he possessed it himself while knowing he did not.

Morgan caught his glance and smiled.

'There is little to say,' said Ditto, turning his gaze on to the backs of the houses whose gardens ran along the other side of the wire-mesh perimeter fence. Were they being spied, he wondered, as others had been before, by one of the unoccupied occupants who would report to the Headmaster by telephone that two of his pupils were lurking behind the sports shed and why weren't they engaged more fruitfully in scholastic activity. 'I do know though that home is claustrophobic.'

'The suffocating womb.'

'Maybe.'

'There's an answer to that.'

Ditto took from his inside pocket a twice-folded page from a school exercise book. 'Which brings me to the business of your *Charges Against Literature*.'

'By what unlikely route?'

'I'll tell you,' said Ditto.

Ditto's Progress from Collapse of Father to Moment of Previous Conversation

Course of Events: Collapse of father. Summoning of ambulance. Father, accompanied by Mother and Ditto, rushed to hospital, where treated for heart attack. Ditto and Mother remain until Father reported 'out of danger', when, at 10.30 p.m., persuaded to return home. Mother sits up all night, unable to lie down or to sleep. Ditto goes to bed, sleeps fitfully, but wakes finally at 4.45 a.m. and cannot sleep again. So gets dressed, has tea with Mother, then sits in own room coping with Emotional State (see below). During this time sees possibilities explained in *Some Truths about Ditto*, para 6, below. Writes *Replies to Charges*. Has breakfast, 8 a.m. Leaves for school. Sits through first two·lessons distractedly. Meets Morgan for coffee during break.

Emotional State: From supper at 6.30 the previous evening till conversation with Morgan, suffers succession of assaults:

SHOCK at father's sudden collapse;

PANIC while waiting for ambulance;

HORROR at sight of emergency treatment—efficient, fast, crypto-violent—leaving no doubt that father in danger or of prospect of father's imminent death;

GUILT at his part in bringing on the attack;

SORROW for same;

RESIGNATION: What could he do now? What would be would be, etc;

DESIRE to amend;

RESOLUTION to effect amendment;

RELIEF when told by telephone that father likely to recover, even if in no better state (and, so implied, perhaps even worse state) than before;

NEED to talk to someone about it all: thus conversation with Morgan.

Physical Effects: Intense activity, followed by trembling debility, succeeded by aching coldness. Sleep, fitful. Early waking, feeling washed out, listless, discordant, nervy. Remained thus throughout morning, with aching tiredness slowly drowning the discordance till afternoon when body felt hot inside, cold out, and filleted.

Intellectual Effects: Mind at first unable to cope. A tumble-drier of pictorial images passing chaotically before inner eye. Psychedelic derangement. But after early waking, begins to re-assert some semblance of control. During this period, physically cold and uncomfortable, begins to see connections in clear-minded strobe, which become by breakfast a coherent rationale. In other words, understood matters before obscure to him. As if the events of the night have somehow 'blown off' meaning in his head. This understanding he composes into *Some Truths About Ditto* and *Document: Replies to Morgan's Charges*, in order to focus and record his thoughts, and give his hand some dis-placement activity, thus diverting himself from the horrors of the memory of the last twelve hours.

Some Truths About Ditto

In the past few hours a number of things have become clear to me. Reaching this understanding has been painful. It is not comfortable being honest with oneself. I have no intention of reliving the painful self-examination, nor of plodging about in a self-pitiful discussion about the things I have come to realize. Instead I shall simply enumerate the Truths.

1. I find myself both loving and hating my father. This appals me and I wish to do something about it. Yet I know that tonight's catastrophe is likely to be repeated—with even more terrible results—because neither of us can cross the barrier of our self-created antagonisms. We cannot, to be plain, talk to each other openly and honestly. And we both fear to show the love we have for each other. Why, I do not know. But struggling to know has decided me about:

2. I must somehow get away from home, for a few days at least. The distance is necessary to help me sort out where I am. More: what I am. I feel this as a bird, perhaps, feels the need to migrate. A compulsion. Do it, or die. It is as though home were making me impotent.

3. Which brings me to Helen. I know now, looking back, that the frustrations bred by her letter, my randy desire unsatisfied, spawned the irritation which spoke at supper and consummated Dad's anger. I want to have it off with Helen, I know. But do I fear the act? If not, why have I not? Starkly, the truth: yes. A truth not easily told.

4. And here around me as I scribble this laundry list of emotional dirty linen are the symbols of my rag-bag being. Last year's toys, other people's gimcrack. What is mine? Me? My own? I feel like a caterpillar chrysalised and about ready to slough off the carapace, that imprisoning lumber from a former life. I will not be so contained. I will not hide among the detritus of other people's beings, or settle for childhood's pleasures. I want more than that. And now I know I must work my muscles to get free.

5. But I have been too cautious. Perhaps that is why I feel so constrained now, when Morgan (so it seems to me) does not. I have not experienced enough for myself. I must set about looking for new moments. Must widen my repertoire of living.

6. So I have devised a plan: Next week is half term, seven days in convenient gift. I shall go camping. That will get me away from home, give me the distance I need to begin sorting out myself and my father. And I shall look for experience, welcoming what comes—pure sensation if that is all that's going—for action, event, drama. I shall test my caution a little. And the main event shall be:

7. The sexy Helen. I shall invite her to go camping (ho ho) too, meet her half way, at mid-point, pointing at her mid, no doubt too, for an encounter with but one goal, one eye to bull. In short —though at pleasant length, I hope—I shall lay her, the first that ever shall be.

And all this shall be raw material to my other purpose: an answer to Morgan's misminded Charges.

Document

Reply to Morgan's Charges
It is crap that literature (I know:
you mean fiction) is crap. I could
Easily reply to you in kind. But that
is not the best answer. It would only
be an argument. And you, Morgan,
being an activist, a doer - as there
ought, by your own confession, to be
many able to bear witness - prefer to
be shown, a demonstration.

So shall it be: I shall
demonstrate.

I intend a jaunt. What I have not
recorded there, however, is that I
also intend recording the events of
my jaunt, as they happen (or shortly
thereafter). And this record shall
be xx my fiction, the raw material for
it anyway.

But to counter your charges, my
fiction shall obey certain rules:
1. It shall not be written in the
manner of our logical stories. It
shall take what form it cares for at
any moment – which means whatever form
I feel like giving it at the time of
wx writing. I do this because you
feel fiction is contrived, designed
to fit certain pre-set ends. I shall
use whatever styles of prose – or
verse, or writing of any kind – I
wish to use and which seems best for
what I want to say.
2. I shall record as honestly as I can
what it is I experience and wish to set
down. And I shall set something down

however insignificant it may seem at the time, and with or without connections with anything that has gone before.

3. We shall see then(to take your charges on):

    a) whether the story of my jaunt is entertaining or not;

    b) whether my experiences are lies, though they are certainly a fiction - aren't they?

    c) whether the ends are tied up or not, and whether their logicality is so weakening;

    d) whether this game is a game at all, or a pretence; or not. Whether it is unlike your and my life or not.

Maybe I'll surprise you.
Maybe I'll surprise myself.
Maybe it will all be quite unexpectedly unexpected.
Who knows?
But before I begin there is a question to be answered:

Who is Ditto?

Ditto is
Thin, wiry, given to being lanky.

Brown-haired, undistinguishedly cut, worn long over the ears, fringy and thickish.

Green-eyed, tending to short-sightedness. (He ought to have visited an optician by now but loathes medical treatment of any kind, dental most of all, and is vain about the owlish effect given him by glasses.)

Slim nose, wide mouth, lips tending to thickness, above a chin that is square and juts too much for his liking.

Complexion pale. (You look a bit peaky healthy adults usually tell him.)

Right-handed. When interested in something requiring manual skill is reasonably able; when uninterested becomes manipulatively incompetent, a state of affairs he calls being psychologically spastic.

Dresses to the left—as he looks at things.

Has thin legs he prefers to conceal in trousers, rarely venturing into the machismo of showy beach clothes.

Feet, size 9 narrow.

Height, five feet eight inches (work the metric out for yourself, genius).

Total income per week: £3.00 pocket money from mother (which makes him feel guilty under the present circumstances but which he rarely refuses); £4.00 on average from work as window-cleaner's mate, an earned income dependent on the weather and the mood of his employer as well as on the fickleness of his will to get out of bed each Saturday morning early, as:

Hates getting up in mornings and likes staying up late at nights.

Temper uneven. When discouraged tends to sulkiness. When on a high, tends to impulsive loquacity.

Generally, and when on best behaviour, much liked by mothering older women. Among contemporaries, liked by a small group of those who know him well and by everyone else, as are most people, entirely ignored. Feels no need to belong to what he calls 'mobs of people'.

So far, if you are none the wiser you are a great deal better informed and may add in the space provided any other attributes you think important and which you note or deduce from a study of these pages, previous and to come:

....

....

....

Of course, we must not forget:

A virgin. Though, as we have seen, a virgin not without urgent desire to change his state, nor without surrogate practice in preparation for that transition when it comes, if you'll pardon the pun.

Three Conversations

I

Hello.

Hello?

That Helen?

Yes . . . Who's this?

Dee.

Dee?

Yes. Dee.

O! Dee! Well, hello!

I got your letter.

I'm glad.

Got your . . . picture.

Like it?

Certainement. Très jolie.

I didn't do it.

Eh?

French. Didn't do it. Not clever enough.

O, ah . . . but beautiful.

But not clever?

Did I say that?

By omission.

Hey, listen . . .

Can you do anything else with the telephone?

There have been attempts.

Communications pervert.

I wanted to ask you.

That's not possible on the phone either.

You're a telephonic hussy.

Spoken like a true rapist.

Listen, Helen, I've got a plan. This next week is half term for us. You too?

Yes.

Well, I'm going camping . . .

Really! Darling, you should have told me. I'd have understood.

Stop foolin', will ya. I've got only one more tenpence left. I wondered if you'd like to come along. Or rather, meet me half way?

Do you ever talk in anything but double whatsits?

Only when people don't think in them.

Parry. I think, though, I catch your . . . shall we say, meaning?

Ach, zo. And?

Love to.

Great. Here's the plan . . .

2

Hello, love.

Hi.

You all right?

Sure. You?

Tired.

Course.

Been home long?

Half-an-hour I suppose.

Telephoned about your dad yet?

Not since this morning.

I rang at one o'clock.

How was he?

About the same, they said. Comfortable as could be expected.
Whatever that means. Poor man.

Don't cry, Ma. He'll come through.

You coming with me to the hospital tonight?

Course.

Good lad. He'll want to see you.

Next week is half term.

You'll be home then.

Well . . . I thought, if you can manage . . . I thought I might go camping.

O?

Well, it's something for school as a matter of fact. A project, sort of.

Dad won't be out of hospital for a few days yet. Not till I get back anyway. I'll be back before they let him home, I mean.

I see. Probably.

Would you mind?

You won't be far from home, will you? Just in case.

Same place as I went with Morgan last year. I can phone the hospital every day. And if you . . . I could get home easily.

Your dad'll miss you.

He'll be all right, Ma. He'll be well looked after. But what about you?

Me? O, I'll be all right. I can manage. Someone has to.

I always have.

You go camping, love. The break will do you good. Do you good to have a change and some fresh air for a few days.

I'll help you with the supper. Then we'll go and see him.

Ta, love.

3

Hello, Dad.

Hello, son.

Did I wake you?

No, dozing, that's all. Nowt else to do here all day.

Good to see you.

Aye?

Sorry I couldn't come in with Mother. They only let us in one at a time. Ration us, you see!

Aye. Anyway, makes it like two visits, 'stead of one.

Feeling better?

Not so bad.

They look after you?

Fine. Fine. Not like home, you know. But they do very well.

What about the other patients? Do any of them talk to you?

Haven't felt much like talking yet.

Dad, I'm sorry about the . . . the other night, you know.

Aye? Me too.

Not much sense in crying over spilt milk, is there?

Suppose not.

Looking after your mother all right?

She doesn't take much looking after, Dad, you know that. I just get under her feet, really.

All the same, me in here, you're the man in the house. She'll need all the company she can get.

She manages very well, Dad. Really. In fact, if I was out of the way as well she'd get a bit of peace and quiet for a change.

It can't be easy for her, me in here.

It's a rest for her.

She must worry. You know how she is.

It's a break from her usual grind, Dad. Change is as good as a rest.

She always did worry too much, your mother. A wonder she's not in here 'stead of me.

I brought you some grapes. Least, Mum bought them. I carried them.
Thanks.
When she left you just now she had to go off to the social security about something or other.
Couldn't you have gone for her?
They said it had to be her.
Bloody bureaucracy.

Dad, I have to go away for a day or two.
Go away? What for?
I have to. Sort of school work, you see.
School work?
A project. Only a day or two.
Couldn't you explain? About me in here. Your mother on her own.
Mam will be fine. It won't be for long. And it's the last chance before A levels.
Your exams? Can't go wrong with them. But she'll be on her own.
I'll phone twice a day. See she's all right. And that you're okay.
Doesn't matter about me. It's your mother I'm thinking of. On her own, in that empty house, worrying.
She'll be perfectly all right, Dad, and I'll be back before she's felt the miss of me.
I don't like it.
I'm sorry, Dad, but I have to go.

Are you doing all right at school?
Smashing, Dad. Very well.
Working hard?
I think so.

How's that dead woman?

Jane Austen?

Aye, her. All right, is she?

Fit as a fiddle!

Better off dead than alive, then, isn't she.

Wouldn't say that.

No, maybe not.

I'll have to be off, Dad.

Aye, right-o, son.

Good to see you.

Thanks for coming in.

Take care.

I'll try.

And mind them nurses.

Can hardly raise me arm never mind owt else.

See you, Dad.

So long. And here . . .

What?

Mind you get back from yon jaunt as soon as you can. You don't fool me, you know.

Tarra then.

Aye.

JOURNEY OUT

View from the "27"

If this were an old-fashioned story—the kind you, Morgan, so anathematize—this could be the beginning. The foregoing would be excoriated by the inventor's pen and omitted finally, or be revamped as flashback, that worn device of the suspense mongers. But this is not one of those old-fashioned stories, is it? Though it is, for me, a kind of beginning. Journeys always are, aren't they?

The bridge out of town, across the river, allowing passage from County Durham to Yorkshire, humps beneath us, a pleasant undulation, providing glimpse over its grey stone parapet of ling-brown Tees, in swirls, urgent, full-bedded, passing beneath.

The Tees is diarrhoeic today: a consequence of spring rains elutriating Pennine bogs and peat. I digress, Morgan, only to entertain your anti-dithyrambic turn of mind.

Why is it I wish Morgan were here now?

To return to the matter in hand. The tantalizing vision not just of a willing but of a lusting Helen. And of a harassed mother and a stricken-prone father. The pursuit of the one inflames in me guilty feelings at my desertion of the others. But without feeling there is no guilt. So my guilty feelings provide proof of my filial affections for those from whom I seek escape.
  Ha.

Maybe that is what this journey is really all about? Ineluctable

34

evolution. Proving myself to myself, if to no one else. The strivings of my independent spirit.

Getoutthereladandshowthemyoucanstandonyourowntwofeet.
Ffossip.

'She should have had more sense,' said the ageing driver-conductor to a rotund passenger of the female gender standing by the open bay of the driver's cab in flagrant disregard of the bus company's rule published in a notice posted above her head.

DO NOT STAND ON PLATFORM
WHILE BUS IN MOTION

'Well,' said the passenger, 'there's many a slip.'
'Aye,' said the driver, 'nor but it's happened before.'
'And happen it'll happen again,' said the passenger.
'What 'tis to be young,' said the driver.
'Nay,' said the passenger, 'nowt like it, is there!'
They laughed; knowing.

LIMBSOME . . . LITHESOME . . . LOVESOME said a neon-glowing advertising panel above a window.

Picture accompanying words: a pair of dismembered legs of the female gender, arranged like pretty boomerangs, dressed in tan-coloured tights.

Intention of advertisement: to sell women's stocking tights by suggesting that they will transform every wearer's legs into limbs of the sort pictured. Mine too?
Ha.

He took from his wallet, where he had carefully placed it, Helen's previously provocative picture, and smiled. She needed no tights.

There was that time when I was about eight when we still lived in the country at One Row, seven or eight anyway, before you really know what it's all about, Mickey and me were wandering back home down the path through the wood when we saw a gang of older kids ten of them maybe all about ten or eleven as well and all of them crowding round looking at something in the middle of them and they were grinning and nudging and excited but keeping it quiet because, you could tell, they didn't want to attract the attention of grownups who might be nearby but they didn't pay Mickey and me any bother and we went up to them and edged our way to the centre and they had a girl there who wasn't much older than eight herself maybe nine and they'd made her lift her skirt and drop her pants and show them herself . . . None of them touched her they just looked as they would at a new kind of toy in a shop window everybody taking a turn in front of the girl to bend down and look closely so that the crowd was circling slowly and bending and rising like a slow circling wave or an endless queue of courtiers processing round a queen and bowing to her . . . We had a look Mickey and me then went off back into the wood again and sat on a log side by side not saying anything at all just shivering, trembling, giggling at each other . . . When we recovered we wandered down the path home and the crowd had gone and the girl had gone and we had not seen the girl's face because her skirt had been held up in front of her all the time we were there. And when we got back to our street there was Mickey's mother and mine standing outside our back gate in their aprons with their arms akimbo watching us come and muttering to each other frosty faced so we knew we were in trouble. We know where you two have been Mickey's mother said when we got up to them. You nasty little beasts. You get home my lad and don't you dare do anything like that again. But my mother just looked at me not speaking till after she had given me my tea when she looked at me again for a minute before she said You know they could have crippled that poor girl for life . . . I puzzled over that for days afterwards but couldn't understand how she could have been crippled just from us looking at her but no one said . . . When Dad was told he just grinned at me when Mother wasn't looking. And winked.

Ditto beat a retreat from his memory, replacing Helen's photograph in his pocketed wallet. Richmond was in view.

On Richmond hill there lived a lass
More bright than May day morn

Ho ho

RICHMOND, Yorks. Pop. 46,500. Ec Wed. Md Sat. Situated on hill-top dominated by 11th Cent. castle, now ruined, built c1075, commanding superb view across R. Swale. Walls 11th Cent. but most surviving military structure 12th Cent. Castle originally entered from town through gate-tower, converted late 12th Cent. into base for 100ft high stone keep, still standing. At S.W. corner remains of original hall containing domestic quarters. Legend claims Robin Hood held captive in Robin Hood Tower in N.E. wall; also that King Arthur's Knights lie sleeping beneath the castle, waiting for the time when a brave man awakens them to save the world from disaster.

Town built round one of the largest and finest market squares in Britain, continental European in feeling. Narrow alleyways lead off, locally called 'Wynds'. Also: Georgian theatre, in use, dating from 1788. Green Howards' Regimental Museum in crypt of Holy Trinity Church standing in centre of market square, unique example of church with shops beneath. Baden-Powell, founder of Boy Scouts, once lived in tower in S.W. corner of castle.

Apart from historical and legendary associations, this attractive little town possesses considerable architectural beauty and great scenic beauty. Visit recommended.

Bus Stop

Ditto descended into the market square. The bus journey had been an experience. Insignificant, commonplace, undramatic perhaps, but an experience: his reason for journeying.

And what was the nature of this experience, this bus journey? He contemplated the question quarter-mindedly as, hitching his pack on to his shoulders, arranging straps and frame comfortably, he plodded off, boots cobblestone-ringing, into Walter

Willson's, there to buy a can of McEwan's Export pale ale, before making for the castle, where he proposed finding a sunny, sheltered corner which offered a view up the river. There he could sit and enjoy his meal.

Nature of bus experience*: consoling, comforting, contenting. Vehicle warm. Motion tranquillizing. Moving view—seen from his snug seat—of passingly pretty interest despite having seen it many times before. The whole provocative of piquant thoughts and sensational images. Unhurried, unworried. Cocooned irresponsibility.

Is that why so many people like travelling?

Maybe, he supposed, his mind turning to thought of his mother's always perfectly made (just moistly right) tomato and egg sandwiches and wedge of apple pie. And the McEwan's, for which his thirsting tastebuds goosepimpled. One thing about a bus trip, it coated your mouth with dehydrated diesel oil.

He sought out his favourite spot in the castle, where the south-west wall breaks from Scolland's Hall into a tumbling defile, a rift in the defences that slips dizzily to the road and river a hundred feet and maybe more below. There is a ledge wide enough to sit on and stick out your feet, where you are hidden

---

*All right, all right, I admit it! I got this idea for telling my tale from *At Swim-Two-Birds* by Flann O'Brien (which I have been reading recently with, I might add, often puzzled pleasure). But then, to be fair, I expect he pinched it from somebody else. (Nothing is safe these days.) But from whom? James Joyce I'll bet. I've discovered that almost all the interesting things contemporary writers do they get from his *Ulysses*. Which I have never managed to read beyond page 27. (I've only tried twice, I confess. But Midge says everybody talks about *Ulysses* and how it is the greatest novel of the twentieth century but that few people have actually ever read it right through to the end. So I don't feel *that* guilty. I've a few years left to try it again.) But working on the principle that there is nothing new in this world, where did Joyce get the idea from? I asked Midge. He said, 'Good question. Probably from Duns Scotus, or one of those forgotten Jesuit theologians Joyce was brought up knowing about at his ghastly school. It sounds to me like the kind of way Jesuits would argue. But go and find out for yourself, lad. Why expect me to know and do all your work?' Typical Midge!

from treading tourists unless they brave the edge. There today the sun shone uncooled by a breeze, and from there the broad sweep of the river and its vee-shaped valley can be seen stretching away up the dale. So there he sat, bum cushioned on folloped groundsheet, back pillowed by pack placed against Scolland's ruined stones.

Sandwiches, pie and beer he set safely firm on the ground, in reach of his right hand.

Quiet.

But a quiet made of surging Swale, fast, full from rain in the hills; a lark ascended, singing; wind soughing in trees furring valley sides, new green blinking in the breeze, sun-flashed. Blue sky. White flock clouds islanded. Grey stone.

An active peace.

Suntillating

No sooner had I enjoyed my small repast and had settled myself to a sunbathed repose than I was discovered by a youth perhaps a year or maybe two older than myself.

Description of intruder: Tall, well-built, mongrel-handsome. Dressed in regulation jeans, dungaree shirt washed to faded pale blue, open to fourth button, revealing hairless tanned chest, muscled. Hair brown, thick, long, tending to curls, casually (but carefully) arranged. Eyes blue, alert; nose narrow, straight; mouth thick-lipped, wide, smiling. Teeth white, sound, attractively irregular. Donkey jacket slung over shoulder perhaps a touch too self-consciously nonchalant. No other portables.

'Watcher,' he said, sitting himself crosslegged at my in-castle side with athletic, look-no-hands smoothness.

Nature of remark: Friendly, inviting conversation, in Geordie (i.e. Tyneside) accent.

For an irritated moment, I resented this disruption of my cosy, somnolent pleasure. But I reminded myself of my resolve, of the very purpose of my adventure. Here was an opportunity of precisely the kind I wanted, an opportunity for new experience, for something to happen, and it was being offered to me unlooked for.

I shifted my slumping torso into a more welcomingly attentive, upsitting posture.

'Watcher,' I replied, assuming as nearly as I could my new companion's tone and inflexion, as a deliberate means of ingratiation.

'You haven't seen my mate, have you?' he said. His eyes were searching me out.

'Who's your mate?' I asked.

'You don't know my mate?' he said, surprised. 'I thowt everybody knew my mate.'

'I'm not from Richmond,' I said, apologetic.

He regarded my cushioning backpack. 'No, 'course. Sorry,' he said without sorrow.

(I remarked to myself again how not knowing what people without reason expect you to know at once lowers your stature in their eyes. Lowers their interest in you anyway.)

'Mind you,' I said, unable to prevent myself attempting further ingratiation, 'I can't see much from here and there's been nobody in sight while I've been here. And I've been here about half an hour.'

'He's not been then,' said my companion. 'Just like him. "Meet me in the Castle about twelve," he says when I saw him this morning. "We'll go for a drink." We never go into the Castle for a drink so naturally I come here. But he'll be there already, propping up the bar. Impatient swine.'

He laughed.

Nature of laugh: Indulgent chortle, not irritated.

Comment seemed inappropriate; I smiled to show willing.

'I don't know why I bother with him,' he went on. 'Take last night for instance. Meet him half-seven at the billiards, he tells me. "We'll have a bit of a game and a bit of a giggle with the lads," he says. I get there at quarter to eight—I knew he wouldn't be there before then no matter what—and I wait around like a spare part till nine. Then he strolls in, grinning like a ninny, and

40

I can see straightaway that the smile is all show. Really he's got a right beat on, so I don't say owt to upset him, and he just picks up a cue and knocks hell out of the balls for twenty minutes before he says a word. And then he doesn't say much more than "Buy us a pint, kiddo." I could have thumped him.'

He repeated his former laugh.

This time a remark seemed necessary to maintain the conversation.

'Then why didn't you?' I asked, affecting genuine interest.

'I have before now, I can tell you,' he said, giving me a glance.

Nature of glance: Collusive, implying that this confession was just between ourselves and that I would understand what others might not.

'I had a go at him just a few nights back. He'd messed me about all day. We ended up in a pub in Catterick. I was in a right mood by then and he started playing up. Having a go at me, you know, in front of a gang of soldier boys that were boozing in there. He gets ower big for his boots at times like that, shows off a bit. So he's giving me some stick, taking the piss like. Well, I've had enough like, and a pint or two, and all of a sudden me stomach hits me eyes and I grabs him and waltzes him out the back into the car park and gives him a right leathering. He's smaller and thinner than me so he didn't stand much chance with me losing me rag, you know, I'm pretty bloody when I'm in a paddy, but by god he still managed to bend me nose about and make me pant. He's game all right. I think he wanted a fight, mind, and he knew I'd not damage him too bad, us being mates, you know, so he went prodding on till I lost me blob. He knew I would. He knows my limits, like. Same as I know his. And if you can't have a good scrap with your best mate who can you have one with? You know what I mean, I expect.'

Morgan.

'Yes, I know,' I said.

'It's a grand day for the race,' he said.

'Which race?' I said.

41

'The human race,' he said, and laughed.

'It is,' I said, smiling through his mockery. 'So why didn't you thump him last night?'

'Wouldn't have been right.'

'Why not?'

'Well, he has this father, you know. Anywhere for a big apple he is, a right crawler. They don't get on. Always rowing. And I could tell they'd had a set-to last night before he came to the billiards. So I laid off. But I was still fed-up with him all the same.'

'Why didn't you go and join him in the pub then, if you know that's where he'll be?'

'No fear! Last night was last night. This morning's different. You can't be giving in all the time. He can stew in there. After a bit he'll feel guilty and come looking, all apologetic and smarmy and trying to make out it's all my fault. "Why, Jacky," he'll say, surprise surprise. "What you doing here? I thought we said we'd meet in the pub, man. I've been waiting half an hour, till I got worried about you and thought I'd better look for you out here. I'm sorry, mate." Like that, you know. But he doesn't fool me.'

'You known him long?'

'About six months. He picked me up one day when I was hitching from Scotch Corner toward Brough. I was making for Liverpool, as a matter of fact. But he brought me here and we hit it off that well we started knocking about together. I stayed on here, got a job labouring for a builder doing some work round Easby Abbey, down the river, you know.'

'You got digs to stay in or what?'

'No, no. I've got a room at my mate's house.'

He seemed surprised I had not understood his domestic arrangements without asking. At which my courage failed me to inquire further. Nor could I have done. For at that moment a shadow fell across us. There standing in the eye of the sun on the wall behind us was a youth who could be no other than Jacky's mate.

42

Description of Jacky's mate: Please enter below your preferences for Jacky's mate's appearance and features. Note well: he must, of course, be handsome (in your eyes if in no one else's) and he must for the sake of this narrative be about eighteen. Jacky has also said that his mate is shorter than he; but then Jacky is over six feet tall and heavyish, so there is plenty of room left for your own imagination and predilections:

Proposal

'I'm sorry, mate. I've been waiting for half an hour, till I got worried about you and thought I'd better look you out. I thought we said we'd meet in the pub, man? What are you doing hiding here?'

'What did I tell you?' said Jacky to me but squinting up at his mate, his eyes dazzled by the haloing sun.

'Like that, is it?' said Jacky's mate, smiling.

Nature of smile: Acidly competitive, inviting tart rejoinder.

He jumped down from the wall and sat on the sloping bank facing us, his hands bracing his body upright. A puff of wind, it seemed, might send him scudding down into the valley deep at our feet, like a child skidding down a helter-skelter.

'This is my mate Robby,' said Jack to me, but still looking at his friend. 'The one I was telling you about.'

'Been telling you about me, has he?' said Robby, glancing at each of us in turn like a cat eyeing two neatly cornered mice.

'The purr you hear,' said Jack, looking at me this time, 'is not Robby's laugh. He has a laugh like a ball of wool.'

'What fun! A new friend!' said Robby with monotone sarcasm.

'You had a bad night,' said Jack.

'And a worse morning,' said Robby. 'But entertain me. Tell me about your—cough cough—friend. What's his name? Introduce me, social moron.'

There was at this point within me an irresistible rise of gall with the attendant side-effect of spontaneous anger. At such moments I have no courage nor any restraint. I merely react. Is that what wins V.C.s? Unthinking, unwishing, I said:

'Why don't you get stuffed.'

There was between my two companions that satisfyingly shocked hiatus which succeeds such unexpected outbursts from an apparently mild-tempered and disadvantaged stranger.

Then Robby rolled on to his side, beat upon the turf with an excited fist, giggled with unnecessary exaggeration, and gasped:

'Great! Marvellous! Terrific! Isn't he beautiful! Hasn't he just drummed us, Jacky!'

While this demonstration was in stagey progress, Jack, grinning but not smiling, leaned towards me and muttered:

'Go steady, kiddo.'

'I'm going nowhere,' I said in matching reply, 'till I'm ready.'

'Here, I say, you two,' said Robby, pushing himself up and climbing across us into the eye of the sun again. 'Let's go to the pub. We'll have a pint. I'll treat you. How about it, drummer boy? You game?'

'If your mate is,' I said.

'Sure he is, aren't you, Jacky? Nobody ever heard Jacky Thompson turn down a free pint.'

Jack stood up, as smoothly as he had sat down, Arab-fashion, and somehow unexpectedly graceful given his size and solidity.

'Aye,' he said, 'come on, kiddo.'

Pubtalk

'Politics,' said Robby when the pints were ringing a table in the corner of the Bishop Blaize, 'now there's a subject to keep off in a pub. Sex and religion being the other two.'

'Nowt much else to talk about,' said Jack, raising his glass.

'Sport maybe, if you like that sort of thing. But you're not going to start on all that again, are you?'

'I've a question to put to our new friend.'

'Look out, kiddo. Trouble.'

'Kiddo can look after himself all right,' said Robby. 'So much is known.'

Jack sucked at his beer. 'A nice drop that Camerons,' he said. 'Good enough to curl your toenails.'

'I take it you're on the right side,' said Robby, ignoring Jack. 'Roughly anyway.'

'Is there ever a right side?' I said. 'Rough or otherwise.'

'An intellectual!' said Robby and honked a laugh that drew staring glances from other parts of the room.

'Listen who's talking,' said Jack. 'Karl Marx resurrected.' He stood, drained his glass, belched. 'My round,' he said and went, casual, to the bar.

'No more for me,' I called to his back.

He flapped a dismissive hand.

'Of course there's right sides and wrong sides,' said Robby in an indivisible tone.

Indivisible: Because earnest, unwilling to banter, arrogantly assuming authority.

But then, I thought, he's been like that all the time, despite appearances to the contrary. There's a manic note in his emotional coloratura. A result of his running battles with his father? And does like always attract like so surely as this? If so, then Jacky is in the deep end with his father too! Must find out.

'You can't opt out of commitment,' Robby was saying. 'Either you're for or against. There are no fences left to sit on. Not any more.'

'Only slogans to rant?'

'You have terminal apathy and gangrenous cynicism.'

'Don't mistake healthy scepticism for pusillanimous indifference.'

'Nor your epigrams for truth.'

'I wish they had Newcastle Exhibition here,' said Jacky returning triple-glass-handed. 'Right nectar that stuff is.'

He sat down, shaking slopped beer from his hand.

'Unlike this beer,' said Robby, sipping delicately from his brimming pint, 'kiddo here is all head.'

'O, aye?' said Jack, 'a bit frothy, is he? And how should he be?'

'You know the trouble with intellectuals?' asked Robby.

'You tell me, clever lad,' said Jack.

'They are so busy sorting out all sides of the argument they never get round to doing anything.'

Jack raised his glass to me in salutation, winked, lifted his eyebrows, and sank his pint in one unbreathing swallow.

'Consider Jack the dripper,' said Robby. 'He doesn't think too much, but he knows where he stands. Knows what it's all about. Don't you?'

'If you say so,' said Jack putting down his glass. He belched again without restraint, wiped his mouth with the flat of his hand and said, 'I could go a nice pork pie, I know that. How about you?'

'See what I mean?' said Robby. He tossed a fifty pence piece among the beer glasses and swill. 'Here, I'll stand you.'

'Not for me, thanks,' I said. 'I had something in the castle.'

'Not our Jack, I hope,' said Robby.

'Lay off, eh?' said Jack, and went off to the bar again.

'How did you meet him?' I asked.

Robby eyed me in sharp, askance amusement for a moment.

'He got fed-up of home,' he said, 'and decided to have a breather for a while. See some places, you know. His dad gives him hell. Always nagging at him . . .'

Bingo.

'. . . Used to thump him about till Jack got too big and might thump him back. His mother tried to interfere once and he gave her a going over as well. Very pretty. You'd think Jack would be the aggressive sort after all that, but he isn't. As placid as flat beer, aren't you, Thompson?'

Jack returned with two cylinders of pork pie clasped in one

hand and a brimming pint in the other. 'Talking about me behind my back, are you?' he said, sitting.

'He's telling me about your father,' I said. 'Fathers interest
me.'

'Nowt much to tell. He's all right really, the old sod.'

'See?' said Robby to me. 'He's not just placid, he knows
where he stands. His father brings him up by hand and our hero,
here, leaves home to taste the delights of travel. Ah, you might
think, a classic case of filial rejection. But you'd be wrong. Our
hero has every intention of returning, actually and metaphoric-
ally, to the familial hearth, there to resume his hard-won place.
As soon as he's bored with the pleasures of the wide world,
home he'll scarper and take up life where it left him off. He's
just having a holiday, aren't you, Jacky lad? All this is just
excursion. Knows his roots, does our Jacky, and he'll be happy
enough to go back to the ground where he was planted.'

'You could be right about that,' said Jack, his pint once again
raised to help on its way the pie he had consumed in two bites.
'Do you want yours?'

Robby pushed his pie towards his friend. 'No, take it. Your
need is greater than mine. We can't have you losing your figure.'

'Ha ha,' said Jack, and consumed the second inadequate
refection.

Robby drained his glass, placed it on the table and stared at
me with that kind of brass-faced grin that means 'your turn'.

'You'd like another?' I said.

'Thanks, kiddo,' said Jack.

When I sat down again, wet-handed, Robby and Jack were
finishing a muttered conversation all too obviously about myself.

'On a hike?' asked Robby nodding at my pack lying by my
stool.

'A few days.'

'On your own?' asked Jack.

'Till tomorrow.'

Robbie: 'Meeting someone?'

'A friend.'

47

Jack's scatological laugh.

Robby: 'A girl, eh?'

'Once aboard the lugger and the girl is mine,' Jack sang, the beer fomenting a tune and an uninhibited performance. 'I'll bet you're a bit of a horizontal champion in your quiet way, bonny lad.' He guffawed and wagged a prim finger. 'Be careful, kiddo, or you'll dip your wick once too often.' He reprised his bawdy outburst.

'Looks like you missed out,' said Robby to Jack.

'O, aye?' said Jack, draining his glass. 'That depends on what I wanted in the first place, doesn't it, Sunshine?'

'Idiot,' said Robby and laughed.

Neither laugh nor conversation included me.

'All right now then are we?' said Jack.

'Champion, man,' said Robby, mock-Jack. 'Much relieved. And it's time you were making tracks.'

Jack looked at his wrist watch. 'It is an' all. Are you going to have a word with kiddo here?'

'I'll see to that. You get to work.'

'See you.'

'So long.'

Jack said to me as he stood up, 'Maybe we'll get together later on. So I'll just say tarra. Thanks for the pint.'

I had suspected for the past few minutes that I was becoming inane. Suspicion now was confirmed. To Jack's goodbye I could do no better than smirk and wave a collapsing hand. It was at that very second I realized the cause of my disintegration: the same as my urging desire to visit the lavatory. With some surprise I heard my voice speaking my ponderous thoughts to Jack's retreating figure: 'I've had five pints.'

Jack turned at the door. 'Down but not out,' he said and was gone.

'He's a nice bloke,' I was saying to Robby. 'I like him.'

'I'm glad,' said Robby, tolerant as a barmaid. 'I think he likes you too.'

His tone was sobering.

'You're extracting,' I said, but with careful effort.

'Never!' said Robby. 'But listen. What are you doing tonight?'

'Dunno.'

'I've got something to do this afternoon.'

'I think I'll have a sleep.'

'But tonight, after six, Jack and me have an amusement planned. Would you like to join in?'

'What you going to do?'

'Come and find out. Don't want to spoil things by telling. It'll be a surprise. How about it? You game?'

'It'll all be experience, won't it?' I said.

'It will for sure,' said Robby smiling.

'Where'll I meet you?'

'Let's say here at six-thirty. Okay?'

'Okay, but listen, I've nothing else to wear but what I've got on.'

'You'll do just fine. Just beautiful.'

'I really have to go out the back.'

'Enjoy a good splash. I'll see you tonight.'

'Half-six. Here.'

'You've got it. And one thing I will tell you. I bet afterwards you'll really know where you stand.'

'Nigmatic.'

'And irresistible!'

Robby went through the street door. I went through the door labelled

Graffiti

FAR AWAY IS NEAR AT HAND IN IMAGES OF ELSEWHERE

49

Ponderoso

Beer has made me tired plus getting up early and being in open
air so much   not used to all that   I'll have a kip in
the sun in the castle just where I was before just here
out of the way   nice   out of the wind too   but
can see up the valley   nice   pretty   ah

Don't know what to make of them two, those two, are they?
Dunno. Interesting. What do they do? if?

Skylark. Pretty view. Thought that before. But still true. Skylark. All that energy, larking about in the sky, all that work,
flying like demented, like in love.   Ah. Sex more like.
Larking in the sexy sky.

I can't even sing, never mind fly. What hope for me with sex?

England: lark, liquid, above a hill, verdant, blue sky dazzled
with pillows of clouds. Wordsworth and Vaughan Williams,
though I prefer Benji-the-jazzman Britten myself, who is
English enough too thank the lord.

And what's this they're up to tonight? Getting brave aren't I,
accepting such uncertain invitations from complete strangers.
What would Morgan say! Ah, Morgan, thou shouldst be with
us at this hour. Crap. He'd say I was a timid sod. Mayhap he'd
be right. How do you get like that? The prisoner is of a nervous
disposition, m'lud, and when attacked by five armed warders
cowed in a corner of his cell in a cow hardly way. Man's a fool.
Yes, m'lud. I sentence you to eternal anxiety and don't let me
hear from you again. Or is it learned? Mother always worrying.
Was she worrying when I was born? Was she at that mystic
moment wondering whether Dad had remembered to leave a
message for the milkman? Two pints today, please, we have an
extra mouth to feed. Was she, even, Shandy-like, unnerved by

some mundane distraction at the climactic moment of my conception? Or maybe Dad's right: that I know nowt except from books, am a pseud. Wonder how the old bloke is, poor chap. Always loathed being ill. Incapable. Like a hobbled animal. Raging against the indignity, the frustration, the loss of control. Rage, rage against the dying of the light, old man. With nowhere else to live except in his body what else do you expect? But that's an insult. To say he can't think. He can think. But he thinks by feeling and knows what he thinks by seeing what he does. Me, I know what I think by seeing what I say, like the poet said. Is that the difference, the real difference between us? Is that why I can't understand him and he can't understand me? Not the generation gap—crap that is—but the education gap? The thinking gap. Is that why he can't explain him to me and I can't explain me to him? He wants me to show him what I am, I suppose. Wants to see I'm like him by acting like him. Is that it? God knows. And He isn't too chatty. Is that why I'm here now doing all this? To try and show him? To try and convince myself I am more than he says? Could be all he wants, if *I* want? And are Robby and Jack what he wants? Jack reminds me of him a bit, as he was before his illness, as he must have been, judging from photographs, at my age. Good boozer, hard worker, one of the lads, a bit of a joker, good looking. A handsome feller, they say my dad was when he was young. They say that about Jack, I don't doubt. But there he is having a hard time with his dad, so what's his dad want of him? And Jack says Robby is always rowing with his father. Though in his case it sounds like he wants his father to be something different from what he is instead of t'other way about. A flipping father trio. Morgan doesn't have

Salutation

'A penny for them.'

Helen. In full flesh bloom. Better than the photograph. I could hardly look at her but in snatched glances. Shyness is an illness and ought to be medically treated.

51

'Hey! What . . .?'

'Meeting you, chump.'

'But I thought . . .'

'To get here I had to tangle a web. Officially, by which I mean parentally speaking, I'm here on a three-day state visit to my father's brother, otherwise known as my uncle, and his family who live in Gunnerside. I told you I'd find a way.'

'Very convincing.'

'In one hour I embark on United's three-o service going forward to Reeth, where I shall be picked up by father's brother's wife, a child-weary mother of eight, one more being imminent, a prolific breeding record I regard as more suitable to rabbits than human beings. On arrival and after a suitable time has passed, I shall casually mention to my bucolic uncle that I met by chance here in Richmond, as indeed I have, an old friend, verily a school pal from my Darlington years, who invited me to a social evening (ahem ahem) . . . well, go on, invite me . . .'

'O, of course, please join me for an ahem social evening tomorrow.'

'Thank you kindly, kind sir. Tomorrow it shall be. And, I shall continue, I would appreciate it if they would allow me to accept and keep the appointment. They, of course, only too glad to be spared an evening of my stay without my adolescent presence, will say yes, but be careful. And I shall meet you where'er you will. Okay?'

'Do you really have to strain the truth so brazenly?'

'Did you?'

'Touché.'

'Maybe I should go out and come in again?'

'Sorry.'

He had had a picture in his mind of how this meeting would go and it was not like this. She talking so much, he tongue tied. He hated being taken by surprise, unprepared. Surprises always turned him sulky. He did not know why but called it shyness.

Helen knelt at his side, bent down, and kissed him. A gentle caress; unmistakably inviting.

'I haven't come sixty miles for a discussion about morality,' she said. 'And you've been boozing. I can smell it. And taste it now.'

'Further apologies. I met a couple of blokes and had to keep my end up in the pub.'

'Masculine crap. And that wasn't exactly the end I thought you'd come here to keep up.'

'Thank you for your confidence in my abilities.'

They laughed at last.

'Why is it always so difficult to be natural when you're meeting someone again after a long gap?' she said, settling herself at his side.

'Any prizes for the answer?' he said, shifting on to his side so that he could keep her reclining figure in view.

'You never know your luck.'

'Try fear.'

'Silly! I'm not scared of you.'

'O, yes, you are. Just as I'm scared of you.'

'How?'

'In case you've changed. Not what I remembered. Or expected.'

'And?'

'Better than.'

'Thanks, kind sir.'

Castle-gazing tourists ambled by, pretending the two recumbent figures they had surprised themselves by discovering were not there. They looked pointedly at the view.

'Are you over your fear yet?' she asked, her eyes closed to the sun.

'I'm recovering fast.'

'Good.'

'Are you okay here or do you want to go somewhere else?'

'The sun is warm, we're out of the wind and nearly out of sight. The grass is soft enough. Why move?'

'There are people about.'

'My, what a private soul you've got.'

She sat up, supporting her body with her arms, her head hanging back full-face to the sun. Beautiful. Provocative. Unknowing? or coy design?

'No,' she said. 'I really do have to get to my uncle's. Mother knows my e.t.a. and will telephone to be sure I've arrived.'

'I know the feeling.'

'Cloy cloy.'

She sat cross-legged; plucked at the turf between her knees. 'Why must they?'

'Yours always seemed pretty easy-going to me.'

'A front. In public they affect a liberal nonchalance.'

'At home?'

'They have three different locks on each of the outside doors, burglar-proof catches on all the windows, and they keep a chromium-plated fire extinguisher under their bed.'

'The latter necessary to douse the ardour of your father's passions.'

'Which explains, no doubt, why the extinguisher has never been used.'

They laughed.

'So they're running scared,' he said.

'For them life is an obstacle course littered with booby traps.'

'And their little girl is always in danger.'

'That's how it used to be. I was ten before they stopped worrying about baby-snatchers.'

'And now they worry that you'll get raped.'

'Wrong. They could almost cope with that. I'd be the injured party, you see. All their expectations about life would be confirmed and they'd have me at home to nurse and coddle all day.'

'So what's the problem?'

'They think I'll do the raping. They don't say so in as many words, naturally. That's the infuriating thing. They pretend to be concerned, and warn me about men who are after only one thing, as they put it. But they can't hide what they are really thinking, that I'll go out and lay any man who takes my fancy.'

'And get yourself pregnant.'

54

'No, no. You still don't understand. That's just what a man would think.'

'So I'm a man!'

'And cute with it. I'm sorry. It's just that I'm all stewed up about them at the moment.'

'Join the club.'

'There was a row, you see, about my coming away.'

'So what should I know that men never do? Tell me, I'm truly interested.'

'Sure? I don't want to bore you. We both came here for some fun, remember.'

'Which is just what you're telling me your parents are worried about, isn't it?'

'You're getting warm, I'll give you that!'

'Fun and games. Hanky-panky. And actually I'm boiling with frustrated passion.'

'I should have brought the aforesaid extinguisher. Actually, they use phrases like that: hanky-panky and fun-and-games. Would you believe? You see, if I got preggers that would confirm their beliefs about life. Another of the traps. And if I liked the bloke and married him that would make it all right. I'd be properly trapped, paying for my mistakes, taking the consequences of my actions—all that guff. And I'd be there, lumbered, for them to cluck over still, giving advice, and, what's best, with a baby for them to feel sentimental about.'

'And all forgiven.'

'Of course.'

'But if you had fun, played hanky-panky and didn't get with child?'

'I'd be a loose woman. I'd be promiscuous and, worst of all, I'd be enjoying it. I'd be an unpaid whore, a happy hooker, a woman of easy virtue. Etcetera. That's what bothers them most.'

'Ugly words.'

'Ugly sentiments.'

'But never said straight out?'

'O, no. That's what makes it so horrible. I don't think I'd

55

mind if they came straight out and said what they think. Trouble is, I suspect they don't even know that they think it. So it all comes out in innuendo, by implication. And somehow, that makes everything worse. Dirties everything.'

Ditto thought of his father; their rows; their straight words. And of his mother, with whom he rarely discussed or argued about anything. (He had promised to telephone home this evening and must not forget; he owed them that, and was glad to discover he wanted to keep his promise.)

'The other way can be as bad sometimes, you know,' he said. 'People say wounding things in anger. And words said can't be unsaid.'

'I'd take my chances.' She stood up. 'My bus leaves in a few minutes.'

He stood up too and leaned back against the wall. He felt an impulsive desire to probe her presence with him now, to hear her reason it. He knew before he spoke that his question was a mistimed curiosity. But could not help himself.

'Just tell me one thing before you go.'

She looked at him, her face still betraying the feelings their conversation had revived. But he could not hold back.

'Why did you send that letter and your photograph?'

'Ask no questions and you'll get no lies,' she said. 'But if it bothers you—'

She turned and all but ran from the castle.

'Helen!' he called.

But she did not stop; and he did not follow.

He pressed his back against the wall. Hard. Bruising stone on brittle bone. Till it hurt. Sharp, clean pain.

His eyes guarded the castle gate against her return. (She *must* return.) While his mind picked himself to pieces.

Fool. Idiot. Clod. There is about you an instinct to disruption. I have noticed it before, often. I could list a number of such occasions but it would be tiresome. Cloth-head. Why don't you just shut up sometimes. You like to get something going nicely and then upset it. You have few talents but your skill in this is consummate. Like a small child building sandcastles and then smashing them down because the sea might get them. You pole-axed or something. What chance again. Stupy. Why. To stop anything coming too close. Is that it. Afraid to be known. To be vulnerable. It's so. Admit. Foolarse. Afraid what you'll learn about yourself. True. It is. Pity 'tis. Twit.

Unthought conclusions sent him sprinting from the castle, belongings left abandoned by the wall.

In the market place he stopped. The Reeth bus was there by the cross, its engine running.

He reached it, panting, searched the windows in panicky haste for Helen's face. He found her in the middle of the farther side, sitting on the inner seat, a solid farmwife between her and the window. She was staring straight ahead, her face impassive, but tears coursing her cheeks. He knew she knew he was there, agitated in the road. He reached up and placed both hands flat against the window. 'Helen!' he called and slapped the glass with his hands. The farmwife turned a fierce, embarrassed face to him. 'Helen!' he called again. But she would not look. The bus door closed, the engine revved, pumping exhaust about his feet. He scrabbled in his anorak pocket, found a ballpoint pen, the slip of paper they had given him at Walter Willson's check-out. The bus's brakes blew off; he heard, as he scribbled, the gear engage. Licked the slip of paper across his writing, slapped it on to the window just as the bus accelerated away.

He had scrawled one word.

Interlude

I've had enough for a while. Am in need of light relief. Anyway, there is now a passage of time between Helen's departure and my next encounter. I did nothing after she left but mope about the place, mentally and emotionally flagellating myself. I have no intention of going through all that again here. It is so embarrassing. So please take it that this space covers the intervening three hours. Use your own imagination to fill in the details. Why do I have to do all the work!

Telephone Call

Hello?

Hi, Mum, it's me.

Hello, love.

How is he?

Not so hot, love. How are you?

I'm fine. Is he worse?

I don't know. They don't tell you anything.

They must say something, Ma.

O, they say don't worry and he's as well as can be expected. But what does that mean to anybody?

Should I try and telephone him?

I shouldn't, dear.

Why not?

It would only upset him.

Why? How could it upset him? I'd have thought he'd be pleased to hear me.

He'd be pleased to see you.

But he can't, can he? He can talk to me though.

That's just it, dear. Your dad thinks you should have stayed at home with me, you know. It would upset him to talk to you on the phone. And that would only make him worse.

He might get another attack.

Another attack would kill him.

Do you want me to come home now?
I'll manage, it's all right.
But do you want me to come home?
You're there now, love, you might as well do what you went to do.
I'll come if you want.
Ring in the morning. He's low but he's not on the danger list. He'll be all right.

Goodnight, love.

Goodnight, Ma.

Downer

Six-fifteen: Ditto is in the public bar of the Bishop Blaize. By six-thirty he has downed two pints of best bitter and is staring at his half-consumed third. Never in his life has he consumed so much alcohol so quickly. A sharp-pained headache is brewing across the left side of his skull. With fierce concentration he tries to deal with a confusion of conflicting emotions.

He feels guilty at leaving his father and mother for a less than necessary purpose. He is annoyed at himself for feeling guilty, an annoyance compounded by anger at allowing guilt to oppress him. Helen's rupturing departure adds anxiety to this recipe for depression; and frustration. If she maintains her disaffection, his journey is wasted and his desertion of home and parents a squandered ordeal.

Of course, this self-scourging is accompanied by a chorus of conditional justifications. *If* his father had not been so provocative, he would never have suffered his heart attack in the first place. But, Ditto knew, whatever the cause of the trouble, a break would have happened between them sometime anyway. After all, he had to gain his independence somehow. Etc., etc.

59

The concatenation is universally scripted from an early age; why torture us all by rehearsing it again here?

What disturbs Ditto most of all as he glowers at his beer through inexperienced boozer's wet eyes, is an undercurrent to his storming emotions, the meaning of which he cannot yet be certain about. In that calm centre where our sanity takes refuge at such times, he wonders if it is fear that his father will die while he, Ditto, is nefariously absent from the family hearth that gives him greatest distress? Or is it something less reprehensible?

(In his present self-abnegatory mood, he will not acknowledge himself able to feel anything honest and noble. But between mental brackets he toys for a moment with the prospect that this gripping undercurrent, the real engine of his turbulent feelings, is a grieving love for the man who lies now drugged to unconsciousness in a starched hospital bed attached to bottled life by plastic tubes. But the thought is unbearable and he slams closing brackets across the words.)

At which moment, six-fifty-three precisely, enter in high-stepping temper the awaited pals.

'Kiddo has turned to drink,' says Jacky.

'So we can down him,' says Robby. 'I'm glad you smirk, drummer boy, and glad to find you raring at the ready for our evening's adventure.'

'We'll just have a pint or two before we go,' says Jack.

'If we must,' says Robby. 'Though kiddo looks as if he's had enough already.'

'Get stuffed,' says Ditto, sour from his thoughts and his beer.

'I just have,' says Robby, 'and even I need time to revitalize my vitals, as it were.'

He sits at Ditto's side, patting his arm, which Ditto draws away.

'Fear not,' says Robby, 'there is no danger.'

They wait, silent, till Jack has placed three pints on the table and sat down facing them.

'Our friend,' says Robby to Jack, 'is on a downer. I recognize the symptoms. And know the remedy.'

'A good stiff drink is what he needs,' says Jack.

'No, no. Adrenalin. That's what he needs. The smack we manufacture for ourselves without aid from doctors and other pill pushers.'

'Stop nattering and sup your beer,' says Jack.

'One last word, executioner. I'll lay you both a bet—nay, will lay you both if you like—our adventure tonight will revive kiddo's flagging spirits a treat. You still game?'

The question is unavoidable.

'Maybe,' says Ditto, not without difficulty. 'Depends what you want to do.'

'Don't toy with your glass then,' says Robby, 'and look at me when I'm speaking to you.'

Ditto cannot help an involuntary glance and an unwilling smile.

'Ah, so it's the old gags you like best! We have vays of making you vile,' says Robby, his laughter infectious. 'As for this evening, dear friends: we begin with a public meeting, after which —doubt it not—you will be only too happy to engage in the titillatious romp I have in mind, a mystery escapade, an assault upon the bastion of boredom, an attack on high-toned hypocrisy, an antic night of convention breaking.'

'You're a right windbag when you try,' says Jack, drains his glass and stands. 'Come on then, Sunshine, one more before the fray, then we'll be off.'

Party: Political

Seven twenty-six. The market hall. Stale with aftertaste of festering vegetables. A cavernous hangar with concrete floor, windows high under iron-strutted roof-without-ceiling. An assortment of stackable chairs laid out in melancholy rows. A gaggle of forty-or-so people scattered about, leaving the first two rows and six ranks at the back yawningly empty. Down one wall, three trestle tables, scarred and bruised from their more usual market duties, bearing cups on saucers, plates of plain biscuits, bottles of milk, bowls of sugar, and a tea urn, all attended by a balloon-bosomed daleslady in blue print dress. At the front, another trestle table, this time its market-worn skeleton shrouded in a motheaten green velvet covering. Two chairs behind. Pinned, botchily, to the front of the covering a poster, wrinkled with crumple-creases: GET GOING WITH LABOUR.

Enter the three escapaders.

'I hope you are going to behave yourself tonight, young man,' says a voice from behind. A cockerel of a fellow peers at Robby, a knotty, tweed-jacketed, open-neck shirted man with a toothbrush moustache. A man with a mission, a belligerent in the Great Battle.

'Why, comrade,' says Robby in mocking astonishment, 'we can assure you categorically that at this time we have no intention of disruptin' the deliberations, though I must take this opportunity to warn you that we reserve our constitutional right to engage in legitimate dissent if we feel it necessary and any attempt to prevent us exercisin' our democratic rights will effect consequences for which we cannot be 'eld responsible.'

'Look, laddie,' says the man, 'don't get cheeky with me. I don't give a damn who your father is, if you start messing about, out you'll go—along with your poncey pals.'

He pushes our three friends aside and parades down the aisle to a seat in the first occupied row, where with nods and thumb-jabbings and animated mutterings, head turnings and hitchings of his body-bulging jacket, he indicates to his companions the presence of (and, no doubt, his recent exchange with) Robby, who, during this pantomime, seats himself in the empty back row, Jacky on his one side, Ditto on the other.

As soon as I sat down I knew I was not normal. Since leaving the pub I had felt like an arthritic marionette. Stiff but unable to stand unaided. My headache, during the two-minute walk supported on either side by my companions from the pub to the market hall, had gone from volcanic eruption to flushing soda-syphon. In my inside, I wanted to be sick; on my outside, I was uncannily aware, my face wore a popeyed grin. I did not know where I was being taken, nor by now did I care.

'Why are you fetching me to the dungeons?' I said as we entered the hall, for so it seemed.

An exchange took place between Robby and a cantankerous custodian. I listened and understood their conversation entirely.

'We must behave ourselves and damn our fathers or he will mess us about,' I said earnestly to Robby when we were seated and I had recovered from not having to stand up.

'That's about it, kiddo,' he said and patted my knee.

I considered the room carefully.

'Why are we attending a prayer meeting?' I asked.

But received no reply.

'Or is everybody sleeping?'

'Dreaming,' said Robby. 'Wakers asleep. No more.'

'Someone should tell them,' I said.

'I doubt if they'd listen.'

'He's never that tight on five pints,' said Jack.

'Who?' I asked, leaning across Robby to hear Jack's reply.

'Never mind, Sunshine,' he said. 'We'll look after you.'

Robby pushed me back up straight in my chair.

Two men appeared at the table in front of the serried rows. One sat. The other stood. The seated one disturbed me. I felt I knew him. The face: features of it instantly recognizable, other parts unknown. A disturbing visual cacophony.

'Comrades,' the standing man said in a gravel voice. Tall, balding, mush-faced, prunesqualler. 'Our guest this evening needs no introduction. We all know of his many achievements and of his commitment to the working class struggle.'

I watched and listened and sawheard in minddazzle.

Went on the standingman, 'government people solidarity people people party people policy party left people party-strugglesocialistwelcome'

A waterfall of fryingpan exploding lightbulbs.

The standingman sat, the sittingman stood.

And spoke; an eloquent precision.

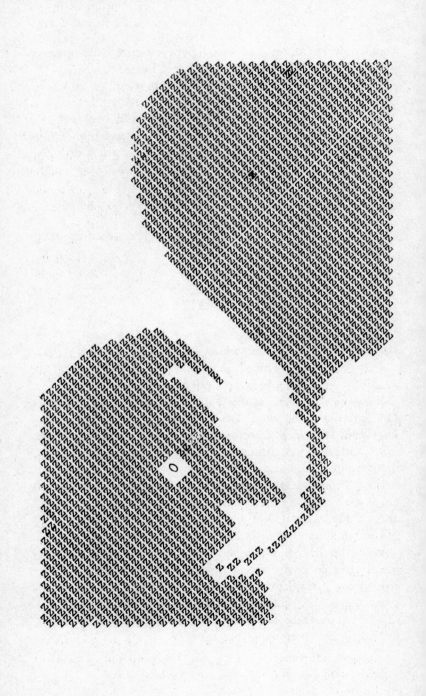

The sittingstanding talking man sat.

Fryingpan exploding lightbulbs waterfalled again.

'That was a load of elephant's,' yelled Jack through the cascade.

'All balloon,' said grin-grimacing Ditto.

Robby was Vesuvius before Pompeii got its historic come-uppance.

The hall silence. The standingsittingman stood again.

'stimulating honest peoplecomrade grateful socialist questions'

The again standing standingsittingman sat again.

Robby suddenly was standing at Ditto's sittingside, leaning forward, hands white-knuckled grasping the green tubular steel frame of the infront canvas-covered chair.

'I would like to ask our speaker when, if ever, he intends to demonstrate his solidarity with the working class by putting his considerable income where his not inconsiderable mouth is?'

'Furthermore, does our speaker condemn absolutely the hypocrisy of those who live by preaching the doctrine of socialist change, let's not use the dirty word revolution,'

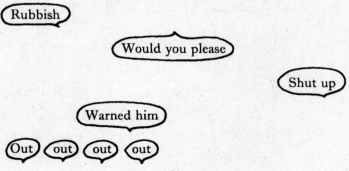

65

'while they themselves hold shares and directorships in important capitalist firms,'

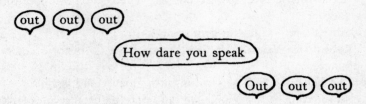

'not to mention their willingness to compromise on such matters as nationalization, the public schools, the maintenance of the House of Lords,'

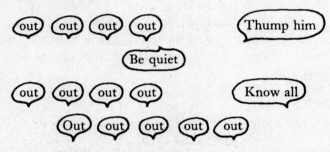

'and the careful use of backhanders, sinecure jobs, personal gifts and spurious business deals to sweeten local party officials'

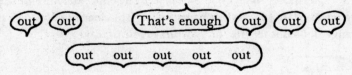

outrage	*thought Ditto*	shout out
outspoken	*rising*	lash out
outlandish	*to his*	lout
outmoded	*feet*	get out
outsider	*like*	fall out
outside	*a skinned diver*	move out
outback	*surfacing*	flout
outwit	*from the depths*	shout
outcast	*of an echoing*	cry out
outright	*pool*	right out
outstay	*into the*	stay out
outpour	*drumming torrent*	pour out
out	*of a thrashing waterfall*	out

'When will you sleepers wake!' yelled Robby as the surge engulfed him.

Ditto panned for Jacky; could not find him.

'Don't potter, Thompson,' he yelled, ablaze and hurling himself at the trembling surge breaking over Robby.

Chairs atomized.

A table subsided beneath assaulting bodies, spraying coruscating china in smithereens.

Trip in regain dodge balance fling forward to rescue and combat support, did Ditto.

An advancing bonewall.

Party: Paean

When he woke to consciousness, he wondered if it was really him lying there.

Sound of water.

Sound of trees.

Sound of breeze in trees.

Sound of water.

Feel of stone.

Hard feel of hard stone.

Feel of breeze, cool.

Smell of green.

Smell of brown.

Smell of breeze over water.

Smell of sick.

Beer-vomit.

He retched. Jack-knifed up, sitting, doubled, turned, threw up. Was clinging to an edge of stone and heaving into a flow of water inches from his obeisant face.

'Back in the land of the living at last, kiddo,' said Robby. 'We thought for a while we had lost you for good.'

The spasm remitted. He swilled a hand in the refreshing river. Performed with his palm a reviving baptism. Carefully lifted himself from the brink and took his bearings.

Late evening; a sunglow in the low sky, enough to pick out warmly the familiar lines of Easby Abbey poking from the trees above a bend in the river, upstream. There was opaque squint and sparkle on the wrinkling backwater pool at his feet, further out a grassy little knot of an island all but reached by humping boulders, the river curling into frothy little rapids between. On the bank, across, trees cushioned upwards, a fringe to the belly-ing field uprising beyond to the arching blue sky sweeping dome above the cave of trees under which he and Robby and Jack were.

Robby and Jack stretched out in luxurious ease on either side of where he must have lain, each with open cans of beer in their hands, their evening-paled faces regarding him with amusement.

'That was better out than in,' said Robby. 'Sit down before you fall down.'

'I'm okay, I feel better.'

'Have a swallow,' said Jack, holding out to him his beer can. He sat between them.

'Seeing I've just unloaded the last lot, I doubt I should.'

'Hair of the mongrel,' Jack said. 'Make you feel on top again.' He took the proffered can.

'How did I get here?' he asked.

'Brought you in my car, then carried you the few yards down here to this Elysian waterhole,' said Robby.

'I must have been knocked out.'

'Either by the thug who rammed his fist into your face or by the floor you fell upon. No one bothered much with the finer details.'

He drank a tentative mouthful of the beer. Surprised: he enjoyed both taste and swallow. Then, reminded of the blow to his chin, he prodded and gently manipulated his jaw. No damage, but a sore bruise.

'I have to tell you,' said Robby, chuckling, 'that that was not the only time you spewed this evening.'

'O, god, not in your car?'

'Nothing so ungracious.'

'Where then?'

'Shall I tell him?' Robby said to Jack.

'You will anyway,' said Jack.

'You must understand,' said Robby, snuggling his back into the bankside, 'that after you were so rudely despatched, the fracas came to a sudden stop. Which is just as well, considering you were prone in the path of the stampede. Our venerable chairperson—you remember him?'

'Vaguely. The standingsitting man.'

'Eh?'

'Never mind. Go on.'

'Well, he steps forward, our brave captain, folds you master-

72

fully over his shoulder—he's learned all the fireman's lifts, has our Hector—and marches down the hall. Just as he reaches the door you decide—or rather, your stomach decides . . .' Robby tries to restrain the laughter welling in him, '. . . decides . . . it has had enough of Hector's . . . of Hector's . . . Hector's shoulder stuck in it . . . and you . . .'

'O, no!'

'O, yes . . . threw up. All down his back.'

Ditto too is laughing now. 'Like a waterfall,' he gasps out.

'Just like!'

'Out, out, out!'

'Right out and down the back of Hector's best blue Sunday suit!'

'O, glory!'

'You're a daft pair,' says Jack, but he is holding his sides too.

'It was great,' says Robby. 'I've never seen a crowd lose interest in anybody so fast. Our Hector dumped you like a bag of garbage on the pavement, and disappeared double quick into the bog. I was hustled out after you by my friends and neighbours. The doors were slammed behind our backs, and presto! All was over!'

'No more than you wanted, I'll bet,' said Jack, recovered and able to drink his beer again.

'Could never have hoped for such a magnificent finale, bonny lad. Pure delight.'

Laughing so much made Ditto feel ill again. Vaguely, not specifically. The river at their feet swirlgurgled, sounding cool and clean and of melancholy purity.

'I feel filthy,' he said unexpectedly.

'And sound solemn,' said Robby. 'We can't have that. What you need is a good bath. That would work wonders. We've no bath, but we have plenty of water. Take a swim.'

'Leave him alone,' said Jack. 'You always have to be messing folk about.'

'I'll settle with you later, deserter,' said Robby, and stood, grabbed Ditto's feet, heaved on them, swinging him at the same

73

time so that he was lying along the edge of the river bank.

'No, gerroff,' he shouted, clawing at the ground to save himself from the water.

But Robby was laughing again; giggling rather.

'Strip him!' Robby yelled at Jack.

Jack did not move. 'Do your own dirty work.'

'No no!' Ditto shouted.

'Yes yes!' Robby replied, lunging for Ditto's trouser belt.

'Off! Off!' screamed Ditto, grabbing Robby's clawing hands and with desperate effort trying to turn himself and his assailant away from the water and his trousers.

Jack sprang to his feet to save himself from the rolling, struggling pair.

'Grab him, Jack,' Robby called.

Jack climbed higher up the bank and sat on a mossy boulder, vantage for the fray.

Suddenly it was essential to Ditto that he be free. No longer a game. His frivolous dissipate energy at once focused bleakly to that end. Firmly, he took grip of Robby's wrists, twisted body and arms, pulled, lunged, leaped, hurled himself in clean rhythm.

Robby was carried, surfing, upon the wave of Ditto's determined bore. Clasped together like lovers they rose from the scuffled ground.

'Submit, fool!' Robby cried.

Each pushed the other away; but each held to the other.

Their push-pull upset the poised balance of Ditto's determined rise.

They hit the water like felled trees with snared branches, at the same instant.

Robby rose from the shallow depths first, like a jack from its box.

'Victory!' he crowed, and danced a plodgy jig in the churning pool.

Firemuse

They made a fire of flotsam and dead branches, stood by it, sat by it, lay by it, and dried. Jack did not help, but sat on and on on his boulder, drinking his way through a six-pack of Newcastle Brown, saying nothing.

Night came, starry, still. The wetness steamed from their clinging clothes in the glowheat of the fire. Activity left them now happier to be cosy and unmoving, with nothing to say, each more comfortably comforted by his secret thoughts.

Ditto was remembering another fire, another chilly night, hardly more than two years ago before his father's illness prevented them living a normal life.

Together he and his father had been fishing up the Tees on some private water. They had lashed the river all the warm sun day but with little luck. Nothing to show, in fact, but one or two middling-sized dace, nothing special, no trout which they would most like to have landed and had hoped to catch when they had set off that morning almost at dawn in a sharp clean sun, the country washed by rain overnight, the air frostdew bright. A glisten. A sparkle. A kind of carnival in birdsong silence. A good day all day, a companionable day. They had not talked much, a few words now and then about bait or pools promising to cast upon. Nothing dissentient. They did not row then; that came later. Over lunch—coffee from a flask, mother's meat pie, cake, an apple each—they had twitted one another and joked, his father in good form, anecdotal, as he always was at his best and when happiest, but not frenetic as he could be when he had had a drink or two in the evening. Relaxed. Ditto had liked him then, loved him, felt proud in a way he could not explain to himself or to anyone else. But he knew now, thinking, that it was the man's simple delight in his day of freedom from work, in the beauty about him, his absorption to the point of obsession with his fishing: these were the things which gave him his self and were attractive and made Ditto proud. And Ditto knew at once then, that evening as they sat by their makeshift fire his father and he, that he was not as this man. Knew that he fished to please him by pretending absorption, not living it as his father did. He had spent the day like this to please his father not because it gave himself the kind of pleasure his father took from it. And did that matter? He did not know, could not decide, knew only that finally he did not want to do anything simply to please this man his father. Wanted to please him of course, but not to please him by pretence. He wished to do what was of himself, his own-him. And he wondered if his father knew this.

Whether his father did or not, from that day Ditto found he could not quite, ever, please his father again. No matter how much he tried, no matter how he acted out the pretence or how fervently he wished to recapture the closeness of that day, the last day of so many that had gone before, he could not. It was as if knowing he had pretended made it impossible ever to pretend again, whether he wanted to or not. His father always seemed to sense the lie. And it was from that time that the arguments, the disagreements, the fractured days began.

From that time, too, his father's illness took hold. Was that coincidence? Or consequence?

He did not know that either. And groaned aloud in the firelight, as people do when they want to push guilt and fear from their thoughts.

'Sounds like you're ready for some more excitement,' said Robby, rousing from his own reverie.

Fireplan

Soon after midnight Robby proposed that we now set out on the second part of his plan for the evening's escapade. I asked what he intended. He said he planned for us to burgle the home of that evening's guest speaker at the public meeting from which we had been so unceremoniously ejected.

Jack was against this.

JACK: You're an idiot, man. Leave well alone. You're just getting your own back.

ROBBY: I'm not asking you, deserter. I'm telling. Either join in or push off.

JACK: You never give up, do you!

ROBBY: Look, you copped out once tonight. Do it again and that's it. Okay?

JACK: So it's a test for me now as well, is it?

ROBBY: You treat it how you like. You know the score.

Their animosity was undisguised. I was not able then to untangle all that lay behind the exchange; this only became clear later, as you will discover in due time.

I was not, of course, myself happy about the proposal. When I voiced my unease, Robby delivered a somewhat lengthy diatribe, of which the following is an abridged version, reproduced as accurately as memory allows in Robby's own words:

'Look, this man is a socialist, right? And supposed to be a champion of the working class, at least that's what he's always claiming. He goes on endlessly about equality and the capitalist oppression and about a fairer distribution of wealth. He shouts about workers' control, nationalization of all the means of production and the institutions of business. You know the kind of stuff, you hear it every day. I believe it, as it happens. Not the slogany side of it, not the bandwaggoneers. I can't stand them any more than that collection of time-servers you saw tonight. But do you know how this paragon of socialist action lives? Eh? He has a house worth upwards of sixty thousand quid, he's got shares in half-a-dozen well-heeled companies and the last thing he'd want is for any happy band of workers to tell him what he's got to do. In other words, he's like all the rest, all he wants is a big slice of whatever there is going. He's a manipulator, that's all, and he mouths socialist doctrine because that's what he knows he has to do to get where he wants to be. It's the fashionable philosophy. You know how he got where he is? Good degree from respectable university. Into a trade union. Organized a nice little strike that he managed to keep going long enough to get sympathetic publicity but not so long that he lost it. From that straight into the national office as a blue-eyed boy. Then a quick side-step into the political corridors at Westminster and bingo, before you know it he's on TV all the time, he's advising unions about companies and employers about trade unions, he's all set for Parliament and is doing all right thank you out of fees, journalism, union support, sinecure salaries and kick-backs. Four hundred years ago he'd have gone into the church, written a classy book on ecclesiastical authority or burned a few heretics and been made a bishop in double-quick time. Bit of sex on the side, not mattering which sort, good food, nice house, secure job. And power. That as much as anything. Status, influence, authority, money. That's the name of the game. Always was, still is. His politics aren't a philosophy and they aren't a mission. And he's not crackers. His politics are a business, a career that gets him what he wants—being one of the elect of the earth.'

As this monologue went on, Robby showed many of the signs of stress which you, Morgan, as a budding M.D. would have been interested to note. He began trembling with anger, his voice became proclamatory as if he were addressing a public meeting. He broke into a sweat, beads of perspiration winked on his forehead, reflecting the firelight. By the end I knew I was watching a fanatic promoting his cause. If the sittingstanding talking man would have done well as a corrupt bishop, Robby would have matched him as a ruthless officer in the department of the inquisition. It was the kind of outburst you cannot reply to; and you cannot politely dismiss or change the subject afterwards.

There was a pause. Robby recovered his composure. (I realized then, watching him, that the thing I had felt vaguely about him all day and had not been able to pin down was that all the time he was on the edge of hysteria, that somehow this was part of both his attractiveness and unattractiveness. Like watching a bomb to see when it might explode. There was rumbling violence always just under the surface of his skin. And I could not

78

tell just at that moment what caused it. I was soon to discover.)

I said, as calmly and as amenably as I could—as though humouring a madman!—that though what he had said was no doubt true, I could not understand why he wanted to burgle the man's house.

I had, he replied, entirely missed the point. Words were no longer enough. Actions were what counted. Only actions revealed intentions truthfully. This man said he was a socialist but acted like any other grabber. This showed his true beliefs. He claimed to believe in equality, in fair distribution of wealth, and to be against greed and privilege. Okay, let him live by that. And as he had so much more than most people let us take some of his unequal wealth and redistribute it. Obviously he would not willingly allow us to do this, so it must be done by a people's tax, by an act on behalf of the people which we, representatives of the people, would execute.

DITTO: I agree with your theory. But not with the action you want to take.

ROBBY: You're a fool, then.

DITTO: Talk sense or not at all.

ROBBY: Okay. You're naive. You've swallowed all that junk they serve up at school about being a good citizen. You're allowing your upbringing to condition you to the morality of the status quo. Just what the cruds want.

DITTO: Crap. I'm saying that if you go around burgling people's houses,

You will have noticed, Morgan, that one of the difficulties of attempting to set down such an account as I am here engaged upon is to reveal simultaneous thoughts and feelings, with concurrent words and actions in such a way that you, dear reader, accept them as being at one, in the moment. Paralleling, as it were, the conversational exchange set down opposite I experienced an interior monologue of influential effect on my decision regarding Robby's criminal suggestion. What he proposed touched, not my mind, but my emotions. My nerves not my thoughts. You

79

however you justify it, it won't be long before everybody is at it whenever they feel like getting something for nothing. And that means nobody comes off best. Certainly not the ordinary bloke, who always comes off worst anyway.

ROBBY: You've no proof that that will happen.

DITTO: Don't talk stupid. It's human nature.

ROBBY: Human nature isn't absolute. It can be changed. And it is changed by conditions.

DITTO: And when your Great Socialist Society finally dawns, there'll be no need to burgle, I suppose.

ROBBY: That's right. Need makes burglars. And there'll be no need.

DITTO: Meanwhile, mayhem on the way to the Great Day.

ROBBY: If necessary, yes.

DITTO: And hard luck on the innocent victims.

ROBBY: To start with, no one is innocent in this fight. Second off, you can't make a cake without

know, Morgan, how often we have inveighed against the narrow restrictions of our education. How we have attacked, between ourselves and to our teachers, the false assumptions made about what we must do in life, how we shall—indeed *must*—live. How we have discussed the possible ways of breaking from that strait-jacket and of reforming it so that others who follow after are not subjected to similar pressures. (Robby was not alone in possessing hotly held ideals!)

I thought, at the same time, of my father, whose whole life has been lived by an honest regard for, a belief in the very system that makes it so that now he lies ill and has for two years suffered for simple want of the means of ease, want of the kind of attention that would alleviate him.

Solemn thoughts; telling emotions. But I have to admit that most persuasive of all was an irrational desire to chance my arm. I wanted to commit a dangerous act, wanted to know what excitements were to be had in crime, wanted for a smashing eggs. Third off, there's no gain without sacrifice, no healing of this sick man without deep surgery. Fourth off, I'm fed up with all this bloody chat. Are you coming or aren't you? Or are you like the rest of them, all hot air?

night to play the outlaw. Had I not set out to take indiscriminately what life offered? Could I turn away because it offered something that might offend a delicate sensibility? Of course not. And I knew then what a ghastly tyranny both causes and logic can be.

I said, 'Let's get cracking.'

Jack said, 'You're mad, both of you.'

Robby said, 'Who asked? And who cares whether you come or not?'

Jack said, 'I'm coming, but just to see the kid gets into no trouble.'

Robby said, 'How touching! Or have you yet?'

I said, 'Look, pack it in, you two. If we're going to do it let's go now before I change my crazy mind.'

Robby said, 'We're about a quarter of a mile from the house. We'll leave the car where it is and walk. All we pinch is a few things, valuable, small, resaleable and light. I know just the stuff and I know where it is, so leave the selection to me.'

Scenes From a Burglary

I need hardly remind you, Morgan, that I am not exactly accustomed to burgling houses. True, when climbing up and down my ladder during my Saturday stints of window-cleaning, I have sometimes imagined what burgling a house at night might be like, how I might do it, with what stealth and cunning I would execute the operation—never of course being caught or leaving behind one tell-tale clue to betray my identity. I would even vary my *modus operandi*, thereby foxing the police, whose routine minds would fruitlessly look for a pattern in case after unsolved case.

But such idle fantasy was no more than pastime speculation, self-hero daydreaming, a hedge against the boredom of polishing vertical glass hour on hour.

This was to be the real thing.

As we walked up the dark lane away from the river, sweat rashed my body.

I am a fool, I thought. What am I doing here?

Was this a dream? A sleeping fantasy too really felt? A nightmare? I had had a hard day, an unusual day; I was not myself; was sleeping without rest.

But I knew it was not so. I had felt similar symptoms before. While going to the dentist to have a broken tooth pulled. While walking to school for examinations. Most recent and vividly of all, while in the ambulance with my father.

Not a dream. Just fear.

I was scared.

My body did not move as it normally does. An act of will was required. I had to make myself walk. Had to monitor myself, as an engineer monitors a faulty engine, making certain I walked toward this unknown house with apparently normal ease, revealing none of my alarm to my accomplices.

But fear itself is a heady excitement.

*

When we reached the house, large glooming in the nightlight dark, solid (how much more solid than in daylight!), forbidding, Robby put up a hand to stop us in our stride as if he were a marine commando in some wartime raid behind enemy lines.

Fear is also a stimulating fantasist.

*

'Round the back there is an unlocked window that lets into the kitchen,' Robby whispered, we huddled head-to-head.

'How do you know?' I asked.

82

'I drummed the place today,' Robby said.

'O, god!' Jack said, derisive, and muffled an unrepentant guffaw.

*

Gravel crunches like boiled sweets when you crush them in your mouth with senseless regard for your teeth. And the noise abraded a sleeping world.

'Keep on the grass, fool!' puled Robby.

*

A house about to be burgled is like an animal being hunted. As you stalk closer, you expect its eyes to open and discover your malign purpose and you, its mouth to growl a warning. You wait for it to stand up and charge away. Or, worse, to charge at you. That a house does none of these things makes it all the more menacing.

'Bloody silly this is, kiddo,' whispered Jack into my face as we stumbled into each other.

*

'Nobody ever pinches me,' said the burglar's wife to her husband.

*

We reached the cliff face of the house itself, fleas clinging against an elephant.

'The window is to our left,' Robby murmured. 'Edge that way slowly.'

My feet trod soft soil.

'We're in a flowerbed,' I said. 'Leaving footprints!'

'Shut it!' Robby said. 'Who cares?'

'The police will care, that's who.'

Jack's mouth to my ear, lips tickling as he said, 'There'll be no police, Sunshine.'

'Optimist,' I whispered.

*

The soles of my feet were tingling in an electrically shocking way. My legs were freeze-dried jelly.

I had felt this before only in one kind of place: when looking down a deep, steep drop, like a precipice or over the edge of a high tower.

*

I needed to urinate. Urgently.

*

'This is it,' said Robby, drawing the other two of us close to him, his arms gripping our shoulders. 'This is the window. It's pretty narrow, and high up. But I reckon if Jack bends down and you, kiddo, stand on his back you'll just be able to reach your arm through the ventilator window, open the catch of the window itself, get in, and then open the back door for us.'

> [*And now, for the first time Oliver, well-nigh mad with grief and terror, saw that housebreaking and robbery, if not murder, were the objects of the expedition. He clasped his hands together, and involuntarily uttered a subdued exclamation of horror. A mist came before his eyes; the cold sweat stood upon his ashy face; his limbs failed him; and he sank upon his knees.*
>
> '*Get up!' murmured Sikes, trembling with rage, and drawing the pistol from his pocket; 'Get up, or I'll strew your brains upon the grass.*'

'O! for God's sake let me go!' cried Oliver; 'let me run away and die in the fields. I will never come near London; never, never! O! pray have mercy on me, and do not make me steal. For the love of all bright Angels that rest in Heaven, have mercy upon me!'

The man to whom this appeal was made, swore a dreadful oath, and had cocked his pistol, when Toby, striking it from his grasp, placed his hand upon the boy's mouth, and dragged him to the house.

'Hush!' cried the man; 'it won't answer here. Say another word, and I'll do your business myself with a crack on the head. That makes no noise, and is quite as certain, and more genteel. Here, Bill, wrench the shutter open. He's game enough now, I'll engage. I've seen older hands of his age took the same way, for a minute or two, on a cold night.'

Sikes, invoking terrific imprecations upon Fagin's head for sending Oliver on such an errand, plied the crowbar vigorously, but with little noise.]

'Are you listening?'
'You mean, I've got to go in first?' I said.
'That's it.'
'Now look, Robby,' Jack said.
'Knock it off!' Robby snapped. A threat, no doubt of it. Then, temperate, 'He'll manage. Won't you, kiddo? All experience, eh?'
'I'm out of my tiny mind,' I said.
'Isn't everybody?' Robby said.

*

Q. *What did the burglar give his wife for Christmas?*
   A. *A stole.*

*

'Why don't you go first? You said you'd looked the place over.'

'Know it like the back of my hand. But I can't reach the window catch. My arm isn't long enough. There's a door just to the left of the window. Open it. One bolt and a Yale. All you do is slip them quietly and we're in.'

'I won't be able to see a damn thing in there. What if I knock over something in the dark? What if there's a dog?'

'There's no dog, and I've got a torch. Just by chance! Here.'

*

There was a poore man on a tyme, the whiche vnto theues, that brake into his house on nyght, he sayde on this wyse: syrs, I maruayle, that ye thynke to fynde any thyng here by nyght: for I ensure you I can fynd nothing, whan it is brode day.

By this tale appereth playnly
That pouerte is a welthy mysery.

*

Other people's houses exude their own smell. House odour. This one smelt of my own armpit fear. My entrance into it was a violation.

*

'The stuff we want is through here,' Robby said, taking the torch from me as he came through the door, and leading the way with alarming lack of caution.

*

A comfortable room. Thick-pile carpet. Big, enfolding chairs. High-polished dark oak antique furniture. A wall of books. Ornaments, knick-knacks, many, the kind you do not touch without feeling the depth of your ignorance and the shallowness of your pocket.

I wanted more than anything to cry out, to shout, 'You are being done!'

*

'Grab this,' said Robby, plunging into my involuntary hands a book, leather bound.

'What is it?'

'A book.'

'Fool. What book?'

'*Das Kapital.*'

'Karl Marx.'

'Educated creep.'

'Why?'

'English edition, 1887. Rare. Worth nearly two hundred quid. Maybe more. Not traceable to present owner. Savvy?'

'Very symbolic!'

'That too.'

'Stop arsing about,' Jack said. 'Get on with it.'

'The trouble with you, Jack,' said Robby, 'is that you've no imagination.'

*

Robby's hand, cadaverous in the torchlight, reached for a luxury china vase, splendid on the high oak mantel of the fire-place, picked it up. Held it.

    slipped/dropped
    on to the stone flags of the firehearth
    like chippings on a grave
    A blaze of shiversound.

*

'You dropped that flaming thing on purpose!' Jack said out of the shock.

'Rubbish!' Robby said.

There was a scuffle-movement: Jack and Robby together.

The torch dived to the floor. Extinguished.

'You want to be caught! That's it, isn't it!'

'Sod off!'

Jack said, 'Where are you, kid?'

'Here,' I said, the word all but choked.

Jack said, 'We're getting out, quick.'

Stumbling, furniture-blocked steps towards the door.

When the door opened.

Room lights arrested us.

He stood, framed in the doorway, the sittingstanding talking man. At once, sober now, I knew why I had felt I had seen him before.

!! Zap !!

We were burgling Robby's own father.

We were burgling Robby's home.

I'd been a fool.

Again.

And fooled.

Meet the twentieth century's Olympic champion dumdum. The world's prize turniphead.

The light dawned. *Pow!*

Too late.

GazZamWamZap.

Pappatalk

'And what, may I ask, have we here?' Mr Hode said. 'What little party game is this? May I join in?'

We none of us replied, but stood like small boys caught scrumping. As we were. Robby's mouth was bleeding at a corner. Had Jack hit him?

Hode looked at each of us in turn. Robby. Jack. Myself. His eyes brooked no brazen stare. He came to me. Took the book from my unresisting hands, examined it as if for damage.

'Herr Marx,' he said. 'More talked about than read. What was your intention, young man?'

He gave me no time to answer, even had I been able to find my voice.

'Never mind. The question is purely rhetorical since you cannot stay.'

I glanced at Jack, who nodded peremptorily towards the door.

Robby was still unmoving, his face an agony of anger frustrated by filial embarrassment. I recognized that look at once, I had felt it so often myself. But was this really how one appeared at such times? So peevishly crushed, so lacking in control? So ugly? Just as I recognized the look on Robby's face, the whole gripped-in stance of his tense body, so I knew too that inside he was a seething confusion of feelings and thoughts: resentment and self-pity and a desperate but ineffective desire to hurt, yet, at the calm centre of his being, also wishing that none of this were so. Wanting, longing even, for it to end. Regretful that his father and himself had come to such a pass. Had Jack been right? Had the accident with the vase been a Freudian slip, or a deliberate act? Whichever, it had a necessary purpose: to get Robby (and us too?) caught.

All along Robby had known how this would end, had willed it to end this way, no matter how he might try to convince himself, as he would, that it had not been so. I knew because I had done the same, and had now to admit it to myself. Standing there in the sullen silence of that unfamiliar room I could admit it to myself, if yet to no one else. Looking at the tortured figure by the cold fireplace made any further self-deception impossible . . . Undesirable.

(It might seem strange to you, reading this, that these thoughts should strike me at that moment. It seems strange to me now too, writing them down. But they did, though as a flash of insight rather than in the linear logic of printed words in neat procession across a page.)

All day I had felt drawn to Robby. I had not been able to resist that underskin of violent energy, that blush of fanatic charm. But in this same instant of insight, fascination vanished as mysteriously and as rapidly as it had seized me. In that second Robby had shown me myself.

Was it cruel selfishness, an ugly weakness in me (another?!) that at this same second I lost all interest in him? Whether it was so or not, I must confess that I did. I knew him, you see, what he was and why he was. All sorts of jigsaw moments from our day together fell now into place, and I knew him. Besides, too much of what I now understood spoke to me about myself, reflected me as if I were looking in a mirror. Perhaps my abrupt loss of interest was an act of self-defence as much as of selfishness? I acted to save myself while there was still time; I could not help but sense that Robby was already lost.

'You can find your own way out, I take it?' said Mr Hode. He turned to Jack. 'I think you too had better leave, Jack. I'm sure you would not want to overstay your welcome. Do call and pick up your things another day, if you'd rather.'

'Turn him out and I go as well. For good,' said Robby, clench-mouthed and still unmoving.

His father did not take his eyes from Jack. 'I think Robby and I ought to discuss matters in private, if you wouldn't mind, Jack.'

'You heard me,' said Robby.

There was a moment's silence. Tense. A fulcrum. Whatever was to be done had to be done now. Afterwards would be too late. A private war and a private peace turned on this point in time.

Jack sighed. 'I'm going, Robby,' he said. 'It's best. There's nowt now, you know that.'

'I'm glad you're being sensible,' said Hode.

'Sensible!' shouted Robby. 'O, Christ!' He turned and sat, hunched, in a chair that flanked the fire, dabbing a hand at his bleeding mouth.

'Well?' said Hode to Jack and myself.

Our final cue to leave. But despite my loss of interest in Robby, I felt a twinge of guilt at leaving him to such defeat. Not he himself, but he anyone.

'Perhaps we should talk all this over together?' I said with pale conviction.

Hode rounded on me. 'Young man,' he said, 'I do not know who you are, nor why you are here. But I saw the trouble you helped cause tonight, and that is enough for me. As far as I am concerned you have no business in this house, nor is there anything I wish to discuss with you. You may leave now, or I shall call the police and have you charged with breaking and entering. Which shall it be?'

One of the worst things about being our age is the way an adult like Hode can beat you down with words—or me anyway; I expect you, Morgan, would have withstood him. Your only answer—mine anyway—is either to stand there flabbergasted or to lash out in uncontrolled anger and make an idiot of yourself. This time I was reduced to an angry flabbergast. From which Jack rescued me.

'How-way, kiddo,' he said. 'Let's go.'

Nightcap

Outside the night was frosty. I realized I was lathed in sweat, was flushed.

We paused in the road, the moon shining through the leaves of overhanging trees, brindling the surface.

'What now?' I said, feeling suddenly lost. Abandoned. Empty. Shock, I suppose, after the excitements.

'I'm going to doss down in the shed at work,' Jack said. 'It's just down the road a bit. There's some sacks and we could brew up on the stove. Want to come?'

I had heard him; but my mind was still catching up.

'What gets me,' I said sullensick, 'is that all the time he was just using me.'

Jack laughed, a sound like the call of a preying night bird. 'O, aye?' he said.

'Well, wasn't he?' I said, defiant.

'Aye, I suppose he was.'

'You know he was. He was planning it with you all along, from when we were in the pub at lunch time.'

'Yes. I didn't know all the details. But I knew the kind of thing it was likely to be.'

'And you didn't warn me.'

Jack said nothing; gazed at me in the moongloom.

'All right,' I said, 'so he was your mate.'

'And you were like a rabbit spelled by a fox. Even if I'd told you, you'd still have done what he wanted.'

He was right, I knew.

'Maybe. But it was the way he used me that gets my gut.'

'So he used you, Sunshine. What were you doing?'

'What d'you mean?'

'He used you, sure. But you must have been using him. And me an'all.'

Experience. It's all experience.

'How do you know what I was doing?'

That bird of prey laugh again.

'Because everybody is using everybody else all the time, kiddo. We're all users. That's what people *are*.'

Why did I laugh? For I did. And felt myself again. Almost refreshed, even if tired. Very tired.

'You're a cynic, Jack, you know that?'

'I know I'm nowt of the sort. Now are you coming with me or not?'

It would have been another experience; but I could not. It was too much. Like everything else, it seems, you can have too much experience for one day.

'No thanks, Jack, not tonight.'

'I can promise you a good time.'

'I'll see you around, eh?'

'I hope, bonny lad.'

'What'll you do now?'

'Hang about Richmond for a day or two, just in case Robby . . . But he won't. It's done.'

'And if it is?'

'I'll move on somewhere. Dunno where. Doesn't matter. There's always sommat wherever you go.' That laugh again.

'So long then.'

'So long. Take care. Sunshine.'

He turned and walked away up the moonspeckled road, a slight figure in that chequered light, despite his bulk. His feet made no sound. He might have been a ghost.

When he was out of sight, I walked back down the lane towards the river and Robby's car where I had left my pack. I thought of spending the night there, where we had sat earlier.

As I turned to go, there came from the Hodes' house the sound of voices raised in argument. I could not make out what was being said, only the hard, brutal clash of anger. Nor could I distinguish son's voice from father's. They were as one sound, one voice, like a man battling against himself.

THE LEAP

How to set this down? How to describe it? It happened to me, but not me. I was him, but not him. Haven't you, Morgan, ever been through a day when you were not yourself? When it was not you who experienced your events but some other you? This day was like that for me. So how to describe it and make you believe how it was, how it seemed? How to show you me-him this day?

Begin at the beginning. As I-I. As eye.

Slept solidly. A cuckoo woke me. Unexpectedly refreshed. Fit. Healthy. Happy, I suppose. (How do you ever know? What's the proof?) Optimistic, certainly; full of energy. And hungry. Yet, as I say, not quite myself. Somehow other.

A bright day. Crystal light glaze-blinking the tingle-crisp river, where I plunged myself, in-out, quickish. Naked. Like the day. Skin-sizzling afterwards.

Yesterday seemed a shaggy dog story. Had it been? Why bother to wonder? Why consider? Consideration is for recollection in Wandsworth. (The day's first terrible witticism. Apologies. The crazed light made my brain flippant.)

Packed pack. On back. Strode into Richmond. There: breakfasted—bacon, egg, sausage, beans, toast, marmalade, tea, tea, tea, tea (I was bottomlessly thirsty), tea. At Johnny's Cafe (truly!).

'Why not just buy the urn, love,' said the busty waitress, bodied as undulatory as the dales, at my sixth request. 'Where you putting it all? Softens the brain, too much tannin.'

'Not to mention its deleterious effects on other parts,' I said.

'Cheeky,' she said, unflurried. 'An early bird. Have you shaved yet?'

'No, does it excite you?'

She rubbed her hand, lascivious, down my jaw. 'Know what I would do?'

'What's that?'

'Put some milk on and let cat lick it off.'

'Ah, well,' I said. 'You can't win 'em all. Thought maybe you liked them young.'

She put my bill down on the counter. 'Chicken, I like them any age, but I'm busy just now.'

A nymphomaniac waitress! A narrow escape!

Time to make a quick getaway before she rips off her pinny and assaults me on the prepacked bacon in her storecupboard.*

A limbering up for Helen! Which reminds me, where's the telephone? Outside Woolies.

Riffle through the telephone book (cigarette-smokey-sniffy, dogeared pages, scrawled messages, e.g. *Come and lay me, cooky 3694758. Tringaling my dingaling 6256943.*) And I'm away.

Hello?

Could I speak to Helen, please?

Just a minute, the baby's crying.

I'm sorry, that's better.

Could I speak to Helen, please?

O, yes, just a minute, who shall I say?

Tell her, it's the boy she left behind.

It's who . . . the baby's crying again. Just a minute . . . Helen! . . .

---

*The worst case of unexpected sex education I have so far heard of was told me by Simon Feldman, who claimed that Lisa Pringle, whose father was an undertaker, trapped him in the workshop behind her father's office one Saturday afternoon, backed him into an upright coffin and there molested him. Had the coffin not been de luxe lined, Simon said, he did not think he would have survived the ordeal, which has understandably left him with a strong prejudice against undertakers, whose profession he was at one time considering as a career because, he said, as an undertaker he would never be out of work.

She's just coming.

Hello?
Help.
O!
Pee.
It's you.
Go to the top of the class and give the penicillin out.
You're chirpy.
Cheeky, I've just been told.
That too. By whom?
Waitress in Richmond where I purchased sustenance.
And anything else?
She was too busy.
Not that you weren't willing.
No. She was a little Massy Harris for my taste.
Have you any?
Can you have, without experience to teach discrimination?
Always one for the words.
The currency of intercourse. I thank you for the compliment.
Take it how you like.
You're still mad at me?
Am I?
I'm asking.
I'm wondering.
Words it was did for me yesterday, eh?
Perhaps.
I'm sorry.
Are you?
I think so. Will you forgive me?
I'm not sure.
If I say please?
I don't like being called . . .
Promiscuous?
Yes.
You knew the word.

Yes.

Ah, I see! You can't talk?

No.

The baby's stopped crying.

Yes.

We could conduct this conversation much more comfortably somewhere else. This phone box stinks.

I'm not sure I want to.

Look, Helen, I meant what I said on that note.

Embarrassing!

At the bus?

Yes.

Desperation breeds disregard. But I'm sorry if I embarrassed you.

Two apologies in one day. What's the world coming to!

Never mind the world. What about us?

Whatever have you been doing, watching old movies?

Nothing so exciting. What have you been doing, by the way?

Nothing so exciting.

You too? We must meet at once and swap notes.

As they say.

But I am—desperate, I mean.

For what?

Do you want the graphic details on the telephone? We might be bugged.

All right. Don't bother.

You'll meet me?

What'll you do if I don't?

Throw myself off Richmond Castle into the Swale?

Not imaginative enough.

Streak through Gunnerside at tea time on Sunday?

There's nothing you've got that they haven't seen here in abundance. Boring. Anyway, most of them here are Primitive Methodists.

And you've not had any excitement? Tut, tut. Well, let me see. Dress in drag as a district nurse, call on your aunt saying I've come at the request of her visiting niece to check her for pregnancy.

You've a putrid mind.

Desperation, as they say, knows no squalor.

Okay, where?

The 11.44 from Reeth, arriving Hag Wood by the caravan site 12.10. I'll be waiting in the bushes disguised as a weary rambler.

All right but under protest.

Protest as much as you like, but give in in the end.

Anyway, how did you find this number?

Elementary, my dear Watsonia. Your uncle's your dad's brother. So much I knew. Your dad's brother is likely to own the same surname as your dad. And therefore yours. A quick ogle at the invaluable GPO reference manual. Three are listed. Only one in Gunnerside. Bingo.

Smarty pants.

See you.

If you behave yourself.

O, and Helen . . .

What?

Don't bother to bring your pyjamas.

The town was busying. I wanted to leave before anyone who had been at last night's fracas recognized me. This town ain't big enough for both of us. But I had things to buy. I wanted everything right for Helen.

The food was easy. Brown rolls, still warm from the oven; lettuce, cos—the crispy kind; a couple of soused herring for starters. Two fresh-cooked meat pies with flaky pastry from Fawcetts and a small tub of sauerkraut (we'd have to pig it with our fingers) for seconds. A quarter of Wensleydale cheese, a couple of pears for afters.

But what to drink? Beer was the obvious thing. But cans are bulky and weigh heavy and I was already overloaded. I had had to tie a plastic bag containing the food on to my pack. So I settled for a couple of large McEwans and set off out of the square, making for the High Gingerfield road out of town, up on to Out Moor above Whitcliffe Scar. But I was not happy about the drink. There was not enough and beer was the expected thing.

In Victoria Road I passed Saccone and Speed, the wine shop. *Voilà!* In I went.

I know nothing about wine. I would like to. What little I've drunk I've liked. But wine is another case of plenty of indiscriminate experience being needed to breed discriminate taste.

At those prices, who can drink enough of the stuff ever to know?

Enter a grey-suited middled-aged gent of retired military appearance. An imbiber. Sharp, red veins laced his face.

'Sir?'

Pointless to prevaricate; he would know. Bull by horns.

'I know nothing about wine. But I would like a reasonably priced bottle that would go well with a picnic. Could you suggest anything?'

'I'll do my best. Of course, it all depends on your preference —your palate, you know. And on the food.'

'I don't know what I prefer. But the food is soused herring, meat pie, and Wensleydale.'

His eyes scanned the shelves. Soldier bottles on parade, labels at the present. Some flat out.

'With the meat and cheese, I'd suggest this.'

A baby laid in my dubious hands.

'A youngish Côte du Rhone. Not too heavy. Nothing special but a pleasant wine that can stand a little . . . ill treatment.' A laugh. 'If you'll pardon the presumption.'

'I'll take it, thanks.'

I was left with a pound by the time I'd paid for the bottle, which cost me as much as all the food put together.

'You have a corkscrew, sir?'

'On my knife.'

'Could I suggest? Allow me to open the bottle for you. I'll replace the cork securely but leaving enough for you to pull it out when you're ready. And, if I might advise, I would remove the cork a couple of hours before drinking. Let the wine breathe, you understand. It will taste all the better. Not left in the glare of the sun, but not kept cold.' He eyed my pack as he disgorged the cork. 'And keep it upright as near as conditions allow.'

'I'll do my best. Thanks for the help.'

Laugh again. 'Delighted. I'll just tuck the bottle into this side pocket, shall I? Safe there, and upright. You shouldn't have any trouble. Just be careful when you dismount.'

We enjoyed his joke together this time.

'Have a good picnic. Wish I was going with you myself. Lovely day for it.'

Off up Hurgill Road and Belleisle Hill at a steady plodding pace, in high spirits. The morning—nine thirty by now—still spring-brisk enough to make walking with a loaded pack pleasant work. As I slowly left behind the last houses of the town, rising above them till Richmond itself was a cluster below, I felt again as I always do going up into the dale an almost explosive sense of release, of unfettering freedom. Like leaving a hot, stuffy room crowded with people, and stepping out into an elevated garden laid out in sparely planted folds that carry you up, one beyond another, always one more beyond, into the stretching sky. Earth breakers surfing you on to the skylimitless shore of space.

I love highpoints of unbroken landview. I love carved cliffs, scooped valleys, distant rivers mirroring the sky.

Whitcliffe Wood and Scar.—Towards the west end of town, through Quaker Lane, is the *West Field*, a beautiful open walk full of delightful prospects, which succeed each other in endless variety; and at the upper end of it, is *Whitcliffe Wood*, and the frightful precipice called *Whitcliffe Scar*, 'where,' to use the words of Mr. Clarkson, 'we see the violent convulsions which the surface of this globe must have received at the great deluge, when the earth was torn from its centre, and

> rocks, water, and woods, separated from their old habitations, were removed to a distance.' On ascending the bold romantic Scar, we behold the wild and sublime rocks projecting on every side, and wooded to the very edge of the precipice; and on its summit is a spot known as *Willance's Leap.—History and Topography of the City of York and the North Riding of Yorkshire, Whellam, Vol 2, 1859.*

For Dad it is the sea. The sea and the sky. A ship and a star. His romance. His image of release. His break into space.

At Redcar a flimsy-seeming (to me, fourteen) fishing smack-boat, a cobble, famed for seaworthyness and tough as rawhide. But out we went though weather worrying, wind and waves rolling with white horses on their spines. Into the troughs and seasick rolling with the curling sea above one second and below the next and Dad laughing and handwringing his pleasure, his release, while I groaned and puked and wished for home and still landed fish quick as I could drop my line, one flapping, gasping, scale-glistening, glaze-eyed, musclebound, cold-blooded, fin-spiked, salt-smacking vertebrate after another as though every gill-breathing member of the rollercoasting North Sea swim wanted to join us in that heaving tub, perhaps in order to escape the tide of bile I was pouring into the waves.

But when our pleasure jaunt was over, we back ashore like all jolly sailor lads grinned undaunted courage at our perilous exploit while pitiful landwalkers crowded our ark to buy at knockdown bravado rates the rewards of our daring. And Dad might have been salted Neptune himself as he gazed with longing a last time at the now high-treacherous ocean before we drove inland home.

It was his last time: never again since.

In his hospital bed does he now fancy himself becalmed on a sunless windless sea?

How do I tell you, Morgan, that there, just above High Ginger-field and just below Rasp Bank, I suddenly and without self-warning, wept? I did. Hills and sky before me, sea and sunless bed within my plodding memory met confluent in my flooding eyes and wrecked me. I had to stumble to the road-skirting wall and cling to its cool, crumpled stone for comforting support. And I did not merely weep. I gasped for air like a drowning man, my body clenched in an uncontrollable spasm.

Lamentation for dying boy and dying man.

Subdued, and at last calm, I set off for the Scar, sly-eying around me in case I had been observed. (Why is it we are so ashamed to cry?)

Just by Out Moor radio beacon you cut across quarter of a mile of mirey coarse-grass field, then through a gate, and you are there: on Whitcliffe Scar. The double-monument: one, a square-based obelisk imprisoned in an iron-rod cage; the other, twenty-four feet away and ten feet lower on the slithering valley side, a grave stone, triangle topped. Each inscribed with the same celebratory message.

1606

HEAR US

GLORY BE TO OUR

MERCIFUL GOD

WHO MIRACULOUSLY

PRESERVED ME FROM

THE DANGER SO GREAT

He wishing to be heard was one Robert Willance, a Westmor-land man by birth:

> who had pushed his way to wealth as a draper in Richmond. With his name is connected the following marvellous story, thus told by Canon Raine:—

'In the year 1606 he was hunting near his own estate, on the high ground between Clints and Richmond, on the northern bank of the Swale. The hunting party were surprised by fog, and Willance was mounted upon a young and fractious horse. To his horror it ran away with him, and made right for the precipitous rock called Whitcliffe Scar, which looks down upon the Swale. The horse, no doubt, as it neared the verge would become conscious of its peril; but as is very frequently the case, the danger that paralyses the rider only makes the steed more fearless. As soon as it left the level platform above, three bounds, each covering twenty-four feet, brought it to the verge of the cliff, down which it sprang. About a hundred feet from the top of the scar there is a projecting mass of rock and earth, upon which the horse alighted, only to throw itself upon the ground below, some hundred feet further down. It was killed by the fall, and Willance's leg was broken. With wonderful presence of mind, he disentangled himself from the dead horse, and, drawing a clasp knife, he slit open the belly of the animal, and laid within it his fractured leg, to protect it from the cold till help arrived. This precaution in all probability, saved his life. His leg, however, was amputated, and he would hunt no more. As a memorial to his wonderful escape, he marked with an upright stone each of the three bounds which his steed took before it sprang over the cliff. On two of them he put the following inscription: "1606. Glory to our merciful God, who miraculously preserved me from the danger so great." And he had indeed great cause to be thankful, for no one can look at the grey cliff over which he was carried without a shuddering

feeling of astonishment that any one could
survive so fearful a fall.'—*History, Topography
and Directory of North Yorkshire*, T. Bulmer &
Co., 1890.

Willance's Leap on Whitcliffe Scar was to be my riding place
too.

My tent-site I already knew: a flat grassy ledge, thirty yards
down valley from the monuments, and nicely below eye-level of
anyone strolling along the scar edge. From view below it was
screened by bushes, yet over which, lying in my valley-facing
tent, I could see the inward-curving ribbon of Swale glinting in
its bed. Hag Wood rose opposite up the fist of moor ending in a
straight edge just below the top, leaving the moor bald headed
and grained with a fish-net grid of dry-stone walls. Bluegrey
misted hills touched the sky beyond.

My eyrie.

(I say that, but have never wished to be a bird. Cannot say I
have ever thought about it, in fact. But it is a good image of my
site, and my feeling that day: poised and predatory. Not like an
eagle, though; all too grand. More like a modest kestrel.)

Ten-fifty. Only just time to pitch my tent, stow the food behind
a keep-cool rock, the wine, uncorked in the shade of my tent-
flap, and then a careful scramble down the scar, across the river
(hoping the rope bridge was still there, its frayed demise having
long been expected) and up through the caravan park to the
road in time to meet the 11.44 from Reeth. If the bridge had
collapsed at last, I was in for a wet crossing.

Filled my water bottle at the caravan park. Then, early, not late,
after all. Ten minutes to spare. Patrolled the road, eyes restless
for sign of moving metal-green. Mouth dry. Limbs in a faint
tremble. Nerves.

She climbed down. Stockingless feet in open sandals, scruffy-smart blue jeans perfectly faded, smoothly fitting; loose cheese-cloth shirt in subdued stripes of colour, revelatorily tantalizing; long hair, light brown, shampoo bouncy; old patchwork shoulderbag bulging and nonchalantly swung. A desirable cliché.

Ditto stares untongued, not sure how he wishes this adventure to begin now it has begun. Helen stands in the road confronting him, as bus noise and engine fumes vanish into the distant air.

'I can't be so stunning,' says Helen. 'And it would be nice to leave this road in case we're seen. . . . I said I was going shopping . . .'

There was a moment when he might say goodbye.

But it passes.

He smiles, feeling a corncob boy.

'Stunning!' He hopes his tone displays his doublemeaning mind. Pointing to the road at their feet, he says, 'From here.' He raises his arm, straightstiff, slowly, till pointing finger directs Helen's eyes to the no more than nipple-point of Willance's caged obelisk intruding into the sky, 'To up there.'

'Hmm,' she says. 'Quite a stretch.'

'A vertical stroll to give you an appetite for lunch. May I take madam's bag?'

They saunter off towards the river, through the bungaloid urban order of the caravan park, affecting casual uninterest in the face of curious caravaners ogling Helen.

The slewing rope bridge brings the first shedding of pretence.

'I can't cross *that*!' she says. 'It's crazy!'

'Fairground fun,' he says. 'Here, grab my hand. Just swing with it, don't fight it. Bend at the knees. And don't look at the water.'

She is giggling with excitement and has lost her magazine-phony sophistiwalk. Like a bather testing the water, she treads suspiciously on to the footboards of the slippery bridge. Her laughter clams into eager concentration and he sees her prettier self. Stepping backwards that he might face her and give her reassurance, he thinks how self-forgetfulness brings out the beautiful in people.

They reach the middle. Low point, they are but ten feet above the river, the bridge swaying its dizzying worst. He makes her pause.

'It's so scarey!' she says but with confidence now. Her speaking is almost drowned in the riversurge. She hazards releasing his hand to push back her hair from curtaining her face, where the breeze has blown it. But grabs again as she loses balance. He finds enjoyment in her dependence. He squeezes her hand and she smiles with all her face through the veiling hair, eyes and mouth confirming the truth of the shared moment.

'You get a smashing view from here,' she shouts.

Their heads turn. Suspended above the water, they see the river sweeping into perspectives, trees and bushes and rocks serrating the lines of its banks; and the valley rising beyond. Nowhere else, he thinks, can you feel the river's energy, its own life, as here. From the bank it seems almost placid, certainly contained and gentle. From here you knew it for what it was, maker of the valley, a powerful force. Here you knew the river did not belong to the dale but the dale to the river. Swale's dale.

'Ready?' he asked when they had looked their fill, and the bridge had settled its thrashing. She nodded and with surer feet they climbed the slope to the bank.

On firm ground again, she exhaled her tension and looked back across the poppling ropes.

'Mmm,' she crooned her satisfaction.

He turned and led the way, zig-zagging up the backbending slope, and then on to the wall of the scar, finding footholds and a safe path for her.

They trudge, she two paces behind him, for ten minutes without pause or word. A steady plod is his way with steep hills; but he admires her perseverance and uncomplaining willingness to follow his lead. Occasionally he glances back at her. Each time her head comes up, as though she is waiting for him to look at her, and she smiles. Soon her face glistens with so fine a sweat she seems to glow. The sight of her like that, warm, her loose shirt clinging now so that he can see the shape and movement of her breasts, stirs in him a desire he has not yet felt that day. He begins to tremble again, this time almost uncontrollably, and dares not look back at her again till the emotion has worn to an ache of anticipation. He can hardly wait to reach the top, to be with her in his secluding tent, and has to restrain himself from increasing the pace of their ascent. All the time he wants to turn and hold her under pretext of helping her safely over some supposedly difficult ground. But he resists that urge too, fancying she will detect his real motive for touching her and reject him, something he knows will embarrass him; worse, she might tease his crude duplicity.

(All this was in my mind—and body—as I climbed. But much more at the same time. As I climbed and lusty desires climbed in me, I also thought and felt much more in parallel, so to speak, and in a reasonless stream. Like:

the pleasurable exertion in bone and muscle pushed to the point of pain

which led me to dwell for a minute or two on how often pain and pleasure are but a hairline apart—is sexual pleasure painful too?—as are sanity and madness, laughter and hysteria, hate, they say, and love

but even while these thoughts and sensualities occupied me, I was aware that my pants were snarling my testicles and hitched my jeans to release myself from discomfort

I worried about my feet for a while: would they smell if/when I took off my boots? I'd have to take off my boots, wouldn't I? Would FO put her off? An ironic chuckle had to be suppressed into a cough

rabbit droppings, like raisins, lying in the spikey moorgrass sent my eyes searching for burrows and my mind turning over snatches of Midge holding forth on the theme 'Is *Watership Down* a fascist book?'—he thought yes on the whole and argued undeniably as Midge always does, only Sayers challenging him, as on such occasions Sayers always does

needed to urinate but decided I could wait till we reached the top

suddenly without clue I thought of Robby and Jack. Yesterday seemed a dream away, yet vividly present so that my stomach lurched as if I had suffered a shock, even a blow. 'We're all users,' Jack had said. Me too now, I wondered. And Helen? Of course

would the wine be okay? Would she think it pretentious? Silly?

dad, I wondered about, felt guilty about because I had not telephoned today. But pushed from my mind

Even to list these things like this is to suggest they came in sequence and order. It was not so: they were random, scrambled, disordered. Everybody's being is like a collage. And a mobile. A multimovement of circumsensethoughts. And no one can ever record them all, not at once, or singly, or ever. All literature is incomplete history.

> history is a pattern
> Of timeless moments.

[T. S. Eliot, you'll remember, Morgan.]

So why do we try, why do we make the certainly hopeless effort to record our experience? Why do I? Now, here, on this hillside, and here on this white paper? Because [T.S.E. again]

> each venture
> Is a new beginning, a raid on the inarticulate

Or just because there is nothing better to do? Or nothing to do that's a better way of spending the time between birth and death?

I thought all this too, on the scar as we climbed.)

We reached the graveyard monument to Willance's survival and flopped gratefully down, side by steaming side, our backs against Willance's cooling stone, our beaming faces drinking the conquered view.

Breath recovered, bodies relaxed, I said:

'Want an epulation?'

Without taking her eyes from the curving dale below she said, 'At it again, word child?'

'Only to confirm my consistency.'

'You know, people at school said you weren't very clever, just a plodder.'

'And?'

'You don't seem exactly birdbrained to me.'

'Does it matter to you, one way or the other?'

'Not really. Brains aren't everything by any means. Just interests me. Does it bother you?'

'It did, when I was about fourteen. Not so much now. I've begun to find my feet a bit. I don't imagine I'm a budding genius, anything stupid like that. But I don't agonize about what people think of me as much as I used to. People at school, I mean.'

'But you do agonize about what some people think of you?'

'Doesn't everyone?'

'I suppose so.'

'Don't you?'

'Maybe.'

'Come on, confess. Why should I be the only one to play at telling secrets?'

'Touché. Yes, all the time.'

'You always seemed so confident to me.'

'You always seemed so standoffish to me.'

'So why the picture and the letter?'

'Can you bear the truth?'

'I can bear honesty. Let's decide afterwards if it's the truth.'

'Brum-brum!'

'Pompous. Sorry.'

'But clever. Exactly what I mean about you. The people who put you down couldn't even have thought it.'

'Thanks. Morgan could.'

'Morgan doesn't put you down.'

'Doesn't he? That surprises me.'

'Then you don't know Morgan very well.'

'I thought I did, but . . .'

'Never mind Morgan, let's get back to us.'

'How about my epulation first?'

'Is it nasty?'

'Soused herring, lettuce, brown rolls. Meat pie and sauer-kraut. Wensleydale. Pears. A bottle of wine.'

'And thou beside me. Sounds like a feast.'

'Exactly.'

'However did you manage it? Up here, I mean.'

'To the pure all things are possible.'

'How much longer do you expect to keep your purity?'

She was looking directly at me, our faces only a shoulder apart.

'As brief a time as I can.'

She leaned to me; kissed me softly on the mouth, unhurried.

'Then we had better eat at once,' she said.

'Each other or my epulation?'

She laughed. 'Stop using that silly word. Your feast will be a good appetiser.'

'I'm not going to say I love you or anything of that sort.'

'It doesn't matter. Just pretend. You think too much.'

'Isn't pretence a lie?'

'Not always,' she said, kissing me again. 'It can just be make-believe.'

'You know a difference?'

'Isn't lying a way of deceiving? It can hurt. Is usually meant to hurt. Yes?'

'Yes, I suppose it is.'

'Moral rape, that's what lying is. But everybody makes believe, don't they? Like children playing. Taking part. Making life how they want it to be, what they wish it was.'

'Pretending life into happening?'

'Exactly. Couldn't have put it better myself.'

'I thought I was supposed to be the clever one.'

'I just let you think so!'

She kissed me again, pushed herself to her feet, laughing.

'I think we should eat,' she said.

There are days when everything goes well, when everything fits. This was one of them. We felt now at ease with each other, happy to be together. The food was tasty, the wine (I silently thanked my grey-suited military adviser) was soft and smooth. We drank beer with the herring to help shift the vinegar and take the edge from our climbers' thirsts. Until we reached the cheese we spoke of nothing but the meal and the view and of Willance and his Leap (I was made to tell the story) and the satisfaction of lounging half-in, half-out of a tent, itself hidden yet providing such a vantage. But this was nothing more than chat, entertaining, but, we both knew, no more than pleasantry before the business of our meeting.

By the end of our leisurely meal the wine was settling the thoughts in my head, leaving me happily drowsy.

Then Helen said, 'Are you fortified against the truth?'

'Against your honesty, I thought we agreed. Lay on, MacDuff.'

'The laying *may* come later.'

'Letter and picture.'

As though preparing for battle, she cleared from around us the detritus of our meal, pushing it into the plastic bag I had carried the food in, and stowing the bundle out of sight behind the wall of the tent. That done, she settled herself on her back, comfortably at my side, her head pillowed by my pack, her long legs stretched out and crossed at the ankles. Through the bushes we could glimpse the curve of the valley bending away: focus for our self-conscious eyes.

'I was bored,' she began, as if telling a story. Something in her tone told me she had carefully rehearsed the words. (So she expected the question and prepared a reply; was I hearing an honest account, after all?) 'You've no idea how much I hate living in the country. The country is lovely for days out,' a lift

of the head, turned to me in proffering manner, 'days like this.'
She leaned toward me, brushing her lips against mine; relaxed
back again. 'But to live in it's ghastly. I'm a town mouse.'

She paused. If I was meant to say something, I could not.
Her deliberate performance amused me but irritated me too
somehow. I stared at the view knowing she would go on.

'One day I was tormenting myself by looking through my old
rubbish. You know, the sort of stuff everyone keeps. Old diaries,
letters, silly mementoes, photographs. Having a wallow down
memory lane. Among the photographs was one of a gang of us
on a school trip to York. D'you remember? Charlie Dawson was
sick in the coach. Susan Parker got lost in the railway museum
—so *she* said, I've my own ideas about that ha ha. Miss Cobbs
was goosed by a verger in the Minster and hit high C. A
reverberation of ecstasy such as those ancient stones had not
echoed in centuries. The line was Midge's, you'll recall. All the
usual stuff. Anyway, I was looking at this photograph and thinking that I'd been out with every boy in it except one.'

Another pause. Another turn of the head, this time displaying
a pert grin.

'You, of course,' she said, lying back again. 'I thought, why
should he be the odd man out? Why should he escape my deadly
charms?' She laughed, self-mocking. 'So I sat down, wrote the
letter, chose a suitable photograph, and sent them off. My
stratagem worked. We're here.'

As though a curtain had dropped at the end of a play, she gave
up her role as storyteller, flopped on to her stomach and stared
into the tent, hands supporting chin.

'D'you believe that?' she asked, the flippantly anecdotal tone
quite gone, replaced by a seriousness that betrayed anxiety.

I thought a moment, not quite sure which direction our conversation was taking.

'Superficially.'

She glanced at me, playful no longer. 'Tell me.'

'It *could* have been like that, but sounded phony the way you
told it.'

'If it *was* like that, would it . . .'

Larks. Breeze-brushed grass and leaves. A question hanging.

'Make any difference now?' I said.

She nodded, face held away, as though expecting a blow.

'We haven't come here under any delusions, have we?' I said. 'It was you who said pretend.'

'I know. Now . . . I'm not sure.'

'What does that mean?'

'I hoped you'd tell me.'

I laughed, finding nothing funny. 'I've problems enough of my own to sort out. Sorry.'

She sat up, cross-legged, facing me. Her fingers picked at the ground between us. She seemed then very vulnerable, very attractive. In a movement too quick and awkward, I laid my hand over hers.

'I'm not sure I can explain,' she said. Taking my hand, she began playing with my fingers, a disturbing pleasure.

'Try,' I said but wishing only to attend to our intimate touching.

'Well, I suppose you're right really. Superficially, that is how it happened. You know—that *was* the plot. My plot. But you know what old Midgely says about plots? Plots . . . what is it?'

Fingertip provocation.

I managed to say, 'Plots more often conceal meaning than reveal it.'

'That's it. What a frightening man he is!'

' "Look behind the action, boy, that's where the true meaning lies." ' Mimicking Midge is my one successful histrionic, as you know, Morgan.

Helen laughed, and bending in her laughter kissed my hand in hers.

'What lies behind your plot, then?' I asked.

'I've been puzzling about that one ever since we were climbing the scar and I realized there was more to my plot than met the eye.'

'And?'

She breathed in deeply and out again, gathering herself for something difficult to say.

'I know I've got a reputation as an easy lay and I play up to it. But boys are shocking boasters. You give them a sweaty grope for five minutes and to hear them talk afterwards you'd think they'd outclassed Casanova. As a matter of fact, I've gone all the way only four times. No more. Honest. Well, four and a half times.'

'And a half!'

She chuckled, her brittle everyday school self breaking through. 'The half was a dishy mutual acquaintance from the first fifteen reputed to be an experienced randy stud, a challenge therefore not to be passed up. He enticed me—so *he* thought—into his room when his parents were out one evening. We were at a point of no return when we heard his mother's voice in the street outside. By then I wasn't in a state to care. But you'd be surprised what a mother's voice can do to a boy!'

We neither of us laughed.

Helen released my hand, turned bodily away, facing the dale.

'I'm sorry. That was cheap.'

'Inappropriate just now, that's all.'

We stared at the distant river; she, no doubt, regretting her words, me regretting the withdrawal of touching hands. For a moment we lost contact.

'I can be cheap,' she said after a while, so quietly I could hardly hear her. 'Loud. You know? Blowsy. Maybe I get my reputation as much because of that as because of anything I . . . do. It's just that there are times when I can't help being . . . I don't know . . .'

'Crude?'

'Yes, not to put too fine a point on it. Bloody crude.'

'Like sometimes wanting to fart in public. Just to shock.'

She laughed and flopped on to her side facing me. Closely.

'You understand.'

'I think so.'

'It's as though two people are inside me, quite different

114

people who have to take it in turns at being me.'

The nearness of her body was intoxicating, like the wine, going to my head. My body tingled with paradoxes. Drowsy yet every cell aware of Helen's warm presence. Relaxed yet trembling for her touch. Unrestrained yet afraid of making the slightest wrong gesture which might break the spell. Careless of meaning and consequence yet anxious for reason and purpose.

'Tell me about your two people,' I said, wishing only to preserve somehow the presence of this moment.

'O,' she said, her eyes avoiding mine, 'one of them is always wanting to go new places, meet new people, do new things. The other is scared of all that, is shy, I suppose, afraid, never sure of herself, not wanting to fail and always feeling she has. One of me is always wanting to break the rules and outrage everybody, especially my parents. That's why I'm crude sometimes and like being thought an easy lay. I started taking the pill just to shock my parents. Or was it because the other one inside me was scared things might go wrong? Because the other one hates upsetting people or getting into trouble.'

'Which one is you now?'

Her eyes found mine and held them with a cool firmness a little frightening in its strength.

'Which one would you prefer?'

I tried to smile, to joke, 'Can't I have both?'

She did not smile in reply. 'I've never tried being both at once before. Is it possible, do you think?'

How could I answer?

Her slim length lay patterning mine so closely I could feel the warmth of her body, yet nowhere touching. My eyes explored her face; her eyes travelled mine. But looking was not enough. I raised my hand, ran my fingertips slowly over her forehead, down the curve of her cheek to the soft firmness of her jaw, round the bow of her chin, up to her lips.

She kissed my fingertips, a sensual caress.

I bent over her, kissed her mouth tentatively, but then, finding eager response, with force. She gripped me to her, pulled my shirt from my jeans, thrust her hand beneath, stroked my back, firmly searching.

Time collapsed, obliterating memory.

Clothes were suddenly an intolerable encumbrance. I plucked impatiently at her flimsy shirt as if it were riveted armour.

'Wait, wait!' she said. A laugh as hasty as her breathing mocked my careless urgency. She sat up and pulled the shirt off over her head.

She wore nothing beneath. Her bare back shone before me and then she turned in a quick, self-conscious movement, showing herself to me. The narrow length of her neck, framed by her hair. The fall of her shoulders, marble smooth. The rounded, lifting nipple-budded breasts above her incurving belly. The pale flush of her skin.

The breathcalming pure pleasure of her made redundant any photograph. I felt no wish to rush ahead. Only I had to reach up and touch with privileged fingers the hard bud of each breast. A confirmation of reality; no self-abusive fantasy this. Then feast my eyes a while.

'I was with a bloke yesterday,' I said, needing to clear my throat before I could speak with confidence, 'who said that we are all users, that everybody uses everybody else. I suppose he meant there's no such thing as altruism.' I ran my hands over her breasts, down her bending sides: a tactile fragrance of flesh. 'Do you believe that?'

'I haven't thought about it.'

'And don't want to?'

Her eyes were closed. She shook her head. Waving hair. All of her body focused.

'Don't talk any more, word child,' she said.

She shifted her position, sitting so that *Don't talk, she says, but the mind* she could undo the buttons of my *goes on. Why won't it stop? Give up.*

Patterns of Lovemaking
There is not much point in trying to describe lovemaking—

shirt, which she accomplished slowly,
Give up itself to what is happening?
laying the shirt from my chest. Her
It damn well thinks, damn well goes on
cool, tender hands then moving over me,
thinking, watching what is happening
soothingly inflammatory, a beginning
like a spoiled indulged child. Shut
of physical crescendo.
up, damn you, shut it.
   Her hands ran down my chest,
There is dazzle-blue sky above
across my stomach. Found the clasp of my
framed in the tent door opening flap
jeans. Undid it. Drew down the zip.
door peak. Shut it. Say the nine times
Pushed jeans and pants below my knees.
table   once nine is nine two nines
   Cooling air feathered my loins.
are eighteen three nines are twenty-
A delicious greeting to my nakedness.
seven four nines are something or other
And Helen's hands, coming with the
five nines are more than that
breeze, hardly heavier of touch.
ten nines are ninety is easy
Searching, fondling, encouraging.
you just put the nought on   o god
   For moments that were
the pleasure   shut it   shut head
endlessly short this was all
close down   off the air   off in
I wished for, all I had ever

whether it is hand-
holding, embracing,
fondling or intercourse.
It is experienced as
a matter of emotion
and relationship
more than action.
   Though we think
of lovemaking as
instinctive, as indeed
it is primarily,
the patterns of expression
vary widely in different
parts of the world.
This shows that we
learn many aspects
of it while growing up—
from books,
movies and TV,
from what we notice
in parks and on beaches,
from what we see our
parents doing and
not doing. . . .
   In the more
drawnout love-
making, lips, tongue,
hands may make
loving contact with
lips, tongue, breasts or
genitals—for several
minutes or for many.
Each couple after

the air   ha   o god don't laugh
wanted.
laugh   please don't laugh   it's
   But then rising in me, a
not done   not done   not in the oven
gathering of every lusting sensation
yet   ha   o please don't laugh
flowing from every cell of my body
under my spread arm spread hands I feel
to that straining centre, wanted
grass knife-blade-sharp, coarse
body on body, a clutch of source
soil beneath grasp the crystal
of pleasure to whole possession.
earth no grasp her grasp shut it

   I grasped at her. For a fearful
enjoy enjoy enjoy enjoy enjoy enjoy
moment she was gone. But then
shut it words are like boulders
was back again.
thoughts are like broadsides fired
And naked.
against my bodypleasure   why?
As I was
o why?   o sylvan wyeswale
And as eager
is this what makes body
As blind
is this the howdyado   the I'm all
As grasping
right jack   the deflowering of ditto
As clinging
the cider rosie had

months and years
of variation tends
to settle on patterns
which give the
greatest mutual
pleasure. A few
couples even progress
all the way to the
climax of orgasm
while engaged in
the forms of lovemaking
which most people
consider only preliminary—
because in this manner
they reach ecstasy
more surely or
more pleasurably
than by genital
intercourse. For most
couples, however, the
ultimate desire is
for intercourse, in
which the man
inserts his erect
penis into the
woman's vagina. Her
labia and vagina have
been made more moist
than usual by her
excitement, so
the penis can slip in
more easily. The man
has the instinct to

As sinuous of body
is this the stars in
As flooded with strength
my eyes   my eyes   close my eyes
And energy
in excelsis
And fire.
shut it
She pulled at me,
is this the way
turning me over upon her, urgently,
aboard the lugger
as she fell back upon
and now let
the ground.
battle commence
And gave me entrance
just shut it
with a deep delighting sigh.
shut it
And then there were
shut it
no more
shut
words
it
no more
it
thoughts
It

Nothing but movement

thrust his hips
rhythmically back-
wards and forwards
to move the penis
partly out and in
again, to increase
the sensation for
both. Intercourse
can last fifteen seconds
or a man can learn
to hold back his
orgasm so that
intercourse lasts
for fifteen minutes or
more. As the couple
come nearer to orgasm,
both partners usually
want the rhythmic motion to
become more vigorous
and the woman
may participate in it too.
At the moment of
orgasm—and
generous, experienced
lovers try to make their
climaxes come simultan-
eously—they are
overwhelmed by
five or ten seconds of
intense, pulsating
pleasure
while the ejaculation
occurs, and they cling

Body on

Flesh on flesh on

Mouth and hands and legs and
  thrusting
  driving
  wild
  relief
  felt
  during her
  high
  long
  scream

tightly together. After
orgasm there is
usually a feeling
of complete
satisfaction
and peace
which often
leads to sleep.
—*A Young Person's*
  Guide to
  Life and Love,
  by Dr Benjamin Spock,
  Bodley Head,
  1971.

  Thought returns
  A sense of place
  Of being
exhausted flat-out quenched desireless body able still to pleasure
in the aftertaste of body on body made poignant by a reasonless
sense of loss sweet with gratitude but still no words to speak no
wish to say

Thanks.

You are kind, warm, funny and clever. And pretty good for a beginner. I wish I could be around to help you practice. But I'm not, and won't be. We wouldn't survive. Truly! We'd get all serious.

I'm afraid of that — not ready for it yet — if ever! But you've been a help. I hope I was to you.

I doubt if we'll meet again. Not like today. But I will remember always.

Be loved.

H. xxx

END GAME

After Helen

When I woke, the sun was setting. Egg yolk in deepening blue.

My sleeping bag covered me. Helen's doing, I supposed.

I looked for her. Found not her, but her note lying by my side weighted by a dalestone.

I read it.

Then lay back. Wordless thought.

Then, impulse:

I had to go back home. Whatever I had come for, I now had. But had yet to sort out.

I felt good as soon as I moved, being busy again with purpose. Whatever I am to be, I am not to be a drifter, a taker-or-leaver of life. I know that now, if no more.

I ate the remains of our lunch, being hungry: stale bread, evening dew moist; a mouthful of herring, acid in my dry sleep mouth; a morsel of cheese; all washed down with water, plastic coated from my aging bottle. Then sat again, feeling calmed, reflective; gazed at the view as though wishing to cherish it, the day, that time-and-place.

Till darkness fell. Ten thirty or thereabouts.

I was ready for off. I would have to walk. No buses now, no money for private hire. Fifteen miles. But I wanted to walk.

Penance, payment or pleasure? Who cares?

I was going somewhere. Home.

The only one I have. For now.

I laughed.

An owl hooted. A barn owl. He was sitting on Willance's cold grave stone. As I watched, he took off and ghosted into the valley.

Tramping

Down into Richmond, silent dark town, through Skeeby. On up to Scotch Corner, across the slice of motorway and along the back road to Barton. Then Stapleton and the roundabout, junction of old road and motorway spur into Darlington. Across the bridge humping Yorkshire into County Durham. Then by Blackwell down to South Park, along Geneva Road's dull, stale mile. And home.

Roadwork at night is a kind of torture by monotony. Thoughts adopt a steady repetitive stomp to match your mechanical feet.

My thoughts that night tramped through Jacky and Robby and Helen and me.

Pedestrian stuff; all here, preceding.

Home

Hello, love.

Hi, Ma. Didn't mean to wake you.

I wasn't asleep. How've you got back?

Walked.

Walked? Where from?

Richmond.

At this time of night! It's nearly four.

I'd finished what I had to do so I came straight home.

I'm glad. But you must be worn out.

A bit.

And hungry. I'll cook you something.

No, no, Ma. Just a cup of tea, eh?

Are you sure? You ought to have something.

I'm okay, really.

Well, a cup of tea, eh?

How's Dad?

Much better.

Good.

Not right yet, you know. Never will be, I suppose. But he's sitting up and taking notice again.

That's good.

Thought I'd lost him.

O, I've a letter he gave me for you.

A letter?

Wrote it yesterday. Said if you rang I was to get an address where you could collect it. If you weren't coming back soon, like.

He's never written me a letter before.

He's hardly had need to, has he? You've not been away long before, not on your own.

But he didn't need to now, did he?

What's in it?

I don't know, love. You'd better read it and find out.

I'll take my tea and drink it upstairs, Ma. Okay?
All right, love. And get some sleep. You'll be worn out tomorrow.

The Memorial Hospital
Monday.

My dear Son,

I must be on the mend, because they have let me sit up and write this.

I am not much of a letter writer, as you know, and not much of a talker neither. But being near death, as I have been, makes you think. I have been thinking about you and me, and your dear Mother of course. I have been thinking about the rows we have been having lately. Maybe it is just growing pains. You are growing up and I am growing old. I want you to know that your Mother and me are very proud of you and have always tried to do our best for you to the utmost of our ability.

The school has brought you on well, especially Mr Midgely, and your Mother and me are very grateful. But sometimes I get worried because I cannot always understand what you are doing.

I am not trying to make excuses though. Maybe we should both try harder to see each other's point of view. I know I will if I pull through this present bit of bother, which I hope to do for your Mother's sake.

Now what I am really writing to you about is this. I want you to do something. I want you to look under the hankies in the top drawer of the bureau in our room. There is a little box there. I want you to have it and contents from me with my love and as a token of my sincere regard for you.

Your loving

Dad.

Free Gift

A small, black, firm-bodied box, no bigger than a wallet, edges worn, as though from much handling. Inside, red silk plush. Laid in the plush, two medals, pristine, with bright red, gold and blue striped ribbons. On the medals, raised in bas relief, the picture of a racing motorcyclist. On the reverse an inscription:

NATIONAL TRIALS CHAMPIONSHIP
JUNIOR CLASS
FIRST

NATIONAL TRIALS CHAMPIONSHIP
ALL COMERS CLASS
THIRD

Each also inscribed with Dad's name and a date.

He would have been eighteen.

Kitchentalk

You're still up, Ma.

I'm not tired, love.

He's given me these.

Yes? Very nice.

Why?

He wanted to, I expect.

They mean a lot to him?

They do.

He's never mentioned them. I've never seen them before.

It's just the way he is.

You know about them?

Yes.

Can you tell me?

When he was young, he wanted to be a motorcycle racer. He went to the Isle of Man T.T. races every year to watch. 'Course, then it was bigger than it is now. I'm talking about thirty years ago. He got a bike of his own as soon as he could. Bullied his mother into buying him one on the H.P., I think. And he started trials racing on it.

Racing across country?

Yes. He did well. Won them medals the last time he did it. He was eighteen. He decided after that it was time for the real thing. But he needed a new bike for professional stuff. And he wanted to enter the T.T. Something like that.

And?

His father wouldn't hear of it. Put a stop to it.

Why?

Said it was too dangerous and cost too much.

But how could he stop Dad if he really wanted to do it?

Well, for a start your dad didn't have the money. Not for a new bike, fares, racing expenses, all that.

And his father wouldn't help?

No.

Wasn't Dad earning enough?

As an apprentice joiner? That's what he was then.

So he never did it?

No. His father said he could do what he liked when he was out of his apprenticeship at twenty-one but that till then he'd do as he was told. And in those days you had to pay more heed to your parents than people do now.

But didn't he try when he was twenty-one?

Too late then. He meant to. But he'd never have caught the competition by then. And anyhow, how could he do it all on a joiner's pay? No, he had an old bike and roared round the streets like a madman and went to the T.T. as a spectator. But he never raced again.

Does he regret it?

Why don't you ask him?

Silly question.

Perhaps. But I'd still ask him.

Thanks, Ma.

Get some sleep now, love. Goodnight.

Making Room

I sat a while in my room. Needing to. Not disturbed, but wanting quiet. Peace. Stillness.

But soon the walls were falling on me.

Unhurried, a deliberate act conducted with great care, I began to disrobe the walls of their covering of posters and pictures. Took them all down; piled them one on another in an old suitcase.

Did not stop at the pictures. The ornaments, bric-à-brac, oddments of all sorts. All the left-overs of me. All into the suitcase.

With surprise I found myself adding some of the books. Not all. Those which impulse told me were sloughed-off skins.

Me, past. Other people's me.

Last of all, I placed Helen's letter, her photograph, and Morgan's *Charges Against Literature* into a large envelope. Sealed it. Placed it on top of all else.

Shut the suitcase. Locked it. Stowed it neatly, at the back of a cupboard in the spare bedroom, among all the rest of the family's lumber.

Put the key into my father's medal case beside his—my—pristine medals.

Now my room was nude, but for some books, and, alone on my desk, the medals in their worn case.

Coffeetalk

'An odd concoction,' said Morgan, coffee expectorating from his plastic mug on to the sixth-form commonroom floor as he and Ditto made for two empty seats in a corner.

'We have discussed the inadequacy of the coffee before,' said Ditto.

'I mean your masterwork,' Morgan said.

They sat, pulling their chairs together, side by side, facing a window providing a view of the breaktime mayhem in the playground below.

'Did you find it distasteful?' asked Ditto.

'Not that. But there are some points I want to argue with you.'

'What then?'

'Amusing sometimes, embarrassing sometimes, interesting sometimes.'

'How generous of you.'

'You had quite a time during half term.'

'I did,' said Ditto noncommittally.

'But to be honest . . .'

'Why not?'

'. . . I can't agree that this curious document answers my Charges.'

'You disappoint me, Morgan.'

'Then demonstrate.'

'What a laboratory mind you do have.'

Morgan smiled with self-satisfaction.

'All right,' said Ditto. 'Point by point but briefly. Point one: is it a story?'

'Of a kind,' Morgan conceded with reluctance. 'The events of your week past.' He chortled at his pun.

Ditto allowed the ambiguity to pass apparently unnoticed. Two could play at double takes, and at sleight of mind.

'Point two: you are only concerned with truth. Have you had truth?'

'Allowing for the inadequacy of your skills as a reporter, yes.'

'My modest work convinced you in this respect?'

'Sufficiently for our purpose.'

'Good. Point three: would you agree that my account does not pretend that life is neat, tidy, falsely logical—any of those things to which you objected, you'll remember?'

'Granted. It's a right rag-bag!' Morgan laughed loudly.

'I'm pleased I amuse you.'

'You do, you do.'

'Point four: literature is only a game, an amusing pretence, a lie I think you said. Playing at life, wasn't it?'

'Correct.'

'Is my poor effort?'

Morgan sat up, as though springing a trap. 'I thought that was where you were headed. False logic.'

'Why?'

'Because, matey, I was talking about fiction. Remember! And your little masterwork isn't fiction.'

'O?' said Ditto.

The klaxon sounded the end of morning break.

'Of course it isn't,' bayed Morgan, triumphant. 'We've already agreed about that. It is a record of what happened to you last week.'

'That's what *you* said. I only asked if it convinced you in that respect. You said yes.'

'Are you playing games?'

'Do you mean, have I written fiction?'

'Declare!'

'Could be. How do you know I didn't sit in my room at home all week making the stuff up?'

'I don't believe you.'

'Thank you. That's the best compliment you could pay me.'

'But your father is ill, you're not lying about that, are you?'

'Of course not . . .'

'Well then . . .'

'All fiction starts from something.'

'Look, I've got Taylor now. He brooks no lateness. We'll settle this over lunch.'

'A viva I shall enjoy.'

Morgan made for the door.

'I'm in the thing,' he said as he went. 'Are you saying I'm just a character in a story?'

'Aren't we all?' said Ditto and laughed.

dance on my grave

A LIFE AND DEATH

IN TWO PARTS

ONE HUNDRED AND SEVENTEEN BITS

SIX RUNNING REPORTS

AND TWO PRESS CLIPPINGS

WITH A FEW JOKES

A PUZZLE OR THREE

SOME FOOTNOTES

AND A FIASCO NOW AND THEN

TO HELP THE STORY ALONG

Acknowledgements

The passage quoted on p.66 is from *Slapstick* by Kurt Vonnegut, published by Jonathan Cape Ltd; the lines on p.152 are from the poem 'Lullaby', reprinted by permission of Faber and Faber Ltd. from *Collected Poems* by W.H. Auden.

The author would particularly like to thank Glenys Salway for her generous help with the social work background to this book.

GRAVE DAMAGE

Youth charged

A sixteen-year-old youth appeared at Southend juvenile court yesterday charged with interfering with a grave. Further charges of wilful damage were brought.

Police trap

Inspector Harry White, prosecuting, said that complaints had been received from Mrs Myra Gorman that the grave of her son, Barry, 18, had been damaged soon after his funeral. Mrs Gorman claimed she had reason to believe this would happen again.

Following Mrs Gorman's complaint, a police constable was put on duty in the cemetery at night. On the second night, the accused was caught and arrested while performing what Inspector White described as 'strange antics on the deceased boy's grave'.

Unbalanced mind

The youth refused to say anything in his own defence or to explain his actions. He sat silent and unmoved throughout the hearing.

Mr C. H. Pinchbeck, chairman of the court, told the accused, 'This is one of the most unpleasant cases I have ever dealt with. I cannot believe you were in your right mind.'

The case was adjourned until a social inquiry report could be prepared.

PART ONE

We are what we pretend to be,
so we must be careful what we pretend to be.
Kurt Vonnegut

1/I must be mad.

I should have known it all the time.

If your hobby is death, you must be mad.

Don't get me wrong. Mad I may be. Crazy I am not.

I am not a weirdo, not some kind of psycho who goes around murdering people.

I have no interest in dead bodies. What interests me is Death. Capital D.

Dead bodies scare me. They do terrible things to me. *Correction*: One dead body did terrible things to me. About which I am telling you now.

If you want to know about it, that is. If you do not want to read about Death, and if you do not want to read about a dead body that I knew when it was alive and still a he, and if you do not want to read about the things that happened to he and me before he became it, and about how he became it, you had better stop right here. Now.

2/The beach, that first day, was a morgue of sweating bodies laid out on slabs of towels. Sea and sand at sunny Southend.

We had lived in this Londoners' playground at the mouth of the Thames for seventeen months, my father, my mother and me, and I was still not used to a town whose trade was trippers.

There was talent about, bared to the imagination.

Correction: I could not get used to a town whose trade was strippers.

But school holiday was three weeks away yet, so mostly the bodies were old. Pensioned. White skin, oat-mealed flesh.

3

I had things on my mind. Oatmealed bodies were an awful distraction, talented strippers too few to be distraction enough. Anyway, the few fetching females there were had eyes only for he-men with inflatable muscles and micro-wave tans. They took a positive pleasure in ignoring a sixteen-year-old unstripped stripling still convalescing from acne. And I couldn't have cared less about them, because what I wanted was to get away somewhere where I could think.

There was only one way left to go. I didn't want to sit at home plugged into my stereo just to keep Mother at bay. And I certainly wasn't going in to school, now that I'd finished my exams, until that afternoon when Osborn wanted to see me. So the only way to go now was seaward. Cool. Unpeopled. What Barry (he who became it) called 'the escape route'.

Just off shore Spike Woods' fourteen-foot sailing dinghy, *Tumble*, was poppling about among the other small craft moored at their buoys. Spike had been daft enough to leave his mainsail furled to the boom. A wonder it hadn't been pinched. Everything movable was eventually half-inched from the beach. Even boats sometimes.

Good old happy-go-lucky Spike was in school that day with exams still to sit. I had crewed for him once or twice, cack-handedly. He only took me out, I think, because for some reason he thought I was good for a laugh. And I liked him because he is one of those people you never have to worry about. He's always in trouble at school because he won't wear anything but raggy jeans and a scruffy shirt. Sometimes I think his blood must be laced with anti-freeze because he wears the same outfit summer and winter, no matter how cold the weather gets. But there are other kids who dress worse than he does and who don't get into as much bother. I think he does

4

because he is one of those kids who exude sex. His flesh is somehow more fleshy than other people's. Girls take one look at him and tremble at the sight. In the right mood I tremble a bit myself. On Spike a crummy shirt and well-worn jeans only serve to emphasize his sexiness. I think he knows it too. He certainly takes advantage of everything going. And that just gets adults, especially teachers, even more riled. He'd been up in front of the Head five times that summer term already, ostensibly because of the way he was dressed. And this was apart from daily skirmishes with the more totalitarian and sex-starved members of staff. But nothing and no one ever manage to improve Spike's sartorial neglect or diminish by one ohm his biological glow.

Well, that day last June Spike was sweating it out in the exam room. And I didn't think he'd mind if I helped myself to his *Tumble* and gave myself a free sail while I did my thinking. I'd never single-handed anything more than a beach cushion before, but what the hell, I thought, it couldn't be that difficult. The weather was calm—a steady breeze not strong enough to blow a castaway ice-cream wrapper along the prom, the sun bright and hot, the sea no more than chuckling. The tide was on the flood but the water was still shallow enough for me to wade out to *Tumble* if I went now. What harm could I do?

3/By eleven o'clock on that bright Thursday morning I was away, the breeze kissing my cheek and bellying the mainsail in a gentle, pretty curve above my head. Romantic. Just like the picture on the Southend holiday brochure. The Resort for all Seasons. And the season for all resorts (thinking of the stripped salamandrian beach-folk).

I quickly decided single-handed sailing was a doddle. Maybe I should get a dinghy of my own. I lounged back complacent against the transom, stretched my legs so the sun could dry my wet jeans. Master of the con, captain of the lonesome bridge, I steadied the thrusting bow on a point just seaward of the pierhead and let myself be carried slap-and-splash against the tide towards the level horizon.

Not that the horizon meant freedom and empty space, for the sea before me was all Thames estuary. But everyone had warned me what a treacherous tideway it was, a trap of confused currents and looming inattentive cargo boats. As safe for an incompetently handled sailing dinghy as an urban motorway at rush hour is for a kid on a tricycle. But I would turn back, I promised myself, before life got too hairy. All I wanted was a chance to sit back and think for a while. Alone.

4/If you only want the what-happens-next Bits of this tale, please skip from here to Bit 5. If you want to know what I was so keen to think about out there on the briny, apart from the question of my fascination with Death, read on.

What I needed to think about was this:

Should I leave school this summer and find a job? Or should I stay on?

If I left school, what job could I do?

If I stayed on, what subjects should I study? And what job would those subjects qualify me for when I am eighteen?

Or should I go to university at eighteen? And if so, why?

I was in two minds about everything. Which my stupefied arithmetic says made me therefore in fourteen minds all at once. Painful. (Maths is my worst subject of all. I am even better at French; i.e. hopeless.)

The people who had a say in these earth-shattering conundrums and were helping to keep me in fourteen minds were:

my father (naturally)

my mother (God bless her)

my Headmaster (if reminded of my existence, which disaster I and he tried to avoid)

my so-called tutorial teacher (Ms Tyke)

the careers officer (a man with a catalogue for a mind)

my English teacher (Jim Osborn, better known as Ozzy, of whom more later)

my aunt Ethel (she thought I ought to 'go in for a cook' because when I was eight I stayed with her for the first and only time, and helped her bake me a gingerbread man by putting in currants for the eyes, nose and mouth, a task I accomplished with such success that ever since she has regarded me as a culinary genius)

the television (okay, so it isn't a person, despite the fact that my father talks to it all the time. But it keeps showing programmes about how this job and that job will be redundant soon, usually just after I have made a firm decision that that job would be just right for me).

That's the end of the official list of careers-advising experts. But there's a whole army of unofficial advisers who get in on the act. For instance, there's our milkman, who pressed me for obscure reasons I never understood to go into waste disposal. And then there's my dentist who suggested once that with teeth like mine I could have a wonderful future as a male model and would I like him to help me on in that direction. I never quite trusted him with a drill after that.

In fact, one of the things I was thinking as I floated down the river in *Tumble* was that when it came to my career everyone I met seemed to think s/he was an expert who knew better than I possibly could know myself just what I should and should not do with my life. I even formulated a useful scientific principle out of this experience. I freely offer it to everyone who finds him/herself in a similar predicament. Thus: The confidence with which all and sundry foist their careers advice on to you varies in inverse proportion to the adviser's own success in his/her chosen occupation.

Or, as my father puts it: Them as says most knows least.

One thing I had decided. I would take a summer job.

Correction: My father had decided for me that I should take a summer job. He had made this decision with one sentence: 'You're not sponging off me and your mother all summer, so you can get off your duff and earn yourself a few quid.' My father has an endearing manner when roused, a charmingly elegant way of showing what he means, not unlike a sledgehammer wielded by an irritable Irish navvy. So between this day in late June and the fatal August morning when my exam results would no doubt confirm my lack of qualification for any job whatsoever, I had to find a congenial, paid pastime.

But what? I couldn't stand the usual temporary summer holiday jobs available to the likes of me in a seaside town, such as deck-chair attendant, or donkey-minder on the sands, or counter-hand on a jellied eel stall along the Golden Mile. (The Golden Mile is a stretch of tatty and tacky seafront esplanade east of the pier that passes for Southend's attempt at gaiety and tourist pleasaunce.) That sort of slavery I could do without.

5/Thus was my mind preoccupied as I cruised wantonly

on the opaque Thames. (*Sea* and *sand* at sunny South-end? I ask you! Mud and metabolic liquefaction washed away by daily doses of tidal North Sea salt more likely.) The sun stiffened my jeans as the Thames water's mono-sodium glutamates dried out. I felt like I was wearing paralysed treacle.

I slipped my jeans off, treading them into the bottom of the boat. Underneath I had on only a pair of red jockey briefs with fetching white trim, but who was around to get excited?

I had spent so much time messing about on the beach this year—I even revised for the exams there—that for the first time in my life I was tanned all over, something I was secretly proud about. (*Correction*: I was tanned *almost* all over.) Of course this is nothing exceptional in a macho-spa like Southend. (Being tanned I mean. Or, come to think of it, being proud of it too.) But my normal skin colour till then had been somewhat on the pale side of chickenbreast white, so I used to keep all but my extremities hidden from the public gaze. I even used to wear a track suit for gym class if I could get away with it so as to avoid unseemly comments about my spectral hue. A favourite quip bellowed across the changing room was 'Hey, Dracula did a good job on you last night.' For a while after I arrived in Southend I was widely known as the Bleach Boy and it was rumoured that I was hooked on Domestos.

Having juggled with tiller, mainsheet and jib sheet while removing my jeans, I thought I should check my sailing condition. Maybe my (to be honest) very few marine excursions crewing for the succulent Spike had already taught me some of the precautions necessary for sea-going survival. Like knowing at all times what your own boat, other people's boats, the weather and the sea are all doing. Or maybe some unconscious premonition of approaching calamity was already blinking a warning in my head. Whatever, I looked around.

Ahead, all was well. Sun crinkling on gentle waves. Very few other craft about and none near me.

But behind: Big Trouble. And fast approaching. A heavy black curtain was being drawn across the sky. I had never seen a cloud as menacing. It was a monstrous tumescence. A Thing from Outaspace.

In the one double-take glance I allowed myself before my body splintered in panic, I saw too that the sea beneath the cloud was shining an aggressive gun-metal bright, and that a leading edge of angry waves was churning over white, as if the monster had teeth and was snapping at the tide.

My nerves fused. I did, though, know enough about Southend weather to realize that the space between the snapping waves and the black cloud would be filled with a pretty feisty wind. Also that this unwelcome gust would arrive like a rocket-powered wall of expanded polystyrene—soft and warm to the touch but a knockout just the same.

Not only had my father raised me from an early age to act on the principle that a man must face what a man would rather run away from, but it also seemed obvious at that moment even to my addled brain that safety lay in pointing Spike's little boat into the coming wind, rather than being blown along by it. Therefore, what now looked to me like my frail and inadequate vessel had to be turned to face the gathering tempest fast. There was also the question of whether Spike's beloved *Tumble* was a suitable sparring partner for the rusting iron stanchions that support Southend's famous pier (all of one and a third miles long) among which we were likely to get tangled if the wind took hold of us and carried us away.

Of course if we were lucky enough to avoid that fate, a

worse lay in store. Beyond the pier stretched the real and vasty North Sea. I was not yet tired enough of life, I decided, to wish for a trip into that certain grave. Death I was interested in; being dead I was not.

At all cost I must come about and face the gale.

So much, at any rate, for the theory. The problem was that I had never yet put the theory into practice, and performed the tricky manoeuvre necessary to turn a boat from running before the wind to heading into it, a 180 degree about-face requiring not a little skill. And performing it for the first time at panic stations is not to be advised.

I had seen it done many times as I lay browning on the beach, watching some show-off expert. But only practice makes practice perfect; and this was not an auspicious moment to start practising.

Not that there was any option. Or that I really gave it much thought.

With the decisiveness of desperation, I yanked the tiller over to port and let go all sheets.

Both actions were fatal errors.

I should have pushed the tiller to starboard and kept control of the mainsheet.

The results were technically complicated and instantly dramatic.

Herewith a guide for the non-naval. When running before the wind, a boat's sail spreads out to one side of the boat or the other, thus:

When coming round into the wind, a wise sailor brings his vessel about in such a way that the sail and its boom (that all-too-solid 'arm' sticking out to the side onto which the bottom of the sail is attached) does not sweep across the hull but remains safely on the same side, thus:

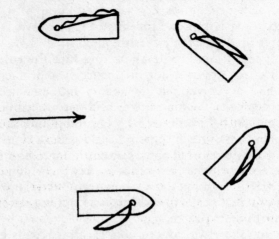

Only a confidently skilled helmsman, or a fool, brings a boat about the other way. Because if you do the boom crashes across the hull dangerously. This event is called making a gybe (sometimes spelt jibe). Only when this has actually happened to you do you really understand why the word 'gibe' also means to mock, to scoff, to make fun of. When a boat gybes it frequently makes a mockery of its crew. Viz.:

The gybe has three dangers. One: you can dismast the boat if the boom smashes across with such force that it jars the mast to breaking point. Two: any unwary sailor can be hit by the boom when it sweeps across, thereby injuring the idiot or knocking him/her overboard, or both. Three: the whole operation can get out of hand and the boat capsizes, endangering the life of the vessel and all who sail in her.

A fourth possibility exists. All three of the aforementioned calamities can happen together: dismasting, capsizing, injuring/killing the crew.

You guessed it: I gybed.

Consolation: I did not dismast Spike's treasured dinghy.

I did, however, capsize.

Consolation: The boom missed me.

The boom missed me because I was not in the boat when it swung across. I had already been flung overboard by the violence of the wind-borne turn which whipped the boat onto its side. I landed in the sea six feet from the wallowing hull.

Consolation: I did not even get my hair wet.

I didn't get my hair wet because I was so nut-cracking scared that as soon as I hit the briny I was dogging it for the wrecked but floating *Tumble*. Even a disabled boat is better than no boat at all. I scrambled aboard its up-facing side before my hair had time to dip beneath the surface.

6/ACTION REPLAY

Everything happens in a couple of seconds.

Yet from the moment I make my mistake with the tiller to the moment when I scramble on to the sloughing hull, everything seems to take place out of time.

I see now that as I put the tiller over, the storm hits me. The wind grabs the sail, slams it as far forward as it can go, then hurls it back again. The boat starts swinging round, responding to the rudder. As it slurs in a tight circle, the sail comes across the hull. On its way, the mainsheet, flapping loose, fouls the tiller.

Once across the hull, the sail fills with wind again. The mainsheet is strained tight, which therefore tugs the tiller, which in turn steers the dinghy on to a tack so close to the wind that the boat cannot withstand the force and is pushed over. I see the bellying sail dip like a scoop into the waves. Water fills it. Sails, mast, and hull slice into the sea, rudely exposing the boat's red bottom above the surface.

I am a useless instrument of jangling nerves sounding in a drum-tight stomach cinched in fright. As the boat goes over I am thrown out and up, somersaulting through the air.

As I perform the curving trajectory common to all catapulted objects, I think: The boat is capsizing. God, what a twit I must look.

My mind refuses to acknowledge what my senses tell me.

I am watching myself. I smile, a kind of crazy, there's-nothing-I-can-do grin of abandon and terror.

I am descending now, emotions shocked by shock into shock-proof numbness. Will I float? I am thinking. Will I drown? Will this be the end? Is this the start of Death?

I am all deflating questions.

But now comes the water. The thick, soupy, solipsistic sea. I enter feet first, a body committed into His Hands. A clean incision that hardly makes a noticeable splash. A neat dunking.

Not unnaturally—but to me at that moment unexpectedly—the water strikes me (literally) as wet. Cold. And surprisingly (why surprisingly?) supportive. Like a large soggy mattress. A sea bed. (Sorry!)

I am sure that if my head is engulfed beneath the surface I will surely meet The End as the sea will meet mine. My feet and hands are piston-props as soon as they feel the water.

At which point, slow motion switches to double-speed timelapse life.

I have not thought of it

and before I can think
I have done it
or know I have done it
I have covered
the distance between me
and the wallowing boat
on its side, the turbulent waves washing sometimes
right over
the forlorn sail rippling in the water like a drenched
shroud
I grab the gunwale
pull myself round to the dinghy's centre-board keel
use it as a step
clamber on to the hull's whale-back side.
A shipwrecked mariner.

Real time returns.
I shiver violently, cannot stop this water-logged goose-
pimpled trembling.
All I can manage to do is hang on.
For dear life.

7/So there I am, sat like a ninny on this dying boat,
dressed only in my Thames-dyed wet-look T-shirt and
briefs, feeling refrigerated, not to say sorry for myself,
when a shining yellow charger with the name *Calypso*
white-lettered on its razor bow comes slicing through the
waves to my rescue. An eighteen-foot racing dinghy surging to my rescue, its sails straining at their seams.
   This yellow slicker executes a neat unshowy spin into
the wind—the kind I have just demonstrated how not to
do—and loses way with disgustingly precise judgement,
slipping quickly to a heave-ho stop beside me, a safe

boat's length away. (Nothing is as impressively humiliating as seeing someone do something well when you have just done it badly yourself.)

Hear:
Much cracking and smacking of now impotent sails flapping in the already (wouldn't you know it) abating wind.

Accompanying syncopation of sucking and splashing waves slopping against our supine hulls.

See:
Overcast gloom above a bellicose sea.
Glancing splinters of metallic light shining from the still sunbright east.

And in the cockpit of 'Calypso':
A head of streaming jet-black hair above a broad and handsome face split by a teasing grin atop a tidy body, medium height, with the build and frame that can dress in worn and weather-bleached blue-jean shirt and pants as if in this year's flashiest marine gear.

Enter Barry Gorman, eighteen years one month. Further details throughout what follows. This is he who becomes it. The Body.

In his yellow flasher, he was grinning, and holding up for my inspection one pair of dripping jeans.

Mine. Like me, lost overboard during the troubles.

8/That image is on instant replay in my head.
It was the beginning; and the beginning of his end.

9/'Yours?' Barry shouts.

I nod, resigned to humiliation.

'Need any help?'

I look helplessly around.

'Get her upright. I'll tow you ashore.'

Upright? This collapsed jetsam?

'Done it before?'

Own up. What gains dissemblance now? 'No.'

'Do exactly as I say.'

Instructions come with firm clarity. Not to be gainsaid, never needing repetition.

Automaton creature of this pelagic Svengali, I meekly follow orders.

10/Trippers crowded round us on the beach, gawping. Lined the esplanade, pointing, laughing. An unexpected spectacle, seeing an idiot ditched and then rescued. Something to add a little pep to their day out and to tell the folks at home about afterwards.

Only when Barry with cavalier gesture handed me my jeans did I realize the real cause of the mirth.

'You'd better put these on,' he said, 'before you're arrested.'

God, they were cold! Clinging, sticky, gritty from sand. Putting them on was the lowest point in the entire fiasco. At that moment all I wanted was to be home; yet the thought of getting there and of dealing with Spike's dishevelled *Tumble* was more than I could bear.

'You live on Manchester Drive, don't you?' Barry said.

'Yes.' How did he know?

'I'm nearer. Cliff Road. Come on.'

He was collecting bits and pieces of pinchable gear from the boats and stuffing them into a sail bag.

'I'm okay,' I said. 'I'll manage. Got to do something about the boat.'

'Don't argue. I know all about capsizing.' He secured the dinghies. 'We're all set up at home for dealing with sailing accidents. What you need is a hot bath. I'll moor both boats later. Come on.'

JKA. *Running Report*: Henry Spurling ROBINSON 18th September. Interviewed Henry in my office. Case passed to me by Probation. Mrs Robinson a client. She needed help after moving to Southend from the North (nervous trouble; unhappiness with new surroundings, loss of supportive friends and neighbours, etc.). Wanted to talk to Henry before making a home visit and talking to the parents.

School Report assesses Henry as above average intelligence, reasonably conscientious, normal health. Henry has settled down well enough, apparently. Gets along with classmates, but the Head thinks he may not have made any close friendships. The parents have been cooperative with the school, and were supportive of Henry during the events that led to his court appearance.

Discussion began at 2.30 p.m. Henry is medium height for his age, fair-haired, slim. Pretty features, rather than handsome, and younger-looking than his sixteen years nine months. Looks more like fifteen. Neatly dressed: blue jeans, T-shirt, bomber jacket, running shoes. Clean. A healthy tan, but he looked tired and was nervously fidgety at first. Tried to cover his nerves by a forced brightness of manner.

Throughout the conversation he avoided questions he didn't like by giving flippant replies—sometimes genuinely funny. In general conversation off the subject of his court appearance he was talkative and open, though I did feel he is a boy whom it might be difficult to get to know. There was also something in the way he talked that made me think he is trying to emulate someone he admires. He can be slightly affected, a little selfconscious. He tries too hard now and then.

The discussion got off to an awkward start. Apparently Henry dislikes his name and thinks Harry is even worse. He asked me to call him Hal. I gathered he had made the change only this summer, but he was cagey about telling me why.

He talked jokily about Southend, but agreed he liked living here. He especially enjoyed seaside life, finding people on the beach entertaining. He seems to have spent a lot of time this summer sailing 'with friends', he said. He talked without strain about school, likes most of the teachers. He frequently mentioned his English teacher, Mr Osborn, during the interview, whom he obviously admires. (*Memo*: see Osborn asap.)

When Hal was settled and more relaxed I tried broaching the subject of his activities at Barry Gorman's grave. I asked why he had done such a strange thing as jump about on a friend's grave. At once, he tensed again and refused point-blank to discuss anything to do with Gorman. I pressed fairly hard, thinking a strong effort should be made straightaway to get Hal to open up. But the harder I pressed the more agitated he became. His hands trembled and his voice kept breaking. I thought at one point he was going to cry.

Explained it was my job to help him face whatever had happened by talking about it. Also that the court had to know why he had behaved in what seemed a very strange way before they could decide how best to deal with him, and that it was my job to recommend the court on the action they should take.

All the time Hal kept saying, 'No, no. This has nothing to do with you or anybody else.' I asked if Mrs Gorman's accusations were true. He refused to say. I said I couldn't understand why anyone would damage a grave, particularly the grave of a friend. Hal said tartly that it was not up to him to educate me about life! But he blurted out that he had not really damaged the grave, that this was what the police said he had done. I said that stamping about on top of someone's grave seemed a damaging thing to do. Not to mention the fact that the headstone on the grave of Barry Gorman's father, next to Barry's grave, had been knocked over. At this Hal stood up and shouted that if I questioned him any more he would leave and refuse to see me again.

I persuaded him to sit down and reminded him of what could happen to him if he went on refusing to cooperate. That he could be sent to a Detention Centre and be kept there while the police, psychiatrists and other social workers looked into his case. He might get fined. He might be thought in need of medical treatment and then a Supervision Order would be made and the treatment specified, and he would have to attend an appropriate hospital. But, I told him, none of those things might be necessary if he tried to explain himself. He might then receive a conditional discharge, or be put on a Supervision Order with perhaps myself, or some other social worker, keeping an eye on him for a while just to see that all is well.

Whatever happened, I said, he could not escape

having to be dealt with by the court and that their decision would be affected by my report to them. So it was in his own interest to help me understand what he had done.

Hal listened to all this morosely. When I finished he said, 'Do what you like. I won't say anything about what happened.'

I decided there was nothing to be gained by further discussion at this time. Asked Hal to be with his parents when I visit his home tomorrow evening.

19th Sept. Reviewing yesterday's notes. Didn't handle the conversation as well as I should have done. And can't quite put my finger on what worries me. Maybe a subject for Team Discussion on Monday. Hal's case is unusual and outside my experience. Obviously something went on between the two boys which led to Hal's activities at the grave. Could Gorman's death have upset him in a strange way?

Hal is charged with *damaging* a grave. Desecration. Is that the action of a person grieving over a friend's death? Been studying the police report on the second attack on the grave, when Hal was arrested and the only time when his actions were actually witnessed. P.C. Hirsh, the arresting officer, says in his report:

The accused approached the grave at eleven ten p.m. He waited for a moment at the foot of the grave. Then he began stamping about on the grave in a sacrilegious manner. At first he stamped slowly and deliberately. But gradually he became increasingly wild. I then made myself known to the accused and arrested him. 'O, no!' he said and began laughing in a hysterical manner.

If I wanted to desecrate a grave would I be satisfied with stamping about on it? It all sounds so feeble.

11/What Barry meant by his home being fixed up for sailing accidents, it turned out, was a large lumpy woman with blue-rinse grey hair who transmogrified into a whirling dervish as soon as she saw me standing dishevelled, damp and dejected in her front hall.

'Barry,' she piped, sounding like a fire siren going off, 'this poor boy is drowned! What have you done to him!'

She took me by the shoulders, cooed at me, patted my cheek, smoothed my tangled locks. I was five years old and she had just plucked me from the clutches of a baby-snatcher.

'He capsized,' Barry said, climbing the stairs.

Don't leave me to this octopus, I screamed to him in my head.

'He capsized!' Mrs Gorman sirened — for this was she. 'O my God, those boats! I keep telling you, Bubby, they're dangerous. Look at the poor innocent. He's expiring.'

She flipped me round and bulldozed me up the stairs.

'Into the bath,' she said. 'A hot bath is what you need. That's what I do with all Bubby's boys when they turn over. Some of them, they do it just for fun, I think. And because they like my baths maybe!' She laughed, and was instantly serious again. 'But the shock, going into the sea like that. A wonder it wasn't the death of you.'

'I'm all right, Mrs Gorman,' I said, panting.

'You're all right! I'm glad. Half drowned and he's all right! What about your mother?'

'My mother? She doesn't know.'

'She doesn't know! My God, she must be worried sick. Give me the number and I'll call her.'

'I'd rather you didn't, Mrs Gorman. She doesn't even know I went sailing.'

'Doesn't know!'

'And we aren't on the phone.'

'You boys! You never think of your mothers. My Bubby, he's just the same. You don't deserve to have mothers.'

She flung open the door to a huge bathroom, bigger than any bathroom I'd ever seen except in films, and shoved me inside. Our bathroom at home is not much bigger than a cupboard that's been fixed up with plumbing instead of coat hangers. There's so little room that if you're sitting on the pan and anyone opens the door you either sustain a fractured kneecap or escape injury only by ejecting fast into the bathtub.

The Gormans' bathroom wasn't just vast, it also glittered. Mirrors bounced concealed lighting from compromising places. Wherever you stood you saw a kaleidoscope of yourself. Glazed tiles decorated with cavorting sea-nymphs and Greek gods covered what was left of the walls. Copper fitments glowed like soft flames on a corpulent, blue-marbled bathtub and a matching hand basin itself as deep as a barrel. A shower cubicle with sliding doors of underwater glass stood in one corner. But there was no lavatory pan, just something I thought was an uncomfortable-looking foot-washing basin. Till then I hadn't even heard of a bidet never mind seen one. My mother could never have brought herself to mention such a thing, and my father would have dismissed it as a suspect device used only by effete foreigners. What surprised me more, though, was the lush blue carpet that covered the floor. At home we would have thought this not merely extravagant but worse: unhygienic.

Water was already tumbling into the tub. Barry's advance-party work, I guessed. (But where was he now?) Steam, billowing up, was beginning to fog the place, sweating the mirrors, splintering the dazzle of light.

'Off with your clothes and into the bath,' Mrs Gorman

said, grabbing a Greek vase from the side of the tub and flinging bath-salts out of it into the water. A smell fumed back, enough to suffocate a sewage farm. Bubbles billowed. The steam turned Florida blue. This woman had blue on the brain.

I stood up to my ankles in the prairie of the carpet, waiting for Mrs G. to finish her ministrations and leave. Instead she stood and stared back at me.

'Well, what are you waiting for?' she said. I didn't move. 'Ah, the shock! It's dazed you. Come on, off with those filthy things.'

I still didn't—couldn't—move.

Mrs G. laughed, a high C that ricocheted off the Greek gods. 'You think I don't know about boys!' she said grabbing my T-shirt and heaving upwards. 'Me, a wife and mother. You're as bad as my Bubby. You know he locks the door when he baths now?'

'Mrs Gorman . . .' I protested, struggling against her attempt to uncover my torso and succeeding only in tangling myself so that her violent upward pulls at my shirt all but strangled me, cutting me off in mid-sentence.

'Locks the door against his own mother! Would you believe? I tell him, you think you got something special that you hide it from me, your own mother?' She tugged again. My shirt let go of my throat and locked itself under my nose instead. 'I brought you into this world, I tell him. You've got nothing now you didn't have then. Everything is still the same, only bigger.' She laughed again and gave a final snatch that yanked my shirt off at last. She threw it in the direction of a wickerwork basket in a corner; it looked like one of those jars they always have in *Ali Baba* for the thieves to hide in. Maybe Barry was in there now?

Not pausing to draw breath, Mrs G. attacked my jeans.

'Mrs Gorman,' I said, hanging on grimly to the waistband. 'Mrs Gorman, I am not used to this kind of attention.'

'Not used!' she said, unbuckling my belt. 'What's the matter? Your mother neglects you? Is that why you didn't tell her you were going to turn over?'

Now she had my belt unfastened and had undone my fly-zip as well. Before I could take desperate measures to protect myself, like crossing my legs and slumping on to the floor, she tugged my jeans and underpants down with one swift (and obviously practised) movement, finishing with an expert flick of the hands that slipped them under my feet. Jeans and underpants followed my shirt in the direction of Ali Baba.

Mrs G. straightened up and stood back, appraising me as if I were a piece of sculpture she had just finished. 'I don't know why your mother should neglect you,' she said, nodding approvingly. 'She ought to be proud of you. Believe me, you're a good-looking boy.'

She smiled at me, patted my cheek, made for the door.

'Now, into the bath before you die of exposure. I'll make some tea. The shock you've had, you need it hot and sweet.'

She was gone.

Some sons do have 'em, and I hadn't met one like this before.

12/Maybe I really was shocked. Mrs G. would come as a shock to any growing boy, never mind the calamity of a first-time capsize. At any rate, when she disappeared into the blue fog all I could do was stare after her gormlessly.

Then I started what I thought must be hiccups, but which turned into a bout of pizzicato giggles. I also started shivering, despite the pea-soup steam and the Turkish-bath temperature of the room.

And suddenly a hot bath was exactly what I wanted:

a refuge	a relief	a restorative
a relaxant	a refresher	a resuscitator
a rest-cure	a revivifier	a reverberator
a revitalizer	a rehabilitator	a reintegrator
a reclaimer	a reactivator	a renovator.

My mind went mad for the eighteenth letter and four-teenth consonant of the modern English alphabet, the alveolar semivowel, as in *red*, and its repetitive prefix *re*. Maybe I really had lost my reason, was raving, rambling, running mentally amok in a dizzying reaction to my recent reprieve from any requirement of a requiescat.

Not to mention the relapse I must have suffered at the mercy of Ma Gorman's predatory pickers and stealers.

13/Bathtubs always remind me of coffins. The Gormans', being so huge, reminded me of a sarcophagus. Its tomb-like hulk had a memorial solemnity and was adorned with a profusion of bits and pieces. Handles to hang on to, soap-cups, a decorated plug-hole plug attached to a love-knot chain that would do terrible damage if you sat on it. A quilted cushion for your reclining head was stuck on with suction pads. A multi-compartmented tray bridged the sides, filled with lotions in exotic-shaped unbreakable bottles, as well as sponges and back-scrub-bers and nail-brushes and face flannels and what-nots unidentifiable. Lost among all this was a cute little plastic duck that quacked when you squeezed it. And who, I asked myself, played with that in the bath at night?

Come to think of it, the whole room reminded me of

the grave chamber in a pyramid. During my researches into Death, upon which I mused as I lay soaking my derangements in this temple to personal hygiene, I read somewhere that the Great Pyramid of Cheops—biggest and best of them all—was built of more than five million tons of stone and rock, was 481 feet high, 755 feet square at the base, and covered in excess of thirteen acres of land. One pretty neat paperweight.

Anybody who wanted a coffin that big had a lot of faith in Death. Most people these days can't raise enough optimism about it even to bother with a headstone for their nearest and dearest. (It was headstones that first got me interested in Death, as I'll explain later, and one of them is partly responsible for getting me into the predicament I now find myself.) I have, though, heard of a few modern memorials that amuse me. There's one in Vancouver, Canada, for example. It is carved to look like an ice-lolly:

Death licked her in the end.

Which is the thing that bothers me most about Death and is one of the important reasons, in my opinion, for taking a healthy interest in the subject. Death gets us all. No exceptions. But every body. Yours too.

14/I did not imagine, though, as I lay leaching in that steaming lavabo, that Death was quite as close as it was.

Once I was warm again, and clean of cloying Thames gunk, I started to feel sane once more. Believe it or not, only then did the nuttiness of Mrs G.'s bathroom attentions seep into my skull. Other people might be able to go out every day worrying about nothing worse than Death and unimportant matters like how to spend the rest of your life, sanguinely borrow a friend's boat only to capsize in a freak storm, be rescued in front of a crowd of entertained and unhelpful spectators, be taken home by a bloke whose mother is a bathroom freak with the hots for Mothering Sunday, and still know what's going on when he meets up with someone like Mrs G. But me—I'm just ordinary. Things like all that don't happen to me. I am one of those people who believes that nothing unusual or strange or exciting or odd ever happens to them.

I am so convinced of this, am so used to thinking of myself as the perfect example of Joe Comatose, the story of whose life would kill you, that when something out of the ordinary does happen I don't even notice. I could walk into the black hole of Calcutta and just think it was rush hour at the doctor's.

In fact, I have a theory that people are nothing more than the sum of the things they think they are. This is not an idea I thought up. I'll be honest, I got it from Kurt Vonnegut, whose books I was reading all the time this last summer. The idea goes like this: If you think you are a handsome, six-foot-three, blue-eyed genius who writes better songs and sings them better than anyone else in the world, then you tend to behave as if you are a handsome, six-foot-three, etc. etc. This explains why there are so many homely, five-foot-four, putty-eyed popcorns gyrating about on stages all over the place, strutting and fretting and hankering after autograph hunters and managers anxious to sign them up for stardom. It's what they believe about themselves that matters, you see. We are what we pretend to be, Vonnegut says, so we had better be careful what we pretend to be.

And it works just the same the other way. I think of myself as an unexciting schlunk so I guess I act like an unexciting schlunk and so grow into an unexciting schlunk. Very attractive, eh?

Now back to me entombed in the sumptuous Gorman wash-house.

As soon as it sank in that Mrs G. might have a triflingly overactive Id, I started worrying about the bathroom door. I had not locked it, you understand. And she had promised (had I heard right?) to return with a cup of sweet steaming tea. (The day was becoming utterly precipitate.) Unfortunately she would, no doubt, return bearing her sweet steaming Id as well. And I could do without the former if having it meant suffering a generous portion of the other. As you'll gather very soon, I like having a bit of the other, but I also like choosing who I get it from. And Mrs G. didn't figure in my list of preferences.

I rose from the Florida blue intending to secure the door. My skin was glowing scalded red from the volcanically hot water and my blushing anxiety. I had one foot in the tub and one foot raised over the edge when the door opened. Expecting the re-entry of Mrs G., I snatched at a towel hanging from a rail just out of easy reach. In my haste I slipped and fell, plunging back into the depths of the sarcophagus and sending a tidal wave over the side.

But it was Barry, carrying the promised tea, who witnessed this further cack-handed—*correction*: cack-footed—goof.

'Swimming again?' he said. 'Want me to dive in and save you?'

'I thought you were your mother,' I said, attempting to

retrieve my dignity by feigning a final rinse before leaving the bath. (Why is it when you're embarrassed you act like an idiot? *Answer*: Because when you're embarrassed you feel like an idiot. See—you become what you think you are.)

'Relax,' Barry said. 'I heard you getting the treatment so I waylaid her on the landing.'

'Not sure which was worse,' I said. 'Being upset in the ocean or tangling with your mother.'

'Personally,' Barry said, laughing, 'I'd rather capsize any day.'

He reached for the towel I'd missed and handed it to me as I stepped onto the prairie.

'Soak a bit longer if you want,' he said. 'I'll keep Mother at bay. Anyway, she has to go to the shop in a few minutes. It's my day off so she has to see to things.'

I took the towel. 'I'm out now, and I've got to moor my pal's boat. Then I have to be in school at two-thirty to meet a teacher.' I glanced at my pile of dank clothes. 'Don't fancy wearing those again.'

Barry said, 'Forget it. Everything's sorted. I'll deal with the boat when I take care of mine. That gives you plenty of time. I've some clean clothes ready for you in my room. First on the left outside here. Come in when you're ready.'

15/AND THEN: In Barry's room . . .

'Luckily you're nearly my size so this stuff ought to fit.'

Laid out on his bed were a pair of light blue jockey shorts, a sweat shirt with narrow blue-and-white stripes (very français, very matelot), light blue jeans, washed pale and worn, blue ankle socks. Too much of the symphonics for my taste, but beggars . . .

'What size shoes?'

'Eights.'

'I take nines. Hang on.'

'I'll manage with mine. They'll dry on my feet.'

He was lounging against the edge of a bench-desk watching me dress. The desk ran the whole length of the wall opposite the bed. I was envious. Not just the desk space, but the rows of shelves underneath crammed with books and records and the gear for a sophisticated quadrophonic system.

'Nice,' I said, nodding at the gear.

'Benefit of owning a record shop.'

Gorman Records on London Road in Westcliff. I'd been there a couple of times searching for cut-price discs. I'd seen Barry serving customers. A small shop. But busy. A Saturday morning hang-out.

The whole room was very neat. Modern furniture arranged almost geometrically in a careful pattern. There was a repro of a picture by David Hockney above the bed, one of his California swimming pool paintings, 'Pete getting out of Nick's pool'. I knew it was Hockney because I liked his work too. Barry's room reminded me, then, of the rooms in some of Hockney's paintings of people in their houses. The way he stood and sat always reminded me, that day and afterwards, of those Hockney people. All part of an arrangement, like a still-life, a little too posed for real life, very clean, bright, clear-cut, airy. I liked their sharp-focus quality, and the feeling that there was something elusive, something waiting behind all that studied informality.

For a second, with Barry leaning there watching me dress, I felt like a Hockney person myself. I quite enjoyed that. But—and I can't explain this—I felt a twinge of fear too.

The clothes fitted near enough. His jeans were an inch

or so too long; I had to turn up the bottoms or I'd have been tripping over myself.

'You'll do for now,' Barry said. He fished a comb from his back pocket and handed it to me. 'There's a mirror on the wall over there. You hungry?'

'Beginning to be. Thought I'd nip home and grab something on the way to school.'

'Soup and cheese ready and waiting downstairs.'

I glanced at him in the mirror. Mirror mirror on the wall . . .

'You've done enough. I'd best get on.'

'All arranged. Courtesy of my mother before she left for the shop. She's taken a shine to you. If you don't eat it there'll be hell to pay.'

I handed him his comb. 'Do you do this for everyone who turns over?'

He led the way onto the landing. 'It's my day off, so I can look after you.'

We went down to the kitchen. Like the bathroom, huge by my standards, and shining with all mod cons. A scrubbed wood table in the centre was set with a lot more than the promised cheese and soup. There were thin slices of cold beef, demure on a plate; a tossed green salad, fetching in a wooden bowl; tomatoes, fruit, chunky brown bread; cans of beer; mugs for coffee that was percolating on an Aga stove, where the soup was simmering in a pan, a thick broth of vegetables.

'Dig in,' Barry said serving me a bowl of soup.

No second invitation needed. Capsizing and Mrs G.'s bathing cure were hungering work.

16/With one appetite being satisfied another surfaced. Curiosity.

Who was this guy who rescued me from the sea and brought me home to be coddled by his mum and dressed me in his clothes and fed me in his kitchen?

I had never met him before; he didn't know me. Why was he doing all this? Out of the goodness of his heart? Pull the other one. Which one of the two? Was that what all this was about?

I knew nothing about him. Except:

'Isn't your shop Gorman Records on London Road?'

He nodded. 'My father started it twenty years ago.'

'And didn't you go to Chalkwell High?'

'Till last summer.'

'Good soup.'

'She's not a bad cook.'

We slurped together.

I said, 'You left to work in the shop then?'

He looked across the table at me deciding whether I was fit to be told. He used to do that: gab away to people till they started getting too close to him, too *inside*. Then he'd stop and stare at them, and think, and if he decided they were okay, he'd answer; if he decided they weren't okay he jossed the question aside.

I passed the test. He said, 'My father died suddenly last year.'

'Sorry,' I said, wishing I hadn't asked.

'It's over.'

I could see from his change of mood that it wasn't.

He took in a deep breath. 'Mother and he ran the shop. Mother looked after the accounts, Father was the music expert and the one that was good with customers. People liked him. He could sell anything if he wanted to. When he died, Mother hired a man to take over Father's work. But they kept having rows. Nobody can replace Dad as far as Mother is concerned.' He smiled to himself. 'And she isn't exactly the easiest person to work for! . . . So I

33

started helping out on Saturdays and after school. But it wasn't enough. Things went from bad to worse. In the end, the problem solved itself. The man left after a row one day, and I knew there was nothing else for it. I left school and went into the shop full-time.'

'But you hadn't meant to?'

'Not till I was eighteen anyway. Maybe not till after university or something. Dad was keen on me going to university. He hadn't had the chance, you see. Thought it was the thing to do. Wanted me to have all the benefits he never had, etcetera etcetera. Have some more salad.'

'Thanks . . . Wasn't there anyone else—anyone in the family I mean—who could have gone into the shop?'

'I've an older sister, but she's married, lives in London, got a kid. And her knowledge of music gets about as far as "White Christmas".'

'Yuk!'

'Granted.'

'Bit hard on you though, leaving school when you didn't want to, just to serve in the shop.'

He smiled. 'I don't just serve in the shop. I run it.'

'But if you wanted to stay on.'

'The shop comes first.'

'Why should it? What you want to do with your life should come first, I think.'

'The shop happens to earn our living.'

'That's important, yes, but your mother could have managed somehow. From my brief experience I'd say she's pretty good at getting her way.'

'It's difficult to explain to people who haven't owned their own business. I had the same trouble when I was trying to explain to the Head why I was leaving.'

'Try me.'

'Coffee or beer?'

'Some more beer, please.'

'My father and mother started the shop from nothing, right? They wanted to do something where they could be together all the time. Dad liked music. The shop seemed the answer. They built up a good business. Regular customers. Big stock. They put a lot of work into it. Now the place is a kind of centre for people interested in music. It was Dad's life really.'

'That doesn't mean it has to be yours, does it?'

'No. But I do feel some kind of loyalty. Music means a lot to me. The business means a lot to the family, and to the town as well. It would be a waste to let it fall to pieces or to sell it off. I just felt I had to carry on what Dad had started.'

'You were right. I still don't understand.'

'Haven't you ever thought about following in the paternal footsteps?'

'My father's a baggage handler at the airport.'

'So you don't want to be a baggage handler at the airport. What do you want to do?'

I shrugged. 'Haven't a clue, to be honest. That's the current problem. Get a job or stay on at school. I think that's what Osborn wants to see me about this afternoon.'

'Trust Ozzy. He'll want to have his say.'

'Why not? Everybody else does.'

'Have some more beef, you'll need it.'

'Ta. But I like Ozzy.'

'A minority taste.'

'People grumble because he makes them work, that's all. He knows his stuff and I think he makes it interesting. Anyway, if I get through O-level lit. it'll be because of him.'

'I'll grant you he thinks Eng. lit. is the only thing that matters.'

'Sounds like you drew blood.'

'Now and then. Drink up.'

'I've had enough, thanks.'

He started clearing the table of the dirty plates. 'When you've seen him you tell me all. Just to see if I'm right.'

I looked at him, the question unspoken.

'Well,' he said breezing it up, 'you'll have to collect your clothes. Mother's already got them in the washer. And you'll be bringing my stuff back, won't you? You can tell me then . . . Okay?'

17/That was how it was.

Correction: That was how it was not.

We said all that. But there was more going on behind our faces so to speak.

But if I'm going to get it right—and I have to get it right or why bother with all this in the first place?—I'll have to make a cringing confession that will help explain. The sort of confession people only make when they are drunk or hypnotized on a psycho's couch. Or are mad. Loony. Like me. The sort that wakes you up afterwards, in the middle of the night, shaking your head and groaning 'No, no!' in an agony of sweaty regret. But what the hell, I've told you too much now anyway. You might as well hear the rest. And you can't skip it because if you do you'll miss something that makes sense of everything that happened.

When I was a kid of about seven I watched a television programme, I'm not sure whether it was a play or an old film, about two boys. If I saw it now I'd probably rupture myself laughing at the incredible banality and pukiness of its story. But when you are seven, if you can recall those far-off days of last year, a TV sci-fi monster made from plastic foam and kitchen foil is frighteningly convincing;

even the newsreaders look real. In short, at seven you still believe.

These two boys were a couple or three years older than me, and together they had a series of adventures of the kind that, at seven, you think must be the most exciting events known to man. In the first adventure they found an old tin can that was supposed to be full of magic beans. These magic beans possessed the power of transporting people back in time. So Our Heroes had day trips to such wonders as Robin Hood in Sherwood Forest, the Spanish Armada on the High Seas, Hadrian's Wall at the time of the Romans, and the Court of King Arthur during a period when the knights weren't getting on too well together. Wherever they went Our Heroes sorted out everybody's troubles by dint of native twentieth-century knowhow and stunningly precocious intelligence, like commonsense. I am ashamed to admit that I was thirteen before I stopped enjoying that kind of gunk. As Barry used to say about me in a slightly different circumstance, there are times when I can be a late developer.

The important thing is that at one glorious moment near the end of the first adventure Our Heroes swore eternal fealty, one to another, by each cutting his hand with a forage knife freshly sharpened on King Arthur's stone, and then, holding their bleeding wounds together, mingled their blood while chanting a solemn oath and gazing deep into each other's eyes.

'Now,' said one of them afterwards, 'we are bosom friends forever.'

I remember those words exactly for two reasons. The first reason is that I had just that week learned that a woman's breasts are sometimes called her bosom. (The fact that bosom also means chest, man or woman's, had not yet become clear to me.) One of those TV boys calling the other the friend of his breast was therefore a little startling to a small boy with a fresh interest in mammary glands.

The second reason isn't so easy to explain. It wasn't so much the phrase 'bosom friends' that struck me, but the idea behind the phrase. It put into words something I have always wanted since I can remember: an out-and-out, no-holds-barred, one-for-both and both-for-one, totally faithful, ever-present friend. And I do not mean a pet dog.

Here was this bilgewater TV show putting words and pictures to my till then unspoken desire. Ah-ha!, I must have said to myself, or whatever gasp you emit when you are seven and talking to yourself about something as surprisingly illuminating as a flash of mental lightning, Ah-ha! So other people want to have friends like that as well! I am not alone, I must have thought. Somewhere out there is someone looking for me, just as I am looking for him. A boy with a can full of magic beans.

I've thought about that moment of surprise often since. The only way I can explain it to myself is to suppose that because I did not have any brothers or sisters to knock romantic ideas of friendship out of me at an early age, this irrational desire for a bosom pal took hold. Or maybe my mother should have let me roam the streets and get beaten up sooner than she did. Or maybe it was all genetic, or had something to do with what I ate, or didn't eat, or maybe it was the result of not being taught to say my prayers at night because my father is a raving atheist.

I might add that nobody warned me at an appropriate age about wet dreams, and maybe these had something to do with the persistence of my desire for a bosom buddy into adolescence so that it was still with me, as strong as ever, when I was sixteen. But then, nobody warned me earlier about television and how a little of it tends to corrupt the mind and a lot of it corrupts the mind completely. And, after all, it was television which gave me, during one of its frequent wet emissions, the words and pictures to imagine this idea of a possible reality — the hope for a bosom friend. Remember Vonnegut: We are what we pretend to be. So in the end it is probably all television's fault that I became a bosom-pal freak.

Whatever, here I was at sixteen years six months corrupted by a long-lasting desire for a bosom friend without ever having found a friend to be truly bosomy with. Mind you, I did have some close calls in my search for a soul mate. There was Harvey, for instance.

Harvey came to live in our street when I was nine and growing despondent, having by then searched for two years without success for someone to cut a hand with. Harvey, I was sure, was He. And for a while everything went just like on TV. We had adventures. Not, sadly, with a can of magic beans, but more routine stuff like sleeping at the bottom of our garden in a tent made of an old blanket over a washing line. (God, the daring! The day it was due to happen I broke out in a rash at the excitement of it all.)

In the middle of the night we swapped our best jokes, by which you'll recall, everyone at nine years old means their dirtiest jokes. The joke that kept Harvey and me giggling longest that night was this one:

There's this little girl and this little boy and the little boy says, 'Can I come to your house?' and the little girl says, 'You're not supposed to, but seeing you're my friend I'll let you.' So they go to her house and the little boy says, 'Can I come to your bedroom with you?' so she says, 'Well you're not supposed to, but seeing you're my friend I'll let you.' The little boy says, 'Can I get in bed with you?' so she says, 'Well you're not supposed to, but seeing you're my friend I'll let you.' The little boy says,

'Can I put my finger on your belly-button?' so she says, 'You're not supposed to, but seeing you're my friend I'll let you.' So the little boy does, and the little girl says, 'That's not my belly-button,' and the little boy says, 'No, and that's not my finger.'

Of course, when we'd gone through it two or three times and worn ourselves out with giggling, we tried acting it out, which I enjoyed very much and couldn't understand why Harvey got tired of the game so soon.

Another time we built a secret den behind a back yard garage rarely used by its owner. Harvey said the owner was a 102-year-old man who lived on Coke and mashed cornflakes. A young and pretty District Nurse visited him a lot, which gave rise to much speculation between Harvey and myself about the extraordinary properties such a diet must possess. We tried it for a while, but it did nothing for Harvey.

Before long Harvey turned out to be a disappointment. His idea of bosom friendship was all for him and none for me. For days I supplied every demand of this self-indulgent creep, hoping my unselfish devotion would eventually win him for the cause of true and lasting amity. But the more I did to please him, the more his appetite for slavery increased. I've noticed since that this is how a lot of friendships are. I soon decided palship meant more to me than being dogsbody to an egotist. We split up after a nasty row that ended in a scuffle on the pavement outside Harvey's house, and remained sullen enemies thereafter.

Next there was Neill. He came along about a year after my friendship with Harvey broke up. Harvey had had one good effect. He had made me suspicious. Harvey looked clean-cut, open-faced, honest. The sort of kid your mother says you should try and be more like. But behind that innocently cute phizzog was a scheming and selfish mind. People are not always, I realized after Harvey, just what they look. Even less are they what they say.

Neill was overweight, mother-coddled, and quiet. He had a long nose that was fat at the end and sometimes dripped on cold mornings, like a leaking pear. He was also an only son. After Harvey I felt safe with Neill. Life was never exactly sparkling and he certainly did not possess the can of magic beans. But he was always there, willing and faithful. We went to school together every day, watched TV, flew kites, shared meals, sat around talking. Also Neill was a big reader; he took me to the local library and made me join, which I hated him doing at the time, but now I'm grateful because it was something I would never have done on my own. We spent hours thereafter lying side by side on his bedroom floor with our noses stuck in books.

But none of this is really what kept me friends with Neill for three years. What did was one thing: obsession. In this case, Neill's, not mine. Neill knew exactly what he wanted to do in life. You'd never have thought so to look at him; you'd have thought he was a wet slob with a mind as flabby as his overfed body. But not a bit of it. He fascinated me because till I met him I had never known anyone else but myself who had an obsession. And he had something more. He had a concentrated personality. He did not just have an obsession, he devoted himself to it totally. What we did as we apparently did nothing but lie about talking and reading, was to talk and read about Neill's obsession. Neill wanted to devote his life entirely to *experimenting* with electricity. It was this that provided a few mind-blowing moments of such high excitement that the long boring stretches of life with Neill were well worth suffering.

These big moments happened because it never occurred to Neill that you are supposed to wait till you are grown up before you engage in scientific experiments of the kind that might push out the barriers of human knowledge but might also kill you in the process. He was already getting on with the job when I met him. He had commandeered the spare bedroom and turned it into a laboratory stuffed with gear he had begged, bought and filched—wire, and meters of various sorts and sizes, and inexplicable gadgets, and control units as ominous as robots. And from time to time the entire house seemed to be nothing more than a testbed for Neill's latest experimental wizardry.

What I could never understand was the way Neill's mother encouraged him. In everything else she smothered him with maternal protection. Even in summer she made him wear a sweater, a thick jacket, an overcoat and a scarf if the sky went cloudy. And he wasn't allowed to go into town on his own in case he got lost. Neill never protested; I suppose he couldn't be bothered. But I was a godsend to them both. Neill's mother trusted me for some reason (motherly women always trust me, to wit Mrs Gorman, I put it down to my sad eyes) and regarded me as a safe junior child-minder who could take care of her son for her when he was out of the house. Neill knew that if I was with him he could go places and do things otherwise forbidden unless accompanied by mum. Both showed their gratitude. Neill's mother never stopped trying to feed me up to similar proportions as her son, and Neill allowed me to help with his experiments, a privilege no one else enjoyed. (I never saw Neill's father, by the way. He was a merchant seaman and came home only rarely.)

Not that I ever understood a thing Neill was doing. But the experiments provided the excitement. The first such I witnessed was when Neill set his next-door neighbour's house on fire. He had designed a gadget which somehow involved the mains electric circuit. With my nervous assistance he rigged up oddments of equipment to the electricity meter controlling the household supply, which was located in a cupboard under the stairs. All seemed to be going according to Neill's plan when we heard the unmistakable noise of a fire engine hurling itself down the street and skidding to a fierce stop, as we thought, outside Neill's house. We raced to see what was going on only to find the engine had stopped next door, which was already smoking badly from every crevice. I'm sorry to admit that we watched with amused interest while the fire was put out. People are cruel when they are twelve. How Neill's tampering with the mains supply accomplished such spectacular results neither he, nor anybody else, ever discovered.

On another occasion Neill exploded himself through the kitchen door, luckily open at the time, into the back yard, where he scattered the dustbin in an elaborate and noisy landing which exaggerated the violence of the explosion and from which the dustbin never recovered.

On a third occasion, and for what electronic purpose I cannot remember, we were bending glass tubing over a bunsen burner. Neill got over-confident, went too fast, snapped the glass, and was cut by a flying splinter on the vein that passes over the knuckle of the thumb. Blood spurted like an oil strike, splattering the kitchen walls in a profusion so alarming as to make Neill, who could never stand the sight of blood even in the Sunday joint, suppose death must be only seconds away.

Before I could think what to do, Neill raced screaming into the street, where he literally ran into his mother who was returning from the shops burdened with food parcels to keep Neill alive for the next couple of days. A scene of Mediterranean proportions ensued. Voices were raised in arias of panic, hands were waved, people rushed to the rescue from all directions. Blood and emotion flowed like lava.

Eventually an ambulance arrived. Neill was sirened away. Only to return an hour later by public transport, his thumb patched with a humiliatingly minute piece of sticky tape, his devotion to science quelled but by no means quenched. By evening we were busy with a wholly new electronic project which had suggested itself to Neill while he was at the hospital. He had seen some clinical machine or other, the purpose of which remained obscure to me but which he understood perfectly, and which he was certain he could improve on in a design of his own invention.

In the end I decided Neill was a genius. But I tell you—if geniuses are all like Neill, they aren't much cop as friends. They're interesting, no doubt of it. And eccentrically companionable. But Neill made me realize that there was something more I wanted of my bosom pal than cosy companionship.

Not that I could then have described what that extra something was, not even after Neill, by which time I was fourteen. Except that it had to do with cutting your hand, and blood, and grasping your friend's wounded mitt and swearing a binding oath.

I was to learn about the missing something when I came across another potential BF a few months after I gave up seeing Neill all the time, and just before we moved to Southend. I won't bore you with the unhappier details. I'll just mention that the candidate's name was Brian Biffen, better known as Buster. He was two years older than me, and a lock forward in the school's rugby team. He was the only one of the three who wanted me to be his friend and chased after me, rather than me setting the ball rolling and wanting him to be mine.

I guess it was flattering to be chased after instead of

44

chasing after someone else. Which is why I agreed to watch Buster perform on the rugger field—not something I'd usually be seen dead doing. And it was after I'd watched him play in a match one evening that he took me behind the gym and taught me the pleasures of mutual comfit (or, rather, dis-comfit when Buster was your instructor), a learning process that slotted the missing piece into my understanding of bosom palship, even though Buster proved himself undesirable because being hugged by him was like being hugged by a teenage cactus with large biceps. I have avoided rugger players ever since. 'I wish you were a girl,' breathed Buster at the climactic moment. As I did not wish Buster were a girl, only less cactal and overpowering, an essential difference between his ideas about himself and mine about myself became all too clear to my astonished mind.

There remains only one more item to add to the fraying emotional embarrassment of this confessional catalogue:

One day a few months ago Holy Joe Harrison, our religious teacher unextraordinary, read out from the Holy Bible certain unexpected passages about David (the little guy who gave Goliath the chop with a sling stone) and Jonathan (the tearaway son of fierce King Saul). David and Jonathan got a thing going between them, apparently, because they started talking about the soul of Jonathan being knit with the soul of David, and Jonathan loving David as his own soul.

I'm not sure Holy Joe can have realized what he was getting into, because this isn't exactly the sort of Biblical revelation it is advisable to read out to burgeoning sixteen-year-olds, especially if you are as uptight and morally fundamentalist as HJH and have poor classroom discipline into the bargain. Everybody woke up and hooted of course, and there were scrawny cries of 'Hello-o-o-o-o!' But I found myself sitting up and taking notice just like I had all those years ago in front of the telly.

To be honest, the can of magic beans and the cut hands were losing their potency as images of bosomry by this time. They were tainted with kiddishness. But this stuff about souls being knit, and all of it Biblical too, was a lot more engaging. So afterwards I got the reference from HJH—who must have thought he'd made a convert because no one ever asked him anything—and read it all for myself in 1 Samuel 18 *et seq.* I then discovered the even more riveting information that D. and J. found their love, as the Bible puts it, 'passing the love of women'.

This really set the juices flowing. Whatever had I stumbled upon? The two boys with their can of magic beans as processed as TV dinners disappeared into the mists of babyhood in one evening's Bible reading. Here was meat far more nourishing to feed a growing lad.

Not that the Bible goes into too much detail. It never does. That book is full of all sorts of terrific ideas, and is always telling you what you should and should not to, but it never gets round to telling you how to do them and how to stop yourself from doing them. So here I was with a tantalizingly dazzling phrase cried out by David at the death (DEATH!) of Jonathan—'Thy love to me was wonderful, passing the love of women' (2 Samuel 1, 26)—but left to wonder what it meant, and, more importantly, what exactly had happened between them to make David think like that. For God's sake, what had they *done* to—with?—each other?

One thing was sure. David and Jonathan were archetypal bosom friends. No question. This explained also the message I had seen scrawled on a wall under the pier a few days before: BRIAN LOVES JONATHAN. To which someone else had added the words: SO DID DAVID. READ YOUR BIBLE. Since then I have come across further evidences of the same fun. BATMAN LOVES ROBIN, for instance.

David's illuminating cry stalked my mind for weeks. And was still haunting me the day Barry Gorman hove into view waving my jeans from the cockpit of his yellow *Calypso*. So, you see, I wasn't exactly all wide-eyed innocence that day, whatever I may have tried to pretend—to him or to you.

18/Which explains why things were happening under the surface (if you'll pardon the expression, given the seaborne nature of our meeting) from the time Barry begins his rescuing pick-up until the moment we sit facing each other across his kitchen table scoffing his mother's nosh. So I'll try again.

RETAKE

He comes alongside, and I know who he is at once. I've seen him around during my first two terms at school here before he left. And since he left I have passed him on the street, and caught glimpses of him sailing. Each time I size him up, as you do people you come across now and then. Nothing more than that: just pick him out of the crowd and think, 'Interesting' or 'Nice'.

But it isn't part of my nature to seek out people who I think I might like, and try to win them. I wouldn't trust the result, not after Harvey and Buster. Besides, I don't like rejection; it hurts. I also get some of this caution from my mother who has an old-fashioned, doomsday view of life. She says that what you have to ask for you don't deserve and shouldn't get. What's more, she says if you do get it, retribution is bound to strike, like a kind of spiteful lightning. Ask and it shall be taken from you, and great shall be the pain thereof. My mother believes all this superstitious gunk. I don't, of course, but sometimes I catch myself acting as if I did, like the people who don't believe it is bad luck to walk under ladders but don't take the chance anyhow.

So I never make a pass at passing attractions, whatever the sex. But when Barry appears alongside, though I am cold and wet and miserable and expect to die, I take one look and I know he is the latest contender for the role of the boy with the can of magic beans. My death is imminent in this watery waste and there I am sitting on a wrecked dinghy thinking of acquiring a Jonathan for my David, and wondering how long you need to find out exactly what it is that passes the love of women.

The irony of this does not escape me. (Isn't he a clever boy.) But I do not laugh aloud. O no. Instead I slip into a lost-and-hopeless-kid routine. Not deliberately, not by scheming design, you understand. I really am being freeze-dried in the angry Thames, after all; and anyway I am not *that* scheming even at the best of times. It all happens instinctively. As if there is something about Barry that triggers off this reaction. But all the same, I can *feel* myself acting the part. I almost watch myself perform.

What is more, I enjoy it. I put myself into his hands and love it. He tells me what to do be saved. I do what he tells me neatly, straightaway, as if he is working me by remote control. And how do I explain that feeling to anyone who hasn't had it? Well, in the days when I was watching Buster play rugger, I remember seeing those hearty athletes revel in some moment when everything went just right between them. They said they felt like they were one man. They go flip afterwards in their amusingly bullish fashion. I used to wonder about it, and envy it too, secretly. Maybe this inter-being I am feeling at this moment of rescue is the same kind of experience? I don't know, not just then. What I do know is that I glow inside.

Barry gets me ashore. I protest about going home with him, but this is all show. Of course I want to go home with him. I really do feel miserable, foolish, shocked. (Especially on the beach; that bloody gawking crowd!) But I don't feel as bad as I put on just to keep the calamity alive and the mutual interest going. I've noticed before: there is nothing like a catastrophe that leaves you helpless for stoking up other people's interest in you.

So we get to Barry's house and there is all that fandango with his mother. But I enjoy my bath. Mrs Gorman is right about it as a cure for capsizing. Afterwards I know Barry is sizing me up while I dress in his room. I know I am sizing him up too. And the more I see the more I like him. Which is one of the great conundrums: how do you *know* that you like someone in just a few minutes? How does it happen with this person so quickly and not with hundreds, thousands of other people who cross your path every year? I've thought about that a lot and still haven't a clue. Because it isn't just that you like the look of a face or the shape of a body or even how someone lives that makes them attractive. It's something else, something you can't ever quite put your finger on. You just know it has happened, that's all. And it happened that morning.

And then we are guzzling at his kitchen table, and I am pretending now to be cool, calm, collected, and O so mature. When actually I am coming apart at the seams with the blood-tingling thrill of it all. Hey-nonny-no.

19/'Finished?' Barry asked. 'Want anything more?'

'Great, thanks. I'd better be going . . . '

We cleared the table, loaded the dishwasher. Our dishwasher is my mother, hindered by my dad on Sunday afternoons, if he isn't working.

'Listen,' he said. 'I'll see to the boats while you attend the wizard of Oz. Why not drop in this evening? You could tell me what Ozzy says, and maybe we could go to a film or something?'

'Okay, sure.'

'See you about half six then?'

Hey, Nono: nonny-no.

20/When I found Oz that afternoon he took me into an empty classroom and handed me an essay I had written just before the exams started.

'Your work, I think, Robinson,' he said.

Ozzy is tall, wirily thin, balding. When he gets you at close quarters and peers at you through his glasses with their lenses like the bottoms of bottles you feel like you are trapped by an inquisitive shark afflicted by myopia and possessed of an over-active thyroid. Not a pretty sight. It took me weeks to realize that when he is putting you through the mill of his attention, he isn't trying to pulverize you with the force of his superior intellect, but only trying to sharpen your powers of thought. 'He could have fooled me,' other kids say when I try to explain this. 'It is a well-known fact,' they say, 'that even the Head is afraid of him. And that he eats new boys for breakfast.'

He sat me down and drew a chair up beside me.

'Be good enough to read out what you have written.'

TIME SLIP

I was thirteen at the time. We had
been visiting relatives for the day,
my parents and I. My uncle — my
father's brother — insisted on showing
us the family grave in the little
churchyard lost among fields near his
farm. The family plot was big enough
for five graves laid side by side.
There was a low marble wall all round,
and a big tombstone at one end with all
the names of the dead carved on it.

The names went back to the last
century, and each one was followed by
a date of birth and a date of death.
For people like me, who cannot do
arithmetic, there was also the age of
the person. <u>Charles Robinson</u>. <u>Born
5th March 1898</u>. <u>Died 10th May 1962</u>.
<u>Aged 64 yrs</u>. Fifteen names, one on top
of another. A death list.

As I stood looking at this bed of

dead bodies I suddenly thought: There
are people lying under there. People
who are connected to me. I saw a
picture in my head of a long row of
dead bodies stretching back away from
me in time. And beyond them, others;
people I did not know about but who
belonged to this queue of Robinsons.

I giggled. Everyone was being
very solemn and my mother glared at me.
She thought I was going to show her up.
But I wasn't giggling because I thought
there was anything funny. I was
giggling because I had suddenly been
struck by the foreverness of time.

This forever time was not filled
with minutes and hours and days and
years, but with people, people's lives,
one after the other in every direction.
Hundreds and thousands and millions of
them. They stretched not only
backwards in time, but across time as
well, and away into future time. Time
in all directions, all over the world,
for ever and ever, measured by people.

I started giggling because it was
all too much: all that time; all those
people. I couldn't grasp it with my
mind. But I knew it was there. That
they were there. That it was true.
I could _feel_ it.

I went wandering about among the
graves because I could not stand still
any more. And I couldn't keep my eyes
off the gravestones. Some of them
leaned over at clownish angles as if
they were performing a slow-motion
collapse, which of course they were.
Some were so old and eroded I couldn't
read the names and dates carved on
them. Some were new and smart and
somehow smug in their well-kept
neatness.

I read the names and ages and kept
thinking: Every one of these people
must have been alive and must have felt
like me once. They were inside themselves, like I am inside myself now,
looking out of themselves seeing other
people looking out of theirselves at

them. But then one day they weren't
inside themselves any more. They were
dead.

Is that what _dead_ means? Not
being in your body? Died aged 64 yrs.
Died aged 80 yrs. Died aged 36 yrs.
One said: Died aged 2 yrs 3 mths.
They only put the months on babies, as
though months matter then but don't
matter any longer when you are grown up.

Some things you know, but you
don't _know_ them. They don't mean
anything real. Before that day I knew
people died. But for the first time
that day I knew all of a sudden, so
that I felt it, that not being inside
me would happen to me as well one day,
and could happen at any moment.

When this thought hit me, I
nearly fainted. I had to sit down
on a tombstone and put my hand under
my sweater, feeling for my heart. I
wanted to be sure it was beating. And
I listened for my next breath. Each
time my heart beat I felt relief and

immediately then was anxious again,
waiting for the next one. And the same
with each breath I took.

But you cannot go on all the time,
and all through time, feeling relieved
and then anxious and then relieved
again seventy times a minute. You would
die of exhaustion. My own attempt
lasted about two minutes and seemed
like an hour.

Gradually I calmed down and
returned to normal. I went back to my
parents. They were talking, laughing
at memories of relatives buried in the
family grave. And I started to wonder
when we would be given something to
drink and when it would be time to go
home. And I forgot about the startling
foreverness of time.

Since then, though, Death has
always been something real to me,
something present, and not just a
subject people talk about. And every
day I wonder what time will be like
when I am dead.

22/'Does it please you?' Ozzy asked, typically deadpan, nothing in those laser eyes or the crisp voice betraying his own opinion.

'When I wrote it, sir.'

'And now?'

Caution.

'Don't dither.'

'I think so.'

'You worked at it?'

'About five drafts. Rough versions, I mean. This neat one made six.'

'You changed a lot each time?'

'Mostly it was cutting things out, sir, trying to get it clearer, more exactly what I wanted to say. Trying to get it tighter. Like you told us to, sir.'

'I'd prefer "as" to "like", but I regard that as a losing battle. "They were inside themselves, *like* I am inside myself . . . "'

'I guess it is, sir.' I chanced a smile. 'A losing battle, I mean.'

The smile was returned; he must be pleased!

'You bring the language tumbling round our ears, Robinson. Is it ignorance or preference?'

'Preference in that case, sir.'

'No bliss then. I grow old . . . Tell me, what are you reading?'

'I'm on a patch of Vonnegut, sir.'

'From which comes the Americanism, no doubt. Ah well, you could do worse, I suppose. *Slaughterhouse-Five?*'

'I started with that, sir.'

'Hence this interest in death?'

'No, sir. I caught that a few years ago.'

'Then would you say this modest piece of prose is fiction or non-fiction?'

I hadn't thought about it. I shrugged, 'It's about things I've felt, sir. But I invented the incidents.'

'You might safely call that fiction. And, Robinson, I'll be frank with you.'

'Sir?'

'This is quite a promising essay.'

Surprise, surprise. 'Thanks.'

'Do not mistake me. I am not saying you are a literary genius. Far from it. Ridley, Wilson and Carter are all in your year and produce consistently more impressive work than you.'

He picked up my pages again and flicked his eyes over them.

'But you have learned a lot since you joined us.'

He slipped a pencil from his pocket and began underlining phrases. (He always seems to have the same pencil and it's always a stump of a thing with a sharp point. It is never new and never blunt. Yet no one ever sees him sharpen it; and when does he ever begin a new one and wear out the stump?)

'"Lost among fields" must be rejected as cliché by now, I think. The "long row of bodies" suggests corpses laid out head to foot, but "a queue of Robinsons" suggests bodies standing up in packed lines. The images clash, you see, which reduces their effect. . . . '

He went on, devastating, paragraph by paragraph.

' . . . The last sentence makes a well-judged end but it stands too starkly separate from the sentence before. Maybe the uncommitted conjunction is the fault. You're fond of a conjunction as a sentence opener, but it must be wisely handled. The connection between your last sentence and what precedes it needs firmer statement, in my view.'

I was feeling crushed by now and combative.

'Could you show me what you mean, sir?'

'Well, let's see . . . Try this: "Since then, Death has been something real to me, something present that forces me to wonder what time will be like when I am dead."'

'That flows better, sir, but isn't as interesting.'

Ozzy smiled. 'At least I've got rid of "though" and "always", which are redundant, as well as "not just a subject people talk about", which is weak. But I'll grant you the case could be argued. However . . . ' he looked at his wristwatch, 'I've a class in five minutes and there is something else I want to discuss with you.' He slipped his pencil back into his pocket. 'Tell me, have you decided what you'll do with yourself from September?'

I shook my head. 'Not a clue, sir.'

'Your parents?'

'I think my father would like me to get a job.'

'He hasn't said so?'

'Not in so many words, no.'

'Your mother wants you to do what you think is best?'

I smiled. 'Yes.'

'Does your father offer any suggestions about work?'

'He's hinted he could get me something at the airport. He's a baggage handler there.'

'Does the idea appeal?'

'No, sir.'

'What does?'

'That's the trouble. Nothing specially.'

'What about staying on at school?'

'I wouldn't mind. I quite like it here. But there's something of the same problem. What to take. And what to do with it afterwards.'

Ozzy stood up. 'This is my two pennorth, Robinson, and then I'll say no more. Should you decide you would like to stay on I would be happy to have you in my English Sixth. You have an aptitude for the subject and I think you are developing a taste for it. You would certainly, in my view, be an asset to the school. So I would support your staying on. I also think, for what it is worth, that you need time to mature and sort yourself out before deciding on a career. In your case you would do that better at school than in some stop-gap job.'

I managed to mumble, 'Thanks for telling me, sir.'

He gave me one of his predatory shark grins. 'I think I should add that specializing in English literature is a very foolish thing to do.'

'Sir?'

'Because it qualifies you for little else than teaching English literature. Do you want to teach?'

'I don't think so. I've thought about journalism though.'

'I should have thought even you could see from one glance at any newspaper that most journalists know little if anything about English and nothing at all about literature. The best of them are specialists in some other subject. Politics—the twentieth-century fag end of religion —or industry, for instance. No, if you have any sense, you'll enjoy the delights of the science labs or indulge yourself in the intricacies of computer technology. Are you good at such matters?'

'I enjoy some science. But I wouldn't say I was any good at it.'

He led the way into the corridor.

'Well, be sure to think carefully before you take my advice. Come in and talk again if you feel the need.'

He swept off with the kind of confident stride that always makes me feel tired. Today I felt punch-drunk as well. A capsize, Mrs Gorman, Barry, and now Osborn. Maybe I should have looked at my horoscope before I got up this morning.

I say that, but really I was zinging with excitement. Apart from anything else, it isn't every day that Osborn

59

invites—actually *invites*—someone to join his Sixth. Usually he tells people he wouldn't have them if they were the last students left on earth. Not that you're safe once you're in. He usually starts with about ten and weeds those down to half that in the first term, either from intellectual and emotional exhaustion or by summary banishment. When Nicky Blake dropped out last year he said he would rather go through a term of torture by the KGB than a week of Ozzy's English seminars.

The idea of staying on and taking English hadn't occurred to me for a minute. I thought about it as I strolled home. Sure, I was flattered to be asked. But I didn't get any closer to making a decision. Except that I'd try the idea on Barry that evening.

PART TWO

Once, and but once found in thy company,
All thy supposed escapes are laid on me.
John Donne

JKA. *Running Report:* Henry Spurling ROBINSON
19th Sept. Home Visit.
The Robinsons live in one of the smaller, older houses
on Manchester Drive. I visited just after they arrived
in Southend when Mrs Robinson experienced some
difficulties as a result of the move from her home
area. She felt lonely and distressed by the loss of her
friends and relatives, on whom she had obviously
always relied a lot for company and support.

The house was just as I last saw it. Neat and tidy,
well cared for. The sort of home that always puts me
slightly to shame because I feel it must be spring-
cleaned every week and repainted inside and out twice
a year.

Mrs Robinson, a little woman, thin and now
disturbed by her son's trouble, was as nervous as
when I first met her eighteen months ago. The doctor
has recently increased her dosage of Valium to try and
help her through the court case.

Mr Robinson is medium height with a slim frame
but going to fat, and his hair balding. He is a blustery
man. His speech still retains his northern intonations
especially when he gets worked up. He let me in. Both
parents were polite and welcoming, anxious to do all
they could to help.

When I arrived, Hal was upstairs in his room. Mr
Robinson did all the talking at first. He told me that
neither he nor his wife could understand what had
happened. They had hoped the court appearance
might jolt Hal out of his present state and 'bring him
to his senses'. 'He goes round like a zombie,' Mr
Robinson said. He was not angry, but puzzled and
tired, I think. Neither parent can get anything out of

Hal, who seems to spend most of his time in his room or roaming the sea-front. Naturally, his parents are beginning to worry seriously about him, his health and his future.

At one point Mr Robinson did burst out with the opinion that it was time Hal was given a sharp shock. Maybe we are all being too kind to him, too soft: etc. I tried to persuade him that perhaps Hal had had enough shocks already, and that what we need to do is gain his confidence so that he can begin to talk to us.

I went through the events leading to Hal's arrest as they knew them, but they could add nothing to what is already on record.

After this, Mrs Robinson began talking. She said that Hal was kind and considerate, not like many teenagers today. He was clever, and she thought this was the trouble. She and her husband couldn't keep up with him because they couldn't understand what he was talking about half the time. Besides that, she said with some emotion, she and her husband did the best they could for their son whom they loved very much, and that whatever had happened she was sure there was a reasonable explanation, and they were determined to stand by him.

By this time, Mrs Robinson was very distressed and began to weep. Mr Robinson comforted her, though clearly embarrassed by the situation. When she had recovered herself a little, Mrs Robinson said that in her opinion Hal—whom both parents call Henry, I noted—was still very upset by his friend's death, and that even though it seemed strange, this must be the reason why he behaved as he did in the cemetery. 'Henry changed a lot after he took up with Barry Gorman,' she said. I asked what she meant exactly.

She said she didn't know, but just felt this explained everything if only Hal would tell us about it.

All the time she spoke, Mrs Robinson twisted the edge of her dress between her fingers, and sighed heavily as though it were hard for her to get her words out. I tried to change the subject so as to give her some relief, and asked what they thought Hal should do now. Mr Robinson said that one thing was certain: Hal could not go on hanging about the house for much longer. It wasn't doing Hal any good or his mother. He thought Hal should be made to get a job.

Mrs Robinson said she didn't know what should be done now, but that Mr Osborn had said Hal should go back to school. Mr Robinson was against this plan. I asked about Mr Osborn. Mrs Robinson said he had been very helpful during the summer and since Hal's arrest. They relied on him now whenever they needed to do anything about the school because, she said, 'The Headmaster is always too busy and we don't like to take up his time'. This reinforces my previous impression that a meeting with Mr Osborn might be necessary and useful. I have arranged one for 22nd at 10.15 a.m.

I felt enough had been said for now, and that Mrs Robinson would be too much upset by further discussion. So I asked if they would mind if I saw Hal on his own. Mrs Robinson called upstairs and asked Hal if I should come up to his room. He agreed.

Hal has turned the very small spare bedroom into a kind of study. He had made a desk and bookcase from oddments. He has an old portable typewriter and a good but well-used stereo set and a considerable collection of discs and tapes. He was playing music to himself, but he switched this off when I came in. A copy of Kurt Vonnegut's novel *Slapstick* lay on his desk.

To try and ease the conversation, I asked him why he liked Vonnegut so much. He said, because of the way Vonnegut looks at life and because of his humour. He read out some of the jokes from *Slapstick*. I said I had not read the book. He said it was the only book of Vonnegut's so far that he found hard to understand. He couldn't quite see what Vonnegut was trying to do.

I encouraged him to talk some more about this because he was chatting without any apparent reserve. He is an articulate boy and his enthusiasms show when he talks uninhibitedly. (I was also enjoying myself. This was not the sort of interview I am used to!)

Suddenly, Hal said he must read me a passage from the beginning of the book that summed everything up. It explained a lot, he said. He read this passage (I borrowed the book from him before I left, feeling this might establish a friendly link, and that I ought to look more closely at the passage, as it obviously meant so much to him). Vonnegut is writing about the films of Laurel and Hardy, which apparently Hal likes watching on TV:

There was very little love in their films. Love was never at issue. And perhaps because I was so perpetually intoxicated and instructed by Laurel and Hardy during my childhood in the Great Depression, I find it natural to discuss life without ever mentioning love.

It does not seem important to me.

What does seem important? Bargaining in good faith with destiny.

I have had some experiences with love, or think I have, anyway, although the ones I have liked best could easily be described as 'common decency'. I treated someone well for a little while, or maybe even for a tremendously long time, and that person treated me well in turn. Love need not have had anything to do with it.

'That says it exactly,' Hal said. 'That's what it is all about.' I asked if he meant it was what life in general was all about, or what his present predicament was all about.

Hal drew back at this and looked sharply at me for a while. I knew I had made a mistake in putting the question. His flippant front returned. 'Who's the clever social worker then!' he said. He very coldly told me again that he would not discuss his arrest. I argued with him for some time, trying to get him to see that his parents were very worried about him, that he was not helping himself with the court by keeping silent. But he stubbornly refused to say anything more.

I left feeling very angry with myself for making another mistake in dealing with Hal. But he is so different from any other case I've handled that I find myself puzzled about how best to tackle him. I think I must discuss him at the Team Discussion next week.

Arranged to see Hal at my office at 2.30 p.m. on 22nd.

1/'Bubby, it's the boy who turned over this morning,' Mrs Gorman carolled when she opened the door that evening. A fog horn on bennies.

'Fetch him in then.'

His voice came from the kitchen along with a whiff of curry.

Leading the way, Mrs Gorman said, 'He's been a bad boy, my Bubby. He came to the shop this afternoon. On his day off. I tell him he shouldn't. Week in week out I tell him. All work and no play . . .'

'Hi,' I said. He was at the table, finishing a meal.

'Thanks for the clothes.' I put the bundle down on a spare chair.

'But still he does it,' Mrs Gorman said. 'On his day off!'

'Smells good,' I said.

'Want some?'

'Just eaten, thanks.'

'What good is a day off if he goes to work?' Mrs Gorman started clearing dishes from the table, clattering them under a tap before stowing them in the dishwasher. 'He's worse than his poor father, who was a slave to that shop. For twenty years a slave. And look what it did to him. Dead.' She rounded on me. 'And I thought you were his friend!' She flicked her fingers at my nose. 'Ha!'

I looked at Barry for help, not knowing whether to treat what was happening as a joke.

'Well,' he said, comedian to fall-guy, 'answer the lady. *Are* you my friend?'

Routining the patter, '*Am* I your friend?' I said.

'I don't know,' he said, exaggeratedly puzzled, 'I *think* you're my friend. But are you my friend?'

'If you *think* I'm your friend . . .'

'. . . then you *must* be my friend. In which case I think we can safely say . . .'

'. . . that I *am* your friend.'

'There you are, Mother,' he said, holding out his arms. '*He* thinks we're friends. *I* think we're friends. So we *must* be friends.'

Mrs Gorman sniffed with polythened disdain. 'Some friend! He lets you go to work on your day off when you should be enjoying yourselves together. Having fun. Relaxing.'

'He didn't know I was coming to the shop, Mother. He had an appointment to keep. It wasn't Hal's fault.'

'Hal . . .?' Mrs Gorman turned her full measure at me. It was like being turned on by a brontosaurus. '*Hal!* What kind of a name is that? Is it short for something? Hal . . . Halibut? I didn't know people were named after fish.'

'It comes from Shakespeare, Mother.'

'Shakespeare? I thought he was a William. Halibut was also his name?'

'You're being deliberately cussed.'

'Henry the Fourth, Mrs Gorman.'

'Shakespeare had four first names! What extravagance! What was his third?'

'No, no, Mother,' Barry said with heavy patience. 'Hal is short for Henry.'

'Well I'm glad it's not short for a fish. He doesn't look a bit like a fish.' She took my head between her damp hands and smacked a suction-cushion kiss firmly on my brow. 'Even though he is good enough to eat.'

'You've already had your supper, Mother dearest,' Barry said, getting up from the table. 'And aren't you missing *Take a Card*?'

'It's time? My God, and I haven't finished the dishes!'

'We'll do that. Then I'm taking Hal to a film, okay?'

'All right, my darlings. Have lots of fun.' She left the room, which suddenly seemed twice the size. 'But Bubby,' she fog-horned from the stairs, 'don't stay out all night, you hear?'

Barry winked, shrugged, called back, 'I hear.'

'And Hal . . .'

I went to the kitchen door. Her face mooned at me over the banister. 'Yes, Mrs Gorman?'

'You see he keeps his word,' she whispered at ten

megahertz. 'You're his friend. And you're a nice boy, I can tell. Straightaway this morning I could tell. I can trust you. He needs a friend, my Bubby. Some of these other boys he knows, well . . . they lead him astray—'

Barry came up behind me, putting an arm over my shoulder, leaning. For the first time I smelt him, his clean bodywarmth.

'You'll miss your programme if you stand there gabbing, Mother,' he said mocking.

Mrs Gorman peered at us, mouth pursed. 'He's all I've got now, you know, Hal,' she said. 'Since his father—'

Barry's hand pressed down on my shoulder, a warning for silence.

A pause. Glass threatened by a brick. Then suddenly Mrs Gorman smiled. The brick a feather duster.

'But you're a sight for sore eyes, the pair of you,' she said and clumped away upstairs.

2/What was all that about?

'Forget it,' Barry said, the question unasked. 'She thinks I work too hard. That's because the shop is work to her.'

'Not you?'

'I told you. I love it. I like music. Like people. Like selling.' He grinned, aping greed. 'Like money.'

'Who doesn't.'

He was stacking the dishwasher, reloading it after his mother's attempt. He was one of those people whose movements are as natty as a conjuror's. I handed him odds and ends so as to feel helpful.

'And what about the ineffable Oz?' he said. 'Had he a master plan for your brilliant future?'

'Only wants me to join his English Sixth, doesn't he!'

A melodrama of dishes. I'd tapped a nerve seemingly.

'Never!'

'Split my tongue and hope to cry! He also told me in the same breath that Eng. lit. would be useless to a genius like me.'

'He said that?'

'Words to that effect, yes.'

'The crafty pillock!'

'Why?'

'Obvious. He asks you to join his Sixth. You feel chuffed at the rare honour, right?'

'Right.'

'Then he tells you what he has to offer won't be any use. And you think, "How honest! This is a man I can believe." Right?'

'Something like that.'

'But telling you that is like putting up a "No Trespassing" sign. Anybody with any gump thinks there must be something worth trespassing for and wants his bit of the action. Besides, if you tell anybody who's worth anything *not* to do something, they go and do it right off, don't they?'

'So?'

'So he's testing you. If you take the bait against all opposition, even from him, he'll know you're really keen.'

'Isn't that good?'

'Marvellous. Wonderful. One more disciple in his ranks.'

'And now comes the coup de butt.'

'The boy's a giggle in every bite. *But*—what he's telling you is still true, idiot!'

'There's no future in Eng. lit.?'

'You said it.'

'No. *He* said it. I haven't made up my mind yet.'

'Oo, you Fierce Northern Tribes! You're so *strong*! So *independent*!'

I slung a teatowel at him.

'One long laugh, you Southerners,' I said.

He snatched the teatowel from his face and came round the table stalking me with it. 'You should have called yourself Hotspur,' he said, flicking the towel at my thighs.

I dodged round the table, grabbing up a chair as a shield.

We both started giggling, like kids in a playground.

'Careful what you're doing with that thing,' I said. 'I've need of my vitals yet.'

'Maybe my need is greater than yours,' he said.

'You trying to tell me something?' I said, fending off a torrent of damp cloth with the chair.

'Not a lot,' he said. 'But I thought you and me was going to be chinas.'

'Whatever gave you that idea!' I said.

He suddenly stopped trying to flense me and tossed the cloth over my head. When I'd put down the chair and unveiled he was eyeing me frankly.

'Right though?' he said.

I might have run a mile. 'You talk in riddles,' I said.

He turned away, switched on the dishwasher.

'We could stay in if you like. Instead of going to a movie, I mean.'

I was glad his back was to me. It was getting harder to look honest.

I said, 'I think I'd like a movie.'

'Have a butcher's at the local rag,' he said, making for the door, 'see what's on while I have a jimmy.'

He dashed out, like he was needing to escape.

3/Know what I made of that? A can of magic beans offered on sale or return is what I made of that. Hence the sudden symptoms synonymous with sprinting the five thousand metres.

I could hardly read the newsprint announcing this week's filmatic attractions because my eyes were palpitating to the rhythm of hard rock in my head led by the drummer, high on $C_9H_{13}NO_3$ in my chest. No surprise. The rhythm stick was forcing.

And I might have been wrong. Which added to the excitement, as the possibility of being wrong always does.

But was I to proceed to the cinema through Southend's crowds with my hands held before me like a defrocked choir boy? I could hardly stand up straight even now. Which wouldn't do at all.

So three deep breaths, a no-nonsense juggle with my pudenda, a readjustment of my round me's, and the newspaper came into focus at last.

'Porno or sci-fi epic,' I said when he came back, by which time I had recovered some calm again. 'That's the choice.'

'Sci-fi for me,' he said, checking the kitchen was safe to leave. 'There's enough porn in my head without needing more.'

4/He stopped on the pavement outside his house.

'We could ride if you like. I run a Suzuki.'

'Whichever, I don't mind.'

'Better walk. I haven't a spare helmet and the old Bill is heavy handed in town. Every biker a Hell's Angel. But we'll have to buy you one.'

'We?' I said. 'And are we going somewhere?'

'Why not?' he said.

We strolled to town along the esplanade, the tide in

and the bathers mostly gone. But plenty of sea-watchers. And the weather was cool and gentle now after the storm.

'So you're chucking your lot in with Ozzy,' Barry said after a while.

'I told you,' I said, 'I haven't made up my mind yet.'

'You will.'

'How do you know?'

'You've got that lean aesthetic look.'

'I'm not sure if that's a compliment.'

'Anyway, you'll be a gentleman of leisure till September.'

'Not if my dad gets his way.'

'Wants you earning, does he?'

'Part-time at least.'

'Quite right too. Schoolboy layabouts!'

'Yes, grandad!'

'I was thinking about that after you went this afternoon.'

'You're keen. I haven't even started thinking about being a dad yet.'

'Har har,' he said. 'You'd slay them at the Palace. About you being a layabout, I mean, knucklehead. What sort of thing are you looking for?'

'I'll do anything except anything.'

He stopped and leaned on the railing at the edge of the pavement, looking out to sea.

'How about Mondays, Tuesdays and Wednesdays, four till six, and all day Saturdays?'

I'm so thick I really didn't know what he was playing at.

'Where?' I said.

'Gorman Records.'

And he really did take me by surprise.

'Are you having me on?'

'Serve in the shop, help keep the stock in shape, chat up the customers, that sort of thing.'

'Why?' I was watching him carefully, but he wouldn't look at me, just kept his eyes on the view.

'Because we need somebody. Mother's a genius with the accounts. But she's hopeless in the shop. We get busiest in the late afternoons. Mostly kids wanting to hear the new discs. They drive Mother crazy. And Saturday is the worst time of all. More than I can manage on my own.'

I said nothing for a minute or two. Leaned on the railing beside him and stared at the sea. Another bout of symptoms synonymous started up as the light began to dawn. If all he wanted was a shop assistant he could have found plenty of people at the job centre who were eager for that kind of work and who had experience of it.

We set off for town again and I said, 'I've never worked in a shop.'

'You'd soon pick it up.'

'But what about your mother?'

'You heard her. She trusts you. Can't think why! But she'd be all for it.'

'I'll think about it.'

'Stop fighting me, will you!' he said, stopping me by the arm and making me face him. 'Give it a try, eh?'

I felt he was hustling me and I didn't like that. It was his worst side. If he wanted something he prodded and pushed till he got it. And if he didn't get his way he pouted and sulked and went sour. I didn't know that then, and wouldn't have cared if I had. I wasn't going to be hustled.

I said, 'Look, Barry, I've told you. Give me time. I've got to work myself up to things.'

'All right, all right. Relax!'

'Well, you're not just offering me a job, are you!'

'You'll be okay. You're a natural. Just smile a lot, be polite, and stay cool. That's all it takes. Honest. The customers will lap you up.'

'It's not the customers I'm thinking about.'

'What then?'

'Look, is this a game of telling truths?'

He started walking again. 'If you want it to be.'

'All right. It's you. That's who I'm thinking about.'

'Me!' The comic exaggeration! 'What have I done?'

'Ah come on, Barry, stop mucking about. You know what it is. You're pushing me too fast.'

'Why waste time?'

'I told you. I've got to think things out a bit.'

'Okay, okay. I'll say no more. But you'll give it a try? Just for a few days? A week? We'd be a great team.'

'I'll tell you tomorrow.'

'Done.'

5/There's always a moment. The point of no return, when you know if you go on you can't ever afterwards go back. I know that now. I learned it with Barry, then. And Ozzy showed me some lines the other day. They sum it up. They're by T. S. Eliot in a poem called *The Waste Land* which Ozzy keeps trying to make me read. Here are the lines:

> The awful daring of a moment's surrender,
> which an age of prudence can never retract.

It happens in the moment when that small word 'Yes' will be enough to change your life. Your stomach gets the jitters—or mine does, anyway. Your brain melts inside your head. Your tongue feels like it's contracted elephantiasis and will shortly choke you. Your mouth gets lock-jaw, and your hands get cramp. You start keeping an eye out for the nearest lavatory because your bowels indicate an imminent onset of dysentery. You tend to yawn a lot, and also grin, stammer, giggle, hiccup, shiver, sweat, break out in facial ticks, itch in crevices awkward to scratch in public, and unexpectedly to fart.

You'd think your body had declared war on you just because you are on the point of taking a risk. Nothing dangerous of course, in this case. Just telling someone for the first time what you really think of him, what you want of him, what you hope he wants of you.

I guess you—I—feel like that because knowledge is power. Once somebody knows that about you—knows how you *really* feel about them—once you've declared yourself, then they know about you, have power over you. Can make claims on you. You're giving yourself into their hands, the Bible says, as I found out at the same time as I was finding out about D. and J.

The boys with the can of magic beans didn't have anything to say about this. They didn't go pale with dementia when they gazed into each other's eyes while grasping their bleeding hands and swearing their pal-hood. Nor, I might add ruefully, did David need twenty-four hours to think about whether he wanted Jonathan to love him as his own soul and in some manner surpassing the love of women. Or if he did, he wasn't telling. And who can blame him? It's not the sort of thing you print in the school mag or rabbit about on the way home after school, never mind spilling it all out to a reporter from the Holy Bible so that it can be recorded for posterity. Heroes have to be made of sterner stuff. No dithering from heroes. We can't have them getting the runs just because some bit of cheesecake wants to be friends with them. How could anybody believe in their heroism if we knew such things as that about them?

Not being any kind of hero, I admit myself glad that

evening to get inside the cinema and sit down in its dark cocoon. Public privacy. Reality-with-consequences exchanged for reality-without-consequences for the price of a ticket. A womb with a quadrophonic heartbeat and an image of the world-to-come moving tantalizingly on the membrane of the uterus.

My embryo mate twinned beside me, shoulder, arm, thigh and knee making us Siamese if you please. Which was close enough for now. Enough to rest on. Suspended animation. A still from coming attractions.

Everybody needs a rest now and then.

And I had had enough direct action for one day. The movie's simulations were what I needed. I wanted to be a spectator for a while.

I also thought that would be the end of it for today. We would see the film, wander home, let today slip comfortably away.

But life isn't like that.

I had reckoned without The Drunk.

And without Barry. Who never gave up.

Ever.

6/Scene: Southend High Street.

Time: 22.45 hours. Thursday. Summer.

People: a jostle of holiday-makers, most of them young and hearty, behaving themselves in that joyously decorous way that distinguishes civilized homo sapiens from all other beasts. Happy bantering words fly across the traffic-busy late-night street, between rival groups of mob-handed mates. They sometimes smash the odd window here and there as a mark of the affection in which they hold their playground by the almost sea. Their home away from home.

78

Barry and I weave our way from the cinema through this milling throng of gaiety, out of the pedestrian precinct, under the railway bridge and onto the traffic-driven part of the High Street leading to the pierhead. Just there, at the corner of Tylers Avenue, comes stumbling across our path The Drunk. He has on his face that concentrated, pole-axed expression of determination, and the floppy-doll body that betrays in his system the presence of enough alcohol to give a Breathalyser a nervous breakdown. He has some purpose in mind, but whatever desire the drink has provoked it is also taking away in the performance.

Even so, he manages to stagger to the kerb unhindered by the passing hordes, who avoid him by pretending he isn't there. Without pause for consideration of the dangers he might encounter by doing so, he hurls himself head first into the road as if taking a dive into a quiet swimming pool.

Luckily the traffic is moving at funeral pace. The Drunk flops down, full length splayed between two cars.

Brakes screech. Horns blow. 'Run him over!' quips a happy holiday-maker from across the street.

No one does anything but carry on as though nothing untoward has happened. As indeed, given what passes for normality at such times on Southend High Street, nothing has.

Barry however darts into the road, drags The Drunk to his feet, and hauls him onto the pavement, where I join him in holding The Drunk upright.

'Wanna swim,' The Drunk says, making movements that might be either an attempt to escape our rescuing clutches or a few practice strokes for the crawl.

'You can't swim here,' Barry says.

'What are we going to do with him?' I ask Barry.

The Drunk smells like a midden and I am not keen to remain too long in the vicinity of this human gasworks.

'Get him somewhere safe.'

'Try the morgue.'

'You have death on the brain.'

'Have you caught a whiff? He's decomposing already.'

The Drunk has attended to this exchange like a tennis spectator who is a head's turn behind the flight of the ball. Now he says, 'Ss the tideout?'

'Yes,' says Barry.

We struggle with a renewed attempt to test the popular theory that God takes care of babies and drunks.

'I'll av adip in the Ray,' The Drunk says.*

'Where you from?' Barry says, speaking with that slow and extra loud voice people reserve for babies, foreigners and inebriates, apart from the deaf.

'Ackney,' says The Drunk after a pause for thought.

'Wouldn't you like to get the train home?' Barry says, Adult humouring Child in Difficult Circumstances.

The Drunk grins with pixilated devilry into Barry's grinning face. (My God, I thought, Barry is actually

---

* For those who have yet the pleasures of Southend in store let me explain about the Ray, a most important feature of this watering place. At Southend the tide goes out a long way. Some people say it goes out all the way to the other side of the estuary. Be that as it may, when the tide is out an amusement often enjoyed by the resident locals, the younger of them especially, is to plodge through the gooey mud left behind by the receding waves until you reach, half a mile or so from shore, a deep, fast-flowing channel of water known on the maps with delicate felicity as the Ray Gut. Here only the brave and foolish swim, for the current is dangerously strong. Everyone cavorts on the comparatively sandy and hard Ray bank, having messy picnics or bottle parties (and, as you can imagine, much else besides) before trudging back through the sludge. Set off for home too late and you are likely to be trapped on the sandbank by the fast in-coming tide and be eventually drowned. So the jaunt is not without its frisson of danger. For a drunk to make the trip would therefore be unwise. But whoever heard of a wise drunk?

enjoying this!) 'Lass trays gone,' he says, naughty-boy, and giggles.

'Great!' I say, my cool hotting up. 'We'll be here all night. Let's dump him. Why are we bothering?'

'He'll do himself an injury if we leave him. You saw.'

'So what!' I say, exasperation and argumentative displeasure doing the talking. 'He got himself into this state. Let him get himself out of it.'

People, remember, jostle past us as this chat goes on; cars slur by in the road endangering our swaying persons. It is night. I am tired. It has been, as they say, a long day.

'You didn't say that,' Barry snaps back at me, 'when I helped you this morning.'

I think: Our first row. Jolly hockeysticks!

'O, thanks!' I say as tartly as I can and with a dash of real bile for flavour. 'Sir Galahad to the rescue again, ducky. You're so dashing!'

Barry is glaring at me. The Drunk is metronoming again.

Barry says, 'I can't see much difference between him being drunk and you single-handing someone else's boat when you can't even sail a rubber duck in your bath without sinking it.'

I am rendered speechless. Also angered, piqued, resentful, hurt, aggrieved, dismayed, subdued, nettled, and put in my place. So I pout.

What a rich life I lead. All that at one go.

'Less av a drink,' The Drunk says.

'Too late. The pubs have shut,' Barry says, the Brusque Adult now.

'Nar,' says The Drunk, The Irascible Wilful Child. He struggles to get free again. We do a tippy-toe tango down the pavement till a shop front gets in the way, barking my shin on its doorstep. The pain is inflammatory.

'I don't give a toss what you think,' I crump. 'I've had it with this lark.'

'Go suck!' Barry says. 'I'll cope.'

He will too, I know. How I hate such unyielding competence. I've had it laid on me all day.

7/At this very moment I spy in the throng on the other side of the street a patrolling Boy-in-Blue. The badge of his Noddy hat glistens in the neon. His walky-talky bristles on his chest. Another knight to the rescue.

'Hang on,' I say to Barry and nip off before his dissent restrains me. I am not going to waste my chance to become the competent organizer for the first time today.

'Could you help me, officer?' I say in my best law-abiding voice.

'Not unless I have to, sir,' says the P.C. He grins faintly to show he really has made a jest. Life in the nick's canteen must be a permanent side-split. Perhaps I should join the Force. (It has been suggested, of course. The Head offered it as his opinion that as the only thing presently flourishing in Britain is crime, the Police Force as a career has a bright future. It took Ozzy's daring to point out that the logic of this argument made it more attractive to join the criminals. The Head smiled painfully and changed the subject. The Head, being a sociologist by training, isn't too great with language and hopeless at logic.)

I return the B.-in-B.'s grin to show willing and say, 'There's a drunk over there trying to chuck himself into the traffic. Could you take him in for the night?'

'O no no no,' says the B.-in-B., sucking at his breath like I'd given him an extra strong mint to tease his mouth ulcers. 'I can't help you there, squire.'

'But he'll cause an accident,' I say, 'and we can't stay with him all night.'

'If I was you,' says the P.C. confidential-like, 'I'd take your friend to the beach. Let him sleep it off.'

'He isn't my friend. He's a drunk.'

The B.-in-B. expresses surprise. 'You're with him, aren't you?'

'Yes, but . . .'

'Well, then, you must be a friend of his, mustn't you? Can't arrest a member of the public for being a bit tiddly when his friends are looking after him, now can I? How'd you think that would look on the charge sheet?'

Suddenly I begin to understand Kafka's *The Trial* for the first time. I say, 'But we are not his friends. We just happened to stop him killing himself. Do you have to be friends to do that?'

'No. No. But a friendly sort of act, isn't it? And he's not dead, is he?'

'No. Because we saved him.'

'There you are then. But I've only your word for that, haven't I?'

What a Sherlock the man is.

'All right,' I say, 'let me put it this way. What would you suggest we do? Let him go so he can chuck himself into the road again?'

The B.-in-B. takes my arm. Bends his head to my ear. 'Look, mate,' he says, 'I'll be honest with you.'

Does he mean our wonderful police are sometimes not entirely honest? My God, after all these years, now I find out! How can I ever again believe in the basic goodness of the human soul? What a cruel night this is turning out to be.

I compose myself for the shock of hearing the truth.

'You see, sonny,' the P.C. goes on (and I note the declension from sir to sonny), 'if I arrest your friend, I'll have to trot him down the nick, charge him, lock him up. You never know what some real villain will get up to here

83

while I'm gone. Then I'll have to get up early tomorrow morning, after working the late duty tonight, because I'll have to get your friend ready for court. And putting him through court will take all morning, which I'm supposed to have off. Now what's the point of all that aggro when your friend is just a bit under the weather and safe in your good hands? If I arrested every drunk I see along here I'd never be finished.'

I'm like a balloon tonight, puffed up and deflated by turns. The wind has been taken out of me again.

'Well we can't just leave him, can we!' There's desperation in my voice now. And worse, there's the squeaky sound of boyhood breaking through. 'He'll only chuck himself under a car if we do, then you'll have real trouble on your hands. He can't stand up, never mind walk, so we can hardly drag him down to the beach, can we?'

'Look, tell you what I'll do, kid,' says the copper. *Kid* now! 'But it's between ourselves, okay? If anybody asks, I don't know anything, right?'

'All right. We can't mess about forever.'

'Get your friend to the corner of Clifftown Road there, okay?'

'It'll be a struggle. And he's not my friend.'

'You'll manage. I'll be with you in five minutes.'

When I get back, Barry is pressing The Drunk up against the shop window.

'Wa bout the boatin pool,' The Drunk is saying. 'Tide's all ays in there.'

Barry says to me, 'What the hell were you doing talking to the law?' He is having trouble keeping Our Friend upright because of the slippiness of the glass.

'Just getting a little help, that's all,' I say tartly. 'We've got to take stinkpot to Clifftown Road.'

'Why?' says Barry. 'You're not turning him in.'

'Fat chance. The law isn't *that* helpful.'

The Drunk laughs coyly. 'Ere,' he says with simpering confidentiality, leaning into both of us. 'I gotta sprise f'you.'

'What's that?' Barry says with thin patience.

'I juss piss mesell!' The Drunk announces in a raucous shout like he's just won the pools.

'Bingo, our kid,' yells a passing comrade, hardly better for wear than Our Friend.

Barry creases with laughter. 'Well, you wanted to go swimming!'

'Hey, thass right!' says The Drunk, and they laugh together as if this were the century's wittiest quip.

'For God's sake let's get shot of him,' I say.

Barry draws a straight face. He's beginning to act as unpredictably as The Drunk. Maybe he's getting inebriated by the fumes we're breathing in.

'Will you stop beefing,' he says. 'What's the matter with you? You're getting hurt? You're going somewhere? Eh? Look, you want to go—go. I care?'

Puling, I say, 'But what are you bothering with him for?'

'You want reasons?'

'Yes, dammit!'

'Because he needs help. Because we were there. Because nobody else wanted to know. Because it amuses me. Because I wanted to be bothered. Because I felt like it. Because I *like* him. Okay? Does that satisfy you? From me you want the sermon on the mount? Now do we get him to Clifftown Road or not?'

We did. Discordantly. The butt of passing jests. Pungently. But we got him there.

8/There is nothing, I discovered that night, like being

sober in the company of an incontinent drunk for bringing home to you the eggshell brittleness of your pride.

I found myself remembering—I comforted myself with —graffiti collected from the town's more intelligent loos.

REALITY IS AN ILLUSION PRODUCED BY ALCOHOLIC DEFICIENCY

I DRINK THEREFORE I AM. I'M DRUNK THEREFORE I WAS

IS THERE A LIFE BEFORE DEATH?

I am especially pleased and encouraged, as we stagger to our rendezvous with the constabulary, by this last remembered scrawl.

9/Our friendly neighbourhood Plod turns up ten minutes late. He must have been keeping police time.

He doesn't say anything, just points his flashlight towards the railway station entrance not far down the road, and gives a triple flash.

A taxi comes gliding up to us.

'The usual,' says the B.-in-B. to the driver.

'He's not going to throw up, is he?' says the driver, as we pile Our Friend inside. 'I'm not cleaning up after him if he does.'

The B.-in-B. ambles away at the regulation saunter. It is as though the taxi and we bumbling three are in the twenty-sixth dimension of the planet Aora for all he sees of us. There's nowt so blind as reluctant officialdom. Or was it the Nelson Touch? Not tonight, thank you, Hardy.

10/'If he pukes,' says the taxi man as we settle inside, 'stick his noddle out the window.'

But, like a child exhausted from play, The Drunk is snoring before we even move off.

I look at Barry; he looks at me and raises a questioning eyebrow. I shrug a 'don't know', and he grins. There he is, enjoying himself again. This guy has an insatiable appetite, I think to myself.

Never was a righter word thought. He had.

We soon know where we are going.

It is less than half a mile from the station to the pier-head, the beginning of that once proud symbol of South-end's uniqueness among resorts for all seasons. Blackpool has its tower, Brighton has its pavilion, Southend has its all but clapped-out relic of the longest pier in the world.

The taxi pulls off the road and stops in a darkish corner.

'All change,' says the driver, getting out and throwing open the door against which The Drunk is slumped, and begins unceremoniously dragging him out.

'Give us a hand, then,' he says. We sober two have not moved, being unable to register that this can possibly be our intended destination.

'We stop here?' Barry says as we help from inside to hustle Our Friend.

'Where else?' says the taxi man as though this is a fool question to which we should know the answer already.

By the time Barry and I have got ourselves out after him, the driver has The Drunk pressed up against the car and is making a very professional job of going through his pockets. The Drunk is not resisting, being now apparently incapable of resisting anything.

'What's this then?' says Barry meaning no nonsense.

'Got to get my fare ain't I,' says the driver. 'Why?' He laughs. 'You paying?'

He pulls out a wallet from The Drunk's back pocket. It is a fat wedge of notes.

'Very handy,' says the driver, about to stow the money in a pocket of his own.

'What the hell!' says Barry bracing.

The driver pauses and weighs us up askance. 'Don't worry, squire,' he says, scornful, 'you'll get your taste.'

'Look,' says Barry, 'I don't know what your game is, but you're not taking his money.'

So now he's not satisfied with rescuing a suicidal drunk, he wants to get us both murdered as well. Loyal to the last, I step up to Barry's side as though I am as brave as he. What am I trying to prove? I ask myself. That I really am his friend? In which case I hope he's got that can of magic beans hidden somewhere because when things get rough he'd better give it a quick rub and get us back to the twentieth century double quick. I've got a sensitive skin. It bruises when it's punched.

The driver is suspicious now. 'What's the joke?' he says.

'Just put the money back,' Barry says. If he's scared I wouldn't know it.

'O, I get it,' says the driver, 'you want me to put the readies back and leave you two to split them between you when I'm gone!' He really laughs at that one. 'Good gag that! Great!'

'Think what you like,' Barry says, 'but put it back.'

'Get knotted!' says the driver.

He pushes The Drunk, who slumps onto the ground looking and sounding like a plastic bag full of squashy tomatoes, and is about to climb back into his taxi.

Barry leans against the door. 'All right,' he says. 'Have it your way.'

The driver is cracking the knuckles of one hand in the fist of the other. 'There's a clever boy,' he says through his tight grin.

'Registered plate HX 96310,' Barry says deadpan. 'And if memory serves, the copper who so kindly enlisted your aid was P.C. SO190. How about driving us back to the nick?'

The driver considers each of us in turn for a moment.

'We've got a right one here,' he says to me, as if I'm nothing more than his audience. To Barry he says, 'You crafty young bugger. I've heard of some pretty sells but this one takes the biscuit.'

'The biscuit you can keep,' Barry says. 'Just hand over the cash.'

'They get younger every day,' says the driver eyeing us both with distaste now. 'Here,' he says, 'take the bleeding money.' He slips a ten quid note off the bundle and throws the rest onto the snoring body slumped at our feet. He pushes Barry aside and climbs into his car. 'I'll take my fare though, if you don't mind,' he says, flapping the note through his window. Then he starts up and reverses away fast. 'I'll remember you two,' he shouts as he goes.

11/The pace was beginning to tell. We stood gormless, and watched the taxi lose itself along the esplanade.

A grovelling at our feet reactivates us.

'Pick up his legs,' Barry says, stuffing the bundle of money into The Drunk's trouser pocket. 'We'll bed him down on a couple of deck-chairs under the pier.'

We struggle like corpse thieves with The Drunk's lolloping body, finding him a spot as hidden as we can.

'Am I dead?' he moans as we lay him out on his makeshift bed.

'Not yet,' I say.

'Feel like I'm dead,' he says. He has reached the maudlin stage.

'Nothing to what you'll feel like in the morning,' says Barry. 'Have a good kip. You'll be all right there.'

But he doesn't hear. He's snoring again already.

We stand looking down at him. I see for the first time—or take the fact in for the first time, I guess—that he is not much older than Barry. In his early twenties maybe. Sleep smoothed his features. The distortions of drunkenness had gone. He was handsome, I saw. A strong face, well fleshed. Tender in sleep. Only his hair was deranged.

Barry bent down and carefully combed Our Drunk's hair into ordered shape again.

I knew then, in the way he took obvious pleasure in tidying the sleeping man's hair, why he had rescued him. And was sure now why he had rescued me.

JKA. *Running Report*: Henry Spurling ROBINSON 21st Sept. 0930. Hal telephoned, saying he could not manage our meeting tomorrow, what about today? Thought it best not to question him, and agreed to his request, because I think it better that he talk, if he wants to, straightaway. He also asked why we had to meet in my office, which he said was 'impersonal and official'. I made various suggestions of other meeting places. He did not like any of them. He suggested the end of the pier or a rowing boat on the children's boating pool! I settled for Queen Victoria's statue in the gardens above the esplanade at 10.30.

Hal was waiting when I arrived. He did not see me approach; he was sitting on the grass just beyond the statue watching some children playing nearby. I sat down between two old folk in the shelter and looked across the flowerbed at him on the other side of the monument. I hoped I might learn something by watching his behaviour when he was relaxed.

He was laughing at the kids playing and throwing their ball back to them. Of course, they started 'losing' their ball in his direction more and more. He was enjoying their attention and did not try and dominate their game, just reacted to what they did. I felt he was getting as much from watching them as I was from watching him! Whatever is the matter, or has gone on, the sight of him playing so naturally suggests to me that there is nothing psychologically deep seated to worry about.

I went up to him after a few minutes. He joked and put on his flippant front for a while. He asked about Vonnegut and what I thought of the book he loaned me yesterday. I fobbed him off by saying I hadn't had time to read it yet.

Just the trouble, he said: there was never enough time in what he called my 'official investigations' to talk properly about anything.

I asked him what he wanted to see me about so urgently. He said he had been thinking over the situation and had decided he would like to tell me what had happened. But I would have to give him 'proper time' and he wouldn't be able to talk if we met 'officially'. We would have to talk 'off the record' somewhere else than my office. And at home his parents would always be hovering around.

I listened to all this, relieved in a way that he was now behaving normally: wanting to feel I was completely taken up with his case, giving him my time in preference to other people, etc. I decided the best thing would be to treat this a little firmly. I explained that I did have other cases to look after. That I could never talk completely off the record. That after all the whole point was that he explain to me what had happened so that I could recommend to the court a course of action that would suit the circumstances.

He would think about this, he said. But he couldn't go on calling me 'Mizzz Atkins'. I said that I called him Hal, he could call me by my first name if he liked.

I said I had another appointment and would have to go back to my office. I asked him to think over what he had promised and that we would start from the beginning next time. I fixed a meeting with him at Tomassi's coffee place tomorrow at 14.30 when I'll have seen Mr Osborn and might be better prepared.

Hal was a little sulky when I left him, I think. But I felt the meeting had gone well and put our relationship onto the right footing.

12/I do like bed. I have to admit it. Not that I always did. But for the last few years, since I was about fourteen, I have liked bed. So the reason I did not get up till twelve o'clock (noon) the morning after the night of The Drunk wasn't only to do with the fact that I did not get back home till one o'clock (0100 hrs!). Also, it helps explain why my ever loving father performed his stampeding rhinoceros act round my room on some unexplained slender pretext at seven-fifty a.m., before he went to work. He had entertained me with similar antics on many mornings before.

My doting parent was conducting a campaign against my liking for a lie-in. To show willing, and in hope of ending this latest skirmish sooner rather than later and without the shouting match attendant on a later ending, I gave my well-practised performance of waking up. I boast eight versions of 'waking up' in my repertoire. The day before I had chosen the sudden, startled 'Ah! Eh? Wass matter?' routine, jumping up and looking shocked as though I had just seen a ghost. Effective, convincing. No doubt of it. I could tell from the satisfied smile that spread across Father's face. The only trouble with this version is that all the shouting and jumping about shakes me out of the pleasant, cosy, half-awake, day-dreaming limbo that makes a lie-in so enjoyable in its early stages. I really did wake myself up. Couldn't settle again and so had to get up in the end, disgruntled because, after all, Father had won. Which is why I was roaming the sea-front that memorable Thursday morning as early as ten-thirty—with such notably unexpected results as those herebefore described. Which only goes to prove once again that it is indeed the early worm that is caught by the birds.

I wasn't about to make the same mistake today. So this time I performed my slow, quiet, languorously waking stir. Not that I needed to act much. I really was knackered from yesterday's exploits.

Dad said, 'You're awake then.'

'Hummm?'

'Don't moulder in that pit all day, mind,' he said from the door, adding, 'Your mother's got work to do,' which seemed something of a non-sequitur.

I did a bit of mouth-sucking-lip-smacking, waved a floppy hand, grunted. He seemed satisfied of victory and left, mumbling 'Lazy bugger,' on the stairs, as if to himself but just loud enough to reach my ears.

13/I lay for a while in the same position as I had woken, foetally curled. Womb warm. Pre-natally comfortable. And mused. Had enough to muse about, after all. Images of a Bean Boy. Montage of Gorman. Headbound simulacra of a seductive soulmate that, nevertheless, moved the body, mate, too.

For half an hour of days and nights we did everything together. And I wondered: Could it be? Would it be? Please let it be! But questions are death for wishfulfilled fantasy. You start noticing the improbables, the impossibles, the unlikelies, the life's-not-like-that perfection. All fantasies are full of holes in the invention, and reality pokes through. I guess that's why I can never stand that old fool Tolkien* and his never-never land full of narks and nurds and magic rings. All sublimated sex of course. The same with that lion, witch and wardrobe rubbish by his pal—what's his name?—Lewis. Made me puke at ten when some goofy teacher who drooled over the idiocy read it to us. I can still remember feeling amazed because almost everybody else in the room fell for it and was ooing and ahhing and getting wet-eyed at the death of that lion character, Aslan, while I was enjoying a quiet chuckle. I thought the story was meant to be some kind of spoof, and couldn't believe it when I was told the whole thing was deadly (yes, sir, deadly indeed) serious.

But back to my bean-boy fantasies, and the questions that punctured them. I shifted, taking up what I had come to think of as the Corpse Position. Flat on my back, legs and feet together toes pointing up, hands across chest. R.I.P.

* I said this to Ozzy. 'Not such a fool,' he said. 'Tolkien grew rich on his fantasies.' 'A fool made rich by bigger fools,' I said. He laughed. 'There's hope for you yet,' he said. 'But you've misjudged Tolkien, as time and greater wisdom will show you.' Crunch.

Scenes from yesterday projected themselves. Like a French film. All of yesterday, from capsizing to after The Drunk. But jumbled, not in the right order. And slow motion for some sequences, and action replays for the best bits and the puzzling bits and the bits that needed thinking about. And the whole day ending as we strolled back from bedding The Drunk down under the pier. Neither of us talked about him, or about anything that had happened that day. Most of the way back to Barry's house we walked in silence. Which I liked; it meant we could be together and not have to bother about finding the right words. The wrong ones just then could have ruined everything.

He wanted me to go in, but I wouldn't. I was bushed. We parted at his door.

'Don't forget,' he said. 'I'll be waiting.'

'Waiting?'

'For your answer. About working at the shop. I'll be there all day from nine. Telephone when you're ready.'

'Okay.'

'Better still, come in and tell me. I'll take you to lunch. How about that? Very business-like!'

'I'll think about it.'

'You think too much.'

'Sure. See you.'

'See you.'

'Night.'

End scene: walking away into the moonlight.

All say *Ahhh!*

I played and replayed my mental video. Each time the me that is me detached a little more the me that was me from the me that is me. I became cold observer of me-that-was. Psychotechnology did pre-select close-ups of B.'s eyes and mouth, his hands, shifts of body, tones of voice. Searching for ambiguities. Finding plenty. The lexigraphy of flesh.

Frisson. Of danger? Of passion? Either/or. Take your pick: danger in B., passion in me. Both probably. Which knowledge gave me a frisson of frisson. With which tingle in the testes I drifted into dozy cozy daydream slumber.

14/Surfaced again at the sound of catcalls and fibrilose yelling. The wind must be easterly, the time 10.40: break-time at school blown in gobs up Man. Dr. from the playing fields. Emotional tumbleweed.

My body was still corpsed.

What's it like to be a corpse? Who cares? The point being, presumably, that no one inhabits a corpse, the who having departed for that bourne from which no who returns. A pity really, I thought; I rather like my body. I'll be sorry when the time comes to leave it. Or will I? By then, probably, it will be wizened, my skin blotched and creased like old bark. My breath will stink like an inciner-ator, my body like a sewer. My hair will be thin as the fur on a baboon's bum. My nose be purple veined, a blodge that dribbles like a leaking tube of glue. I expect I'll be stuttering about on slippered scrawny feet, supporting myself with a cane clutched in a clawy mitt. My eyes will be palely vacant, staring with gaga incomprehension at all and nothing while weeping from no other sorrow than the blight of age. I will not be able to control my water; will spill my food down my chest where it will leave festering fungoid spots on my holey cardigan. And chil-dren will laugh at me in the street and call me unhappy names.

Will thoughts still worm in my cadaverous cranium? Will I still juggle with words? Will I remember enough words to juggle with? Will pictures invade my mind with power to give my body some gyp? Will I still feel the rush of blood and the stiffening of sinew? Will I know anything except maybe the longing not to be?

Will anybody make passes at me then? Will geriatric men and women give me the eye? And who will rescue me then from drowning in death and wave my pants from a flashy yellow streaker?

15/No body.

Those hanging about me at that time will be waiting for the moment when my deceased flesh and bones can be stowed safely away six feet under, or be popped into the burning fiery furnace and reduced to manageable proportions, to whit: five ozs of fine grey ash, suitable for the making of egg timers.* And the only thing being waved will be a gravestone or memorial plaque upon which will be inscribed some pertinent epitaph.

* I have not yet decided whether my mortal remains shall be buried or cremated. Some people of religious scruple hold strong objection to cremation and others to burial. So there is no answer in the multiple voices of God. Without such authoritative aid, I cannot decide whether I prefer to rot in the ground, providing food for worms and fertilizer for dandelions, or to be reduced to the aforesaid ashes and dispersed to the four winds. I guess it is some primordial instinct which sometimes makes me prefer burial so that at least my bones will stay together in case of any chance of future need, such as resurrection. But then I get a social conscience about being a nuisance. I mean, if everybody insisted on a six-by-four plot of ground to lie dead in, the country would very soon be covered in graves and become a vast cemetery. Apart from the sneaking suspicion I have that bodies rotting in the ground, however regulated and well-behaved, pose something of a threat to the already unpalatable water supply. All I can say is I hope I've made up my mind before I snuff it.

GOOD RIDDANCE, perhaps, or GONE AT LAST.

Epitaphs have interested me since that day in the churchyard (cf. Part 1 Bit 21). I collect them. How about this one from a postman's grave: NOT LOST BUT GONE BEFORE. Dad found this one in a cemetery near where we used to live up North:

> WHERE ERE YOU BE
> LET YOUR WIND GO FREE
> FOR IT WAS THE WIND
> THAT KILLETH ME

I guess he remembers it because he thinks it gives licence to the explosive excesses of his frequent ventilations.

It really is incredible what some people write on gravestones. Viz.:

> HERE LIES THE BODY OF ANNIE MANN
> WHO LIVED AN OLD WOMAN
> AND DIED AN OLD MANN

and:

> HE HAD HIS BEER FROM YEAR TO YEAR
> AND THEN HIS BIER HAD HIM

16/Back—again—to bed. The next thing I knew, the vacuum was scurling outside my room. My mother performing her daily spring clean with the electronic bagpipes. The paintwork on my door was sacrificed to a fistful of battering biffs disguised as vigorous dusting: a sign of my mother's anxiety at my continued somnolence. Not that she was conducting the same campaign as my father. On the contrary, my mother's preference is always that I should do exactly what makes me happiest—and if that is lying in bed 'all the hours God gave', then so be it.

The reason she was thus indicating a desire for me to get up was entirely the result of her fear that my father might for some unexpected reason arrive home and still find me 'lazing about the place'. In any case, she knew he would question her when he got in from work about every last detail of my day's activities, including the very hour and minute of my arising.

I took pity on her.

17/I spent fifteen minutes in the bathroom inspecting The Body Beautiful in the mirror, trying to see it through Barry's eyes.

To be honest, I have never been completely satisfied with my knees.

The bathroom mirror is only half full size, and is fixed to the wall at a height convenient for shaving. In order to inspect my lower quarters therefore I must either stand on my head, which causes certain features to dangle in an unflattering manner and is difficult to maintain long enough for a proper look, or I must balance myself on the edge of the bathtub. This is a moderately dangerous exploit as the rim of our tub is narrow and curved so that I have to perform something like a tight rope act, risking broken bones if I lose my balance and slip into the tub, or worse if my feet skid off in opposite directions causing me to fall with my legs astride the tub rim.

Knowing, of course, that I would shortly be called upon to display my knees—that indeed, when I came to think of it, I had already done so not only before a grinning crowd but, what was far more important, on three separate occasions before Barry yesterday—I thought I had better survey the limbscape and decide how best to present myself on future occasions. So I climbed up onto the rim of the bathtub and began my inspection.

The problem I have with my knees is that they seem to be too far down my legs. This makes my thigh too long in proportion to the glutei of my nates — which have always struck me as nicely shaped, neat and well set under iliac crests that might on some males certainly look too pronounced but on me seem just right. Of course, if your femoral quadriceps are well moulded and smoothly covered, a slight disproportion in their length doesn't matter, at least when viewed frontally. They can even show off your genitalic drapery to good effect. Providing you are flourishing in that feature and not recondite.

I studied myself in that area from as many angles as my precarious platform would allow. On the whole, I decided, my genitalic modelling was passable, though I would have liked a bit more quantity as well as quality. But my rectus and lateralis were okay; the medialis were well developed but they gave too thin an appearance just above the knees, which I suppose exaggerates the boniness of my patellas and further pronounces the length of my thighs.

By stretching out my left arm and supporting myself against the wall behind the bath, I kept my balance while I bent my left leg upwards and viewed it in profile in the mirror. This had a distinctly improving effect, rounding off my scraggy knee cap and displaying quite attractively the gracilic line. But I could hardly hop about the beach on one trousered leg while holding up the other leg nude for public inspection and approval of my knee exhibited at its best angle.

In order to check the view from behind I had to turn with my back to the mirror and cautiously twist my head round to inspect my reflection. As far as I could see from this limited and wobbly position the appearance of the backs of my knees was greatly helped by a nice popliteal upholstering, which saved them from the scrawniness some people suffer from. But I could not see very well, so I tried bending down far enough to look between my legs at the view in the mirror. This required a pretty skilled balancing act.

I was just about doubled up enough to see through my legs when my mother rammed the bathroom door with the vacuum agonybag. I lost my balance and crashed into the tub, barking various angles of myself on its hard enamel.

'Are you all right in there, our Henry?' Mother shouted above the noise of vacuum and calamity.

Further anatomical investigation had to be abandoned for that morning. And as it turned out for a few weeks after that life was made a good deal easier whenever the need to inspect my body came over me because I could use the multi-mirrored walls of the Gorman bathroom which allowed the closest study of every detail from every possible viewpoint without any need for unnatural contortions or danger to the person.

18/Half way through my breakfast in the kitchen, Mother appeared, duster at the ready. She flicked absent-mindedly at the cupboard doors. Semaphore from a nervous wreck.

'Why not have a cup of coffee,' I said.

'Maybe I will,' she said.

She made herself one—half milk, half water, as always—and sat at the other side of the table, duster cocked for action.

'It's before my coffee time really,' she said, looking guilty.

'Give yourself a treat,' I said.

She sipped from her cup. 'It's a terrible price, you know. Awful. I don't know how they have the cheek to charge the prices they do.'

Silence. I finished my toast.

'You'll have to stop these late mornings, pet,' she said, dabbing her duster along the edge of the table. 'Your dad's upset.'

'How can me getting up late bother him? He's at work.'

'He always asks, love, when he comes in.'

'Then don't tell him.'

'O no, I have to tell him. Can't lie. Not to your father. Wouldn't be right.'

Further polishing of the table edge.

Then: 'He thinks a lot about you, does your dad. Wants the best for you. Wants you to get on.'

A dab at the cooker in arm's reach from where she sat. Most things are in arm's reach from the table in our kitchen.

Then: 'It was after one when you got in last night. It can't go on, Henry. Your father won't stand for it.'

She stood up, made a sally against the cupboard doors again, sat down. Sipped her coffee. Began rubbing the table edge again.

'You'll have to make up your mind soon,' she said. 'About what you're going to do. Your dad thinks it's bad for you, lying about all day. Nothing to do. You know he told you to get a temporary job. To tide you over. Till you've sorted out what you really want to do.'

I pushed my plate aside. 'What do you think I should do?'

She teased at her duster, picking dust specks from it. Dusting her duster. 'I wish I knew, love. It's beyond me.'

'Stay on at school?'

'Your dad thinks you'll be best off with a good job.'

'But what do you think?'

Her pause was as long as this page. Then she shook her head once with distressed slightness. 'Whatever will make you happiest, pet. That's all that matters.'

'You always say that. But I don't know what will make me happiest. How do you know till you do it?'

She sniffed. 'Yes, well, you're not alone. Most people don't know. And never find out. It's the lucky ones who do. Luckier still if they know what they want and get it.'

The duster fluttered. We sat in silence.

'Osborn thinks I should stay on and take English.'

She looked at me. 'What use will that be?'

I smiled. 'Not much he says.'

'Funny way of going on. Telling you to study something no use.'

'He means for a job.'

'It's a job that matters.'

'Yes.'

Silence. A rub at the table top.

'I was good at English myself at school.' She smiled at me. 'Wrote very good poems the teachers said. I was good at spelling as well. Which is something I haven't passed on to you, eh?' She laughed.

'I can't be a genius at everything,' I said, laughing with her.

She got up. Shifted my dirty plate from the table to the draining board. Polished the table with her duster. Sat down.

'I never liked reading though. Not like you do.' Her eyes drifted across my face. 'I don't know where you got that from.' She made reading sound like a contagious disease.

'Would Dad let me stay on?'

A sniff, drawing back inside herself again. 'You'd better ask him, pet. I should think so. If he thought it was right for you.'

Back to Go.

I said, 'Anyway, I've got a part-time job till the results come through.'

She was perky at once. 'You have? Where?'

'Gorman Records. Helping in the shop.'

'On London Road? When did this happen?'

'Yesterday. It was Barry Gorman I was out with last night. He runs the shop with his mother.'

'Well, I say! Tell us about it then. When do you start and how much do they pay?'

I stood up. 'I don't know the details yet. Find out today.'

'I'll look forward to hearing all about it. Your dad will be pleased. They must have liked you a lot to take you on so easy.'

'Yes,' I said, 'I think you could say they liked me.'

JKA. *Running Report:* Henry Spurling ROBINSON
21st Sept. Talked with Sue about the case, and
whether we should include it on the agenda for the
Team Discussion next week. She thought not.
Suggested we go through the objectives together, as I
might be losing sight of them because of the
unusualness of Hal and the events involved.

Purpose:
  i. To find out why Hal acted as he did.
 ii. To discover his attitude to his actions.
iii. To find out how he views his future.
iv. To assess his background.

Our statutory involvement and responsibility in this
case:

To present the court with a report which:
 i. relates what we know about the case;

ii. makes recommendations about what should be done next in dealing with Hal.

We agreed that the boy is not in danger and that this did not seem to be a case which, as far as I can judge, needs psychiatric or other treatment.

The only difficulty is that the client will not talk about what he has done.

We discussed my worries about having handled Hal badly so far. Sue thought those unfounded. But she suggested that I keep a more detailed Report and that she and I discuss my progress after each meeting. I agreed. I could not help feeling uneasy about the case and will feel better knowing Sue is keeping an eye on it with me.

19/I telephoned Barry from a box near home.

'Great!' he said. 'Look, it's busy here today. I can't manage lunch. Come to the shop about five. We'll fix up about your pay and stuff. Then we'll celebrate. Okay?'

'Okay, fine.'

There was a fog-horn noise in the background.

'Hang on, Mother wants a word.'

'Hal? Hello? This is me. You're coming to join us! Barry told me. I'm ecstatic! I won't have to serve all these awful children so much now. And such a friend for Bubby. You're a godsend, you know that? But, Hal—are you there?'

'Yes, Mrs Gorman.'

'I have a bone to pick with you.'

'A bone, Mrs Gorman?'

'Last night. You promised me you'd not keep Bubby out so late. Four o'clock! That was naughty.'

'Four o'clock?'

'I know, I know! You're young, you forget the time. I was young once myself. Mr Gorman used to keep me out dancing, dancing. Sometimes all night. What days! What nights! But you promised, Hal. Four o'clock, that's too late when Bubby has to work next morning. You'll find out when you are working here.'

'I'm sorry, Mrs Gorman, I—'

'Forget it, my darling. It's nothing. Really. I must go. Bubby says I'm holding up business talking like this. He's a slave driver, that boy. You'll find out! Cheerio till we see you soon.'

'Hal?'
'Yes?'
'I'll explain tonight, okay?'
'Okay.'
'We'll be great together, yes?'
'Sure.'
'Shalom.'
'See you.'

20/I guessed what he had done. Gone back to The Drunk.

And I guessed right. He told me that evening when I got to the shop, which excitement is coming soon.

He tried to pass it off by lacing the story with jokes against himself. He'd felt uneasy leaving the poor goy (!) lying there with all that money because someone might happen along and rob him, or the taxi driver might come back and try again. So he'd gone back and sure enough someone was hanging about near The Drunk, so Barry woke him and stayed with him talking (?) till Our Friend sobered up enough to look after himself, etc. etc.

What he missed out of the story was probably as interesting as what he told. And he was like a kid who is a compulsive stealer of sweets trying to pass off his latest failure to resist temptation as a first-and-last-time affair, but knowing that nobody really believes him. Anyway, Barry was never any good at telling a story about anything not even a simple joke. And he had no memory either, which is something a good liar needs. He lived for the moment all the time, so memory was something he didn't need.

I said nothing. Tried to laugh in the right places but couldn't keep from looking squashed. It shouldn't have mattered to me. If I'd thought about such a thing beforehand I would have sworn it wouldn't have mattered to me. But it did. I guess, like the boys swearing eternal faithfulness to each other over the can of magic beans, I thought then that faithfulness was one of the things that was part of bosom palship. I expected it as an unspoken gift.

He couldn't help but see my downcast feelings in my face. I guess that's why he took me out on his motorbike: a kiddish way of trying to make everything right again by a breathless assault of madcap fun and frolics. Results also coming shortly.

I put the telephone down and stood outside the phone box for ten minutes chewing over what must have gone on. The more I thought about it, no doubt making it all far worse than it really had been, the deeper into depression I plunged. For a while I wandered round the streets chomping away in my mind at my distress. Surprising myself by my reaction. Kicking myself for feeling like this. And being completely stumped in deciding how to deal with Barry or myself. Lost, still, later, as Barry spun his yarn.

Now, weeks afterwards I still don't know that I could

handle the same thing better. Maybe I wouldn't feel so upset now, wouldn't feel so betrayed. I'm harder now. I think. I hope. Maybe I'm also more tolerant of a friend being what he is and not what I want him to be.

But I guess one of the oddities about life is that you never really do learn from one experience how to cope with another. Because no two experiences are ever quite the same. You're changed by what happens to you; but each new experience is just as hard to handle as the ones that went before.

21/Have you noticed how, if you get depressed, you start doing all the wrong things? And doing all the right things in the wrong way. You go from bad to worse, sucked into a vortex of deepening dismay.

That happened to me that afternoon. Thinking to distract myself and make some use of this wasted time, I went to school and saw Ms Tyke. Ms Tyke is my tutorial teacher, the one responsible for my 'pastoral care'. That's the phrase they use at school for the member of staff who is supposed to look after your personal interests—like whether you are feeling suicidal or bite your toenails or otherwise display signs of being human. The only thing having a person in charge of my pastoral care does for me is to make me feel like a sheep. Maybe it's meant to. Anyway, Ms Tyke is about as pastoral as a cracking plant and as careful as a bulldozer. She believes the best way of countering male chauvinist piggery in a male-dominated society like England in general and Chalkwell High in particular—about which she waxes deliquescent at the drop of a male gender—is to adopt the worst excesses of male chauvinist piggery for herself, presumably on the theory that if you can't beat them you should join them. I guess she reckons that at least this way she gets her hormones back. Certainly you can be sure that whatever Ms T. says turns into Ms T.

I was foolish enough to put myself in her clutches that depressed afternoon because she was first in line of the bureaucratic hierarchy I had to navigate for careers advice and a decision about staying on in Ozzy's English Sixth. Last in line was the Head. Four obstacles lay twixt he and me, viz: Ms Tyke; my year teacher; the careers officer; and the head of upper school. If all agreed with my hopes for my future, whatever those turned out to be, the Head would grant a two-minute rubber stamping interview. Otherwise return to Go. It has been known for a really determined applicant to succeed in a week, but the average time for this assault course is three weeks, so the sooner I started the better.

'And what's your problem?' Ms T. said through her python grin as I entered her room. She yanked open a drawer in a filing cabinet, took out a thin buff file with my name on it, sat at her desk, waved me to a chair by its side.

'I think I should see the Head,' I said, hoping a full frontal attack might so take her by surprise I would get through to the top unhindered.

Her grin tightened and I knew I had blown it. As I say, when you're depressed you can be sure you'll do the wrong thing.

'What can he do for you that I can't do better?' she said paring her nails with an unbent paper clip.

I hitched uncomfortably in my seat. 'I'm thinking of staying on next year.'

A twitch of the eyebrows told me this announcement really had taken her by surprise. 'I suppose I should feel pleased,' she said. 'What to do?'

'English lit.'

'Eng. lit.! Whatever put such a fool notion into your head, boy?'

Stung (wrong again; always stay cool) I said acidly, '*Whoever* actually, miz. Mr Osborn.'

'That figures,' she said, her grin turning down at the ends. 'And is there some dark secret you've not so far revealed to me about the value of Eng. lit. in your future life? Or are you just into poetry and stuff?'

'It interests me.'

'It interests me too, but that's no reason for staking your future on it. You'd be better off doing something useful.'

'Isn't literature useful, miz?'

'No. Not like physics or chemistry or maths or medicine. The world needs people who know about things like that. Poets it might manage without.'

'I'm not sure about that.'

'Let's not argue the point.'

An unforthcoming silence seemed the best reply.

Her eyes narrowed. 'You're not thinking of becoming a teacher, are you?'

'No, miz.'

Evident relief. She grinned widely. 'Thank God for that. Tell me, then,' she went on with forced professional interest, 'what do you hope to do with yourself? And don't get excited, I only mean careerwise.'

'*Careerwise*, miz?'

The semantic point evaded her. Or she pretended it did. 'For a job,' she said with heavy tolerance.

I affected rumination. 'I don't know.'

An as-I-expected nod. 'You don't know!'

'Not sure.'

'Not sure!' Another rough going-over with her cold green eyes. She hitched in her chair, settling herself with her bare elbows sharp as marlin spikes on the desk.

'Let me tell you something, Robinson.'

Clearly the news was not going to be happy. 'What, miz?'

'You are wet.'

This did wonders for my depression.

Nor had she finished. 'Eng. lit. is just about your size. I expect you still weep over poetry.' She scratched an armpit. Somehow an appropriate reflex, I thought. 'I've been keeping tabs on you this last year,' she said, tapping my file. 'You've sloped around being useless most of the time. You don't like games, you've hidden yourself away in the library whenever there was a vague chance you might get roped into house competitions. You're anti-social. You've no initiative, no go at all. About all you're good for as far as I can see is making smart-alec speeches at the Debating Soc. and writing twitty stuff for the school mag.'

A repeat performance of my unforthcoming silence seemed only further provocation.

'What Mr Osborn sees in you I can't imagine. Well, if he wants you he can have you. But don't expect me to send up a favourable recommendation. In my estimation what you should have is a douche of cold reality. You need to find out what life is all about. A job would do wonders for you. Certainly, in my estimation the school won't benefit from having you hanging about in it for another two years. There are better ways of spending the taxpayers' money.'

I waited a minute to be sure she had finished and to give myself time to calm down. She had; I didn't.

'Is that all, miz?'

'You want more?' Her tight python grin returned. 'Masochist. You're like all the arty lot.'

The end-of-afternoon bell rang. Ms Tyke shuffled the few papers of my life together and closed the file. Stood up. Dropped the file into its drawer. Slammed the drawer.

'Okay,' she said, standing by the desk swinging her car keys from a finger. 'Come see me again if you change your mind.'

I went and stared at the sea.

22/'The sea is *rather* fine, don't you think?'

She was sitting behind me on the low wall that separates the beach from the esplanade just below Chalkwell station. I turned and saw small feet with painted toenails, slim legs in hugging blue jeans, a red T-shirt tight over unobtrusive breasts, a small triangular face, short cropped blonde hair. She stretched out 'rather' in a way that betrayed she was not English, like it was an elastic band.

I nodded. Turned back to the sea.

She slipped down onto the sand beside me.

'You don't mind I should talk to you I hope?'

Usually I don't like talking to strangers: the inconsequential polite natter of the unattached. But sometimes, like now, when people you know have given you a pain in the mindgut, it is a relief to come across someone you don't know who wants to talk. Wants to prattle about nothing. Inconsequentiality then is even comforting.

'Talk away,' I said.

'It is for my English,' she said, raised her eyebrows —pretty eyebrows, brown, like a pencil line—and nodded her head from side to side. 'I am rather rusty.'

'You're doing very well.'

'You think so?' She smiled widely. 'I am pleased. I only arrived two—three days ago.'

'Where are you from?'

'Norway. My name is Kari.'

'Hello, Kari. I'm Hal.'

She shook hands, a comic formality sitting on seaside sand.

'Hal?'

'Short for Henry. I don't like Henry.'

'Hal is nice. I like it *very* much.' She elasticated 'very' also. 'Southend I like too,' she said smiling approval at the Thames and settling herself comfortably. 'It is quite jolly.'

'You've been to England before?'

'Once. That time at Birmingham.' She pulled a bad-smell face. 'Birmingham is not so jolly as Southend.' We laughed. 'I think I shall sun bath if you don't mind.'

'Be my guest,' I said. 'And it's sun*bathe*.'

She cross-arm gathered the hem of her T-shirt in her hands and hauled upwards. 'Sun*bathe*,' she said, pulling the shirt over her head. 'Thank you. Please correct my wrong speech. I learn best that way.'

'You're doing great,' I said assessing her litheness, the small breasts scarfed in a haltered slip of red cloth, her sleek tanned skin.

In a neatly flicking unzipping movement she sloughed her jeans. A daring nappy of cloth curtained her crotch and arrowed the eye down the flow of her trim legs.

I needed to swallow a lot.

'Wouldn't you like to sunbathe too?' She lay back flat on the sand, pillowing her head on her bundled clothes. 'You must be hot in your clotheses.'

'Clothes,' I said, just managing.

'Silly me,' she said, chuckling. 'Always, I get that wrongly.'

I looked at my watch. 'I have to meet someone soon.'

She was staring at me too frankly for comfort. 'Someone rather nice I think.'

'A friend. He might give me a holiday job.'

'Then he must be a rather good friend.'

'I'm not sure,' I said.

But for some reason just saying that lightened my glooms. And her verbal tick, elasticating her rathers and verys, was not only funny and sexy, but reminded me of Barry. He had a verbal tick too. His tongue seems— seemed, dammit, *seemed*; it doesn't any more—*seemed* to go to the side of his mouth instead of to the front when he said sibilants. It wasn't a lisp, but produced an unusual emphasis to his speech, a sexy articulation and movement of the mouth. Just remembering this pushed out of my mind any more sulking about the telephone call, or Ms Tyke, or about drunks visited in the night. The drunk would have gone home. I was still here. B. had just been going on the way he had been going on before we met, hadn't he? Now we'd get together and it would be different, wouldn't it? We'd be a team, a pair; he had said so himself. If I had gone in with him last night, he wouldn't have gone back to The Drunk. It was my fault for deserting him when he wanted me to stay with him. I'd not make that mistake again.

What's more, as these thoughts echoed in my head, having Kari lying right there next to me near-naked in the sun made me want to be with him. It was him I wanted lying next to me in the sun.

I got up. Brushed sand from myself.

'Maybe we meet again? I hope we do,' Kari said.

'I'd like that,' I said, not expecting that we would.

'I am an au pair, you know. At the house painted pink in Chalkwell Avenue. You have seen it? Near the railway bridge? Or perhaps you do not live here?'

'I live here and I know the house. You'll be around quite a time then.'

She stood up. As sliver as a whistle. 'Six months. More I think it might be. If I get along okay with my people. They are rather nice. I think it will be all right.'

'Well, I come here quite often.'

'I'll watch for you.'

Walking away half turned I palmed a salute. 'See you, then.'

23/ACTION REPLAY

I turn and look at her.

She is looking at me.

I turn away.

She slips off the wall and sits beside me, close.

I look at her.

She looks at me.

We both look at the sea.

I look at her.

She looks at me.

She undresses and I am watching.

We are looking at each other.

I am thinking about Barry.

I get up, looking at her.

She gets up, looking at me.

I walk away, looking at her.

She waves, looking at me.

I turn away, not expecting to see her again.

Which shows how wrong I can be.

JKA. *Running Report*: Henry Spurling ROBINSON 22nd Sept. 1015. Meeting with Mr J. Osborn, Head of English, Chalkwell High.

The school secretary showed me into a small darkish room where Mr Osborn was already waiting. The room was chill, even though the sun was shining outside. Mr Osborn indicated a chair on the other side of the table. We engaged in routine greetings.

Mr Osborn is the kind of teacher who makes me feel thirteen again. He has a precise manner, and piercing, slightly crossed brown eyes that glare through thick-lensed glasses. His speech is clipped and sharply pronounced. He often rolls and rasps his 'r' sounds.

Mr O. had already made it clear during our initial telephone conversation when I arranged this meeting that he had nothing to tell me and regarded the meeting as a waste of time. He began by repeating this. He asked why I thought he could be of any use. I said that I understood he knew Hal well. He asked what made me think so. I replied that Hal and his parents had said things that led me to this conclusion.

Mr O. said it was true he had helped the Robinsons, but he would not claim to know Hal well. I said I was beginning to think that no one knew him well, and explained that what I wanted to know was what had gone on between Hal and Barry Gorman that caused Hal to damage Gorman's grave.

Mr O. paused for a moment. He then told me he had little time for social workers. He mistrusted their motives, 'and often their intelligence'. I said that whatever his views about social workers might be, the court had charged me with the responsibility for discovering what had happened in this case and of making recommendations about Hal's future. Mr O. said that none of this had anything to do with him; it was Robinson I should be talking to. I said I had been trying but that Hal would not say anything about his friend's death or the subsequent events, but that things he had said led me to believe that Mr O. might know at least some of the story.

116

'Let us suppose,' Mr O. said in a very schoolmasterly way, 'that I do know. I would regard such information as confidential.' He added very acidly, 'I assume you have heard of professional confidentiality.' I said I needed no reminding, that professional confidentiality was a part of my job. He said that in his opinion this was not just the prerogative of priests and doctors, and even social workers, but that it extended to teachers too.

I tried to assure Mr O. that anything he told me would remain confidential. He replied that I had missed the point. A confidence did not remain a confidence, he said, just because you told it to someone else who was bound by professional confidentiality. In any case, he went on, he was not stupid enough to suppose that anything he told me would not find its way into a file somewhere, if not onto a computer. Wasn't this what social workers did—keep files on people? How else could they compile their reports?

I said that, naturally, we had to keep files. But that they were not available to anyone except those social workers involved in a case. That, said Mr O., mean' they were available to anyone determined enough to get the information he wanted. No file was ever completely secure; surely I understood that!

I could see no point in continuing with this discussion. I began to suspect that Mr O. likes an argument for the sake of argument, and began to see, too, where some of Hal's habits have come from. I said that I understood Mr O.'s position; but what was his opinion of Hal? How clever was he?

Clever enough to stay on in the Sixth and go to university afterwards, Mr O. replied. I made a show of writing this in my notebook.

Did he think Hal was still disturbed by Gorman's death? Of course, Mr O. said; Gorman and Robinson had been close friends for some weeks, everyone knew that. Naturally, the boy was upset and shocked. What Hal needed was to regain his self-confidence—or maybe to find it for the first time in his life. In Mr O.'s view, this would happen if Robinson was got back to school as soon as possible and helped to apply himself to subjects and activities that deeply interested him.

Did Mr O. feel that literature deeply interested Hal?

Ideas deeply interested him, Mr O. said. And Hal happens to discover their best expression in literature.

I asked whether it was literature they had discussed during Mr O.'s regular meetings with Hal over the last few weeks. Yes, he said, but their meetings were no substitute for a full-time course of study and the companionship of his peers.

I said that I tended to agree, but that there was a problem. Only a problem of bureaucracy, nothing else, Mr O. said. I said it was a little more difficult than that. Hal is charged with a crime, and one the court finds hard to understand and which offends public decency. I would like to try and explain this in my report, and to make recommendations that are sensible in the light of the facts. But that I cannot do this if I cannot find out what has happened. Robinson won't talk about it at all, and the only other person who seems to know, I said firmly, seems to be you. Now you say you won't help me either.

Mr O. thought about this for a while. I reminded him that the case comes before the court again next week. If I knew no more by then I shall have to submit a report saying that Hal will not cooperate. The court will then, probably, decide that Hal should be sent to a Detention Centre where he can be examined by psychiatrists and the police as well as the social services more easily.

Mr O. became quite angry. He said such a course of action would be a disaster, a crime in itself. I told him neither I nor the court would have any option. Under the law there is little else that can be done. The offence must be dealt with, and in the absence of further information to explain it, the only thing the court can do in the end is punish the offender for the crime committed.

Mr O. sat stiffly in his chair glaring at me. Nothing was said for a few moments. Then Mr O. said that in his opinion it was extremely important that Hal himself explain what had happened. He felt that Hal was brooding on it all, and that this was bad for him, and might have worse long term effects than any treatment the court might impose on him. But also, he felt it important that Hal's trust in him be kept intact. By telling me what he knew, Mr O. would break that trust, and he would only do this with the greatest reluctance.

I agreed with all he said. In that case, Mr O. said, he would suggest a course of action. He would do all he could to persuade Hal to tell me what had happened, if I would agree to recommend to the court that Hal should be allowed to come back to school, whatever other treatment was also felt necessary.

I said I could not make deals. He laughed at this, and said I was talking like a second rate television crime story. But, I went on, I did think it was in Hal's best interest to keep him out of a Detention Centre, and that his future might be best served by staying on at school, if that is what he wanted. If he did, and there was nothing in what he had to tell that might lead to further criminal proceedings, then I would *probably* recommend either a conditional discharge or a Supervision Order.

This would mean that Hal would be kept an eye on for a while and helped if he needed it, but would not be required to go through any further official investigation. However, I added as firmly as I could, I would need support from someone responsible who knows Hal if I am to succeed in making such a recommendation. Would you, I asked Mr O., give that support and appear in court on Hal's behalf, if necessary?

Mr O. said that of course he would.

We agreed therefore that Mr O. would see Hal and try to persuade him to tell me his story, and that Mr O. and I would meet again next Tuesday to review the matter. By then I hoped Mr O.'s influence would have worked.

24/By the time I got there, it was after five-thirty and the shop was closed. Mrs Gorman had gone home; but Barry was in full view of the window pretending to arrange a sleeve display.

He let me in, all overdone brightness, and locked the door behind us.

'Listen, about last night . . .'

He told me the story. I couldn't raise much enthusiasm. He noticed; but the harder he tried, the less I could respond.

'You don't have to explain,' I said at last. 'I mean, it hasn't anything to do with me, has it?'

I hated all this jiving about; but still his presence fingered me pliant, as it always did no matter how I felt or what he had done. Just the sight of him was enough. (Always? Till once, ending always. When he spiked resistance, rage.)

'Okay,' he said. 'We'll forget it. Now . . . close your eyes. It's surprise time!'

'What are you up to?'

'Do as you're told! Come on, close your eyes.'

Laughing, I blinded myself. I heard him scrabbling about behind the counter.

'Quick,' I said, 'stop faffing about!'

'All right . . . nearly ready . . . Now. Open up!'

He was holding out close to me at eye level a shining red crash helmet. Visored and flash and gladiatorial.

'*Voilà*! *Pour broom-broom*!'

I stared, unmoving.

'Well,' he said. 'Take it. It's yours. Go on. Try it!'

And when I still didn't move, 'Come here!' He lifted it over my head and crowned me with this upturned fishbowl. Stood back and admired. 'Beautiful,' he said, and pushed down the visor. 'Especially as it obscures your phizzog!' He laughed like a kid with a new toy— which he was in a way I suppose.

'What am I meant to do with this?' I said, and the sound of my own voice wrapped in the helmet stunned my ears. I pushed up the visor. 'I don't have a bike, you idiot!'

'Patience, patience. That'll come in time.' He took my hand and led me to a room behind the shop: the office and store for spare stock by the look of it, lit only by an air-vent window high up and a couple of electric lights. 'Till then,' he said, 'we've places to go, and pillion people need protection. The law says so. Here—on the wall. A mirror. Take a glim at yourself.'

25/A headpiece hiding place.

Mask.

For a masque.

The faceless back of Barry's head also within the frame.

Hidden out of frame an extension of two bodies overlapped in the glass.

Hands also, refracting what the mirror could not show. And could not say. The words are never there.

No words ever from its hard and absent surface.

But watch this space. We have ways of making it talk.

Yes in deed.

Yes.

26/And what a night then began for a quiet lad like me.

'How about a ride?' Barry said. 'On the bike, I mean! Give that new helmet an airing. Celebrate your last night of freedom. Tomorrow you'll be a working bloke. Yes?'

'Okay.'

He geared us both in zazzy parkas kept ready behind the office door, and himself in zippy-zappy biker boots. Topped in our spaceman bubble hats we, thus accoutred against the excitements of speed, wheeled from its stable behind the shop his armed and gleaming mount, a Suzuki 250 with a thousand miles on its clock and the click of clear oil plucking in the knuckles of its joints.

'Know the ropes?' he asked.

'First time.'

'Remember: Don't put your feet down. Whatever happens. Keep them on the rests. Relax. Lean with the bike. Don't fight it. Just follow me. And hang on. Tight.'

27/A 250 is a maquette for a sculptor's memorial to brazen speed. And riding pillion with Barry was giving a cuddle to a crazy while he had a bash at scaring death off the roads.

When I mounted behind him he hooked a hand under my thigh and hitched me close to him.

'If you stop short,' I shouted above the revs, 'I'll do you a terrible damage.'

'Joy at last!' he shouted back over his shoulder. 'Here we go. Hang on.'

Up London Road, a well-behaved right at the lights into Southbourne Grove, a flicking left into the stream of dual-carriageway on Prince Avenue, and then away in a dib-dab rib-throar blur up the Arterial, Londonwards.

I stopped glancing over B.'s shoulder at the speedometer when it touched seventy, and gave myself up to fate. If you're going to die you might as well enjoy it.

At the Laynham junction we turned back, jog-trotted at thirty for a mile or so, then slipped into a cart track where we stopped a little way from the main road.

28/'Do you always drive like that or only on Fridays?' I said as we uncoupled from the Suzi's vibrant intimacy.

'Like what?' he said all mock innocence.

'Like dangerous. Like fast.'

'I don't drive fast!'

I hooted.

Emphatic, but laughing, he said, 'I don't! Well—okay, yes I do. But it never *feels* like fast.'

'That's just what it feels like to me. Like speeding.'

'But that's it, you see.'

'What's it I see?'

'Ah shucks, I gonna have trouble with you tonight, kid!'

True; I was biley in the pit of my stomach because of last night. 'Try me,' I said.

He was latching our helmets to the bike by their chin-bars. 'Fast is one thing,' he said. 'Speed is another.'

'You're right,' I said. 'You've got trouble.'

'It's hard to explain.'

'Take your time, we've got all night.'

'Yes,' he said, 'we have, haven't we!'

I ignored him, settled myself side-saddle on the resting Suzi.

'Didn't you enjoy it?' he said.

'Loved it. But fast isn't speed?'

He perched himself side-saddle on the Suzi's other cheek.

'It's like this. Fast is something you do. Or something that happens to you.'

'You go fast, or you're driven fast?'

'Right.'

'So far so simple. But speed?'

'Speed is.'

'Is what?'

'Just *is*.'

I let that gem settle a minute.

'You know something?' I said.

'What?'

'You're weird. You are also crazy. And you are also wrong. For a start, look up speed in a dictionary.'

'Forget the dictionary! I'm telling you how I feel.' A touch of anger showed. 'Do you want to know or don't you?'

I said, 'I want to know. Honest.' And smiled.

He smiled back. 'Fast is what you go to achieve speed.'

I turned that over.

'Sorry,' I said. 'I need a bit more.'

He hitched his seat. 'On a good road, like the Arterial . . .'

'Yes?'

'. . . I never feel I'm going fast. What I feel is that speed is somewhere just ahead, and that I'm chasing it. Always it's just out of reach. So I go faster and faster, trying to catch it. But because speed is always ahead, always the same distance in front of me, I never feel I'm going fast. Or getting faster.'

Silence. I scratched my cheek.

'What would happen,' I said, 'if you ever caught it up?'

He shrugged, looking away. 'I dream about that. It's like being inside an invisible bubble, or maybe some kind of force field. And it could take me anywhere, anywhere at all, in a split second. It's strange. I know I'm moving but there's no effort, no noise or vibration or anything like that. And no danger either. The whole experience is marvellous. I don't want to do anything but be inside that bubble of energy always. Forever.'

That put a stop on me. He turned, watching me to see every twitch of my reaction.

I shrugged. 'Some dream!'

'You've never had one like that?'

I shook my head.

'I'll tell you something else,' he said. 'The best part. When I wake up, I feel the dream is telling me it will soon really happen. I mean happen in real life. Wouldn't that be something!'

I got off the Suzi and walked a pace or two.

'You're even weirder than I thought,' I said, trying to laugh it off.

'So who wants to be normal?' he said.

29/Sauntering back, a gang of motorbikers overtook us, moving in for Friday manoeuvres. Southend: The Resort for All Frissons. They swarmed; Barry accelerated to keep with them. Some had pillioned girlfriends who waved cheeky-cute as they came alongside. Some of the riders might have been girls as well, but there was no way of telling.

Ahead of them, the first of the gang to pass us, was a rider dressed in bright white leathers with black helmet, gloves and boots. He was so small I thought at first he was an under-age kid. Or a monkey. He was balancing with one foot on the saddle, the other stretched out behind him, like a circus stunt rider.

When he was past us, he dropped into his saddle, but facing backwards, hands held out to his sides. His pals, surging round us now, blared their horns, waved, cheered. Acknowledging this applause with a clenched fist, Monkey Boy swung his right leg over his rear wheel, sat side-saddle, left hand on the rev-grip. Thus perilously seated he overtook on the inside a holiday-packed car whose driver went into shock and sent the car veering about in convulsive zig-zags as the tidal wave of bikes swallowed him up and swept on, leaving him bobbing like jetsam in their wake.

On we roared, Barry and me tucked into the middle.

'Staying with them?' I shouted into Barry's helmet where his ear should be.

He nodded. 'Good for a laugh,' he shouted back.

And so Monkey Boy led the pack along Prince Avenue, round Priory Crescent into Eastern Avenue, then right into Bournemouth Park Road and on down Southchurch Avenue to a revving cheering stop in the car park on the sea-front at the end of Marine Parade, opposite the Kursaal's casino-and-fun-fair glittergleam tat.

30/Everyone dehelmets.

'What's this then?' says Monkey Boy approaching Barry and me. 'Them's not us.' (Without his helmet he is indeed like a boyish monkey: big eyes and eye-circling hair.)

'Who's not?' says a six-foot-three monolith bearing down on us from a bullish 500 Kawasaki. His ancient leathers, creased and greased, are sparkling with metal studs.

'Them's not us,' says Monkey Boy.

The tribe gathers.

'Right,' says Monolith. Now we see him close he looks too old to be playing at motorbikes. In his late twenties for sure. And a face that's had asphalt laid on it.

'Where'd you come from?' he says.

One of the tribe has a girl's head. 'They've been with us from just outside town,' she says and performs a simper. 'I thought that one—' she points at me—'was the other one's girl!'

A camped oo-hooing goes up.

'Well,' says Girl's Head adding coals to this fire, 'she could have been the way she was holding on.'

'*She*?' they cry, playing up.

'Ooo no!' Girl's Head exclaims, exaggerating manufactured confusion at her intended mistake and clasping a hand over her mouth. 'I mean *he*!' And she all but collapses in supersonic giggles.

After which begins a procession of catcalls.

'Are we a little Southend pier then?' says Monkey Boy sashaying the inner circle.

'A bit first of May?' says one with a doormat for hair.

'A couple of bottle boys are we?' says another with a surprising absence of earlobes, those he once possessed clearly having been lopped off in the not so long ago, for the scars glow red.

'Now's your chance, Riggsy,' bellows Doormat, and a lamp-post of a lad, ugly and carroty, his head protruding from wrinkled new leathers his gangling body cannot fill, grins sheepish and says, fluting, 'Pretty enough anyroad.'

They all hoot again and Carrot Top turns bright red at his daring.

Monolith has not moved or laughed or even smiled. 'I said,' he says, bunging the chorus, 'where'd you come from?'

There is the zing of focused malice in the air.

'Qwert yui op?' says Barry.

31/Cheeky.

I am trembling in my parka.

ACTION REPLAY

I had not much liked the turn of events from the time we joined the growling throng. I am not keen on crowds. In fact, I think I must be a crowdophobe. (Did you know that in Norwegian the word for crowd is *kryda*, which means *to swarm*? Very appropriate in the circs. I learned this from Kari on one of the occasions soon to be re-counted.)

My idea of hell is being forced to stand for all eternity in the middle of a football crowd which is incensed to the point of rioting because the game is so bad. I hate football; and football crowds I hate even more. They're the perfect example of Robinson's Law. This states that human idiocy multiplies in compound ratio to the number of people gathered together in one place for a common purpose.

I have to admit that standing there in the car park surrounded by this gang of uglies the thought did occur that I might soon be provided with fresh evidence for a revised Robinson's Law. My instinct was to turn tail and run. Fast. But as Monkey Boy lolloped around us and the spangled Monolith came to view the objects of the simian's attention, my ever heroic new friend muttered, 'Stand still and act dumb.'

So still and dumb I remained, though whether at B.'s command or out of paralysing fright I think it best for my ego's sake not to examine too closely.

Luckily, however, the uglies were as taken aback as I myself by B.'s reply to Monolith's insistent question.

32/'Qwert yui op?' Barry repeats after a pause for effect.

'Aaaah!' says Girl's Head, as she might had she just seen two cuddly babies. 'They're foreign. No wonder they're funny.'

At this, most of the rest of the gang lose interest and drift off in the direction of the Kursaal.

'Where you from?' says Girl's Head edging closer. 'You French, are you?'

Monkey Boy slips alongside performing what he supposes is a Parisian sex-bomb's mosey. 'Parly voo franky?' he says, fluttering his eyelids into B.'s face.

'Qwert?' says Barry, much puzzled.

God save us! I think, becoming religious of a sudden.

'That's not French,' Carrot Top says. (Is the child educated?)

Girl's Head puts her face close to Barry's and pronounces with firm deliberation at point blank range, 'Where? You? Come? From?'

The few remaining members of the gang shuffle in, the better to inspect us. The smell of their sweat and oil and faggy breath stings the nose and helps keep the mouth shut.

'Hey,' says Doormat full of sudden excitement, 'maybe they're Ruskies.'

'Nit!' says he without earlobes. 'They're not bloody Ruskies. Ruskies are big. Heavy. With fat noses.'

'Fat noses!' says Doormat. 'Where'd you hear that rubbish?'

'They have, I'm telling you. Them's not Ruskies.'

'They're cuddly enough though, eh?' says Girl's Head. 'D'you think they're Eyeties? Supposed to be great lovers, Eyeties are.'

'Don't think so,' says Carrot Top. 'Eyeties put an *a* and an *o* on the end of everything and pinch your bottom. They haven't done none of that.' (So much for education.)

'Youa speaka da Italiano?' says Monkey Boy twisting his hands elaborately in the air.

'Op?' says Barry.

'Well anyway,' says Girl's Head, 'I think they're cute.'

'Wert quiop,' says Barry. 'It rop we qui?'

'Where . . . ?' says Girl's Head indicating Southend with a sweep of her arm . . . 'You . . . ?' she points at Barry, taking the chance to rub her finger down his face and chest . . . 'From?'

'Ah!' says Barry as if light is dawning. 'Ert Olym Pia.'

'O-lim Peer?' says Girl's Head screwing up her face.

'Qui!' says Barry.

'Where the hell's that?' says Doormat.

'You wouldn't know,' says Earlobes. 'You don't even know where your own house is.'

Doormat thumps Earlobes brutally in the kidney. Earlobes guffaws, whether from disdain or pain I have no time to discover.

'Well, wherever it is,' says Girl's Head, 'I like them. They're nice enough to keep.'

'Here,' says Carrot Top, 'why don't we show them a bit of Southend, eh?'

'Take them a ride in the Kursaal,' says Monkey Boy.

'Yeah,' says Girl's Head stepping between Barry and me and commandeering Barry's arm. 'That's a good idea. Bags I this one.'

Help, no! I am screaming inside my head.

'Let's go,' says Monolith.

33/We are pressganged by camaraderie into the Kursaal, Barry erting and qwerting, ropping and opping, myself as silent as a display dummy and very nearly as stiff from fright. We are backslapped and play-punched, flirted with and teased; reasons are found for kissing us, hugging and gripping us.

At the entrance, the whole gusty party gathers again. We are swept along, taking the Kursaal's fun-fair by noisy rough-house storm. Less mob-handed Friday evening pleasure-seekers scatter like nervous sparrows from our parading bike-booted feet. Attendants yell distant warnings. Fathers and mothers, snatching aside their goggling children, glare and mutter dark imprecations and sometimes bandy words against a chorus of derision and backchat. Beer cans pass from hand to hand; footballed away when empty. Monkey Boy scampers about ahead, leading the pack, excited as a hyper-thyroid ten-year-old.

The roller-coasting Big Dipper, the Dodgems, the Octopus, assorted carousels and side-shows. We do them all in a kind of rowdy military operation before a different kind of military arrives. We pay for nothing, but take what we want and jeer at requests polite or rude for payment. We are cock of the walk, dive and run and jump and skid and turn turtle and have an all-round explosive good time. Monkey Boy, on the spinning Octopus, lights firework flares and fizzing crackers and hurls them into the watching crowd as if he were playing ducks-and-drakes on a pond of faces. The crowds scatter, which pleases him best of all; he whoops and yodels and bellows his satisfaction.

It is shortly afterwards that the other kind of military arrives.

'The filth!' shouts Monkey Boy. He sounds as if he has just caught sight of an indulgent favourite uncle.

There approach all of four Boys-in-Blue armed to the teeth with bare hands and flat caps and rolled up shirt-sleeves. But they might as well have been an invasion force equipped with deathray guns or a battalion from the S.A.S. For at the sight of them our biker pals peel off in all directions at double pelt.

The cavalry to the rescue, I think; escape is nigh.

But no. Faithful to the last, Doormat, Earlobes, Girl's Head and Monolith close ranks around Barry and myself and, with Carrot Top and Monkey Boy dancing rear-guard attendance, they tug, push, nudge and scamper us away, out of the Kursaal, and tow us jubilantly pierwards along the bustling Golden Mile.

And so we process, celebratory, passing Dizzyland Children's Playground (EAR PIERCING £2.50), The Forester's Arms (Lunchtime Strippers), Happidrome, Las Vegas Amusements loud with thumping pop, The Falcon, Kentucky Fair, Ocean Fish Restaurant loud with frying fat and generous with vinegar, on by The Hope Hotel by when I feel we have lost all hope, Coney Island Leisure Centre, Monte Carlo Bingo, Garden Discount House (Closed), The Beachcomber, Harbour Lights Leisure Centre where leisure means hustle, and on beyond Louis Manzi Presents Talk of the South, Tots, The Mississippi, the Papillon (Southend's Victorian Public House), Rose restaurant where Rose wouldn't, Liberty Bell (Take Courage—and we need it, for we are almost breathless now), Clark's Quality Fish Restaurant as loud and as generous as the Ocean, to Marine Sale Rooms and Olympia Entertainment Centre (Prize Bingo), where we scurry across the road, dodging with disdain the hooting cars, onto Western Esplanade, to the pierhead, where we collapse in a panting line along the protective rail in front of the window of the white-painted crenellated Waxworks Including Chamber of Horrors. We stare, gasping, at a perpetually horrified man being perpetually chopped in half by a perpetually swinging pendulum axe, and there enjoy hunter hunted gulps of laughter in which neither Barry nor I can help joining.

'You not careful,' Doormat says to Earlobes, indicating the perpetual waxwork horror, 'that's where you'll end up.'

'And you'll do the chopping,' says Monkey Boy.

'Wouldn't mind,' says Doormat. 'Bit of fun, eh?'

34/ACTION REPLAY

The fun-fair. The anonymity of numbers. The hardboy bully-boy fun. The gags and catcalls and rowdy rabbit. The rough guy, matey body-talk. The cockiness insured by belligerent numbers. The prickling excitement of engineered disapproval. The dangerous satisfaction of stirring up the law.

I feel it all and know it all as it is happening.

And know why these gangboys do it. Their way out. Their way in. Their can of magic beans. Their togetherness. That they wouldn't dare speak or show anyway else. Which, as we gaggle there, I feel the sadness of.

There is an easily contracted infection in such mind-losing thrills. And I am speechless of necessity. One word and I'm done for. Thus trapped, there is no escape.

35/A geriatric gorilla emerges from the waxworks door marked WAY IN.

'Hoy,' he says, addressing our gaggle, 'we got enough horrors inside for people to see. Don't want you lot cluttering up the window giving a free show out here. Piss off. Go on—play somewhere else.'

'Hark at grandad,' says Girl's Head. 'How rude!'

Questions of a rhetorical nature shower upon the custodian's balding head. Viz.: Has he looked in the mirror lately, Monkey Boy wants to know. Earlobes inquires whether the old fruit would like he, Earlobes himself, to stuff him and stand him among the dummies in the window. 'Do you always wax so eloquent?' asks Carrot Top exhibiting a flash of wit he has so far kept hidden from us all. Monolith offers only a hand and arm in a signal advising the old man of what contortions he might practise on himself.

But we move off, huffling discontents about holiday places that do not want visitors to have even a mite of fun.

36/That's when I see Spike.

Correction: That's when Spike sees me.

(Remember Spike? Good old happy-go-lucky flesh-sexy Spike, owner of *Tumble*?)

Correction to correction: That's when, in the backward-stumbling retreat from Fort Waxworks, I bump right into Spike, literally falling into his arms.

There are occasions when I would not object to finding myself in that position. This, however, was definitely not one of them.

'Watch it!' Spike says, crisply shoving me away.

Seeing him, my nerves fail me. But seeing who he is manhandling, Spike becomes his normal generous self at once.

'Hey, Hal!' he says. 'Where you going, kid? There's a party over at Bill Hazel's. Want to come?'

I reply in hiccups.

The tribe closes in, looking suddenly bigger, bruisier, more numerous than hitherto.

'You know him?' says Monolith in his gravel voice, addressing Spike over my head.

Hiccup I say.

'What's it to you?' says Spike.

'Now look . . . ' says Barry boxed in next to me.

Hiccup I say.

'The bleeders can talk English!' says Earlobes. 'I knew there was something funny.'

'Just hang on,' says Barry, 'and I'll explain.'

'Aren't you foreign at all?' says Girl's Head as much in disappointment as in anger. 'Not even Welsh?'

Hiccup I say.

'Look, it was just a joke,' says Barry.

'Who's laughing?' says Monolith.

'Markem,' says Monkey Boy with relish. 'Go on, givem one.'

'Shut it,' says Monolith.

Hiccup I say.

'A friend are you?' says Monolith with scornful implications on 'friend'.

'Yeah,' Spike says and nods at me, 'of him. What about it?'

Hiccup.

135

'Reckons hisself, by the looks,' says Carrot Top.

'Fancy your chances?' says Monolith pushing me aside and smiling for the first time since I have been entertained by his company.

Barry says, 'He's got nothing to do with it . . . '

'I'm talking to the man not the mouse,' says Monolith not taking his eyes off Spike.

Hic I say. 'Why don't you *hic* Bill's party, Spike?'

Spike shrugs. 'No sweat. I'll see you all right first.'

'Does fancy his chances,' says Monolith.

'Depends what you got in mind,' says Spike.

Monolith hitches his shoulders. 'Nothing gross,' he says. 'You being so small and young and on your own.'

This is greeted with jeering cheers from the surrounding braves.

'You could have a try, I suppose,' Spike says.

Monolith snorts. 'Who you kidding, kid?'

Spike says, 'This kid is kidding nobody, kid.'

'Oooo—lissen him!' Carrot Top yelps.

Hic I say, thinking: That's torn it! No hope now.

'What d'you prefer?' Monolith says. 'Your poncy head crunched or your arm broke?'

'Give him both just for luck,' Monkey Boy says.

'Crack his peanuts for him as well,' says Girl's Head. There is no doubting she means it.

37/At this point, I am sorry to relate, I am not exactly sure what happened next. Girl's Head's suggestion suddenly made me very conscious of an urgent need to micturate, brought on no doubt as much by the prospect of her desire being acted upon as by the tensions of the last few minutes. And this distracted me. At any rate, piecing things together from what Barry and Spike each told me afterwards, what really happened goes something like this:

Barry decides to intervene. He steps between Monolith and Spike. (I have since wondered whether this was an act of sacrificial courage, or was motivated by pique at being ignored as hero of the month by both Monolith and Spike.)

The next thing I know, B. is crumpling to the ground. He later explained that he tripped over someone's boot—he thought Doormat's—deliberately placed in his path.

Spike, however, claims that Monolith let loose a short arm jab to Barry's gut and thus felled him.

Barry said that, if this was what happened, he couldn't remember the blow. Or, rather, he was kicked and stood on so much during the ensuing melee that he could never then or after sort out the cause of each individual pain.

Whatever, down goes Barry. Instinctively, I dive to help him. I understand from Spike that at this same instant Monolith launches a blow in the general direction of Spike's solar plexus. But before his fist can reach its goal, it connects instead with my descending head, smashing into my left cheek, nose and mouth.

The force of this (not to mention my reaction to it) spins me round, knocking me off balance, and sending my hands to my face in protective shock (and, no doubt, in an effort to ascertain whether my head is still on my shoulders and in one piece. It felt disgorged).

Twisting in a half-bent posture, my head rams into Girl's Head's lower abdomen.

Girl's Head doubles up, screaming. This means she falls over my stooping body so that she is lying half across my back, trapping my head under her, and pinning me down. To save herself, she grabs at whatever is in reach and finds my particulars.

Thinking Girl's Head is intent on carrying out her aforementioned desire to crack somebody's peanuts, I unbend with such self-protective force that:

Girl's Head is catapulted upwards, through the air, and plummets down between Monolith and Spike, having performed, Spike said, a somersault of quite elegant perfection.

Sadly for Girl's Head, Monolith is at this precise moment taking yet another swing, this time in the general direction of Spike's chin. Spike is stepping back for a second time. Girl's Head comes diving down between them. Monolith's oliver connects with snappy crispness against Girl's Head's protesting mouth, shutting up it and her with instant effect.

Girl's Head slumps onto Barry, who is just managing to struggle to his hands and knees. He collapses to the ground again under the weight of the now unconscious girl.

By this time I have stumbled to the ground, having thrown myself off balance when acting as Girl's Head's launch pad. I find myself lying on my backside in the gutter, from which drain's eye view I observe further progress.

Seeing the knockout assault on Girl's Head by their leader, Earlobes and Doormat both let out a noise of the kind I imagine is made by moose in rut, and charge to her rescue. So intent is each on the object of his passion that neither sees the other coming.

They meet in head-on collision above Girl's Head's supine body. There is a crack of mallet on block, of stick on puck. Doormat and Earlobes rebound, hands to heads, letting out cursing howls of pain and anger.

But Monolith moves too now. He has gazed in astonishment at his recumbent Girl's Head for the time it has taken Doormat and Earlobes to put their heads together.

Their intrusion on his gaze reactivates him. And apparently angers him further as well. After all, Girl's Head is his girl. Yet here are Doormat and Earlobes plunging to her aid with all the ardour of gallant suitors, each thus revealing, I guess, a so-far wisely concealed dedication to her charms. Eyes blazing now with a fuelling of anger, distress, frustration, and failure, Monolith grabs Doormat and Earlobes by their hair and hurls them violently aside.

Doormat goes scudding into Monkey Boy, knocking his feet from under him. Each clutches at the other to save himself but they succeed only in bringing themselves crunching to the pavement at which each vents his annoyance by yelling and punching at the other. Meanwhile, Earlobes careens into Carrot Top with such force that he takes Carrot Top with him over the railings that line the pavement as protection against pedestrians falling into the children's go-kart track fifteen feet below. They disappear from view emitting hollow cries.

Monolith, with fists clenched and body straining in every seam, lets out a mighty bellow:

'ICE CREAM!'

There is some dispute later about what Monolith actually did shout. I have always thought he was really calling 'Irene', which I take to be Girl's Head's given name. Barry, who it has to be conceded heard the noise from beneath the muffling blanket of Girl's Head's leather-jacketed chest, thought Monolith had decided we'd all had enough of this game and was hailing a passing ice cream van from which to purchase refreshment. Spike, however, contends that Monolith was uttering some sort of East End war cry before launching a final fierce attack upon him. As he could see no further impediment to Monolith succeeding, Spike decided he had better do something about it and so launched his own counter-attack instead of taking further evasive action.

Whatever Monolith actually meant, what happened was that Spike steps forward with smooth efficiency and delivers a pile-driver to Monolith's nose, followed by a teeth-clamping uppercut to the chin.

Give him the old one two . . . I said the old one two . . .

Monolith stumbles backwards, a look of disbelief on his face and blood erupting from his snout. Shudders. Then slumps earthwards. Poleaxed.

38/By the way, I think I should mention that all of this (I mean all of Bit 37) took no more than ten seconds, which only goes to show how much faster real life can happen than reading about it (or, worse still, writing about it: Bit 37 took all morning to do). Also I should record as a matter of interest that while we were enjoying our little Bit of Bovver:

+ my mother and father were watching The Friday Film on TV which, that night, was *Butch Cassidy and the Sundance Kid*. They had seen it four times before. My father slept through a lot of it and woke up for the gun fights. My mother looked at her magazine during those parts and would have preferred to watch something else altogether;

+ Mrs Gorman was reading *Miss Pinkerton Came to Die*—a book I have never heard of before or since—and looked through the family photograph album between chapters, when she also drank coffee: six cups in two hours;

+ Kari was dancing in a disco with a bloke she had met (who had picked her up?) on the beach that evening after I had left her. His English wasn't dazzling but he looked *rather* sweet so she took a chance. As it turned out he smelt strongly of nicotine so she ditched him later and wandered home alone (she said);

+ the rest of Monolith's bikers were doing their best to get drunk in the Forester's Arms while waiting for the strip show to start. It never did because it only took place on Saturdays at lunchtime, which fact they would have known had they read the poster outside the pub more carefully. They ended up causing a fracas and being turned out, from where they worked off their pent-up emotions by having a punch-up on the beach with the Benfleet mob. The police wagon eventually carted off those too drunk or too mashed to scat when the B.s-in-B. arrived.

What a happy, busy world we live in.

39/Spike hauled me to my feet. Barry struggled from beneath Girl's Head. The three of us crossed the road, leaving Monolith and Co. to the gathering crowd.

'You two okay?' Spike said. 'No harm done, eh?'

Barry said, 'Nothing a good plastic surgeon can't put right.'

I said, 'Like replacing a face.' I could hardly bear to touch my left cheek; my nose felt like it was the size of a Christmas balloon; my top lip was swollen and split. Both my nose and my lip were bleeding enough to keep me swallowing in the way that makes you feel you'll either choke any second or fill up and drown. Need I add, someone was blasting for rock inside my head.

'You look a bit sorry,' Spike said, inspecting me closely. 'But everybody does in this light.' He meant under the sodium neons of the street lamps. I hadn't noticed till then that dusk had given way to dark.

'What time is it?' I said, dabbing with my handkerchief at my mouth and nose, wincing.

'Half eleven,' Spike said, consulting his wrist watch. 'Bill's party should be going nicely. What about it?'

I shook my head, and wished I hadn't. The movement caused nuclear fission.

'I'd better get him home and clean him up,' Barry said.

'Please yourselves,' Spike said. 'See you.' He walked off townwards.

'Hey, Spike,' I called after him. He turned. 'Thanks, mate.'

'For you,' he said, smiling, 'any time.' He waved and walked on.

Barry and I took the shortest way to his place. We decided to abandon his bike to its fate for the night. (The next day B. went to fetch it and there it was, just where we had left it. They'd been kind enough to restrict their revenge to slashing the tyres, busting the headlamp, and breaking his rearview mirror. But they'd left the helmets dangling from the handlebars. Nothing, those lads, if not honest.)

Luckily, Mrs Gorman was tucked safely in bed and wide to the world under the influence of her nightly sleeping pill when we arrived.

40/We stripped in the palace of mirrors. Tenderly inspected each other's wounds. My swollen face and cut lip. Barry's bruises on his sides and thighs and grazes on his hands and knees from grit on the pavement. Nothing worse.

And no other excuse needed for touching and holding and caressing the contours of our bodies for the first time.

We showered. I cleaned up his grazes with swabs. He patched my lip.

Lightheaded now, high on the smack of adventure and

finding each other, and knowing, we ate, drank beer, lay on the bed in his room, chewing over our evening.

'And what was all that qwerty stuff?' I said.

'Typewriter talk, you goof!'

'Typewriter talk?'

'Q–W–E–R–T–Y–U–I–O–P–question-mark. The top row of letters on a typewriter.'

'You're crackers, you know that! We're about to be taken apart by a gang of bikers and you remember the letters on a typewriter!'

'Dad used to play a game with me. We called it Gormandising. Any time we were bored or, you know, feeling skittish, we'd talk to each other in invented language. Mine was Olympian.'

'Olympian?'

'After my typewriter. An Olympia.'

'Olim Peer! God, their faces! It was all Greek to me as well! I guessed you had funny tastes.'

'Including you,' he said.

And gave me a present from Southend.

Wish you were here?

41/'Stay,' Barry said. 'You might as well now.'

I looked at my watch. Two-thirty.

'I can't,' I said, getting out of bed. 'My mother will worry herself sick. And there'll be hell to pay for being out so late.'

'Then stay tomorrow. You can warn them.'

'You mean today! Okay, but you'll be the death of me,' I said.

I was reaching for my clothes. He came to me naked still and serious as the night.

'You're always talking about death.' He put his arms round my waist, stopping me from dressing. 'Does death bother you so much?'

'No.'

'Then why keep mentioning it?'

'Because it interests me. Doesn't it you?'

'Not much.'

'What about your father?'

'What upsets me is not having him around any more. To be with, I mean. I loved him. Naturally I miss him.'

'There you are then.'

'You've missed the point, stupid.' He kissed me. 'What I'm talking about is me. Being alive and not having my father around. That's all that ever really upsets anybody about death. Not having somebody they want any more. But what bothers you is the *idea* of death. Right?'

'I guess so.'

I broke away; started dressing. He lay on the bed and watched.

'What about the people who are dead?' I said. 'What about your dad?'

'What about him? If dead means finis—nothing— what does he care? If it means anything else . . . Well, I'll tell you: if it means anything else my father will be in there organizing himself a part of it.'

I finished dressing, waited for the moment to be right for leaving. *Correction*: Waited while I tried to make myself leave. I wanted to stay. Who wants to give up the can of magic beans when you've only just found it, even for a second?

'You know what you should do about death?' he said.

I shook my head, not thinking about death anyway.

'Laugh at it.' He raised his eyebrows asking: What do you think of that?

'All right for us to say now,' I said. 'We aren't exactly on the point of death, are we?'

'Look,' he said coming to me from the bed and smiling that dangerous smile. 'I'll make a deal with you.'

'Okay,' I said. 'I'll chance anything once.'

'Whichever of us dies first, the other promises to dance on his grave.' The raised eyebrows again.

I laughed and walked towards the door.

'I've told you before,' I said. 'You're crackers.'

'You think I'm joking, don't you?' he said.

I turned to face him. He was standing in the middle of the room.

'No,' I said. 'You're just crazy.'

He came to me. Flicked at my hair with his fingers.

'We've got to do something about that hair.'

'Like what?' I said, handing him my comb.

'Not sure. I'll have a go at it tomorrow.'

He finished sorting me out, stood back a pace and looked me over, head to feet. Smiled. Proprietorial.

Then he suddenly held out his hand to be shaken. I took it, not knowing why.

His grip tightened so that I could not easily pull away.

'Promise,' he said.

'You mean—' I said.

'If I die first you dance on my grave.'

'Look, Bee,' I said, 'don't be daft, eh?'

'I'm serious. Promise.'

'You'll live to be eighty.'

'Don't raise difficulties.'

We laughed.

'But—' I said when he still did not let go, instead adding his left hand to the grip of his right.

'But me no buts. Just promise.'

'Why?'

'For me.'

I looked at him, wakened out of the mindlessness of the last two hours.

'I'm tired, love. Let me go.'

'No. Promise. Is it so hard?'

'No—'

'What then?'

'I don't know. I don't understand, that's all. It doesn't make sense.'

'Maybe that's why I want you to promise. Because you don't understand. Because you always have to understand. Don't you? That's what you always want, isn't it? To understand. But some things you can't. Can you? Never. So promise. For me.'

There seemed no point in arguing any more. This was something he wanted from me; why say no? He'd just given me something I'd been wanting, hadn't he? Now he wanted a ridiculous oath. A promise it was pretty unlikely I'd ever have to keep. So there he was, the boy with the can of magic beans wanting me to swear an oath. At that moment there was nothing I wouldn't have done for him.

'I promise,' I said. 'For you and for no other reason.'

And it was a split lip on a bruised mouth that sealed the oath, not cut hands in never-never land.

PART THREE

Death is the greatest kick of all.
That's why they save it till last.

Graffito

1/From beginning to end was seven weeks.

Forty-nine days from me being soaked in seaweed to him being dead. He becoming It.

One thousand one hundred and seventy-six hours.

Seventy thousand five hundred and sixty minutes.

Four million two hundred and thirty-three thousand six hundred seconds.

And all that time, and a lot of the time since, I wondered: Why Barry? Why him and not, say, Spike? It can't have just been that I liked the look of him; it can't only have been physical; not sex alone. Can it? Was it? It might as well have been Spike if that was all there was to it.

Maybe I loved him. I thought I did. As much as I knew what the word means.

How do you ever know? I used to think I would know when it happened. Know immediately, without having to wonder about it.

But all I knew for certain was that I couldn't get enough of him. I wanted to be with him all the time. And yet when I was with him that wasn't enough either. I wanted to look at him and touch him and have him touch me and hear him talk and tell him things and do things together with him. All the time. Day and night. For 4,233,600 seconds.

A for instance: He would leave me alone in the shop. I'd wait on edge for him to come back. Customers must have thought I had some sort of convulsive twitch because my head and eyes would keep darting towards the door every few seconds. But they couldn't have been mistaken about what was going on when Mister Wonderful hove into view again, because then I went to pieces. Lost my grip entirely on what I was supposed to be doing and had eyes for nothing but him till I got used to him being there again.

Sounds like a pet dog. And I knew what was happening to me even while it was happening.

At first I tried to stop myself. But I couldn't. It was a compulsion, an obsession. Irresistible. After a while I gave up caring how I behaved or who thought what about me. Trying to hide how I felt was too much strain, and I wasn't succeeding anyway. I was just making a fool of myself. So I let it show, let it happen. I felt easier straightaway. More natural. More in charge of myself. If that was the way I was, I told myself, why pretend anything different?

We never discussed any of this. All the time we talked. But never about this part of us. I knew anyway what Barry would say: 'That's the way I feel, so that's the way I am. End of story.'

Now, I keep going over and over in my mind everything that happened. Everything we said. And did. Every detail. Every little bit. Trying to fit the little bits into one Big Bit. Into one whole that makes some kind of sense. Some kind of meaning. A Meaning. Capital M. Something that explains him to me, me to myself. Explains what it was all about.

These Bits coming now are some of the Bits from the good times. From the Monday after we got together, with me working in the shop and us spending every evening together and most nights as well, to the Friday it came to an end.

2/After the first week I stayed with Barry every Saturday night and most week nights.

'Your mother,' I said, the first time.

'What?'

'Don't you mind?'

'You're a long time dead.'

'What about her?'

'She's very good at knowing only what she wants to know. And medical science helps her blot out what she might not be able to help knowing. She's taken sleeping pills since Dad died.'

But she had to have known. How could she not? Which is why I can't understand the way she went on in court. Saying I'd led Barry astray, made him act wildly . . . all that. She has to be crazy.

3/'Like a plate of ham?' Barry said one night.

'Thought you was a ten-to-two, squire.'

'Don't mess about.'

I hadn't a clue what he meant, so 'Help yourself,' I said, and he gave me a present from Southend of a kind I hadn't had before. He gave me a lot of those: new experiences. One of the things that was exciting about him. I never knew what was going to happen next.

I enjoyed this one, after the surprise had worn off.

4/One morning I woke just after dawn. I liked waking early with him. They were the nicest times. Quiet. Warm. The early morning sounds outside. The drift of sleep. Him. Looking at him. He slept like he did everything else. Flat out.

That morning he was already awake, and looking at me.

He kissed me, said:

'Lay your sleeping head, my love,
Human on my faithless arm;
Time and fevers burn away
Individual beauty from
Thoughtful children, and the grave
Proves the child ephemeral:
But in my arms till break of day
Let the living creatures lie,
Mortal, guilty, but to me
The entirely beautiful.'

I said, meaning thank you, 'A poet and he doesn't know it.'

'So much for your budding genius,' he said, laughing. 'The lines are Auden's. Mr W. H. by strange coincidence.'

'What coincidence?'

'Cor, Ozzy's got his work cut out with you! Shakespeare.'

'What about him?'

'Dear, dear! The ignorance!'

I smiled at the condescension and looked smug. 'Can't have everything, can I? Not when I'm young and beautiful as well.'

'Shakespeare dedicated his sonnets to Mr W. H., widely thought to have been his boyfriend.'

'Ah, I see!' Light dawning. 'Wouldn't have thought you'd go much on the guilt, though ... "Mortal, guilty ..." whatever.'

'No,' he said. 'Nor did Auden, I guess. But times have changed since he wrote that.'

'When?'

'I dunno. Nineteen thirties I think.'

'How do you know it anyway?'

'You aren't the only one Ozzy ever asked into his Sixth.'

I lifted my head, surprised, to face him. 'You too?'

He nodded.

'So that means you were in his English Sixth when you left?'

'He wasn't very happy about me going either. I did have a certain flair.'

'Bighead. But how come?'

'Told you. He's a fanatic. I'm sure he really does think Eng. lit. is more important than anything else. I told him I was leaving. He said I was betraying a talent, selling out to Mammon, giving in to a possessive mother. Didn't mince his words.'

'But you explained? I mean about the shop—how you feel about it. Surely he understood?'

'Did you?'

'Not at first. Now I do. After working with you.'

'So I should employ Ozzy?'

'Hey, that would be a laugh.'

'A laugh it might be to you. Customers might not see the joke.'

'He'd refuse to sell them stuff he didn't approve of.'

'One thing you're going to learn, mate, is that Mr O. is human. And, dearest chuck, can be wrong.'

I let that go. We were too cosy to argue. I brooded instead on what it must have meant to Barry to drop out of the English Sixth. Looking round his room at the books, the pictures, the stacked music, the whole feeling of the place—why I liked it so much—I knew it had to have mattered.

After a while I said, 'You still mind?'

He drew in a breath. 'About Ozzy or about giving up Eng. lit.?'

'Both.'

He took his arm away, stretched on his back, hands behind his head.

'Both,' he said.

There was bitterness in his voice.
We never talked about that subject again.

5/One morning in the third week when Barry wasn't there
and the shop was empty, Mrs Gorman, doing the accounts, said, 'My Bubby hasn't been so happy since
before his poor father died.'

'That's great,' I said.

This was the first time she had said anything about
Barry and me getting together. At the beginning she
treated me like a favourite visitor. I was pampered and
overwhelmed with attention. Then suddenly, as if she
had made a conscious decision about it, she started treat-
ing me like one of her family; I'd be asked for my washing, given chores to do, ticked off if I crossed her. But
never mentioning what she must have known: that B. and
I were sleeping together. I thought she was going to say
something about that and I didn't know what to say if she
did.

'After his father died,' she went on, 'he was miserable.
Went a little wild, poor boy. Out all hours. And with—
well, not nice people sometimes. Not good for him. Worried me sick, Hal. I don't mind telling you; you'll understand, I know. But now he's so happy again. Properly
happy. Do you know? His old self again.'

Pleased, embarrassed (why?) I picked up some disc
sleeves from the counter and put them on the display
rack.

'You are so *good* for each other,' Mrs Gorman said
when I was behind the counter again. 'Maybe *together*
you could make the business better, eh?'

'How d'you mean, Mrs Gorman?'

She put down her pen, turned me by the shoulder to face her. 'I've been thinking. Why don't you work here full-time? It's a good job, good pay. Maybe in a couple of years, when you're older, know the ropes, who knows?—we would open another shop. Have two. One down there in the precinct in Southend, where the trippers go. You could manage one. Or maybe we move to bigger premises in the best spot in town. Mr Gorman always wanted a place there. You and my Bubby together, you could do it beautiful. What d'you think?'

I didn't know what I thought, only that it meant more of Barry.

'I don't know,' I said; then, after a silence because it was the only thing in my head that I could actually say, 'Is that what Barry wants?'

Mrs Gorman raised her eyebrows, shrugged. 'He hasn't said in so many words. But—I know my Bubby. He's *thinking* about it, you bet, my darling. You too, why don't you think about it?'

'I'll think about it,' I said.

6/This morning I reckoned up that during our seven weeks together we:

+ Sailed *Calypso* twelve times, once as far as the Kent coast, where we slept out in the boat for the night and sailed home the next day.

+ Read eight books.

+ Saw four films, including the one on our first evening together.

+ Ate one hundred and nineteen meals together: twenty-three breakfasts, forty-four lunches, thirty-one suppers, nine picnics, and two middle-of-the-night snacks in bed.

+ Motorbiked eight hundred miles approx., mostly just

mucking about, but one Sunday going as far as Norwich for the day.

+ Slept together twenty-three times literally and fifty-five times, one way and another, euphemistically.

+ Went by train to London to see a show (cf. Bit 11 following) and poked about the crap and con of puky Piccadilly.

+ Listened to hundreds of hours of music (because of the shop).

+ Wrote each other five letters. He to me, three; me to him, two.

+ Stayed up all night four times because we were talking so hard and didn't want to stop. (To be exact, we went to bed about five o'clock in the morning each time, but it was dawn by then.)

+ Bought each other six presents—one each week. The present I gave him the seventh week was death.

7/Busy busy listed like that. But at the time, time seemed timeless. Except time apart, which seemed endless. So long as we were together time did not matter; what we did did not matter. We did things to do them together; nothing had to be done. There was only one imperative: the two of us together.

I thought.

8/'What frightens you?' he asked at the end of one of our all-talking nights.

Without hesitation, thinking I meant a joke, I said, 'You!' And then knew I really felt it.

He was silent. I, too, waiting, having taken myself aback.

Finally, he nodded, smiled, said, 'I frighten myself.'

9/His present to me the second week was a black sweat-shirt.

'Why do you always wear the same few things?' he said. 'Is it money?'

'Not just.'

'What else?'

'I can never decide what I'd like to wear. I never know what's right for me. I don't know why. I see things in shops and I think, They look good and I try them on and they don't seem right.'

'Easy,' he said. 'I know just the gear that would suit you. We'll kit you out.'

We did. I still didn't feel right. But I wore them because he liked them.

The other day I took all that gear into the back garden and put it into the incinerator and burnt it. I stood there and watched till it was burnt to ashes.

10/I was going to write pages more about those seven weeks. I wanted you to understand what we were like together. What Barry was like. Like *to me*: how I saw him, knew him, thought of him.

But this morning I got up and read everything I have written so far, and particularly what I wrote yesterday (all the Bits in Part Three up to this one) and I knew straightaway: It can't be done. The words are not right. They just ARE NOT RIGHT. They won't say what I want them to say. They tell lies. They hide the truth. I read the words and I can feel—FEEL—what they should be

157

saying and they aren't. The meaning is hidden behind them. They are like bricks. They make a wall. A wall hiding from view what's happening behind. You can hear muffled noises coming through but you can't quite, never *quite*, make sense of them. They might be coming from someone being murdered, or from a child playing, or from a couple making love, or from someone playing a game trying to trick you into believing something is happening that isn't really.

I almost tore everything up, all these pages. I've sat for an hour, telling myself I am an idiot.

And then I thought: What it all comes down to is this: I do not understand myself. That is why the words don't say what I want them to say.

But there you are again. What did I just say! Look at that sentence: *I do not understand myself.* Does it mean: I do not understand *about* myself . . . ? Or does it mean: I do not myself understand about Barry . . . ?

Actually, when I put it like this I see both meanings are true. But I meant the second. You wouldn't have known though if I hadn't explained. Not for *certain*. The words just are never *right*.

So I'll start again.

When it comes down to it, I do not understand Barry, or about Barry, or about myself, or myself.

So how can I make *you* understand? I thought at first that if I wrote it all down as it had happened, telling as much of it as I could, I myself might get to understand, as well as explaining. But it isn't working. I can't get enough of it down. There is always more. And what is written doesn't ever tell enough, doesn't really explain anything, not anything at all. And so the longer I go on the harder it becomes to understand anything.

A few days ago while I was sitting here trying to fight not-understanding, I suddenly realized I couldn't see

Barry's face in my head any more. After only this short time, a few weeks, I can't see him in my head. I can *feel* what he looks like—isn't that strange?—but I can't picture him. He comes faintly, in flashes, right at the back of my head, and then is gone again before I can look at him properly. Like a camera shutter opening too fast for the film to record the image. There's only a faint blur. A ghost that just didn't materialize.

It wouldn't be so bad if I had a photograph of him. But we never took any of each other; never thought of needing them. We were always together so why bother?

I just went off to Mrs Gorman's house. I thought— hoped—maybe she would have calmed down by now. Might see me again. Talk to me. Let me try and explain. I was going to ask her for a photograph. But she wouldn't answer the door to me. Just shouted from inside. I told her what I wanted. She nearly went hysterical. Yelled and stormed. She isn't any calmer. She's just like she was when it happened that day. So I came away.

11/Which reminds me, I wanted to tell you—though it doesn't matter now anyway—about when we went to London that once to see a show. The show we saw was *Hamlet* at the National Theatre. When we came out a woman just ahead of us burst into tears. Her friend fussed around her, embarrassed, and some people coming out of the theatre saw and laughed. Barry went up to her and said, 'Are you okay? Can I do anything?' And the woman looked at him, tears streaming down her face, and she smiled and shrugged her shoulders and shook her head and said, 'No, no. It's just the play. Just the play.'

We left her to her friend who we could see didn't

understand and walked from the theatre across Waterloo Bridge towards the West End. We were both silent. Half way across the bridge Barry said, not looking at me, 'The remembering is what is so hard.'

I couldn't think what he meant so I said nothing. A little further on he said, glancing at me this time, knowing I was confused, 'The trouble with Hamlet. His father's ghost telling him, "Remember me". He can't, you see. That's why he feels so guilty. Why he wears his father's picture round his neck: to remind him. Why he forces his mother to look at it. He says his mother has forgotten his father. But he's talking about himself really. It's his own guilt that's driving him mad, not his mother shacking up with his uncle.'

We turned into the Strand, going towards Trafalgar Square.

'That's why that woman was crying just now, I think,' he said. 'She knew. You can't remember and you think you should. I mean, you remember in one way. But you can't recall the face, and the remembering doesn't upset you any more and you feel guilty.'

Of course I knew by this time he was talking about himself and his father. I didn't know what to say.

He looked at me and smiled, putting on the normal, everyday Barry. 'Remember me!' he said, sending up that evening's ghost voice in the play. But I knew he meant it too, was saying it to me. 'Swear!' he said, being Hamlet's father's ghost still.

I laughed, trying to pass it off as the joke he was trying to pretend it was. But I knew he was thinking of our oath—that daft, nonsense-night oath I had not taken seriously then and still did not now, even though I felt him meaning it and was frightened by that. He did frighten me sometimes; I had found out a truth when I told him so. I didn't know what frightened me, except that every time it happened I felt at the same time he was wanting too much from me. Wasn't waiting to be given, but was taking. And I always felt at those times that he never got what he was looking for. That I was a disappointment then.

I can't go on. I feel terrible. A headache is squeezing my eyes between my temples like a coconut in a vice. I want to be sick. I'm going to the lav.

12/I was so bad yesterday afternoon I had to go to bed.

I've had the same trouble before. Three or four times since Barry died. A crushing headache with a sharp slicing pain inside. My eyes go mushy and I can't bear bright light. I vomit: biley ugly sick. I feel poleaxed, cold, fragile, battered. My nerves jangle; I can feel them twanging. In the end I get so bad I have to lie down under piles of bedclothes and with the curtains drawn across the windows.

My mother calls it migraine. Maybe it is. But I know what I call it. Fright. Funk. Shame. Guilt. Locked-up anger trying to get out. Self-pity.

All of those. All in one. A disaster area.

I look in the mirror and hate myself. For being stupid and weak.

Before the ache starts, I can't feel anything. Nothing about anything, anyone.

Afterwards, I can't feel anything again. I pretend I can. Behave as if I can. But I can't. Nothing.

Ever since Barry's death I've been like that. Then it all bursts out, like pus. I feel everything in a kind of fit. Then all that feeling gets tangled up inside me and boils over and gives me this headache that's like a pressure cooker about to burst. In the end it sicks itself out, a volcanic eruption of misery.

I told you, right at the beginning I told you: I am mad. I must be. What other explanation is there?

13/You know why I got ill yesterday? I thought about it during the night after the headache subsided and the sicking stopped. I always calm down then, just for an hour or two. Relax. Am drained but relieved it is all over. I can think straight again. Well—almost straight.

I decided the reason I got ill yesterday was that I knew I would soon have to write about Barry's death. I realized I have been trying to put it off all this time because I couldn't face having to set it down in words. For someone else to read about.

As soon as I decided this I decided something else also. It is no use putting off writing about Barry's death any longer. The sooner it is all down the better. Sick the words onto the page and then sicking my guts into the pan will stop.

14/So that's it. All these experiences, and squads of them I haven't told you about. We shared them. He-Me. He-in-Me. Me-in-Him. We.

Do experiences build up in you like money saved in a bank? Do they accumulate interest so that eventually you have enough to buy something really big? A huge supernova of an experience?

What would I buy with all that saved-up experience, all that we were?

Are still. In me. *In my head.*

PART FOUR

1/The end began the morning Barry and I met Kari on the beach by Chalkwell station the Thursday of our seventh week.

Remember Kari, the au pair from Norway? The *rather very* girl. The eye-catcher I never thought to see again.

'Hello, Hal,' she called, rising from the sea like Aphrodite as Barry and I stripped just above the tide line. She came smiling towards us, adjusting her bikini against sea-spillage.

A bombardment of thought-rays split atoms in my mind. That she had—surprise pleasure—remembered me. That a lot of sun had hugged her buff in the last few weeks. That Barry had done a double-take. That at this very instant I was unveiling for Kari's inspection my low-slung knees.

Tripping on my blushing indecision—whether to pull my jeans up again or whip them off regardless of my patellas—I tumbled onto the sand.

'I don't usually have such an effect on people,' Kari said, reaching us, 'but I must say it is *very* amusing.'

Barry seemed to be sharing the gag with her. I struggled to my feet, my jeans crumpled round my ankles.

'Kari!' I said treading grapes to free my hobbled feet. 'Kari's from Norway,' I said to Barry. 'This is Barry,' I said to Kari. 'Kari's an au pair while she improves her English,' I said to Barry. 'Sounds like it's coming on great,' I said to Kari. 'Met her a few weeks ago,' I said to Barry, 'well, the first night—I mean, the motorbike lot, that night, before I came to the shop.'

'O, yes,' Barry said grinning widely at Kari who was grinning widely back. 'Hello, Kari.'

'Hello, Barry,' Kari said. 'Actually, I've seen you both, you know. In a yellow boat, which looks *rather* fast, I must say. It has a pretty name I think.'

'*Calypso*,' Barry said.

'*Calypso*,' Kari said. 'That's right. You sail it so well.'

'You can see her over there,' I said, pointing, 'moored just beyond that green cabin cruiser.'

'O, yes,' Kari said, 'I see. *Rather* beautiful.'

'We'll have to take Kari out sometime,' Barry said to me but looking still at Kari. 'Teach her some nautical terms.'

'That would be rather jolly,' Kari said.

'You can sail?' Barry said.

'If someone is telling me what to do,' Kari said. (Did that turn out to be an understatement! She was better than Barry.)

'Barry is pretty good at telling people what to do,' I said laughing.

'You can swim?' Barry said.

'Of course,' Kari said.

'Just as well,' Barry said. 'Hal's good at capsizing.'

Kari laughed. 'Perhaps you should stay in charge.'

'Don't worry,' I said, 'he will.' To hell with my patellas, she wasn't looking at any of me, never mind at my knees. I whipped off my jeans and shook the sand off them so that the breeze blew it into their smirking faces.

'It all sounds like great fun,' Kari said ignoring the sand storm.

'Why don't you come out right now?' Barry said taking her arm and leading her in the direction of the dinghy.

'Why not!' Kari said.

I grabbed the sail bag of gear and followed them.

2/That, as nearly as I can remember, was how the conversation went, how the end began. Because that is the trouble—*Correction*: That is part of the trouble—I can't remember so much about the end. Which has been one of the problems about telling anyone—the police, my parents, Ozzy, or you, Ms Atkins. Stupid, eh? Other bits I can remember in detail, like being rescued, and he and I sitting together in the cinema that first night, about which there really isn't more to be said than that: We were together. But I could spell it out in heartbeats, every one remembered, and what happened between every single beat. (Well, that's how it feels!) They were the Great Moments. And what made them GMs was Being Together. Nothing else. Physical presence. Body-mind talk.

But the beginning of the end was not a GM. It was trivial. Crass. Can it be all that happened? Am I forgetting the more important bits? They say your memory can block out painful experiences, just as it can record so clearly every second of the GMs. And this must be true or we would all remember terrifying moments, wouldn't we? Like being born. And after it is over, do we remember death?

On, on . . .

3/Together.
His hand on the back of her neck.
Caressing.
To get her.

4/The grass is always greener on the other body's grave.

5/It was half past ten next morning before he turned up at the shop. I was already there. Had been since eight-fifteen. Not out of duty; not out of famished desire to be in the presence of Prince Charming. But out of fury.

Jealous? Me? *Never!*

As he came through the door our eyes met. He could not help seeing in mine the beam of anger. In his I could see—what pleasure!—a mote of shame, a devil's obsequy.* But he was hiding whatever regret he felt behind a mug full of glee.

'Hi, handsome!' he said, parading the empty shop addressing himself effusively to the sleeve displays. 'How's business?'

'Slow,' I said heavily.

'There's no business like slow business,' he said, and when I didn't respond, 'Boom-boom!'

'Had a good night?' I said, pretending to perform tasks of a clerical nature.

'Con-tortious,' he said. 'Inventive. Suc-cu-lent.' He prowled, shafting the words at me barbed with provocation. '*Novel.*'

'Sounds exhaustingly Nordic.'

'A saga of sexual sensation.'

'I can imagine.'

He faced me squarely across the counter. 'Can you?' he said drily. 'And how would you know?'

A challenge, no doubt of it.

'I had *such* a good teacher,' I said, tit-for-tart.

'Philately wouldn't deliver you this male,' he said. 'Not today.'

'I don't accept spoiled goods from Norway,' I said.

---

* When Osborn read this, he said, 'If you go on like this you'll turn religious, you know that don't you?' I said, 'Only over your dead body, eh, sir!' He said, 'You really do have death on the brain, Hal.' I said, 'All unconscious.' He said, 'With death on the brain you would be.'

He leaned towards me, head wagging. 'Are we a little peaky this morning?'

'No more than we're a little traitorous.'

Here began the heavy breathing, sour looks, tight-lipped mouths, raised voices, spewings of verbal bile.

'Don't push your luck,' Barry said, snip-snip.

'*Me* push *my* luck! So who's talking!'

This is ridiculous, I was thinking; I don't want this to happen. Why am I doing it? All last night, every time I woke up, which was often, I'd been telling myself to stay cool, to play it calmly, not to lose my temper, not to show any anger. And here I was doing just the opposite, saying everything I'd told myself not to say, like all the switches in my mind had got mixed up so that 'off' meant 'on' and the 'don't' buttons activated the 'do' circuits. I was a robot programmed for self-destruction.

'You don't own me, kid,' Barry said.

'I didn't say I did. And don't call me kid.'

'You're acting like you think you do, and like a kid.'

'What I *thought* was that we were friends.'

'More than friends, surely?'

'Call it what you like. You know what I mean. You came after me, remember.'

'*Me* . . . after! . . . Cobblers!'

His derision triggered off all the wrong switches at once. I started disliking him. Wanted to hurt him. Any how.

'It wasn't me who came to the so-called rescue waving your jeans in the air,' I said, spitting out the words like gobs of concentrated H_2SO_4 and camping the ac-companying gestures in parody of that first day. 'It wasn't me who gave you a nice hot bath and dressed you in my hello-sailor clothes and made eyes at you over a meal and cosied up at the movies—'

'All right, all right—'

'You're sure you wouldn't like me to go on? There's plenty more where that came from.'

'A proper little acid factory, aren't you, ducky!' He stomped away into the office, sniping from the door, 'I don't remember you putting up much resistance.'

For ten minutes after that we assaulted each other with pouting silences. I guess there must have been a customer or two, but I don't remember. All I remember is standing behind the counter staring blindly at the sleeve racks. There was no thinking going on in my head, only in my stomach.

Then my stomach made me walk to the office door. He must have heard me coming because I heard him move as I approached and when I reached the door and looked inside he was standing in front of the mirror combing his hair.

'Why?' my stomach made me say, quietly, not in anger.

His eyes, in the mirror, left his hair and grazed my face.

'Why?' he said. 'You're always asking why. What's it matter why?' He turned to face me, six feet away, a waxwork of himself. 'Just relax, will you? Forget it. Nothing's happened.'

'Nothing!'

'Nothing that matters. Nothing that need bother you . . . Us.'

'I still want to know why.'

He sighed. 'Hal, you're getting to be a pain in the gut.'

'Tell me why.'

'It's happened before. You didn't make a song and dance those times. Leave off, eh?'

'Not like this.'

'Because it was a girl?'

'That as well.'

'As well as what?'

'As well as dumping me. You were blatant. You made

passes at her in the boat as if I wasn't there. You walked off with her, leaving me to stow the gear and clear up after you. And while I was mooring the boat you disappeared and got yourself nicely lost with your new toy till you flounce in here at ten-thirty this morning expecting everything to be just like normal. Well, I'm not your bloody skivvy, mate, and I'm not your tame catamite neither.'

'O, the words, the *words*! Have you done?'

'No. I still want to know why you did it.'

'I don't think you do, sweetheart, not really. You're a bit jealous, that's all, and I don't blame you, but you'll soon get over it.'

'Don't patronize me, Barry.'

'I'm not, I'm not. Pax! I'm explaining, for God's sake!'

'You think that's an explanation!'

'It'll do for now.'

'Not for me it won't.'

He drew in a deep breath, leaned back against the wall. 'Okay, okay,' he said. 'Let's both calm down, eh? Let's agree I behaved badly. Let's not push each other about it any more. Let's just forget it and enjoy each other. All right?'

I shook my head. 'Sorry. Not this time.'

I don't know when I had decided this. At that moment, I guess. But there it was, said. And I knew at once I meant it.

There was a calm before the storm. Whispering in the undergrowth. Deep silence. Eyes on eyes, waiting: a last gazing look that says this should not be but will be. The end of something. It is/was the saddest moment of all.

Barry said, 'Some things are better left unsaid, Hal. Once they're out, people can't let you take them back.'

Hard and weary and bitter, I said, 'Like oaths of undying friendship. Like swearing to dance on graves. Like those kind of things you mean?'

This brought a glower to his eyes and a blush to his cheeks.

'You want to know? Okay, I'll tell you.'

'Good.'

'I was getting bored.'

'Bored?'

'That's right. Bored!'

'What with?'

'Not what. Who.'

'Who?'

'You asking or exclaiming?'

'Both. So who?'

'You.'

'Me!'

Ridiculous not to have known; but that was the way of it. And I still didn't take in what he meant.

I said, 'I thought we were having a great time.'

'That's the trouble.'

'Trouble? How trouble?'

'You are. I was. We were. Not now.'

'Why didn't you say? We can do other things.'

'*That is not the point!*'

I shouted, 'Then what is the bloody point?'

He shouted back, 'I've told you!'

'Then say it again!'

'It isn't *what*. It's *you*.'

'*What about me?*'

This time he didn't shout, he yelled. 'You Bore Me!' The words separated, pronounced, thrown like punches felt in my stomach. As my stomach was doing all my thinking at the time, they left me speechless as well as breathless and weak.

I turned from him and sat down—slumped down—in the swivel chair at the office desk. I stared, not seeing, at the invoices and catalogues, sample discs, tapes, spare sleeves, letters, accounts, stationery littering the desk top. I thought, irrelevantly, Mrs G. will be in tomorrow, do her weekly blitz, clear things up.

Barry was going on behind me. 'We've had a few laughs, sure. Had a good time. But I like a change now and then. More than that really. I want to get into as many different things as I can,' he chuckled, 'as many different people. One is never enough. Not for me.'

He paused, waiting for me to say something. But I was in slow-motion shock.

He went on, 'So I picked you up because I fancied you . . . but I liked you straight off. Liked you for yourself, I mean. I thought you wanted the same things I do. I thought when we'd got to know each other, we'd do it all together.'

Silence again. I was embalmed.

Then his voice again, quiet. 'But that's not you, is it? It's not what we do together that you want. It's me. All of me. All for yourself. And that's too heavy for me, Hal. I don't want to be owned, and I don't want to be sucked dry. Not by anyone. Ever.'

My stomach decided it was an atomic reactor. Barry's words split the atom. Explosion time.

Suddenly the clutter in front of me was unbearable. So with one sweep of my right arm I scythed the mess to the floor. A compulsion of history: my father assaulting the tea table after a row with my mother flashed as an after-image in my memory.

I did not stop there. Standing and turning to confront Barry was part of the same belly-blasted ballet. And hurling a sea stone at his face was a clone of my father-flashing memory. For as my arm swept the desk my hand caught and gripped in its clawing anger a pearled rock we had found one day on the beach. Barry kept it on the desk as a paperweight. Now it was a bullet for his head.

He saw it coming and ducked.

His dodging body revealed the mirror on the wall behind him.

For a sharp split second I saw my own face snarling back at me before the pearly brickbat shattered the glass and my face fell in splinters to the floor.

6/The slivered glass cut words to the quick. There was no more talk.

A fractured moment let silence in. Then silence too became unbearable.

I turned and ran from the shop. I had cycled to work that morning. I grabbed my bike and pedalled away without looking back.

In my head, now and since, a cry has echoed: Barry calling my name at my back, '*Hal! Hal!*' as I sped through the mid-morning traffic.

Did he really call to me? Or is it the voice of his ghost raised by my regret? I never know.

7/Fifty minutes later he was dead.

They say his motorbike left the road, hit a tree.

They say. Who say? The police. The newspapers. The radio.

What do they know?

He was on the Arterial road just outside town travelling *towards* Southend. Where had he been?

An eyewitness said, 'It was like he was trying to fly. Just took off. Unbelievable. Maybe he was drunk or stoned or something. Or just plain crazy.'

None of that, as a matter of fact. But all of it at the same time. Drunk in his timeless time bubble. Stoned on speed. Crazy because he wasn't himself at that moment of lift-off into flight.

He had dreamed true. Or had made his dream come true. Which?

I keep thinking: It was because of me. He died in anger, because of me.

I keep thinking: No, it was because he was glad to be rid of me. He was celebrating, proving his freedom.

I keep thinking: It was nothing of that. It was because of Kari. Because he was pleased with her.

I keep thinking: Yes, it was because of Kari, but not because he was pleased with her, but because he regretted her. He died in remorse.

I keep thinking: Whatever it was, it was all my fault.

I keep thinking: I wish I had been on his bike with him. I should have been. If I had gone back when he called, maybe I would have been. But did he call?

I keep thinking: I wish he was still here.

Whatever else I keep thinking, the only thing I keep thinking all the time is that I wish he was still here.

That's why it is me that's mad, you see; that's why I've got death on the brain.

8/I heard about his death on the early evening local news.

From the shop I had cycled home, told my mother I had a queasy stomach (not short of the truth), couldn't work, would stay in my room.

Stayed in my room, cans gripping my ears, listening to tape after tape, anything, whatever came to hand, loud stereophony obliterating the soft centre of my cerebrum, eyes staring nowhere, everywhere.

Tea time. Necessary to put on a show of mild suffering bravely ignored. My father's view is: If you're properly ill you go to bed and get a doctor; if you're not, you shut up, put up, and work.

So downstairs I went, shutting and putting. The radio was playing in the kitchen—it always is because otherwise, my mother says, she can't stand the noise in her head. Her mind doesn't have a built-in Dolby.

I wasn't listening.

'. . . Barry Gorman, eighteen . . .'

And then I was.

The news turned me into a compound oxymoron. Hotly cold, limply rigid, mind-racingly stunned, a mess of emotional lack of feeling, I wanted to sit down and walk about, hide in my room and race round talking to everyone who knew Barry and anyone who might know exactly what had happened.

Mother, listening but not attending, made no connection, went on sizzling steaks under the grill.

Food was obscene.

I shook, trembled, a spasm spreading out from the fork of my legs.

'Got to go out,' I said, making for the door. 'Phone call.'

If she protested I didn't hear.

9/I cycled to Cliff Road.

The curtains were drawn.

I rang and rang the front door bell; thumped the door.

No answer. Finally I lifted the letterbox flap and peered through. She was standing just behind the door; she was dressed all in black.

'Mrs Gorman,' I said into the letterbox.

'Stop that! Stop that noise, d'you hear!' she hissed.

'It's me, Mrs Gorman. It's me—Hal.'

'I know who it is.'

'Can I come in?'

'No.'

'But, Mrs Gorman—'

'Go away.'

'—I have to talk to you.'

'Don't you know my son died today!'

She began to weep. Not profusely, but with a searing kind of abandonment.

'I know, Mrs Gorman. That's why I came. I just heard.'

'My son is dead.'

'Mrs Gorman, please open the door.'

Then she let out a strange, strangled wail, and howled at me, 'And you killed him!'

I let go of the letterbox flap. It snapped shut.

10/Such a thing is not said to you every day. It comes as a shock. Even when you have already thought the same words yourself. I had already thought those words: a spool tape of that same sentence, *you killed him*, played in my head all the way from home to Cliff Road. But it is different when someone else says it, aloud, without contradiction.

I gawped at the door. Couldn't move. Couldn't speak. Will-less.

There was a long silence. Of course, the silence can only have been in my self. Cars must have driven by; people, talking and laughing perhaps, must have walked past. Did wandering dogs sniff at me? Birds at least had to have been singing. Children were playing on the pavement two doors away—I remember them now—when I arrived; were they not still squawking at each other? An evening in August: lawn mowers must have been burring grass; open windows must have been mouthing inner dealings. But none of that penetrated. And none of it was changed or affected for one second by unhappiness.

Then I heard Mrs Gorman saying sternly on the other side of the door, '. . . do you hear? Go away. You want me to call the police?'

Cold winter came in muggy August. I started shivering. All I wanted was to curl up warm away from people, and not-think.

Zombie fashion, I got home, climbed the stairs to bed, went on shivering between the cocooning sheets, for hours playing scrabble with my tortured sadness.

11/**Sad** (sæd) *adj.* 1. feeling sorrow; unhappy. 2. causing, suggestive, or expressive of such feelings: *a sad story*. 3. unfortunate; unsatisfactory; shabby; deplorable: *her clothes were in a sad state*. [Old English *sæd* weary; related to Old Norse *sathr*, Gothic *saths*, Latin *satur*, *satis* enough].

Sad: unhappy, unlucky, accursed, unfortunate, doomed, condemned, pitiable, poor, wretched, despondent, melancholic, cut up, heart-broken, sorrowful, woebegone, dejected, weeping, tearful, lamenting, displeased, disappointed, discontented, chagrined, mortified, resentful, sorry, remorseful, regretful.

All of that in the long following night sleepless.

A dictionary is a word mine. Dig and bang.
But says nothing.

12/After dawn I slept, warmed at last and exhausted by my own hellfire.

Seven-thirty, enter the rhinoceros (for those who have no memory: cf. Part Two, Bit 12) but not stampeding today; not even tearing open the curtains. Instead he stood by my bed, rattled a cup on a saucer, pushed at my shoulder in a manner which, from him, had to be taken for gentleness.

'Your mother's sent you a cup of tea,' he said as I stirred (forgive the pun), on this occasion genuinely surfacing from unconsciousness.

He waited a too brief moment for me to take the unaccustomed gift, then put it on the table by my head.

I squinted at him through eyelids of ovenhot fibreglass.

'You all right?' he said. 'Only your mother's a bit worried. You didn't even speak to her when you came in last night. Didn't eat your tea she'd kept for you either.'

'Sorry,' I said. 'I was upset.'

'Aye well.' He fidgeted his feet. 'Owt the matter?'

'Don't you know?'

I couldn't believe he didn't. When you've been thinking about the same thing for hours on end you get to thinking everybody else has been thinking what you've been thinking. Like your head was the only radio station in the whole world and everybody has been listening in.

Dad hadn't. 'How the hell can we know what's matter if you never tell us nowt?'

No denying that. But telling meant I'd have to say it out loud. For the first time. I didn't know if I could and stay in one piece.

He perched himself on the edge of a chair where I chucked my clothes at night, and leaned towards me, elbows on knees, hands clasped in front of him. I panicked. He'd never sat down in my room before, not since I was about six.

'You'll have to say something, son,' he said. 'Your mother—. You know what's she's like.'

Easing myself up, motion covering emotion, I said sharply, sounding like tetchiness but not wanting to, 'Barry Gorman's dead.'

Dad raised his eyebrows and pulled down the corners of his mouth. 'Yesterday?'

I nodded.

'How?'

'Bike crashed.'

I wasn't looking at him now; but could feel him watching me closely. For days, months, we hadn't spent so long alone together.

After a while he said, 'Taking it a bit hard aren't you? I mean, you haven't known him that long.'

'Seven weeks.'

'Aye well, things like this happen. You can't let them get you down.'

Silence. A creak on the stairs.

I could have explained then. Wanted to. Everything. The closest I got to trying to tell him. But there was so much to say. And at that moment, the creak on the stairs sent all the willing part of me into deep freeze.

I could look at Dad again and show nothing.

He said, 'What about Mrs Gorman? How's she taking it?'

'Badly.'

'You'd expect her to. You should think of her. She'll be needing all the help she can get.'

Not from me; but that couldn't be explained either.

'I don't know what I can do,' I said, required to say something but hearing the flabbiness.

'What about the shop? Something'll have to be done about that. You could be a big help there.'

'I suppose.'

'You can't just desert her. She's been good to you. Taking you on, paying you well. You owe her a bit of support, a bit of loyalty at a time like this.'

Another pause. Uncomfortable, lengthy. Awkward for the eyes.

Dad sighed, stood up. 'What d'you think then? You'll get up and go to work, will you?'

Without impossible talk there could be no answer but, 'Yes.'

He smiled. I was ten again. He said, 'I'll tell your mother you'll be down in a minute.' He went to the door, opened it, paused, glanced at me, sniffed. 'If you want owt,' he said, 'any help like—you know where to come.'

I nodded, but could not answer.

'Aye well,' he said, and went.

13/Living it up in the bathroom with the Macleans, the thought occurred (i) that I still had a key to the back door of the shop; (ii) that maybe Dad was right: I would be a help to Mrs G. if I looked after the shop today; (iii) that helping her might make her like me again.

But there was something else far more important that I hardly dared admit to myself. I wanted to be where he had been. I wanted to touch things that were his. And I had a strange sensation, neither thought nor feeling, that I would go into the shop and there he would be, just like always, and we'd joke about our fight and—

I sluiced my face with handfuls of cold water.

I didn't look at myself in the mirror. Couldn't bear to see any part of me.

14/The sensation that he would be there was strongest as I opened the back door into the shop. So strong I believed it.

I even called his name. 'Barry!'

There was no answer, of course.

I rushed into the office. All tidy. The desk neat. No trace of the mess I'd made on the floor. I smiled, for a splinter of time convinced he would be in any minute, that I'd just been dreaming. A nightmare.

Then I turned and saw the broken mirror's empty frame looking blindly back at me from the wall.

I told you I had ways of making it talk.

15/From that instant I knew I *must* see him. Him? His body. His corpse. This was the proof I wanted to have. *Needed.* Of his death. Seeing wouldn't just be believing. It would be *knowing.* And I needed to know. Desperately.

But where was his body? How could I see it? Was it at home? What did they do with people killed in accidents? When would they bury him? Today was Saturday, they'd not bury him today. Tomorrow, surely, the cemetery would be closed? Monday then?

One person knew the answers.

I picked up the telephone and dialled without a second thought.

'Mrs Gorman—'

'Who's that? Is that you again?'

'Mrs Gorman, please listen—'

'Are you pitiless? Without all decency?'

'I've got to see Barry, Mrs Gorman, got to—'

'What! Are you tormenting me? Is that what you are doing?'

'No no! I *must* see him. It's important—'

'You're mad. That's what's happened. You've gone mad. I don't want to talk to you.'

'Tell me where he is. Please, Mrs Gorman.'

'I'll put the police on to you. I'm warning you. You deceived me. I trusted you and look what you did. How you repaid me and my Bubby. He told me all about you. All that you did. Throwing things at him. Breaking up our shop. I cleared up the mess myself. I saw it. Vicious. You're a vicious nasty boy. You should be put away. You're a hooligan.'

'No, Mrs Gorman . . . you've got it all wrong. I can explain. It was only the mirror, that's all I broke, and I'm sorry, I'll pay for it, but Mrs Gorman you have to tell me where he is, I've got to see him, I loved him as well you know—'

'How dare you! How dare you say such a thing! I know all about you. And now you want to add sacrilege to your crimes against my son. As if you haven't done enough. He'd be alive now if he hadn't gone after you. Forget him, I told him, but no, he wouldn't listen.'

'Came after me? How do you know?'

'He told me. Telephoned from the shop. He told me about you making trouble, smashing the place up. He said he was going to find you. I went straight there but he'd gone and the office was a wreck.'

'But, Mrs Gorman—'

'And now you prey on me! The nerve you have! Well, my daughter will be here soon with her husband. See what happens if you plague me again, a defenceless woman. I should take care if I was you.'

She put the telephone down. I listened to the dialling tone, trying to make sense of what it was saying.

16/I flit the shop as soon as I put the telephone down, pushing my key through the letterbox to be rid of it. Mrs Gorman talking of police and sons-in-law made me fugitive. The empty shop, Barryless, made insistent the need to see him. How could I stay there?

The escape route. Room to breathe; time to think.

I cycled to the beach by Chalkwell station, walked my bike across the station footbridge (OZZYMANDIAS RULES OK some wit had spray-painted on the footbridge wall), dumped it by the esplanade, where I could keep an eye on it, found an empty space on the sand with my back against the heavy, grey ridge-grained wood of a groin, from where I could look along the beach towards Southend and the pier, and across the mud and water to the hazy horizon where the Kent coast lay hidden.

The sky was overcast, the weather dull, and almost no breeze. The tide was a long way out. A poor day for bathers and not time yet for sailors. Only a few people were scattered about along the sand, though there was plenty of activity on the esplanade—sightseers and kids on the loose and local folk exercising themselves and their babies and dogs. Not that I paid any attention at the time; I was all inwardness. In fact, I've had to think hard even to remember these few details, which I tell you only to fill in the gap around myself who was huddling from the psychic chill beside the wooden shield, barrier against stormy seas and shifting sands.

17/This morning I read what I wrote during the last couple of days about the aftermath and it is *useless*. Doesn't tell anything like I really *felt*. Which was mashed, minced, chopped, granulated, flensed, mangled, mortified.

That's the word: *mortified*.

Latin *mors* death and *facere* to do, and thus via Old French (in case you didn't know) from church Latin *mortificare*, to put to death: 1. to humiliate or cause to feel shame; 2. to cause or undergo tissue death or gangrene. (Cf. *Collins English Dictionary*.)

What a wonder is language! All that in one word. And still tells you nothing.

I had put to death and was being put to death. But there is no way of telling you about the tissue death of my own self, or about gangrene rotting away my dreams of bosom palship.

Hell, let's take it as read.

JKA. *Running Report*: Henry Spurling ROBINSON
8th Oct. Requested and got a two week postponement of Hal's next court appearance on the grounds that reports are not yet satisfactorily completed.
Emphasized the unusual nature of this case. Impressed on Hal the urgency of his completing his written account for me to see.

11.45. Telephoned Mr Osborn. Told him of the postponement. Asked him to try and expedite matters with Hal. Mr O. said that Hal is agitated because, Hal says, he can't get into his account all the details he feels ought to be included. Keeps telling Mr O. 'the words are never right', and constantly rewrites passages because after a couple of days he is dissatisfied with his first drafts. But apparently he is scribbling obsessively all day. Mr O. is certain writing the account has started to have a beneficial therapeutic effect, and that in addition the act of writing about himself is giving Hal a new and purposeful focus in his life.

I suggested to Mr O. that I might see some of Hal's account so that I could begin to see what is involved. But Mr O. was very strongly against this on the grounds that it might stem the flow and disturb Hal again. I asked whether he couldn't let me see pages without Hal knowing, and received the kind of scornful reply about trust and confidentiality he gave me during our first interview.

I pressed on Mr O. the urgency of Hal finishing the task soon. Mr O. told me he is seeing Hal every day after school, when they discuss Hal's progress, and Mr O. comments on any passages Hal brings for him to read. 'You'd think he was writing a novel,' Mr O. said, and I felt he was as pleased about this as he was about the serious aspects of Hal's case. I tried to explain that all I want is a straightforward record that explains what Hal and Gorman did. I didn't, I said, have time for novels, and said that I hoped Hal wasn't inventing anything.

9th Oct. Received this letter from Hal in today's post:

DECLARATION TO MS J K ATKINS

by Henry Spurling Robinson aka Hal

This is to certify that I, Henry Spurling Robinson (hereinafter called The Author, acronym TA), being of unsound mind and disturbed body, am working to the fullest of my capacity, and seriously intend completing and delivering to you, Judith Karen Atkins (hereinafter called The

Impatient Social Servant, acronym TISS) a
record of my crazy actions relating to the
Death and Burial of one Barry Gorman (hereinafter called The Encomiumed Dead, acronym
TED) with as much dispatch as TA can muster.
TA must however herewith point out to TISS
that the tiss TISS has put TA into regarding
his aforementioned account of TED because
of The Court's impatience to know The Truth
and pass sentence on TA about TED must mean
that from this Bit on in the story of TED
TA will only be able to describe for TISS
the actions TA engaged in without adequate
explanatory detail, and that this gives TA
cause for concern about TISS understanding,
or rather not understanding, everything
about TED and TA.

Hal Robinson.

18/Kari almost literally stumbled across me on the
beach.

She had heard the news from Mrs Gorman when she
telephoned that morning, wanting to speak to Barry.

'I came here to calm myself,' she said. 'Hal, it is terrible.
I just burst into tears. I couldn't stay in the house. Mrs
Grey was wonderful. She tried to comfort me. She

couldn't understand why I was so upset, and I couldn't tell her, you know. But she let me come out here because Mr Grey was not being so nice. He told me to stop blubbing—blubbing?—and get on with my work. But I couldn't do anything with the children anyway. It was all rather awful.'

She was in jeans and a white sweater, with a tired old brown mac over them, too loose—probably one of Mrs Grey's—which she hugged round herself as if the day was cold and wet.

It wasn't. Outward expression of inner feeling. She slumped beside me, glum, on the sand.

Not far from us two boy children of three or four were playing naked in the sand while a woman in a summer dress sat on a towel nearby, watching them. While Kari was talking I watched the children, thinking how I would like to be four again making castles in the sand.

ACTION REPLAY

The image that remains strongest in my memory from that first Barryless day is this still life, like a snapshot, of two naked children kneeling in the sand, their faces bright with pleasure. A mnemonic that revives every fractured sensation of the time. Strange that a mind-frozen moment in the lives of two happy children should memorialize so vividly something so sad. Nor does it simply provoke, this picture, remembrance, for the children seem to embody in themselves the distress I felt as I looked at them. Why should that be? As though every smallest pleasure in the world contains within it all the world's sadness.

19/'We must visit Mrs Gorman,' Kari said. 'Don't you think? When I phoned she sounded very upset.'

I shook my head. 'She won't let me in.'

'Not let you in? But why? You and Barry were so much friends. He talked about you all the time the other day. I was rather envious to have such a friend, I must say.'

I said, 'We weren't just friends.'

She turned her head to look closely at me, her eyes touring my face, searching for a message. She found none in that tundra.

'Weren't *just* friends?' she said. 'Perhaps that is your English way of saying *more* than just friends?'

I nodded.

The children were breaking down their sandcastles with relished violence, the woman laughing at them.

Kari turned from me so that now we sat as replicas, backs bent against the rough groin, legs jacknifed, feet dug into sand.

'I'm so sorry,' she said bleakly. 'I didn't know.'

'Why should you?'

'I ought to have guessed. But it is rather a shock.'

'Moral, or a surprise?'

'O, not moral, not at all. No, a surprise.'

'Because he slept with you?'

A pause. She riddled sand through her fingers.

'You know about that?'

'We had a row about it.'

'O dear, that does make things rather difficult.'

The children were building new castles; the woman, leaving them to themselves, was pouring herself a drink from a flask.

'It wasn't so much about you. Not your fault. I was jealous. He didn't like that. Said I wanted him all for myself. He meant I was possessive and was stifling him.'

'And were you?'

'I didn't think so. . . . Does it matter anyway? He thought I was.'

A pause.

Then she said, 'You want me to go?'

I put a hand on her arm. 'No. Stay. I'd like you to. Honest.'

I think I meant to take my hand away, but before I did she slipped hers into mine and let them rest together between us.

'It is difficult,' she said, 'to give everything to one person.'

'Maybe it's wrong to want that. Maybe it's wrong to try.'

She shook her head. 'I am rather confused about it.'

'Can I join the club?'

She looked at me, puzzled. 'Club?'

I smiled at her. 'Forget it. Just a saying.'

We turned our attention to the kids again: their funny stomping way of doing things before they are manually dextrous. Wanting more than they've the skill to achieve. Miniature Laurel and Hardys. (Maybe that's what's so funny about L & H. They're children who are trapped inside adult bodies and lost in an adult world they can't quite find out how to control, while pretending all the time they know how.)

If I had thought about it before that moment I think I would have said Kari was the last person I would want to be with right then, and that I certainly wouldn't have wanted to talk to her about everything that had happened between Barry and me.

But as it turned out just the opposite was true. She was the only person I could have been with, and most of all she was the only person I could talk to. As though this was the very reason we met that morning, I told her everything, starting with the capsize of *Tumble* and finishing with my rejection that morning by Mrs Gorman. Sometimes we laughed; the first time I had laughed in forty-eight hours. Now and then she asked a question. Towards the end she wept, quietly, without noise or fuss.

Meanwhile, the woman had gathered up her two children, slipped them into their doll-size pants and shoes, packed their picnic oddments, and sauntered away with them chattering at her heels. The numbers of wanderers on the esplanade thinned, gone to lunch. The tide had crossed the mud, reaching the beach; a yachtsman or two were already out and rigging their boats. The sky's greyness had lightened; a veiled sun showed through and was brightening. The afternoon would bring crowds; the beach would be an escape no longer.

20/We moved to Leigh gardens, buying a snack on the way.

'What about your work?' I asked.

She shrugged. 'It will have to wait. Mrs Grey will understand.'

We sat on the grass, our backs protected by bushes.

'There are a couple of things I haven't told you,' I said.

'I would like to know everything,' she said.

I lay on my back, hands behind my head. She turned and lay on her front at my side, supporting herself on her elbows so that she could look into my face.

'When we first got together,' I said, 'he made me swear an oath. He made me swear that whichever of us died first the other would dance on his grave.'

A pause while she took this in.

'But that's . . . '

'Weird?'

'A little.'

Silence.

'You can't.'

'I must.'

'You'll be stopped.'

'At night?'

'At night!'

'An oath is an oath is an oath. Will you help?'

'What!'

'Not with the dancing. I have to do that on my own.'

'How then?'

'Find out where he's to be buried and when. Mrs Gorman won't speak to me, I told you. And I've got to know where his grave is. Mrs G. will talk to you. Say you're a friend, want to attend the funeral. Get the details.'

'I don't believe this.' She turned and sat up, her arms round her knees.

'I'm not sure I do.'

'But—'

I sat up and faced her, cross-legged. 'Please.'

'I'll think.'

I said quickly, 'There's the other thing.'

She said, looking nervously at me, 'What other thing?'

'It's a bit weird as well.'

'I think I'd rather not know.'

'You said you wanted to know everything.'

She looked away across the gardens, her chin planted on her knees. 'All right, go on.'

'I've got this . . . compulsion. It's crazy, I know. But I've got to see him. I mean his body. I have to know for certain. I can't explain. I just have to, that's all.'

She sighed. 'Poor Hal,' she said. 'For you it wasn't just . . . casual, was it? But very serious.' She reached and took my hand in her slim fingers.

'You've been hit rather badly,' she said.

I took her hand in both mine. 'I have to know where they've taken him,' I said.

She nodded, the movement felt through her fingers.

21/'He's in the mortuary at Leigh General Hospital,' Kari said when she returned an hour later. 'I talked to Mrs Gorman's son-in-law. He was rather nice. Mrs Gorman was resting. Her daughter and son-in-law arrived about lunchtime and they put her to bed at once because she was so distressed and tired from not sleeping. Her daughter is sitting with her.'

'In the mortuary? Why there? Why isn't he at home?'

'There must be an inquiry—no, that wasn't the word —an inquest?—yes, an inquest.'

'An inquest! Why?'

'Mrs Gorman's son-in-law says it is all quite normal. When there has been a death because of an accident your law says there must be an inquest by—a coroner?'

'Yes, a coroner.'

'Who has to find out what happened. In case someone is to blame. Mrs Gorman's son-in-law explained everything but it is all new to me.'

'When's the inquest?'

'On Tuesday, they hope, but perhaps later.'

'So when's the funeral?'

'On Wednesday, but if the inquest is over soon enough on Tuesday it will be on that day.'

'Why the rush, for God's sake?'

'There is no rush. It's their rule—their custom.'

'Whose custom?'

'The Jewish custom, of course. Barry was Jewish, Hal, you must have known that!'

'I knew, I knew. But he wasn't practising. He didn't go to church, I mean synagogue.'

'That has nothing to do with it.'

'Of course it does! He was like me. We didn't believe in religion. Or in God come to that.'

'So?'

'So why should out-of-date customs he didn't believe in matter now?'

'Out-of-date?'

'Yes! The Outina Indians of South America used to scalp an enemy's corpse, break the bones in the arms and legs, tie the body into a bundle, leave it to dry in the sun and then shoot an arrow up its arse. Are you saying South Americans should still do that because the Outinas did it?'

'You're being ridiculous and disgusting. I don't want to hear these things.'

'In the Middle Ages in ever-so-civilized Europe they sometimes boiled dead bodies to get the flesh off so they could easily carry the bones around the place in their luggage. They had this thing, you see, about bones being kept in certain places, like nick-nacks with sentimental value. D'you think we should still do that? It was a widespread custom among our ancestors.'

'You're horrible.'

'But they did! When our brave and chivalrous Christian knights of the crusades went off to slaughter the heathen of Islam for the greater glory of the God they were both supposed to worship, they used to take their own cauldrons with them for the purpose. They wanted their nice clean bones carting back home when they were dead, you see. You wouldn't want your left femur to fall into the hands of the rival gang, would you now? Never know where you'd end up.'

'Why should I listen to this rather silly lecture—'

'I'm not lecturing you.'

'—when I'm only trying to help you with your—weird plans.'

'I'm grateful. Honest!'

'Anyway, what would *you* do about Barry? Even if you don't believe in anything as you seem not to, you still have to do something with dead people.'

'I know.'

'Well? You'd just throw their bodies into a furnace and forget about them, would you?'

'No, of course not!'

'Then what would you do?'

'I don't know, I haven't decided yet.'

'O, how wonderful! So the world must pile up its dead people until you decide what to do about them, eh?'

'Don't be so daft. All I meant was that I haven't made up my own mind about what should be done about me, when I'm dead. Barry didn't care about religious customs, that's all I'm saying.'

'Isn't that rather obvious, as he made you swear to dance on his grave? Which also means he expected to be buried, not cremated, wouldn't you agree?'

'I hadn't thought of it like that.'

'That isn't all you haven't thought of either.'

'What d'you mean?'

'You've upset Mrs Gorman terribly, that's what I mean.'

'What about her?'

'You've upset her with your phone calls. Especially asking to see Barry. How could you!'

'She should have been pleased. Aren't friends supposed to visit after a death?'

'No. Not in Jewish families. They don't go and look at their relatives and friends. They're supposed to bury them as quickly as possible, and simply, and everybody in the same way so there is no difference between rich and poor. They show respect for their dead, which I think is admirable and beautiful. And, after all, you should know all about such things, being so expert on customs of death! Or are you only interested in the gruesome kind!'

'So how come you know so much?'

'Mrs Gorman's son-in-law tried to explain to me.'

'He seems to have explained quite a lot.'

'I told you, he was very nice.'

'I'll bet! Ask to view your body, did he?'

Kari sprang to her feet, furious. 'That is a disgusting remark,' she snapped, and began spluttering garbled English, stamping her foot in frustration, and then poured upon my startled head a spew of Norwegian the gist of which her flaming face and vehement gestures translated. Unmistakably vituperative. After which she stalked away, her old mac flapping around her legs, leaving me marooned in bilious turbulence.

22/As it happens I do know what Kari said in her Norwegian invective. You will have guessed that I didn't remember all this chat word for word, not being a human tape-recorder. Kari helped me reconstruct it, so, yes, she's still around, but I don't want her involved in this mess, even though she says she'll tell all publicly in court if I want her to. Remember, TISS, what you promised: TOTAL CONFIDENTIALITY. You wanted the truth and an explanation for yourself *only*. (And just to show how much I trust you, I've changed Kari's name and place of abode, just in case . . .)

What Kari says she said was, roughly translated, 'You are a selfish, nasty-minded little squirt who doesn't deserve any help from anyone and you can go and take a flying @*+/ at the moon* for all I care because all you are good at is wallowing in self-pity and upsetting a nice old lady because you think half-baked ideas are more

* Cf. Kurt Vonnegut, *Slaughterhouse-Five*. This is how I found out Kari had read it.

important than people and are only interested in your own lousy petty piggy feelings.'

I am glad she could only say it in Norwegian at the time. Otherwise there might now be no more Kari in HSR's life.

Being in ignorance of her sentiments, however, I worked myself instead into a sweat that evening about being friendless and having no one to turn to for help, and how all this was my fault and how I might as well be dead. Which led to imagining various ways of achieving the desired state.

A knife to the throat or wrists. I rejected this as too messy and slow, not to mention painful. Pills would be okay. But none were available except aspirins and they didn't even cure my mother's backaches, and I'd also heard somewhere you have to take so many they make you spew before you've swallowed enough to kill yourself. (She kept her Valium locked somewhere in her bedroom.) Jumping out of my bedroom window wouldn't have worked either. I was only one storey up and would have landed on the tablecloth lawn of our front garden. Poison? My dad's aftershave or my mother's hair shampoo were the nearest thing to poison in our bathroom, though I did remember some slug pellets in the back garden shed. But they didn't seem too good at getting rid of the slugs so I decided not to chance them. Hanging myself. The ceiling would come down, even if I got a hook into it without being heard. Suffocation? Holding a pillow over my nose till I expired didn't seem quite me. Guns were romantic, but the only one in the house was a water pistol I used to have when I was a kid and the inner tube that holds the water leaked anyway. *Willing* myself to death. I'd read about some tribe somewhere who could decide their time was up and lie down and think themselves to death.

I tried this for half an hour and all it did was make me feel more awake than before I started.

I gave up after two hours of sorting out the options. It does seem that if you want to do away with yourself you have to plan pretty carefully for a long time previous. Unless, that is, you're prepared to give yourself the chop in some disgustingly messy manner that leaves someone else to clear up after you. And I didn't/don't think that's fair. Which is all very discouraging when you're in the sort of depressed state I was in that night. At such moments you want a simple, quiet, comfortable croak that provides just long enough before your last gasp for you to relish a few of the zizziest scenes post mortem. Like the satisfying devastation caused by your discovery. The sumptuous distress at your crowded funeral. The way everyone bewails your passing and wishes they had done this for you or that. The speeches of praise. The lavish regret for past offences against you. The gap they all feel in their own lives for the rest of their natural. Ah, the loss you'll be to the world—and serve it right! And the deep and gratifyingly painful GUILT they'll all feel they didn't do something to save you.

After a long soak in this sort of candied vinegar I got fed up. Slept an hour or two. Woke. Shoved on the cans and played a tape of Britten's Quartet No. 3, which offers cauterizing passages of unsentimental sadness. A couple of times through and I was asleep again. Woke at dawn when one of the cans got pushed off my ear and trapped my nose as I turned over in bed. (Audiosphyxiation might, come to think of it, be a novel and amusing means of expiration.)

Sometimes you go to sleep grated, like me that night, and wake up in the morning spun-dried, but all of a piece again. I did that morning. Didn't have to think about it, just do it, thus:

*Kari: SORRY I was an idiot. Will you see me
again? You're the only person I can talk to about
B. and I have to talk to someone about him. If I
wait for you on the beach by Chalkwell station,
where we were yesterday, will you meet me? I'll
be there today—Sunday—from 10.30 until
12.30. Please come. Hal.*

I folded the note, wrote her name on it, slipped it into
the window of a cassette box, with a tape of the Beatles'
Let it be inside. Then I sneaked out of the house before
my parents were up—Sundays they lie in till about
10.30—cycled to Kari's house and dropped the package
through the letterbox.

23/What happened next I can't quite believe happened to
me. If anyone had told me beforehand I could do such
things I would have clocked them one for being so
cheeky. No, I wouldn't; I forgot, I'm a pacifist. No, I'm
not; I'm just not very good at fighting so I don't go
around laying them on people in case they lay a few back
on me. But you know what I mean. Which is that the
following events are so astonishing to me, are so unlike
my imaginings, so out of character, that I can only assume they were aberrant. (It is a relief that Mr Oz agrees:
in fact he suggested this in the first place.) Still, I can't
write it all down as me, as 'I'. I'd feel too uncomfortable.
  All yesterday I chewed over this problem; wrote nothing. (Usual stunt: cans on; tape after tape; doodle on a
note pad waiting for a thought that wants to be written
down. Odd, I'm always certain which few thoughts want
to be written down out of all the chaff blowing in the
cerebral wind. And all the time, feeling physically weak,

heavy, lethargic. Mute too: there is nothing sayable to anyone. Never thought, starting this lark, writing down what has happened to myself would be so difficult. It isn't what happened that causes the sweat, but how to tell what happened. Like jokes—some people can tell them, some people can't. [Barry couldn't.] I guess the same is true about telling terrible tragedies like mine. Anyway, this next Bit was one of the hardest to decide about.)

Only very late last night did the idea I needed turn up, and then I was so whacked I had to leave off till this morning. Solution: If what happened feels like it happened to someone else, then tell it like I was someone else. Simple? Seems like the simple answers always take the longest to sort out.

24/ A DAY AT THE MORGUE
Starring Henry S. and Kari Norway

Here is how Henry S. Robinson got to see the dead body of his mate Barry Gorman with the assistance of his new friend Kari Norway.

When Kari suggested the plan that Sunday afternoon, Henry thought she had gone mad.

'You've gone mad,' he said to Kari.

'I am not mad,' she said. 'You are, otherwise you would not be wanting to do this thing. Well, maybe I am a little mad for helping you.'

'But,' said Henry, 'I can't dress as a girl and walk up to the door of a mortuary and calmly ask to see one of the corpses.'

'That is the only way,' Kari said.

They had argued the ins and outs of this plan for hours. Kari had found out by telephoning the morgue that only official visitors were ever allowed to view a body, and then only by appointment.

'So the only way in is by deception,' she said to Henry and Henry thought to himself how cold and calculating Kari could be. 'There is bound to be a man in charge of a place like that,' she said. 'On Sunday he is likely to be a relief person, just to keep an eye on things and deal with emergencies. That means he won't know the regular details so he'll be easier to bluff. And a man will not resist a distressed girl who only wants to view her dead boy-friend but isn't allowed to because her boyfriend's mother is being against her. Which is half true anyway. Still, you will have to play-act well.'

'I can't do it,' Henry said many times, but he knew all the time he would have to try.

'Let's get on with it,' Kari said. 'I have had enough of you pussypawing about.'

'Pussyfooting.'

'Don't quibble.'

'You said to correct your English.'

'You are just trying to put off. Strip to the waist. We'll start with your hair.'

All this was going on in Kari's room in the Greys' house, which was deserted because the family had gone to visit Mrs Grey's mother in London for the day, leaving Kari in charge.

First she clipped at the longer ends of Henry's hair with sewing scissors. Then she pulled on a curly blonde wig, which, she said, came from Mrs Grey's store of clothes. She tucked and fitted till she decided it was right.

'The damn thing feels like a hairy crash helmet,' Henry said.

'Good enough for now,' Kari said, removing the wig. 'Your face next.'

She sat Henry on a stool in front of her built-in wash-basin and dressing-table, part of the wardrobe unit that occupied all one wall opposite her single bed (which sported a coverlet blazoned with a large NO ENTRY road sign. Did she plan, Henry wondered, to be single for ever? Though the sign seemed often violated.)

'You must shave,' Kari said, rubbing a hand down Henry's cheek.

'Why?' Henry said, peering round her hips to look into the mirror.

'Your fluff will give you away.' She left Henry exploring his fluff and came back with a disposable razor. 'Use this.'

Henry stood at the washbasin. Kari watched from behind his shoulder. He tried a tentative stroke of the blade down his cheek.

'*Yeow!*' he whimpered.

'Stop fussing,' Kari said.

'Hurts!' Henry said, trying a second swathe.

'Nonsense. All men are babies.'

'All women are bullies.'

'That's a sexist remark.'

'No it isn't. No more than yours.'

'All men were babies once,' Kari said, 'and most of them stay that way. Ask any woman.'

'I'll not bandy words when I've a razor in my hand,' Henry said. 'This is my first time, you know.'

'Then it is past time you started. Put some soap and water on . . . Here, let me.' Kari reached over, rubbed soapy water briskly onto his face. 'Your beard is softer than the hairs on my legs.'

'You don't have to shave your legs though,' Henry said through puckered features.

'Of course I do!' Kari stood behind him again, watching in the mirror.

'What?'

'What what?'

'You shave your legs?'

'You don't know? Men want women with soft hairless legs, so we give them soft hairless legs.'

'By shaving them?'

'That's the easiest way. You really didn't know?'

'No.'

Kari laughed. 'You are rather innocent after all, dear Hal, aren't you!'

She bent towards him, kissed him on the ball of his shoulder.

Henry nicked his chin and yelped.

Kari, laughing again, said, 'First blood to me!'

Henry finished shaving himself. 'What now?'

Kari said, 'A very little make-up to emphasize your prettiness. But nothing that might call attention to you. Discreet.' She considered his face, sitting him on the end of the bed and herself on the dressing stool between Henry and the mirror. 'A little foundation, a touch of lipstick, a hint of mascara to sharpen your eyes. That will be enough.'

'I don't like this,' Henry said.

'You are not asked to like it,' Kari said, getting busy.

Henry endured being worked on. Had the purpose not been so daunting, he would have enjoyed such pampering. He liked being handled. *Correction*: By some people he liked being handled. Kari's fingers were soft, precise, firm. Pencils drawing sensational sketches. But she was working quickly, anxious to be done. Was she, Henry wondered, already regretting her crazy notion?

Reminding himself of why Kari was drawing on his face put a silence on him which Kari heard through the fingers. Her eyes carefully avoided his till she finished.

'Yes,' she said when it was over. 'Stand up.'

Henry tried looking in the mirror; Kari blocked his view.

'Not until you're dressed, then you'll see the proper effect.' She handed him a pair of honey-coloured tights. 'Put these on.'

'No,' Henry said.

'Yes,' Kari said. 'You can't wear jeans. They show you are a man. The only suitable dress I have will show some of your legs. They must be properly covered. Men always look at women's legs. At their breasts and their legs. You must be right.'

'This is awful,' Henry said.

'Do you want to change your mind?'

He thought about this, vacantly, finding no answer.

'Did you—what is the word?—dither like this with Barry?' Kari said briskly. 'He was not a person who dithered. No wonder he was losing interest.'

'Shut up!' Henry said, stung.

'Then get on with it. Perhaps it is a mistake. Perhaps you can't do it after all. You haven't the courage.'

Henry scowled at her.

'Well?' she said.

'Are you going to stand there and watch me?' Henry said.

'O, for heaven's sake! What are you afraid of? Is there something special about your body? You are a prim! I'll turn my back, but I am not leaving the room. It would be ridiculous.'

Henry was so angry by now he tore off his shoes and socks, his jeans and underpants, throwing them on the floor.

'And,' Kari said, arms akimbo and her back to him, 'be rather careful with those tights or you'll ladder them. They're expensive and I do not have another new pair.'

Henry huffled, concertina-ed the nylon hose, sat on the

bed, slipped his feet into the legs, pulled them up, wriggled his thighs and bottom into the tights, smoothed them, hated the feel of the stuff against his skin.

For fear the tights would slip and fall about his ankles, he pulled his underpants on over them. Besides, wearing his underpants helped him retain some sense of still being himself.

He said, subdued, 'What next?'

Kari turned. 'A bra.'

'O, God!' Henry said, drooping.

She helped him into the straps, adjusted them to fit, fastened the hooks, stuffed wads of cottonwool into the cups.

Henry watched Kari fiddling to get the bra looking natural. The strange sensation of entrapment round his chest brought back a memory of childhood: his mother strapping a halter round him so that he could play safely in a kind of bouncing swing. He remembered giggling with excitement and anticipated pleasure, his mother smiling and trying to restrain his exuberance while she fastened the clips. How old would he have been then? Three? Younger? Was this his first memory?

Kari tugged gently to snug the bra firmly to his chest.

Now it was the two boy children on the beach the day before who came to Henry's mind, with the woman slowly, patiently dressing them after their play while they babbled to each other, taking no notice of her while submitting to her attentions, like princes attended by a body slave.

'Now the dress.'

Kari held it, bunched above his head. He entered, stooping under it and straightening up, as he might a long shirt, his arms up into the sleeves, and then, the dress released, its folds of light cotton falling about him loosely.

He put his arms down. Kari circled him, smoothing, arranging, adjusting, assessing.

'Stand properly,' she said. 'Look like you're wearing the thing, instead of it wearing you.'

Obedient, he posed himself, blotting from his mind what he was, what this made him. He was acting, he told himself, playing a part. He must pretend; that was the only way.

'Let me see your hands.'

He held them out.

She inspected, holding them in hers.

'They're slim enough, but bony. Try not to draw attention to them. No, I know. Wait. Sit down.' She took some unisex sandals from a cupboard and dropped them at his feet. While Henry worked his toes into them—they were a shade too tight—Kari left the room but was back quickly, before he had managed to fasten the straps.

'Whose are these?' he said. 'They pinch my toes and ankles.'

'Hobble all you like till you get there. But you must walk properly then. Suffer. You deserve to.'

'You're really kind, you know that!'

Kari pulled the stool close to him, sat with a small box on her lap, which she opened. Henry saw inside a jumble of jewellery: bracelets, rings, bangles, necklaces, brooches. She tried first one thing, then another, holding each trinket against him. A brooch and a necklace at his throat but rejected both for a kind of medallion on a short gold chain. Various bracelets on his right wrist, settling for a jangly tangle of thin wiry silvered bangles. On the third finger of his left hand she finally slipped a ring with a mock diamond set in the gold circle.

'You're supposed to be engaged, visiting your dead boyfriend,' she said. 'I think that might do. Stand up again.'

Awkward, pinched, uncomfortable, feeling manacled, he obeyed.

Kari took the wig from the dressing-table, pulled it carefully onto his head, touched up its hair with a comb and her fingers. Stood back. Surveyed him, up and down.

'You're not quite ready yet,' she said, 'something is missing.'

Henry sighed, his breath crushed between panic and dejection.

'Or there is something there that shouldn't be perhaps,' Kari said, after further scrutiny.

'Can't I look?' Henry said, desperate.

'All right.' Kari opened the wardrobe door hung behind with a full-length mirror, and stood back for him to see.

And suddenly there was Henry, facing himself. But not.

He recognized nothing that was him. Except . . . ? Yes, except for one feature. His eyes. They gazed back at him from the glass. His. And pained. Even frightened at that moment behind their astonishment.

He was gazing at a girl with fluffed, slightly frizzed blonde hair that haloed a tanned face touched with a blush of colour on high cheeks. She had a wide, generous mouth, perhaps a too prominent chin. She wore a loose white summer dress, with narrow dark blue circling stripes, that buttoned closely round her thin neck and fell away in soft folds that clung just enough to suggest the shapeliness of the body it covered. The sleeves of the dress tapered from deep loose shoulders to cuffs gathered tight at the wrists.

As Henry gazed, Kari passed round his waist a long matching white-and-blue striped ribbon belt that she tied just enough to nip the dress in a little, emphasizing the girl's breasts and hips without making them prominent.

With a coldness that also surprised him, Henry found himself wondering whether this girl would attract him. Would he fancy her as he passed her in the street? Would he think, 'Nice!' For a thrilled moment he thought, yes, yes, he would! But then he met his own eyes staring back at him and felt again that shock of recognition behind the disguise. Saw the panic he felt. Yet still, that strange ambiguity of himself in himherself puzzled, even fascinated him, teased his memory for a long time afterwards.

'I don't know,' Kari said. 'Perhaps you'll pass.'

'It's taken an hour and a half to get this far,' Henry said with a touch of petulance as much in disguise of his feelings as his clothes were of his body.

'So?' Kari said. 'Many women spend as long every day just so men will think well of them.'

'But there is something wrong,' Henry said, studying himself more coolly now he was getting over the shock. 'I think the trouble is my eyes. They give me away.'

'Ah!' Kari said. 'Of course! Here, try my dark glasses.'

They examined the effect like painters examining the latest brush stroke on a new picture.

'Better,' Kari said.

'Yes. That's it,' Henry said. 'They even make me feel better.'

Being now eyeless, Henry recognized none of himself. He relaxed inside himself. But his chest and loins still felt like they were in a straitjacket and his head like it was crammed into an itchy helmet. Worst of all were the synthetic sheaths suffocating his legs.

Trapped. Covered head to foot. Yet vulnerable, somehow exposed to everyone, as though this flimsy dress was transparent, not clothing at all but simply decoration. He felt more naked than he had ever felt undressed. Was it like this for women too, he wondered, or did you get used to it?

'Come on,' he said, 'let's get it over.' Pushing himself into action, he bundled his shoes and socks and jeans and sweater. 'Should we cycle there? Quicker, and people will have less time to notice me.'

'Just watch out for your skirts in the wind,' Kari said. Laughing, she led the way out, Henry taking a last look at himself in the mirror. He was already sweating coldly under his arms.

Outside, he felt like an actor dressed for a part and out of his element, not disguised any more but exhibited. A freak. He had to force himself onto his bike—carefully tucking in his skirt—blanking from his mind everything except the mechanical operation of getting from Kari's house to Leigh morgue.

Half way there Kari, riding alongside him, said, 'See, no one is looking. No one even notices.'

Henry had been staring studiously ahead; now he glanced cautiously at people on the pavement. No one even looked.

'And why should they?' Kari said, smiling at him. 'What's odd about two girls taking a bicycle ride on a Sunday afternoon?'

And so, encouraged, Henry arrived at the morgue.

They parked their bikes out of sight of the side door. Kari looked Henry over, touched up his wig, adjusted his dress.

'You do want to go through with this?' she said.

'Now you ask!' Henry said, nodding, and no longer certain about anything.

Kari said, 'Then you must act with conviction. You must be a girl distressed. I will speak for you at first. Try not to say anything at all. Nod or suchlike if you have to answer questions. And use your handkerchief a lot, but be careful not to smudge your make-up.'

Henry instinctively tried to put a hand into a trouser pocket.

'All right, all right!' Kari said, stopping him. 'Have mine.'

She dug into her shoulder bag and pressed a piece of cloth the size of a postage stamp into his hand. He grasped at it as at a straw, thankful for anything to hang onto.

Kari said, 'Wait here out of sight. I'll come and get you.'

She went. By the time she returned Henry's stomach was full of exploding Brillo pads.

Kari grinned. 'It is arranged,' she said, her accent stronger now than it had been since Henry first met her. Maybe the strain was telling that way? 'He has agreed. But we must be quick. He will be dismissed if he is found out. All this is terribly against the rulses.'

'Rules,' Henry said. 'Rules!'

'Yes, the rulses. His name is Kelly, by the ways. Yours is Susan.'

'Susan! I hate Susan!'

'You should have thought of that before here. We forgot names. I had to manufacture on the spot.'

'O, God.'

'You don't believe in Him. Now, come . . . *Come!*'

Kelly was waiting for them, lurking behind the half-open mortuary door. A big man in a long white lab coat, he had crinkly black hair, greying at the sides, and a heavy black moustache that drooped. Henry took a dislike to his face at once. His eyebrows were thick and bushy; bristles sprouted from inside his fleshy ears. He looked like a hispid butcher.

'Now, my darlin,' Kelly said in a voice that matched his hair. 'Come in, girl.' He shut the door behind them.

They were standing in a large oblong room; shining white tiles covered every surface. The air was glazed with light and astringent disinfectant stung in the nose.

'Not a nice business this, my dear,' Kelly said.

Henry put his hanky to his nose and shook his head. One of the walls was covered in square white doors with big stainless steel door handles. Banked three high, there were twenty or more, and Henry knew at once they were refrigerated compartments for corpses. Filing cabinets for the dead.

His knees weakened. He slumped. Kari's hand supported his elbow.

'Been in one of these places before, have you?' Kelly asked.

Henry shook his head.

'I shouldn't be lettin you in at all, darlin, you know that?'

Henry nodded, keeping his head down and the hanky over his mouth.

'We'll have to be quick I'm afraid.'

Henry nodded.

'Not very talkative, your friend,' Kelly said to Kari.

'She is *rather* distressed, you know,' Kari said. 'It has been very much a shock.'

'Ever seen a dead body before, Susan, love?'

Henry shook his head, snuffling into his hanky which was no longer a plaything.

'Think you'll be up to it, sweetheart?'

Henry nodded.

Kelly, his hands bulging bananas in his coat pockets, said, 'I don't know . . . I shouldn't be doin this . . . '

'We're here now, Mr Kelly,' Kari said.

'Well . . .'

'*Please. . . .* !' Henry said from behind his hanky and the make-up and the dark glasses and his desperation.

Kelly studied him.

'All right. This once,' he said at last. 'Just wait where you are for a sec.'

He went to the wall of refrigerator-files, opened one on the bottom row, pulled out a kind of long metal tray on which lay a body completely wrapped in a white cloth that was held together along the top by safety-pins. With a delicacy and care that reminded Henry of a mother arranging the coverings on a sleeping baby, Kelly undid the pins and laid back the cloth.

The body was dressed in a white linen gown, the hands resting one on the other across the stomach. Otherwise only the head was visible.

From across the room Henry knew without doubt who this was. He heard himself exhale as if he had at last let go of a deep breath held painfully long.

ACTION REPLAY
I can't move. My muscles seize up. My joints fuse. I cannot take my eyes off that head, his head, Barry's head, lying flat on the metal tray, lying mysteriously silent and with an unpossessed stillness. My eyes are engraved with the sight.

Kelly stood back a pace, like a reverend guard, waiting.

When Henry did not move, he came, took Henry by the arm, led him with gentle pressure across the room to-wards the patient body. Kari, welded to the spot by the sight, stayed where she was, by the door. Henry's steps looked to her, felt to him, like the stiff-legged gait of a paraplegic.

Kelly stopped Henry by the body's side, placing him so that Henry could look down into Barry's face. Into Barry's death.

The eyes were closed. Of course. Why did Henry ex-pect them to be open? The mouth also.

The tanned skin was bathroom fresh. But without glow.

Every feature familiar. Every slightest blemish known. The chart of his beauty. Everything in place.

The nick in his right eyebrow where a stone had wounded when he was a boy. The narrower opening of the left nostril. The bevil of his nose. The mole, hardly bigger than a freckle, hidden under the right jaw. The trim neat ears set close to the skull and half covered by the shock of crow-black hair.

And the folded hands, unmistakably Barry's. And tied round one wrist a label. Like a label on a parcel in a lost property office. Henry forced his eyes to focus and read: a name, a description.

Barry as Body. Barry as Object.

Death. The truth in negative. It proves something, being nothing itself.

ACTION REPLAY

I am looking, staring. I am wishing. I am wishing for the body to move, the eyes to open, the mouth to speak, the hands to reach and touch. I am wishing for this body to become him again.

My wishes battle, batter against the unyielding body. The last battle.

I stare down from the cliff edge of my life at the shore of his death and feel that seductive tingling urge in the gut to plunge down through the separating space and join him. To battle Death in death. Enter that eternity with him. Become by not being. Join in Forever.

As Henry throws himself at the corpse, Kelly grabs him. The mortician catches the neck of Henry's dress, and pulls.

Kari screams.

Henry struggles against rescue, twists and turns in an agony of distress.

Cloth rips, tears, riven by his determination to reach Barry's body and the equal determination of the mortician that he shall not.

'Leave me alone!' Henry hears himself screeching, and gives a final brutal push against Kelly's hefty frame. Which ends the struggle abruptly, for Henry's summer frock can stand the strain no longer and rips from neck to hem, so that Henry is flung, reeling, out of it, tumbling headlong in bra and briefs across the slippery floor. His wig, torn from his head in the commotion, is left behind like an afterthought, dropping at Kelly's feet. Dark glasses somersault in the air and land on Barry's chest.

'What the!' cries Kelly, unhinged, Henry's tattered frock now drooping from his fingers, his eyes wide and tracking Henry's helter-skelter progress.

'Hal!' screams Kari, again, this time hand to mouth.

'Hal?' says Kelly.

'O, God!' says Henry, barking the wall.

'. . . hands on you . . .!' bellows Kelly, enraged and abandoning frock to wig and bulling towards Henry.

'Hal!' screams Kari, this time meaning it would be advisable to scarper while scarpering is still a possibility.

Henry needs no such advice. The spectacle of an angry Kelly advancing upon him is enough, his own embarrassed shame another reason for leaving this place as fast as his stripped body can take him.

But he is not quite fast enough. He skids on the slick tiles as he turns for the door, losing a vital stride. Kelly lunges, manages to grab the back of Henry's bra. Again the mortician pulls, and with such furious violence that the bra's elasticated bodice stretches to its full limit and then snaps at the fastening, thus catapulting Henry on his journey doorwards, a human missile, cottonwool dugs exploding from his sundered boob-bags as he goes.

At this same instant Kari is opening the morgue door, intent, she later admits, on effecting her own escape, having reached the conclusion that Henry is rather done for.

As the door swings back, supersonic Henry streaks through, pursued by mortifying execrations hurled at his back by the fulminating Kelly.

THE END
except that Henry went biking like the clappers through the Sunday teatime streets, flashing his bare chest and his confused blushes, his low slung knees, men's briefs and women's tights. No one noticed. Correction: No one who noticed did more than jeer cheerfully. Thank heavens for the resort for all sorts. When Henry came to, and realized what he was doing and had done, he stopped in Bonchurch reccy, caught his breath, subdued his shame and panic, pulled on his jeans and jersey, and, thus better composed, slunk off home.

25/Three days to write Bit 24! But I learned something.

I have become my own character.

I as I was, not I as I am now.

Put another way: Because of writing this story, I am no longer now what I was when it all happened.

Writing the story is what has changed me; not having lived through the story.

Do you understand? Probably not. I'm not sure I understand myself. I think it has something to do with putting the words on paper. You become your own raw material. You have to contemplate what you were and make something of what happened to you.

Doing this seems to make you see yourself differently.

Also, you stop thinking about your self so much and think more and more about The Work—the Writing! Isn't that crazy! But it is exciting too. It has kept me scribbling day after day, the way I have been. Making this Book of Bits. This Mosaic of a Me-That-Was. This Memorial to Two Dead People.

So you see, Ms Atkins, I am no longer wallowing in the emotional sludge of reluctant confession. Not any more. Instead, I am making you this object: this story. When all the words are written out and fixed the best way I can fix them, I shall type them all out beautifully—or as beautifully as I can, being a two-finger expert only—and I shall bind all the pages with all the words on them in a stiff red cover. Red for danger, passion, socialism, blood, fire, wine, anger: Aren't you lucky! And I will give you this version of a Me-That-Was.

But there is something about it you don't know that I guess you had better know now. I began writing all this stuff down not because you asked, Ms Atkins, but because Jim Osborn suggested I should. He put me up to this job, with his corkscrew eyes, and kept me going when I got fed-up and wanted to pack it in. I wonder if he knew all the time what would happen to me and the way I was—the state I was in—after B.'s death if I wrote about everything in detail? Anyway, it is nearly finished now, and I thought I should tell you The Truth about how I got started.

26/By the way, in case you like loose ends tying up: Yes, my mother did see me when I got home from the morgue that Sunday evening. She caught me as I came through the back door.

'O dear!' she said at the sight of my face. 'You're not taking that up, are you, love?'

'Taking what up?' I said.

'Make-up and suchlike,' she said.

'No no,' I said, scrubbing at my face with a kitchen towel, having forgotten by now I had any make-up on. 'Just trying something out—with a friend—for a play.'

'I thought you might have taken to it permanent.'

I laughed nervously. 'Would I do a thing like that?'

Mother said, 'Your Uncle Jack did. Clothes as well. Women's I mean. You never know, it might run in the family.'

'I've never even heard of Uncle Jack.'

'Your dad won't hear him mentioned.'

'Good God! Just because he wears women's clothes?'

'I should never have said anything.'

'Don't fret, I'll say nowt.'

She took up her duster from the kitchen table. 'Give your face a good wash before he comes in, pet.'

'Where is he?'

'In the garden.'

'I'm going upstairs anyway.'

'You're all right, are you, love? You seem upset still.'

'I'm okay. Really. Don't fuss, eh?'

I went. Locked my door. Never locked my door before. What/who was I trying to keep out? Or keep in?

I sat at my table. Didn't know what to do. Couldn't read. Couldn't bear the idea of music dinning in my ears. No one to talk to. Longing. For him, of course.

As a kid I sometimes kept a diary. Like most people do, I guess, when they are kids. I always got sick of it pretty soon. Never knew what to say.

Now it seemed like an instinct. I took a piece of paper,

wound it into the typewriter, and started typing. Without pause for thought. Under remote control. A robot amanuensis rattling down all the things I wanted to say. A word processor pouring onto white pages black letters in minor key. I kept this effluent diary for the next ten days. Talking to myself about what had happened, what was happening. About B. On the tenth day I was arrested. The diary ends then.

A lot of the stuff in it I've used to help me write this account—memories of Barry and what we did together. I think now that what I was trying to do with that diary was to write him back to life.

I'm going to burn the pages of my diary as soon as I've finished writing this account, because they are too embarrassing to keep. Like keeping your own excrement.

But some of the entries are about the time post mortem, and they tell that part of the story best, because they were forged by the present moment. They're hot from the press of life, and I want you to have a glimpse of how I was then. The chewed-up mess that was Henry S. R. So:

27/EXTRACTS FROM THE DIARY OF A MADMAN

Sunday: dead dead dead dead dead dead dead
Never send to know for whom the bell tolls for who knows if life is not death, and death life, and silence sounds no worse than cheers after death has stopped the ears and I don't think I can live without him for I know death hath ten thousand several doors for men to make their exits but why his now this way and me still here not gone with him because all I do is remember remember remember me remember when to the sessions of

sweet silent thought I summon up remembrance
of things past, I sigh the lack of many a thing I
sought, and with old woes new wail my dear
times waste; then can I drown an eye unused to
flow for precious friend hid in death's dateless
night and weep afresh loves ne'er long cancelled
woe and moan the expense of many a vanished
night.

Yes. But no drowned eye for me. No tears
because my eyes have gone cold. Only know
what I feel by watching what I do, hearing what
I say, reading what I write.

His face. I see his face. Not his living face. His
death face. The skin like plastic, his tan gone flat,
his hands the hands of a shopwindow dummy.

I wish I had not gone to see him. His dead him
is the only him I see in the dateless night.

I want a photo. I want a picture of him before
death set in. I need one. MUST HAVE ONE.

Later: Went out and phoned Mrs Gorman. Said:
I've got to have a photo, won't you give me one,
please give me one. I was polite. But all she did
was swear and scream till a man's voice came on,
though I could still hear her yelling in the
background, and he told me this was enough,
stop phoning or else he would sort me out, or get
the police. But, I said, there's the question of the
dance, I have to dance, you see. Dance, he said,
what the hell are you talking about? On his
grave, I said. WHAT!! this man said, all capitals
and exclamations—WHAT!! (like an amorous
bullfrog). I promised Barry, I said, to dance on
his grave. He would have danced on mine, I said,
if I had died first, it was an oath. WHAT!! this

man shouted again, you're crazy, get off this
phone. I said, Only it's hard, because now I can
only see him dead and I want to remember him
how he was, you must know that, must
understand, surely?

Then the dialling tone. He must have put the
phone down.

This is followed by a very long entry all about my
first meeting with Barry and what I thought of him and
what we did together the first night. I remember it took
me hours to write, well into the night, and that I only
stopped when my father came pounding in, livid, and
storming about the noise keeping him awake. So I packed
up and went to bed, but as soon as I lay down, this awful
fierce headache started, so bad I was moaning and tumbling about. It went on all the rest of the night, till my
mother heard me spewing in the bathroom about five
o'clock and came to see what was happening.

Next day I wrote about it in my diary and went on:

Monday, late: That headache was a migraine. So
the doc says. I spewed and groaned and shivered
and couldn't stand a light on because it was like
having needles pushed through my eyes into my
brain.

Mother called the doc this morning. All day I
lay in bed drained. The headache abated to a
rumble like a departed thunderstorm circling on
the horizon of my mind. The doc arrived
sometime this afternoon; I don't know exactly
when, I didn't care. Peering, prodding, poking,
tapping, questioning: the usual routine. Mother
standing at the foot of the bed, watching,
crumpling her pinny between her fingers, even

answering. 'You should tell the doctor about poor Barry Gorman, love.' 'And then there's his exam results, doctor. He's worried about them, I think.' 'And his career. He's worried about that as well.' 'When he was little he had a nasty fall. Cut his head badly. You never know.'

Pills, of course. 'To relax you.' And: 'Keep rested. Nothing seriously wrong. Stay in bed a day or two.'

Outside the door: 'Just overwrought, I think. Nothing physically the matter as far as I can see. Watch his diet. No cheese . . . Keep him quiet for a while . . . If the headaches go on I'll put him in hospital for a few checks . . .'

They muttered their way downstairs. Why do adults always think that a door is soundproof?

Then Mother waitressing the invalid with boiled egg and thin sliced bread-and-butter on a tray. And blooming. Not a fluttering duster in sight.

But I can't bear the cans on my head and music is like road-drills, and the only way I can write this is with a pencil on a pad as I sit up in bed because I can't stand the sound of the typewriter and if I get up I feel dizzy and the headache starts coming on worse. It is still there, rumbling in the back of my head.

Barry. Barry. O Barry.

There is a long passage of badly scrawled stuff after this, all jumbled memories and descriptions of us together in bed. I'll spare you the details, Ms A.!

Tuesday: Are they burying him? Will I know? Will I know where? Will his be the only new

grave? How many Jewish burials are there every
week in this town?

I've just looked up in my death book about the
customs for Jewish funerals. They don't put up
memorial stones for at least a year after burial.
How will I know which grave is his?

The headache is getting worse again.

Later: Dad has taken to sitting by my bed when
he gets home from work. The weather. The
garden. Work. How am I? Then silence.

He sits avoiding my eyes, except for occasional
curious glances. As if he were trying to weigh up
a stranger he can't quite understand. This evening
he tried talking about the books, the music in my
room. But abandoned the attempt after ten
minutes. He was here for an hour. An hour!

I studied him tonight as I sat up in bed. He's a
littler man than I thought. He seemed to shrink
as I looked. I'm as tall as he is. His face is fatter
than mine, his body is thicker, tougher as well.
But he's always seemed to me bigger than he
really is. If he were a stranger, I'd pass him in the
street and not even notice him: a middle-aged,
tired-looking, balding little man.

I am surprised by this discovery. When I look
at him again he will seem a different person.
Someone I hardly know.

I felt sorry for him.

Wednesday: Headache again, all day. Spewing.

Thursday: His burial is in the paper. Mother
showed. And a report of the inquest. Accidental
death. Accidental!

Gone. All that weight of soil on top of him.

The darkness in his coffin. But he isn't there? Is he? Is he in his bubble of speed?

This bloody rotten stinking puking headache again.

Friday: Seven weeks.
And seven days ago.
We fought.
He died.
I live.
Headache again. Spewing again.

dance dance dance dance dance dance.
Dance of Death?
Dance for Death?
Whose dance? Whose death?

Dance.

28/That night I danced the first dance. Didn't know then, of course, that I would dance a second time. All I knew was that I had to dance because I had sworn an oath that I would.

I woke at ten past two, headache registering about force seven on the Richter scale. I thought: I'm stuck with this till I've kept my promise, I just know it. Might as well get on.

I pushed a couple of the doc's pills down my throat and got up.

Night was the only time: I would have been stopped and caught during the day.

'What are you doing up?' My mother, sotto voce from their bedroom, its door always at the ready, half-open.

I paused on the dark stairway, my shoes in my hand.

'Having a rest,' I sotto voced back.

The rustle of bedclothes, and my mother, ghostly, on the landing. 'You shouldn't be up. You're in bed to have a rest.'

'I want a rest from having a rest. I'm sick of it.'

'What have you got on? You're dressed!'

'I'm just going for a walk. Some fresh air.'

'At two in the morning! You'll catch your death.'

'I'll wrap up.'

'I don't know. I'd better ask your dad.'

Reaching up, I put a hand over hers on the banister. 'No, leave him. He'll only create if you wake him.'

She waited. Put her other hand over mine.

'You've got me properly worried, pet. I never know what you're up to these days. You never tell us anything. And these migraines . . .'

'I'll be all right.'

'There's sommat wrong.'

'Growing pains,' I said, trying to smile through the dark.

'We should never have moved,' Mother said.

I crept downstairs. She followed, her slippers plopping behind me.

'Leaving the place we knew,' she said. 'I never felt right about it.'

'Well, we're here now,' I said pulling on an anorak. 'You go back to bed. I'll be okay. Honest.'

'Let me make a cup of tea.'

'I just want a change from lying in bed.'

'Put something warm inside you.'

'I don't feel like eating.'

She waited. I could feel the anxiety coming out of her like heat from a radiator. I thought: All the time she worries about something, about somebody—me, Dad, what's happened, what's going to happen, what's not going to happen. Expecting disaster. And who worries about her? I never do. She's always just been there, when I wanted, ready. If I think of her when I'm on my own, she's like she was when I was little. Laughing, busy, always on the go, and talking all the time—to me, to Dad, to her friends who were always popping in, to shopkeepers.

I thought: But she isn't like that now. Now she's a frightened woman who hides. I knew I had seen her changing. I must have done: I was there. But I hadn't noticed. Hadn't wanted to notice, I guess. Because I didn't understand? Because I hadn't wanted to do anything about it? Because I didn't know what to do? Because it embarrassed me? Or got in my way?

She said, snuggling my clothes, 'Don't know what the doctor will say.'

'Then don't tell him. I'll take care.'

'Don't stay out long. And don't go far. This time of night, you don't know who could be about.'

She reached up and felt my brow. Leaned further, kissed me awkwardly on the cheek.

'Go back to bed,' I said.

She looked at me, a featureless wraith in the dark, then turned, slipped back upstairs.

29/Getting into the cemetery was easy. I cycled a safe distance past the entrance, because the lodge at the gate is lived in. The stone wall is about waist high; I lifted my bike over to hide it from any stray police patrol. A grave length behind the wall is a man-high hedge, too thick to push through. But an avenue of trees grows between wall and hedge, their lower branches lopped off. I scrambled up one nicely supplied with amputated knobs in just the right places to assist a climber, grabbed a branch, swung from it and pitched myself onto the ground inside the cemetery. I didn't bother to wonder how to get out. By this time all I felt was a desperate determination, a singleness of mind that left no room for any other thought except getting to Barry's grave and dancing.

And I might as well have been guided by radar — controlled by whom? Barry's ghost? — because I have no memory of the weather or the kind of night it was. Not a memory I could swear was accurate. No rain, because I would remember being wet. But how dark? I close my eyes, try to recall. I see the wall, grey, shadowed deeply but catching a glim of light from a street lamp some distance down the road. (Subconsciously I must have chosen this spot because it is in a darker patch of road.)

When I drop onto the ground on the other side I am among graves. Older ones. Stately and aged. Their headstones stand like old folk parading in an ordered silent crowd. The night is even darker here; gloomier, even more shadowed. Now, remembering, I am afraid. This is, after all, a burial place. But then, all I worried about was the living. Me being caught.

I waited, listening. A car purred by on the road, its headlights flooding the trees. After it, no footfall, no cough, no voice, no husp of breath. Rustlings among fallen leaves. Mice?

I'd brought a small flashlight. Shading its face with my hand, I switched it on. Let a beam find the ground at my feet. Guide me through the graves to find the path, a warm sandy glow in the night. Switched off.

The Jewish burial ground lies at the back of the main cemetery, separated by a hedge. The path, worming through the lines of graves, would take me to it. I set off, keeping to the grass at the path's edge so that my feet would not give me away on the crunchy gravel.

Pain thumped in my head at every step. But there was relief in knowing I was doing what I had promised. Somehow it was easier to breathe; and the cool night air on my forehead was soothing too.

30/Looking across the dark line of hedge, the Jewish part was a ruckled white sheet laid over the centre of a square field of cropped grass. I had no difficulty pushing through the loose bushiness of the privet, and did not pause for thought. I was urgent, spelled. Wasn't even wondering any more how I would know Barry's grave; I felt I would when I saw it.

Began searching along the first line of graves, walking down the row. Inspecting the troops. Stand by your graves. Most were decked out with white headstones and surrounds, black-lettered epitaphs in English and Hebrew scored into the faces. Some were topped by a plain slab of stone, like a lid on a box. A few were marked by shiny black memorials, lettered in gold. One or two leaned precariously, as if the body beneath had turned over in its bed and tipped the stone askew. Singles, doubles; here and there gaps between, waiting no doubt for relatives to join them. And every so often a mound of soil, mostly unmarked except for a little metal stake at the foot with a number printed on a disk. They looked like big lollipops, and marked the new graves occupied during the last year.

Barry's had to be one of these. In the first three or four rows none was new enough to be his. Their soil was dry, crusted. But then came one that was fresh. I switched on my torch. Played it over the hump of dark earth. Barry's. But how to be sure?

The grave was at the end of a line, on an aisle that

separated the square patch of burial ground into two blocks, like seats in a theatre. The lollipop stake was no use. I pulled it out, inspecting it closely back and front. But nothing; only the number. And what's in a number?

I walked round the grave, hoping to find some sign, as though Barry, before they stowed him away for eternity, might have dropped some clue, telling me he was there. Ridiculous. Nothing, of course.

The headstone on the grave next door was larger than most, and one of those that leaned on its side. As I edged past along the narrow strip of grass separating it from Barry's grave, the light from my torch spilled across its white face.

The black letters of the name DAVID GORMAN spoke out at me. I had found Barry; this man next to him had to be his father. The dates on the headstone fitted. And on the other side was a grassy gap, space for two more graves before the next memorial staring ghostly into the night.

31/I don't much like telling what happened next.

I started crying. Stood there between Mr Gorman's grave and Barry's, staring at the pile of earth spotlit at my feet, tears began streaming down my face. At first I thought they were beads of sweat caused by the exertion of getting here. But my eyes filled, my nose ran, my breath erupted in my throat, and I knew in the numb core of myself that I was weeping.

The thing is, I didn't know what I was weeping about. That probably sounds crackers. (But I am—I told you so at the start of this.) What I mean is, I wasn't crying *only* because of sadness. I was also crying because of anger. In fact, I felt angry more than I felt sad. I didn't know why—not then. (I do now, I think. But if I am to keep everything in its right order so that you'll understand properly, I can't tell you why here; it comes later.)

Being angry as well as sad, but not knowing why I was angry, made me even more upset. I started gasping for breath as the tears choked me. This made me worry about being heard. I switched off the torch. Didn't know what to do. Walked this way and that beside Barry's grave. Felt weak. Unthinking, sat down on the lid of Mr Gorman's grave. Blocked my mouth against my knees. But this only restricted my breathing even more. Stood up, gasping, tears blinding me now. Staggered. Tripped. Found myself tumbling over Barry's grave. Went sprawling across it.

Scrambled to my knees astride his heap of earth. And in a frenzy began hacking, stabbing, digging, using his lollipop number-stake as a spade, flinging the soil aside in any direction. Some I heard skittering across the table top of Mr Gorman's grave, making a hollow sound.

32/Did I want to reach him? (Reach for him?)

Did I want to join him? (Join in him?)

Either/Or². Take your choice. Squared or not. I didn't know. Wasn't, by then, in a fit state to think at all. As mindblind as I was tearblind.

I don't know how long the fit lasted. Seconds only I guess. I gave up when the metal spike of the lollipop bent so that it was useless any more for digging with. I threw it away in an exhaustion of failure and slumped onto the pitted mound.

I was panting, sweating, shaking all over.

One thing: My headache was gone.

Probably washed out of me by sweat and tears.

I calmed down. Slowly.

I did not come here to dig holes, I thought.
But why this? Why any of it? Why?
Why   why   why   why   why   why   ?

33/I felt as though I had been asleep. A long sleep. That I had woken and was refreshed. But yet empty of energy. A tide at slack water between ebb and flow.

I came here to dance, I told myself. I promised. So I must dance.

I've seen films of foals getting to their feet soon after being born. That's how I was, standing up now. Bendy-legged. Knees wobbling and buckling. More struggle than strength. I stuttered about, trampling on the disturbed soil of Barry's grave. A kind of dance I suppose. I tried raising a foot to perform an improvized jig, stumbled, brought my foot down into the pit I had scooped in my frenzy, and, twisting my ankle badly, pitched forward, stifling a yowl of pain.

I flung out a hand to save myself. Found the corner of Mr Gorman's tilting headstone. Grabbed. And hauled myself towards it, hopping on my good foot.

The headstone held me for a moment and then came away in my hand. With a slow grace it toppled, and with a hefty thud dropped sideways across the top of Barry's grave, then collapsed face down upon it. Chop and splash. The ground seemed to shake, and the noise, in my ears, was thunderous.

I leapt away from the falling slab, forgetting my hurt ankle. Only to be reminded of it again as I landed, this time not able to smother a yell of agony.

So here I was, rending the silent night with bellows and thuds. Suddenly I was scared. Someone must have heard. I had to get away. Scarper. *Now*.

I scrambled on hands and foot, wincing, back to the hedge. Thrashed a way through, regardless of spikey twigs and clawing thorns. Hobbled back round the winding paths of the gentile boneyard to my place of entry, and paused, listening hard for any sign of pursuit.
None.

Breath regained, I searched for a way out my gammy foot could manage. Found one at last: a hole in the bottom of the hedge big enough to crawl through into the space between hedge and outside wall. And then, a careful shuffle over the wall, and a slow, one-footed pedal home unseen.

34/ EXTRACT FROM THE DIARY OF A MADMAN

Saturday. . . . Awful. Terrible. Lost control. Went crazy. Digging up the grave, for God's sake! What's happened to me? Never felt anything like that before. Like someone had taken hold of my brain and turned it back to front inside my skull.

I'm beat this morning. Ankle swollen. Told Mother I fell down some steps in the dark. She took my clothes away because they were in such a state. Mucky, torn. 'I'm glad you had a good game of football as well,' she said. She can be funny sometimes. So I'm back in bed aching at both ends and not feeling too terrific in the middle.

And still I haven't danced. I'll have to. Don't know what to do. Couldn't bear it if I went berserk again. Too scary. Really losing my mind. People say that: He's out of his mind. I never thought of it being true; that it could be true. As ever happening. But it does. It happened to me. And another: I was beside myself. Well, I really was. Standing beside myself, watching myself in a frenzy. All the time a cold unmoving-me watching the mindgone-me going crazy.

I wonder if mad people, the ones they lock up for being mad all the time, I wonder if they have a cold unmoving part of them who knows all the time they are mad, who watches it all happening. Watches what they do; what is done to them. That would be horrible. Because if madness is like that then the real pain for the mad person is knowing he's mad and watching himself, feeling himself being mad every minute of every day. That would be hell. If that happened to me, I couldn't bear it so much I'd kill myself. Maybe that's why mad people do try to kill themselves so often? And when people stop them killing themselves, maybe they go berserk, not because they're mad, but because they know they're mad and can't do anything to help themselves and can't stand it any more.

I've got to talk to somebody. I can't sort this out by myself.

Later. Kari's the only one I can talk to. She's the only one who knows everything. I've written, asking her to come and see me. Asked Dad to deliver the note because it was urgent. I said, 'You told me to ask if I wanted anything. Well, I want this letter delivered. Will you take it for me?' He looked at the envelope and grinned as if I'd given him a present. 'A girl?' he said. I said, 'A friend. I promised to meet her, but I can't when I'm stuck in bed, can I? I thought I'd ask

*her to pop round and see me. Is that okay?' He
looked at me a while, still grinning. 'All right, is
she?' he said. I said, 'How d'you mean?' 'You
know,' he said. 'A smart lass, is she?' I said, 'I'll
put Ms Tyke onto you. You're a male chauvinist.'
'Aye well,' he said, 'I could teach her a thing or
two an' all.' I said, 'She's Norwegian.' 'Foreign,'
he said. 'They usually are,' I said, 'except in
Norway, of course, and then it's us who's
foreign.' His grin went. I only meant a joke but
he took it as snide. Why do I always get it wrong
with him? I was sorry. 'Is it all right for her to
visit?' I said. 'I don't care,' he said, retreating into
his usual self again. 'Nowt to do with me. I'll ask
your mother.' He turned to go. 'But you'll deliver
the letter?' I said. He stopped. 'Aye,' he said,
fingering the envelope. 'Might do you some good.
Doctor's no bloody use, that's for sure.'*

35/ACTION REPLAY

Strange, reading my Mad Diary now. When I was
writing it, I just shot the words onto the page like bullets,
not thinking about them, but only wanting to get them
out of myself because I had no one to say them to. But
now when I read it I find it tells me things I didn't know at
the time, didn't *see*. Like this conversation with Dad.
Reading my diary brings that moment back vividly. I can
feel the weight of the bedclothes on my legs, the heat
around me inside the bed, the jangling aches in my body.
And best of all I can see and hear Dad in a kind of
microscopic blow up.

And what hits me is that smile when he looked at the
envelope addressed to Kari. I even wrote *'as if I had given*

him a present'. His silly chat about Kari and then his parting shot about the doctor being *no bloody use*. More than a grumble. I can hear in the tone of his voice: he was saying, 'What I think you need the doctor can't do anything about'. But Kari—a girl—might? There's hope yet, he was thinking.

Playback.

He knew. He knows. Somewhen or other after I took up with Barry he sussed out what was going on. That Barry was a mate in more ways than men usually mean when they use that word about a friend.

Why should I have thought he wouldn't? Because I've been *assuming* that Dad can't think? That he's too thick to notice? God, if that's right, what a condescending ape I've become.

But of course he knows. I haven't been exactly hiding it, have I? I just haven't been talking about it.

Maybe one day we'll be able to talk about it, Dad and me. But not yet, Mz A., not yet. Not till I've sorted myself out and know for certain what I am. Which I haven't yet.

36/'This is the first time I've had a girl in my room,' I said to Kari while we talked when she visited on the Sunday evening.

'Lucky you!' she said.

I'd hobbled to the bathroom before she arrived, spruced myself up, changed into a clean sweatshirt for the occasion, while Mother spring-cleaned my room, ready for royalty.

'As a matter of fact,' I said, 'this is the first time I've ever had anyone else in my room—except for family of course.'

'I nearly didn't come.'

'Why?'

'You abandoned me. Left me to that angry man.'

'Did he catch you?'

'O no! I'm much too fast.'

'Well then!'

'Well then nothing! He might have done.'

'But he didn't.'

'With no thanks to you. You ran off and left me, after all I had done to help.'

'I was nearly naked. How could I hang about?'

'You had clothes in your bike.'

'Yes. But I forgot about them till I was nearly home. I was in a state of shock.'

'You were also in a shocking state!'

We both laughed, even though the joke was not *that* funny.

'I will forgive you a little bit,' Kari said, 'because the experience was so awful.'

'I wish we hadn't done it.'

'It was you who said it had to be done.'

'I know.' I looked at her for a while. 'Now there's something else.'

'I think I do not want to know.'

'Yes, you do. You're dying to know.'

'You're not supposed to say such things. You're supposed to persuade me to listen till I give in.'

'Let's pretend we've been through all that, eh?'

She eyed me suspiciously. 'Just this once. I don't like being taken advantage of. It makes me angry, which brings me out in spots.'

I told her about going to Barry's grave and what happened to me there. When I finished she shook her head and shrugged.

'This is terrible, Hal,' she said. 'Worse than the morgue.'

'I know, I know,' I said. 'I could understand the morgue, why I had to see him, even if it turned out to be the wrong thing to do. But this . . . I don't understand. I thought you might.'

She shook her head again. 'I don't know . . . Perhaps it was guilt. Feeling guilty for his death.'

'I thought of that. But it didn't *feel* like that.'

'Then how did you feel?'

'Sad. Angry. I don't know. All mixed up.' I thought some more. There was something I wasn't saying and I didn't know if I could. I had to gather myself together, force myself to say it. 'Like I was trying to hit him.'

We were both silent for a long time, not looking at each other. Kari kept her eyes fixed on her feet. Mine flicked here and there, taking her in now and then, watching for some kind of response.

'Hit him?' she said at last still not looking at me, and her face giving nothing away.

'Yes. And trying to reach him.'

'Trying to reach him so you could hit him?'

'I suppose. Sounds mad, doesn't it? Said like that. But I felt both those things. Not like you said them though.'

'Now I'm confused!'

'So am I! I mean, I didn't feel I wanted to reach him in order to hit him. One thing connected to the other, see? Not that. They were separate. I wanted to reach him. And I wanted to hit him. Just like I was angry with him, and sad at the same time. Different things mixed up.'

She was looking at me now, searching my face as if there was something to be found there that wasn't in what I was saying.

'Does any of that make sense to you?' I said.

'Yes . . . and no,' she said.

'Great!' I said. 'We're certainly making progress!'

'It isn't so easy,' she said. 'People are too complicated

for anything like this to be simple. Just one thing. Something you can explain in straightforward words. You read too many books that make it seem possible to sort life out and know about it.'

'No, I don't.'

'Yes, you do. You think there is an answer for everything. A reason you can find and know about. You want everything to be clear cut, like some silly maths formula you can then go away and live by. You keep on looking for somebody who will—O, I don't know—make you know how to live your life.'

'No, I don't.'

'Yes, you do. All that childish nonsense about a bosom friend . . . If you want to know what I think . . .'

She stopped dead in her tracks, glaring at me. And me glaring back at her.

'Mrs Grey will be wondering where I've got to,' she said, standing up. 'I should go.'

'Not now,' I said.

'Yes. We shouldn't argue when you are ill.'

'I'll be a lot iller if you go now.'

'No, you won't,' she said, laughing. 'You're ill because you are upset at your friend's death. That's natural.'

'It's more than that and you know it. These headaches. They aren't only about Barry's death. They're about me.' All this was coming out without my having thought it before, as though something had just punctured a membrane and these words came spilling out through the rupture. 'I get them when I try to think about Barry and me and what we did . . . No . . . what we *were*. That's it, what we *were*. What happened at the grave was only part of that. I thought you might help me but all you do is—'

Silence. Kari stood by my bed looking down at me. She was frowning. 'You tell friends what you really think,' she said, 'the truth about them and—well, they resent it.'

She sat by my side on the edge of the bed, looking closely at me.

'Try me,' I said, a touch too defiantly.

She smiled. 'You are very nice, Hal. But you do want to eat people.' She lifted a hand and held it over my mouth without touching. 'Don't speak. I might not be able to say any more if you do. It is difficult, you see. I have thought about you and Barry. About everything you told me the other day. I can see why you liked Barry, wanted to be his friend. He was exciting. I liked him too. He was full of life. Full of energy. He enjoyed himself. Had a lot to say. But with you, I think there was something more.'

She paused, considering what she wanted to say, I guess, or maybe deciding whether to say it or not. Anyway, she was frowning again.

'I said you like eating people. Perhaps that is the wrong way round. Perhaps I should have said you like being eaten. What I mean is you liked Barry because he—' She checked my face for a reaction, judging how right she was to be saying this '—Because he made you come alive. He made you do things you wouldn't have done on your own. You wouldn't have dared. He decided everything for you, didn't he? Everything important. Where you should go, what you should do, how you should do everything. He even told you what to wear, how to comb your hair, what to eat. When he wasn't with you, you waited for him to be there again. When you were with him you did whatever he wanted.'

She paused. I almost held my breath. I wasn't liking what I heard, but couldn't help wanting her to finish saying it. Like the doctor two years ago telling me I had a grumbling appendix and would have to go into hospital and have an operation. I'd tried not to think why I was being sick and had such a stomach ache. I told myself it was just wind, or nerves at moving, or something bad I'd eaten. But all the time I knew there was a worse cause. And when Mother finally called in the doctor and he said I had to have the op. I held my breath the same way, knowing I might as well face the truth and get it all over with as soon as possible. The same now with Kari: she was saying something I knew was true but hadn't admitted, and I didn't dare interrupt in case she stopped before everything was said.

She waited in silence. I knew she wanted me to say something.

'Go on,' I managed to mutter.

She sighed, not wanting to. 'For a while, I'd guess, Barry enjoyed you depending on him like that. Enjoyed being your teacher, showing you about life, about yourself. I think he got a thrill out of playing your big brother, and your lover, and your boss, and your guru all at the same time. But, being Barry, he'd get tired of it after a while, because what he liked most was the beginnings of things. You know what I mean? He got pleasure out of making people like him, and give in to him. He liked to be in charge. But once people had given in to him, the challenge was over, you see, and he dropped them. Got bored with them. Like he did with you. That's why he had no close friends. He didn't, did he?'

I shook my head. 'Not that I ever met, or heard him talk about.'

'He was exciting, but he liked excitement rather too much. And no one can ever be exciting all the time. Not even him. You just thought he was because for you, everything you did with him was new, different. He liked sailing and motorcycles because they were always exciting. They can always be dangerous. He could always get a new thrill out of them by pushing himself close to disaster whenever he wanted to.'

She got up from my bed and sat down on the chair

again. I felt I should say something, but didn't know what.

'If you really want to know what I think,' she said after a silence, 'I think you went a little wild and beat on Barry's grave because he wouldn't be here any more for you to lean on. For him to take care of you. You couldn't face being on your own again, responsible for yourself, having to make your own decisions. All along it wasn't Barry you wanted. It was your *idea* of Barry you wanted. Because the truth is that Barry wasn't what you thought he was. Really he was just as scared as you are. Or as I am. Or, I think, as scared as most people are. He just pretended he wasn't. Put on a rather good performance. As much for his own benefit as for yours. I think the truth is, Hal, that you fell for a face and a body and then put the person inside you wanted to find there.'

'You're saying he was just a figment of my imagination,' I said, trying to laugh.

She smiled. 'Maybe he was.'

'Rubbish! He was there. I've been with him. Slept with him. So have you. You know he was there.'

'Yes, someone was there. But not the person you believed was there. Or even maybe the person I believed was there.'

'You're saying we invent the people we know. That's daft!'

'But perhaps we do. Perhaps we even invent ourselves. Make ourselves appear to be what we want to be.'

I nodded. Shrugged. There was another silence, a long one this time, while we looked at each other across the length of my bed. Then Kari suddenly blushed, as if from embarrassment, the way people do when they think they have said too much, and she looked away, stood up, fidgeted with her clothes.

'I have to go,' she said.

I was speechless. Not tongue-tied, just without words to say.

She said, 'You asked. That's my opinion, Hal.' She was trying to be her jaunty beach self. 'I expect I am wrong.'

I nodded. 'Ask a silly question—'

'It wasn't silly!' she said.

'No,' I said, 'just a saying—'

An awkwardness. Neither of us wanting to part. She hesitated with a hand on the doorknob.

'Hey,' I said, my turn to try breezy friendliness. 'I really am grateful for helping me the other day. The morgue.'

She grinned, taking my cue. 'Any time,' she said. 'What are friends for if they can't get you into the morgue.'

She was gone before I could play the flip side of her joke.

37/When Kari had gone I slipped into a sort of stillness. My headache was properly gone for the first time in days. I meant to chew over what she had said. But instead I very soon drifted into a deep, undreaming sleep—also for the first time in days, or nights. I half-woke some time later, vaguely aware that someone—Mother, I expect—was rearranging the bedclothes around me, and then plunged deep again.

I finally came to suddenly, lying in the Corpse Position. My watch said nine thirty-five; morning light filtered through my curtains. No rampaging rhino; no agonybag scurl of the vacuum.

I stirred, my body cosily stiff from being too long in one place. Immediately Kari was in my mind. Snatches of what she had said replayed.

The bathroom. I needed to pee.

'Is that you, love?' Mother called from below as I crossed the landing.

'No, sweetheart, it's the milkman,' I called back.

As I came back I realized I was walking without any trouble from my ankle. I stopped and looked. The swelling had gone down.

'How you feeling?' Mother asked from the bottom of the stairs.

'Okay. I'll get up.'

'Take care, pet,' she said, hesitantly climbing a couple of steps so she could look through the banister. 'Your dad thought you should get plenty of rest.'

'Makes a change,' I said, but not acidly, only amused.

'I'll get your breakfast,' she said, retreating.

I spent most of the rest of the day brooding on what Kari had said and scribbling in my diary.

38/That Monday night I waited, knowing I would dance as I had promised this time.

By ten-thirty my patience ran dry. I wanted it over.

The same pretext: I was going out for some fresh air and to give my foot some exercise.

'You in training for a job on the night shift?' Dad said. 'Or is it that bird again?' He had been chirpy ever since coming in from work, twitting me at every opportunity about Kari.

The same way into the cemetery (though being earlier there were more cars to dodge and one or two people on the road). The same path to the Jewish section.

I paused at the hedge, looking for movement among the graves. Saw nothing. Pushed my way through the divide and went straight to Barry's grave.

At once, as I approached, I saw that his father's headstone had been re-erected, firm and square now, and the hole I had dug had been filled in and the soil smoothed over. A new number plaque was staked at the foot.

The thought flashed through my mind: If they've repaired the damage maybe they're on the lookout for me. But I paid no heed. Since then, I've wondered whether I wanted to be caught. Like they say criminals often want to be caught and punished for their crimes, and even unconsciously leave clues to their identity, and return to the scene and make themselves conspicuous.

Well, I was conspicuous enough that night. I just stood there at the foot of his grave, nothing clear-minded going on in my head, and my torch shining like a spotlight on the oblong heap of his deathbed in front of me. I was quite calm; none of that anger and madness of three nights ago. Tears started down my face again, but I wasn't heaving or distressed at all, but making, I think, a kind of farewell. Letting him go.

After a few moments like this, I heard in my head the funny little tune that Laurel and Hardy films always begin with. *Tum-ti-tum, tum-ti-tum, tumpetty-tum, tumpetty-tum . . . cuckoo! . . . cuckoo! . . . cuckoo!* The Cuckoo Song. Ridiculous, sad; always makes me smile. It wasn't exactly music I'd have thought of dancing to on someone's grave. Not that I'd ever thought of dancing on anyone's grave till now. But it was all I could hear. So I picked up my feet to its gawky rhythm and set about a knees-up as best I could. And soon the music faded and the beat became something of my own, quickened in pace and vigour, a tattoo In Memoriam of Barry's needless death and in celebration of what he had been to me, which no one else could ever be again.

It was when my dance became more celebration than memorial that the black shape of the hidden B.-in-B. rose, like Death himself, from behind a gravestone only a row away and came swooping down upon me in a flying rugger tackle. We both crashed to the ground on the path by Barry's grave. Instantly the B.-in-B. was on his booted feet again, grabbing me by the collar and an arm, and braying with evident satisfaction, 'All right, sonny, that'll do for now. You're under arrest.'

What he, poor bloke, couldn't understand, was why I burst into squalls of uncontrollable laughter.

39/You know the rest.

So I'll add only this. Yesterday, after I'd written Bit 38, I wandered down to the beach by Chalkwell station, thinking my Record of Death was finished, and feeling happy-tired. Happy to have finished, tired because I've done nothing much else for three weeks now but write everything down and relive my seven weeks with Barry, and face his death again.

I was feeling relieved too, but sad, in a way, to be done with it all—except for my court appearance, which seems now like an irrelevance. I don't care what they decide to do with me, because I've decided what I have to do with myself. I'm going back to school, for a couple of years in Ozzy's Sixth. Not that I want the exam qualifications; and I don't have any ambition to go on to university. What I want is the time. To let everything settle. I want to read more, and write some more too, because I've enjoyed doing that so much. There's something ahead for me; I can't see what it is yet, but I know it is there, waiting. And I just feel I'll get to it better by staying on at school than by getting a job.

I was thinking all this as I sat on the wall between the beach and the esplanade gazing out at the sea, when someone tapped me on the shoulder. The sensational Spike, succulent as ever, and a paintbrush in his hand. He had pulled *Tumble* on to the beach and was overhauling her, ready for laying up during the winter.

I gave him a hand; I reckoned I owed him for borrowing his beloved boat and turning her over so ignobly. We laughed a lot and larked about while we worked, and talked school and sailing and sex and jobs. He's starting as a labourer for a painter and decorator next week, and glad to be free of school. He's been sculling about all summer, doing as little as he can, but now he's broke and his father won't stump up for him any longer.

He thought I was mad to be staying on, of course, and mad without hope of rescue for opting for Ozzy's Sixth. I tried to explain, but it was all too confused still, and so I changed the subject.

All the time I was getting a charge just from being with him, but for the first time—and this is the important bit of this Bit—I didn't wonder once if Spike might be a boy with a can of magic beans, the real and everlasting bosom pal. Because it doesn't matter any more.

'Look,' I said to Spike, 'how about a movie tonight?'

'I told you I'm skint. I really am,' he said.

'It's okay,' I said. 'I'm flush. I've done nothing for weeks. Feel like a night out. We could grab some land-and-sea somewhere when we've finished here and catch the five-thirty showing.'

'What's on?'

'Couldn't care less,' I said laughing.

He looked across the upturned hull at me and laughed as well. 'You're crazy, you know that?' he said.

'So who wants to be sane?' I said.

And that night I gave him a present from Southend.

Wish you were here?

40/I wouldn't want you to think this is the end. How can it be the end when even I don't know what the end is yet? Maybe it's just the beginning. And not even the beginning either. Maybe it isn't anything at all. Not beginning or end. But just a bit of the middle of something that has a beginning and an end so far out of sight you might as well forget about them, as if they weren't there at all, which they aren't when you come to think about it. I have written all this so you can see how I got to be what I am. But that is not what I am any more, because what I am now is someone who is making sure that he is no longer influenced by what made him what he has become.

The only important thing is that somehow we all escape our history.

Youth's Pact 'To Dance on Friend's Grave'

A sixteen-year-old youth, who damaged the grave of a friend who died in a motorcycle crash, was told by Mr C. H. Pinchbeck, chairman of the juvenile court, yesterday: 'To desecrate a grave as you have done is repugnant to normal decent people.'

The court heard how the youth, a pupil at Chalkwell High, had made a pact with his friend that if either died the other would dance on his grave. The motorcycle crash had occurred after the two youths had had an argument over a girl.

Social inquiry reports revealed that the youth's behaviour was caused by a mild depressive illness, which, the court heard, often shows itself in adolescence, and which was brought on in this case by the friend's death.

The magistrates placed a Supervision Order on the youth for one year, and accepted the youth's apology for any distress he may have caused the family of his dead friend.

Afterword

When I began *Breaktime* in 1975 I didn't know that it would be the first of six novels, that they would be related in so many ways that I would come to think of them as a sequence, and that it would take me thirty years to finish the set. I had written many books before *Breaktime*, but they hadn't satisfied me. All of them were written for young readers, trying to give them what they'd told me they wanted. None of them was 'mine'.

Breaktime began unexpectedly and unplanned. Looking back, I think the trouble was that I was bored, so bored I couldn't write one word of another book of the not-me sort. I sat at my desk in a state of verbal paralysis for eight days, and on the eighth day, in a fit of anger and panic – how could I not write a novel? I certainly couldn't give up; it was the only thing I wanted to do – I made myself write down the first words that came into my head, and go on until I told myself to stop. The first words that came into my head were '"Literature is crap," said Morgan.' (You'll find them on the second page of the story, where they ended up after one of the many revisions of the book.) I had no idea who Morgan was or what he had against literature. He was answered by a character who didn't seem to have a name, so I wrote 'Ditto' whenever he was mentioned, intending to substitute his name when I found out what it was. After a while I realised 'Ditto' contained several meanings appropriate to him and his story and so Ditto he remained.

It took three years to finish what turned out to be the simplest and shortest of the sequence. I had to stop twice – about one-third, and about two-thirds, of the way through – in order to work out what was going on, what the book wanted to be (rather than what I wanted it to be), and how best to tell each of its scenes. In the process, it taught me everything I needed to know about myself as an author of my own books rather than a writer of other people's, about what I wanted to do with 'the literature of youth' – novels in which everything is seen through the eyes of the central characters, who are people in their mid to late teens – and the ground rules that would guide me.

For instance, it taught me that I write the first draft best with a pencil on large pads of paper, and then rewrite subsequent drafts on a typewriter (as I'd used for all drafts till then) or a word processor (which I have used since 1985). And the ground rules? That I will not compromise with language or subject, just because some people regard them as 'too difficult' or 'too controversial' (that is, taboo) or too long or too anything. That I will only write scenes for which I have 'a reference point of truth', by which I mean that I have evidence that they have happened or can happen. And I do not write *for* anyone or any particular readership, but only in order to make a novel that has its own being, its own shape, pattern, layers of meaning, its own voice, and its own 'way of telling' the story.

Breaktime is the novel I would have written if I'd been capable of it when I was fifteen and first decided I was a writer. It's about what interested and mattered to me then, about what I longed for and didn't ever achieve. Because of some of the scenes in it (the sex, of course), I didn't expect it to be published 'for young people' of the age of Ditto. Nothing quite like it had appeared before. But by good luck, I found the ally every author needs: a great editor. In my case Margaret Clark of The Bodley Head. She looked after everything I wrote from then until *The Toll Bridge*, the fourth book in the sequence, when she retired. I owe more to her than I can say here.

Though *Breaktime* was the first of the sequence to be finished and published in 1978, *Dance on My Grave* was begun long before, in 1966, when I read a newspaper report of a sixteen-year-old boy charged with desecrating a grave. He told the magistrate that he had sworn on oath with a friend that if one of them died the other would dance on his grave. His friend was killed in a road accident after they'd had a row about a girl, and he had kept his promise. Nothing more was revealed. But as soon as I read the report, I felt I knew what had really happened, the title came into my head and I felt compelled to write the story. I tried twice but failed each time. The fact is I wasn't ready. I hadn't learned enough about myself as a person or as an author. I needed more experience of life and the lessons *Breaktime* taught me before I was fit for the job. It took until 1982 before *Dance* was ready for publication.

When I began the final version, I thought it was quite separate from *Breaktime*, but by the time I reached the end I had an intuitive feeling – nothing more concrete or specific – that these novels weren't only a pair, but belonged to a group of six, each of which would explore aspects of youth. They would each be a story about love in one or other of its manifestations. Each would be a story about the interior life of its central characters and about the importance of the individual. Each would be a drama of everyday life, of place, of language, of states of being, and each would reveal the secrets of the body, the mind, and the heart – in other words, each would be a drama of the 'essence of your being' that we call the soul.

The novels came to be called 'The Dance Sequence' because they are like a dance, in which a group of characters move to the music of life in a variety of relationships and interactions, which I hope entertain and enliven, provide food for thought and reasons for living, and, in one way or another, give us a better understanding of who we are and how we came to be what we are, individually and together.

The other novels, in companion editions and with their own Afterword, are:
Now I Know and *The Toll Bridge* in one volume,
and in separate volumes:
Postcards from No Man's Land (winner of the Carnegie Medal in the U.K., the Printz Award in the U.S.A., the Andersen youth fiction award in Italy) and
This Is All: The Pillow Book of Cordelia Kenn.
You can find out more about these books and all of his work from Aidan Chambers's website www.aidanchambers.co.uk

now i know
Aidan Chambers
the toll bridge

TWO FANTASTIC NOVELS IN ONE VOLUME

In *Now I Know*, a body is found hanging from a crane in a scrap yard and Tom, a young detective, sets out to investigate the bizarre case. Nik is researching a film about Jesus when he meets Julie, a girl whose belief in a Christian God is so strong she has no doubts about the rules by which she lives. They embark on a love affair that carries them into a spiritual experience and changes them both for good.

The Toll Bridge is the place Jan takes a job to escape the pressure from parents and teachers who want him to decide on his future. Living alone in the toll house, he hopes to find out who he really is. Then he meets Tess and Adam, who also face turning points in their lives. But for one the experience is so traumatic that the choice is not to face it, but to avoid it, with the most devastating result.

The third and fourth books in The Dance Sequence *– six ground-breaking and provocative novels that explore different aspects of teenage love and self-discovery.*

ISBN 978 1 862 30287 7